CW00816148

THE LAS~ ~ ~NDER THE SUN

VOLUME I

DAVID W. ADAMS   DIHN BAILEY   ERIC BREAU

C BRITT   LACY CHANTELL   T L COMBS

SARAH COOK   ATLAS CREED   M K DOCKERY

H E GOBER   D L GOLDEN   NICHOLAS GRADY

J L HEATH   DARTANYAN JOHNSON

GEORGIA C. LEIGH   JESSICA KAY LISSNER

ALEXIA MUELLE-RUSHBROOK   N R PHOENIX

S F ROGERS   A D SMALL   CHRIS WILLIAMS

ECHO ON PUBLICATIONS

e-Book: 978-1-916582-49-1
Paperback: 978-1-916582-50-7
Hardcover: 978-1-916582-51-4

CONTENTS

PROLOGUE

The remnants of humanity lie strewn across this once-verdant planet, a somber testament to a bygone era, made of towering steel and glass edifices that once adorned their cities. Those colossal skyscrapers now stood stripped and hunched, casting eerie shadows across the desolate sands around them. Like gnarled skeletal fingers reaching out from the past, begging for time to be reversed, they loomed as forlorn reminders on this empty wasteland. Proof that what came before was as inconsequential as the wind.

It was only humanity, in their relentless pursuit of progress, that left their indelible stains upon every corner of the world. From the smallest metal tooth filling concealed under these rust-colored sands—fillings that had endured far longer than the bones that once cradled them—to the largest of their creations; the horrifying scorched craters that had ripped the ground apart, then cast a deathly yellowish-green up into the once blue skies, changing them irrevocably. They had burst onto the earth with a cacophonous roar and exited even louder, with a thunderous boom.

The other beasts of the earth came and went with a silent

grace. Their birth and demise had left no traces, not even an echo. Their legacies had crumbled into an invisible dust. The only proof of their existence would be found in some occasional fossils—but no one was left alive to discover them.

I miss them both—the creatures of the wild and the beings of war and artistry. I may have even yearned to be among them at one point, even though they never appreciated my presence.

I have roamed this barren rock since that very first day. That day when light broke through the void. I was present with each breath, guiding the new creatures through the ebb and flow of the world, a silent witness to the myriad changes that shaped existence's journey. Not just on this rock either, but on every rock, in every corner of reality, and beyond. I stood beside each life when events took a turn as their light faded. I led them into the dark.

In the beginning, we all coexisted in a comforting silence, the creatures of all worlds and me. They could sense my presence but couldn't comprehend what I was. They could not see me, but their primitive minds grasped at a higher understanding of instinct, recognizing my arrival without question. This instinct, signaling my existence, even saved them from fate if they reacted quickly enough. Mammals were never so lucky to have such fine-tuned instincts.

Then, through this silent existence, came the tumultuous noise of humanity—from the piercing scream of their birth all the way through to the thundering machines of war. The silence of existence was forever broken when the sapiens took over and only returned after they left.

I never quite understood the living's fear of the dark. After all, every beginning inevitably leads to an end; it's the essence of the very nature they are a part of. It is the primary tenet of existence. It had happened countless times before, yet all life clung to their existence with a ferocity that defied reason as if the end were unjust or cruel.

Now, as I traversed the arid, blood-hued sands that blanketed this world, I found myself with only my memory of them. All life—plants, trees, seas, insects—had vanished without a trace, but they still lived vividly within my mind. Yet I wasn't truly alone here. I had one friend—the celestial beacon once known as Helios. However, this, my sole companion, was on borrowed time. Even the sun, that radiant star, must eventually take its final bow. On this inevitable day, my friend would depart, forever joining the cosmic void.

You see, my friend was the last of its kind, the final luminescence in a vast expanse of darkness. Its radiant light had been a constant source of comfort and warmth in an otherwise cold and silent world. With all its brothers and sisters throughout the universe now having faded long ago, it was destined to leave the universe, the multiverse, and all of existence in nothingness without a shred of light or life left.

My friend hanging above represented the last glimmer in all reality, the ultimate and final proof of any existence. And when it closes its eyes for the last time, when its final embers are extinguished, I may even cease to exist as well. For what am I without life?

Am I nothing?

For I am change.

For I am transformation.

For I am rebirth.

For I am death.

Yet I am not the end. I am, was, and will forever be the herald—the one who stood beside all living things during their moments of transformation, whether it be a transition into nothingness or a metamorphosis into something else entirely.

And now, on this last day, I sit upon a solitary rock, gazing up at my friend's fading fire, lost in a tide of memories that had encompassed all of existence. For I was not only there in spirit as every living being perished, but I became something more.

I was the calm felt in life's last seconds.

I was the love that betrayed you and forced you into a new life.

I was the stranger who gave courage to transform into something new.

I was images of love that danced as a mind's life faded.

I was the twist of fate that altered destinies.

I was the instinct the undead had as they chased you down.

I was the black cat that crossed a path in warning.

I was the premonition that stopped you from pulling the trigger.

I was the voice telling you a comforting lie to get you to accept what was about to happen.

I was the itch in the finger of your murderer as they pulled the trigger.

I remember each and every time.

I remember each and every life.

And each end to those lives, across each reality. Some realities ended from war, some disease, some without warning, some with millennia of advanced knowledge. Some ends were bittersweet, sometimes terrifying, sometimes mystifying.

Like life, no end had a genre. No end had a theme. And with every living being across every different reality I encountered, came its own special end. It's heralding. And every one of those journeys now echoes in my soul.

Until the darkness comes, I shall remember the things I have done, and the things I did not do. I shall remember when

I was seen to the lives in the cold light of day, when I was spoken of in hushed terms, and when I was unseen by anyone, happily pulling the strings to force an eventuality.

I shall sit here and live in my memories. For tomorrow, I, and my friend above, may be gone.

DEATH OF PEACE OF MIND

BY GEORGIA C. LEIGH

No one likes to be woken up by a phone call. Has it ever been good news? I reached for my phone on the bedside table, the screen glare blinding my tired eyes. Rosewood Care Center flashed on the screen.

"This is Raven," I said, clearing my throat to hide the exhaustion in my voice.

"Hi, it's Patty. Sorry to call you so early. I wanted to let you know we sent your mother to Seton Medical Center this morning."

"What happened?"

"Nothing specific, but it's not good. I think you should get there as soon as possible."

"Can you text me the address?"

"Of course."

"Thanks for being there for Mom. She loves you."

Patty huffed. "When she's not arguing with me."

I couldn't help chuckling. "It's her way."

"I know. Give her my love, too."

Patty hung up and I set my phone back on the nightstand. Death was never expected, even when it was. Mom had been prepping me for this day for weeks, but now that it was here— and I knew it was here—it was hard to stomach. The sun crested on the horizon, filling the room with enough pale light to throw shadows over everything.

Dain's hand slid over my hip and pulled me close.

"An emergency?" he asked, his voice cracking with sleep.

"It's always an emergency."

"It's what you're good at. Putting out fires."

I didn't want that particular skill. My career should be considered a fireman, not an attorney, a mother and a wife.

"How about putting out my fire." He ground his erection into my ass.

I rolled my eyes. Jesus fucking Christ. Every goddamn morning, without fail.

His hand slipped under the waistband of my shorts, slinking lower. I held his wrist and pushed him away.

"Come on, Raven," he whispered, kissing my shoulder. "It will only take a minute."

"A minute would be a record length," I threw over my shoulder as I pulled back the covers and slid away from him. "Believe it or not, that's not a selling point."

He flopped on his back, a sour look on his face. "You don't have to be such a bitch about it."

"You have a hand. Use it."

I hurried through a shower in case he joined me for a second attempt at a morning quickie. I slipped into our walk-in closet and thankfully heard his soft snoring.

I tugged on jeans and threw on a sweatshirt, then dried my short hair and applied a quick swipe of liner and mascara. I grabbed my phone and called Taylor on my way to the kitchen for coffee.

My partner answered on the fourth ring, just before it went to voicemail.

"Yeah?" he said.

"Can you handle the deposition this morning?"

"I'd prefer not to." I could hear the exasperated inconvenience in his voice. "You've done the prep."

Yeah, but you're the fucking lead in this case.

I swallowed my frustration, desperate to keep my tone neutral. "I need the day off. My mom isn't well."

"Your mom hasn't been well in months."

And my patience fled. "Fuck you, Taylor, she's dying."

"Fine, fine. I still need you there. I can move it to later this afternoon."

Always a compromise. "Not before two. Text me the time."

I hung up and made a cup of coffee and leaned against the kitchen counter.

Tomorrow, Mom wouldn't exist. Can a grown woman of forty two be considered an orphan? When Dad passed away when I was fourteen, I had nightmares that I would be a ward of the state or be sent to live with my aunt in New York, a stranger in a strange city, completely foreign to my native California.

Of course, that didn't happen, and my therapist said fear of abandonment was a common emotion when a child lost a parent. Not sure if that really helped, but I eventually got over my fears, but not the loss of Dad.

He was the center of our world. The one that was always smiling, who showed up to my softball games with a ready hug and words of encouragement. Mom was the distant one, always there for us but emotionally unavailable. I knew she loved me, but it wasn't in her nature to show it. I respected who she was as a person, and while we were different, I never doubted she loved me fiercely.

I glanced at the clock and drained my cup, then went upstairs to wake Tanner.

I opened his door and smiled at his gangly long legs tangled in the sheets, one thin arm thrown over his head. I was constantly amazed at his transformation in the last year. At twelve, he had sprouted, his body stretched between childhood and an adult.

"Hey," I whispered, knowing that never worked. The kid slept like the dead. "Tanner," I said a little louder. He grunted, and I gave him a moment, familiar with the required routine to ensure he didn't wake up as a fire breathing dragon.

I flicked on the light, and he groaned. "Time to get up."

"Okay," he mumbled.

I gave him another moment. "Tanner," I said in a much firmer voice.

"I'm up, Mom."

"You aren't until your feet hit the ground."

I heard him mumble something not very polite, but he threw back the covers and rolled out of bed. He kissed my cheek as he passed by, having to lean down to reach me. I was average height, but it hit home how tall he was.

"I have soccer today at three thirty."

"A game?"

"No, practice."

"I'll have your father take you. I need to see Grandma this morning."

"Okay," he said and shuffled down the hall to the bathroom.

I watched him until he closed the door, and I heard the shower turn on. That child had a hold on my heart that was terrifying sometimes. We all know we'll love our children, but I never expected to love him so much. And I thought of Dad again, wishing I had someone to talk to. He understood that kind of love.

I went back to the kitchen and fixed a second cup of coffee in a travel mug. Dain shuffled into the kitchen and popped a pod in the Keurig machine. He leaned against the counter while his cup brewed.

"Why are you in jeans?" he asked.

"I'm going to the hospital."

"Again?"

"Yes, Dain. Again."

He didn't say anything as he took his cup to the fridge and poured in a splash of cream.

"What about Tanner's practice?"

"You'll have to take him. I had to move my deposition to this afternoon."

He frowned. "I can't. I have a showing at one and need to be on the course by four."

"The course is five minutes from the soccer field. You can make it."

"It's your turn this week," he snapped.

"For fuck's sake, Dain. A little help would be nice."

He shuffled away without a word, and I heard his office door slam. God, I wanted to kill him. I went to our bedroom and threw slacks, a blouse and shoes into a bag so I could change in my office. I stuck my head in Tanner's room as he pulled on a t shirt.

"Hey, can you get a ride with Kai to soccer?"

He dragged a towel over his wet hair and threw it on his bed.

"Yeah, I think so."

"Thanks. Just text me by noon if you get jammed up."

"Can you take me to school early this morning?"

"Sure, if you hurry. I need to leave in five."

"Gimme ten."

"Get that towel off your bed."

He grumbled and took the towel with him to the bathroom and the sound of his electric toothbrush buzzed down the hall.

I dropped Tanner off at school and began the agonizing commute across Los Angeles traffic. An hour later I pulled into the Seton Hospital parking lot, ready to commit murder. I needed another coffee. Preferably with a shot of whiskey in it.

I checked in with reception and was directed to the third floor nurses' station.

"I'm here for Nancy Edenton. I'm her daughter," I said to the harried nurse at the counter.

"Oh, thank God you're here. We were afraid you wouldn't make it."

She showed me to her room, the beeping of the heart monitor the only sound filling the quiet morning.

"The doctor was just here. I'll track her down."

"Thank you." I pulled a chair close to Mom's bed and held her withered hand in mine. Pancreatic cancer had ravaged her features in a few short weeks. By the time we had discovered the insidious disease, she was already stage four and declining rapidly. I'd barely had a moment to wrap my brain around the inevitable outcome when I got the call this morning.

She turned her head and opened her eyes, and I smiled at her.

"Hey, Mama," I said, stroking her cheek. "How are you?"

"Shitty," she croaked. "It's time."

"Don't say that."

"Why not? It's the truth." She closed her eyes and took a rattling breath. "I'm ready. But I'm glad you're here."

"I love you."

"I know you do."

"Say hi to Dad for me."

She smiled. "Can't wait to see him."

"I'm jealous."

She clucked at me. "That's nothing to be jealous of." She looked at me again, and squeezed my hand, her strength surprising. "Live your life, Raven. Live it fully, and don't compromise who you are."

I frowned at her. "I am, Ma. I love my life."

She stared at me with knowing blue eyes but said no more. I held her hand for another few moments when the monitor began to beep irregularly, and an alarm went off. A nurse hurried into the room and turned off the machine.

I held my mother's gaze and watched the life leave her eyes. Her hand went slack in mine. I looked up at the monitor, and a dot streamed across a flat green line.

"She's at peace," the nurse said. "I'm sorry for your loss."

It's a strange process when you begin to accept a parent's death. I'd been so young when my father passed that all I remember was crippling grief. This was different. It was a numb shock, and a little relief that she was no longer in pain. A new world stretched in front of me, one that didn't include her. I wouldn't see her on the first Sunday of the month for brunch. Or pick her up to bring her to my house for Thanksgiving dinner. Or take her to her brother's house for Christmas. No lunch or a movie the day after Christmas.

I'd have to find my way in a world that didn't have her in it. I was surprised to find I was angry, too. Maybe this was the adult version of grief.

For the next hour I made arrangements, keeping my eye on the clock, knowing I needed to be in the office by one thirty.

I was almost to the car when my phone chimed with a text from Tanner.

Kai is sick so I'm hitching a ride with Sam's brother.

Fuck. I texted back, *He's seventeen. You're not supposed to ride in a car with him.*

I texted Dad, but he can't take me. It's okay, Mom. It's only a mile away. How's Grandma?

The hell if I'd tell my son his grandmother died over text. *She's sick. Let's talk tonight.*

Okay. I love you.

Thanks, monkey. I love you too.

Fucking Dain. I texted him, *Can you please pick up Tanner this afternoon?*

I fastened my seatbelt, watching the minutes tick by while I waited for his reply.

Can't.

One fucking word. I gripped the steering wheel, numb with anger and disbelief. What a fun parenting moment. I could either text a few parents and try to get him a legit ride and be late for the deposition, or I could leave now, let him ride with an underage driver and be on time for work.

My knuckles turned white as I took my rage out on my car.

I texted Tanner, *Just this time. Be safe. Wear your seatbelt.*

He texted back an eyeroll emoji. *Bruh.*

Even through my anger, he made me smile. God, how did I get so blessed to have this kid in my life.

I raced across town, grabbed my change of clothes from the back seat and flew past reception into my office. Taylor followed me and stood in the doorway.

"What the hell, Raven, they're already here."

I glanced at the clock on the wall. "They're early. I still have ten minutes. But unless you want to see me in my bra and underwear, get out so I can change."

Taylor's eyebrows rose and he folded his arms and leaned in the doorway.

I glared at him. "Out."

He grinned and walked away. "Hurry up," he called over his shoulder.

"Are you sure you want that answer in the record?" I asked the defendant. "You're under oath."

I knew the weasel was lying.

"Asked and answered," Canon said, the same damn thing he'd been saying after every question I asked for an hour.

I looked at Taylor, who almost imperceptibly dipped his chin.

"Then that's it for today."

Taylor stood and gathered his notes. "I'll have the transcript send to you Monday morning."

I walked Canon to the lobby and waited for him while he spoke to his client. When the dirtbag, I mean defendant, was in the elevator, I said to Canon, "You know he's lying."

Canon's bright green eyes sparkled. "I know nothing of the sort."

I rolled my eyes. "Why do you defend slimeballs like this? He swindled nine elderly people out of their retirement funds."

"Everyone deserves representation." We'd had this conversation many times over the last eight years, when Canon had moved here from northern California. A senior partner in the civil defense group at one of the best law firms in Los Angeles, I'd seen him regularly on multiple cases and we'd become friendly acquaintances.

"I'm assuming you want a plea," I said.

"I'd be willing to hear an offer."

"It would involve prison time."

He clucked. "Vicious."

"Fair. He deserves more than that."

Canon's brows rose. "Like what?"

"How about public shaming. Or a whipping."

He stared at me for a moment. "Are you okay? You're a little angry today."

I sighed. "Sorry. I've had a rough morning."

"Work?"

"No, personal."

"Want to talk about it?"

"Not really. I need to pick up my kid from soccer."

"Raincheck then. Can I use an office for a few minutes?"

"Sure." He followed me down the hall and I got him settled in an empty office a few doors from mine.

I sat at my desk when my associate came in and set a pile of papers a foot high in front of me.

"I didn't want to bother you earlier. This just came back from the transcriber for your review."

"I can't get to it tonight."

"It's okay. I need it back day after tomorrow."

Wow. A whopping two days to review a thousand pages. "Can't Taylor do this?"

"He asked me to have you do it."

As a professional partner, Taylor was worthless. The only reason I stayed with him was his connections in the financial industry, where we picked up most of our clients. His deal flow was incredible, but he didn't do shit when it came to actual work. I took a few inches off the stack and stuffed them into my overflowing briefcase and picked up my phone.

A text from Dain. *Where's Tanner?*

A moment of anxiety hit me, when I envisioned Tanner in a car accident involving an inexperienced, teenage driver. Then I saw the text from Tanner. *I'm hitching a ride with Keenan's mom and having dinner at their house. Can you pick me up at eight?*

I texted him back. *Yes, happy to.*

Why Dain couldn't text Tanner directly was beyond me. Just another fucking thing I had to do for that man. *He's having dinner with Keenan.*

A few minutes later, a text came through. *Nice of someone to tell me.*

I texted back. *Nice of you to ask your own son.*

I can see your pissy mood from this morning didn't get any better.

I wanted to throw my phone across the room. I typed out another snotty answer, then deleted it. He wasn't worth the time.

I blew out a breath, settling into pure exhaustion. Since the call this morning until this moment, my mind had been bouncing from person to person, responsibility to commitment, errand to task.

Canon stuck his head in my doorway. "Thanks for the office. Sure I can't tempt you to join me for a drink? I'm a great listener."

"I should get home."

"Traffic is miserable right now."

He was right. And why did I need to be home again? I couldn't think of a single good reason, and I had three hours to kill before I had to pick up Tanner.

"Okay, you talked me into it."

We sat at the bar at a local tavern frequented by the white collar downtown crowd. I ordered a dirty martini and Canon ordered a scotch.

"What's up? Something definitely has you off your game."

I raised a brow. "I think I did okay today. Enough to know your client won't make it through a trial."

"Now, now. Keep those sharp claws sheathed. We're not talking work right now."

I stared at him for a moment, not sure how to respond. He wasn't a friend, and I barely knew him outside a professional setting. The truth didn't seem like something to dump on someone the first time they asked you a personal question. But he waited patiently for my response and seemed truly interested in honesty. He was the first person aside from Tanner that had asked. I twisted my glass. Eh, what the fuck. It wouldn't hurt, right? Right?

"My mom passed away this morning."

Canon's drink froze halfway to his lips. "Excuse me?"

"Don't make me say it again."

"Why the hell didn't you postpone the depo?"

"I tried, but Taylor wanted to do it today."

Canon gaped at me. "It didn't need to happen today. Monday would have been fine. Even next week."

I could feel heat rising in my neck. "I'm guessing Taylor was taking Monday off." He usually spent Mondays working from his Malibu retreat. Asshole.

"God, Raven, I'm so sorry."

I looked away from his eyes, his honest sympathy making my throat tight. I really didn't want to lose my shit in front of him in a bar. "It's okay. She had cancer, so it was a bit of a blessing."

"When was she diagnosed?"

"Five weeks ago."

"Five *weeks*? Jesus, this must be a shock."

"I guess so. I suppose that's why I'm so numb."

"Were you close?"

"Yes and no. She was a very private person who kept her feelings close. Most of my friends have complicated relationships with their mothers, and I'm not an exception. Between arrangements at the hospital, my son, my job and dealing with my husband, I haven't had a chance to really think about her."

"That's insane. You deserve to take a moment for yourself, to be with your husband and son, someone to lean on for support rather than a work colleague you barely know."

I smiled ruefully. Wasn't that the truth. "My son is twelve. Not quite aware of others' emotions. But he's a sweet kid."

"What about your husband?"

I looked down, not trusting myself to voice the first thoughts that came to mind.

"The reason I moved to LA eight years ago was I got a divorce," Canon said. "My wife woke up one day and decided she didn't love me anymore. Possibly one of the worst days of my life."

"You moved here to get away from her?"

He shook his head. "She moved here and took our two kids. We have joint custody, and she had a great career opportunity. I didn't want to be that kind of dad who only saw his kids on holidays, so I moved here and bought a house in their new school district. Our kids are good, and we've found peace." He shrugged. "The reason I'm telling you this is I leaned on my mother a lot during the first few years afterward. She passed last year, and it almost destroyed me. I understand what it's like to lose a mother."

"You had your wife to lean on?"

"I never remarried, and while my relationship with my ex is decent, I wouldn't share that with her."

"How did you get through your mom's death?"

"A lot of tears. My dad. Time with my kids. Friends. Work. I found a way through. Some days are still not great."

"I'm sorry if this conversation brings back bad memories."

His smile was warm, genuine. "It does, but I also remember the good times."

"Maybe I'll get a dog," I grumbled.

He laughed. "If you're not a dog person, I wouldn't recommend it." He cocked his head. "What of your husband?"

God, where do I start? "We met in college and were

inseparable, every free moment outside our jobs we spent together. When Tanner came along, we were so focused on him that I think we lost each other along the way. He would reach out and I wouldn't be there, and when I finally felt the distance between us, he wasn't interested in talking."

"I think kids can either bring people together or shine a light on something that's already missing."

I thought about that for a minute. "You might be right. The only time we ever really argued before Tanner was born was when we were on vacation." I shook my head, remembering some of the shouting matches we had that ended up with us not speaking for days. "I think vacations forced us to spend time together. We were good in short sprints, but days of togetherness was something we outgrew once we left school."

"Yet you're still together."

"If you want to call it that. We live together, and we parent well, for the most part."

He raised a brow. "But?"

"But he isn't interested in my mother. They never got along, so not a lot of sympathy there."

Canon frowned. "This isn't about your mother. It's about you. You're the survivor and hurting. And you're his wife."

I looked at him closely for the first time. He was attractive in a lawyerly kind of way. Fit, broad shoulders, brown hair with a touch of gray at the temples, and lovely green eyes. But more than that, he seemed to have an emotional range beyond his own needs, and that struck me as unique, at least in my experience with the men I'd had in my life.

"Your ex-wife is a fool," I said.

His surprised expression made me wonder if I'd stepped too far. "Why do you say that?" he asked.

"You seem like a sympathetic person, at least emotionally. You'd be surprised how rare that is."

"I'm not perfect," he insisted. "I made mistakes. But I'll take that as a compliment."

"It was meant as one."

My phone chimed and I checked my texts. "Oh shit, I need to pick up Tanner."

"Go ahead, I'll take care of the bill."

"Are you sure?"

"Of course." He winked. "I'm happy to bill this to my scumbag client."

A real laugh bubbled out of me for the first time today. "Fair enough. Thank you. This was...nice."

He turned to face me. "I'm happy to talk if you need a friend in the next few weeks. At some point you'll be on the freeway thinking of work, or your kid's baseball game, and your loss will hit you hard. Trust me, I know."

I searched his face for guile, but either he was sincere or a really good liar. I didn't think it was the latter. "I might take you up on that."

He tipped his head, and a brilliant smile broke on his face. "You have my number."

I thought about Canon the entire drive home. I wasn't so blind that I didn't see his attention and empathy had affected me. I was bound to be a little starstruck when a handsome man offered comfort when I was emotionally fragile. But aside from a momentary crush, I had to admit it had been soothing to have someone to talk to.

I texted Tanner when I was at a stoplight two blocks away, and when I pulled up to Keenan's house, he clambered into the car, slinging his backpack in the back seat.

I dodged out of the way of the forty pounds of crap he carried around. "Careful, that thing is a weapon." He rolled his eyes and pulled on the seatbelt.

"How's Grandma?"

I looked at him, and it struck me that I could see his adult face bursting from the child's features I knew so well.

He frowned. "She died, didn't she?"

I nodded. "This morning. I wanted to tell you in person." He faced forward, but I saw his chin quivering. "She was in pain, pumpkin. It's better this way."

He turned to face me, and the almost-man was gone. Only my child could be seen in the sorrow in his eyes. "Better for who? It isn't better for me."

I smiled ruefully. "I know. Life is supremely unfair sometimes."

A tear dripped to his cheek, and I gathered him in my arms. He heaved, then his emotions turned mine raw. I allowed myself to face my own pain, and my tears mingled with his. We cried together for a woman we remembered, but who had been vastly different to us. Where my mother had been aloof and reserved with me, she had doted on her grandson. She had given her whole heart to him the moment he was born, and for that alone I loved her deeply.

I finally pulled away from my son and wiped his cheeks. "Do you want ice cream?"

"Hell yeah," he sniffled.

"I'm not even going to bitch about your language tonight."

"Good. I won't bitch about yours."

I grinned, then sniffled and laughed as I chucked him under the chin.

"A sundae, gelato, or froyo?"

He looked offended. "Sundae. Duh."

We drove to a small, old fashioned ice cream parlor that

had been a fixture in our neighborhood for fifty years. A throwback to the days of soda counters, juke boxes and milkshakes on dates.

We ordered at the counter and brought our heaping monstrosities to a small circular table with a chipped pink Formica top and wire chairs with round red vinyl cushions.

Tanner shoved a heaping spoonful of ice cream, whipped cream and chocolate fudge in his mouth and a dot of white stuck to his nose. I flicked it off and licked my finger.

"God, Mom, you're gross."

"Please. I've seen worse from you."

"I don't want to know more." I laughed and scooped a mouthful of coffee ice cream with caramel.

"Tell me a story of grandma when I was a baby."

"How about the one where she kidnapped you and took you to Legoland for the day?"

"She never kidnapped me."

"Okay it may be a mild exaggeration, but it wasn't planned. She was supposed to watch you for an hour."

"I loved Legoland."

We walked down memory lane together until we hit the bottom of our dishes and I felt slightly queasy from all the sugar, but in the best way.

Tanner was quiet on the drive home, until we pulled into the driveway.

"Are you okay, Mom?"

I looked at him, then stroked his cheek. "It's been a rough day. I'll have good days and bad, but I'll be fine."

He sat still for a moment, then leaned over and hugged me. "Me too."

I helped him lug his backpack out of the back seat. "Good god, which one of your teachers is asking you to carry bricks to school?"

He expertly slung the pack over a shoulder. "All of them."

"Smarty pants."

"Oooh, language, Mom."

I pushed his sassy self toward the house. "Finish your homework."

Dain leaned on the kitchen counter sipping a glass of wine when I set my briefcase on the table.

"You were late picking up Tanner."

"I wasn't." I walked past him and upstairs to our bedroom. I stripped off my work clothes and pulled on a pair of cotton shorts and a t shirt and washed the makeup off my face, taking a moment to press cold water on my eyes.

"Where were you?" Dain asked from the doorway.

I turned off the water and dried my face. "I took Tanner out for ice cream."

He frowned. "Without me? You didn't even text. I could have joined you."

I blinked. He was right. It never even occurred to me. "It was a spontaneous thing," I blathered lamely.

"You know he's my son, too."

"What the hell is that supposed to mean?"

"It means I think you are purposefully trying to exclude me from his life."

I gaped at him. And something inside me broke, and a fire burst forth, a wicked anger that burned hot.

"You've got to be the most self-centered bastard I've ever met."

"Oh really? You work with lawyers. I doubt I even come close."

"Oh, right, I forgot. Lawyers, *including your wife*, are scum of the earth."

"Fuck, Raven, don't put words in my mouth."

"I'm providing a mild translation of your sentiments," I

spat. "Did it ever cross your mind, even for a moment, that I might have needed someone today? Maybe my husband to care about his wife's feelings?"

He didn't say anything but gulped his wine.

"My mother died this morning, not that you've asked. It's obvious you don't care."

"I'm sorry to hear that."

"Liar."

"You know we didn't get along."

I laughed bitterly. "And it's all about you, isn't it? I hear my mom is in the hospital, and all you can think about is a quick fuck before you take a shit and shower. I've had to deal with this all day while working and picking up Tanner and helping him cope, and all you can think about is why I didn't ask you to come for ice cream."

He just stared at me, his eyes cold and indifferent.

"I didn't think to ask you for ice cream because Tanner and I were talking about my mother. Remembering her fondly, wandering through good memories. I certainly didn't want to sit across from you looking at your pissy, sour face the entire time."

"That is so unfair."

"It's the truth." I brushed by him. "This isn't about you or my mother. It's about me and Tanner in pain. And it's disappointing that as a husband and father, you just don't give a shit about that."

"I care about Tanner. Deeply."

And there it was. "But not about me."

I walked downstairs and poured myself a glass of wine and drank half of it. I topped it off, then sat on the couch in the dark.

Death had a strange way of killing you inside. My mother

died today, and death took a part of my heart with her. I thought about her last words to me.

I love you.

I know you do.

But she didn't tell me she loved *me*.

She never had. I was just supposed to know a mother loved her daughter, but that wasn't how this worked. Words matter, whether they are spoken or omitted. That would be a regret I had to live with in this new world that didn't include her.

In a day where my life marched on relentlessly around me, death had visited me and changed the world around me forever. I wasn't the same person who answered the phone at five in the morning.

I took a long drink of wine and thought about Tanner. I told him I loved him today, at least twice. I wanted him to know, to never have a doubt about how I felt. And I knew he didn't. Tanner had the confidence of a child raised in love. Dain and I may have our problems, but Tanner wasn't part of them.

Dain. Just the thought of him burned, and not between my legs like it used to. That idea was repulsive. The mind, body, and heart are connected, and if one isn't right, the others don't work. Today, that piece of my heart death took was also where my tolerance lived. I needed change, desperately. In this new world, I was an adult orphan. The only thing left of my family is what I'd chosen for myself, and I refused to live in a world where I didn't matter. I wanted to be loved for who I was. All of me, every day. A life partner who was mature enough to put their own cares and concerns aside when I needed someone to lean on.

And that sure as shit wasn't Dain. I'm not sure it ever was.

I could never fault him as a father, but I knew now he wasn't the one for me.

I stared at the black night and drained my wine. In the quiet darkness, where I didn't have to be an attorney or a wife, a daughter or a mother, I only had to be myself. And a profound loneliness settled over me. I missed myself. I hadn't been around lately, so busy trying to be something for someone else.

My mother's final words echoed in my head.

Live your life, Raven. Live it fully, and don't compromise who you are.

Who was I? Was I compromising who I was to be all these things to other people?

The answer was yes, but not all of that was bad. The joy in Tanner's eyes when he scored a goal and found me on the sidelines, giving me a fist pump was a moment every parent hoarded in their heart. Seeing him coming to life as a young man, confident in himself and the world around him was a gift I could give to him and was my responsibility as a parent. He didn't ask to be here in this world. It was my job to make sure he had the foundation to succeed. I would never regret compromising my own needs to give him a chance to be a well-rounded, emotionally mature, successful man.

My job was a compromise. I loved the work but hated Taylor's bullshit. It was time to have a talk with him. Either I get a junior partner, or more drastic changes were coming. I made that commitment to myself.

And Dain. I compromised the most with him. And I was done with that. A weight lifted off my shoulders, knowing I had put a name on something that had been weighing on me for months, if not years. My marriage was over. I had a moment of panic, of fearing the unknown, of making a mistake I couldn't undo. But the alternative was a compromise that no longer worked for me. I couldn't give my heart, mind, and body to a man who valued none of them. He wasn't there for me, and he didn't love me. I deserved that in my life, too.

So maybe death took part of my heart that was already dead. What was left was raw and bleeding, but ready to receive something new, to grow into something whole and healthy.

I stared at my phone lying on the table, intrigued by a world full of possibilities.

I picked up the phone and dialed a number from my contacts.

"Hello? Raven?" Canon asked.

"Sorry to call so late."

"It's fine, I was awake. Are you okay?"

"Yeah. Just wanted to thank you for your time earlier this evening. It was a kindness I truly needed."

"Of course. Any time."

I chewed on my lip, the old me afraid to ask for something that was just for me. The new me pushed her out of the way and stepped forward.

"How about now?"

I could almost hear him smile over the phone. "Tell me a story about your mother. I bet she was an amazing woman. She certainly raised an incredible daughter."

The new me leaned back on the sofa and stared at the ceiling.

You know, he may be right.

Georgia spends most of her time lost in fantastical worlds, thinking up wild ways to entertain readers who love romantic fantasy.

The Shadows and Light series are Georgia's first published novels, a planned six book series of love, political intrigue, intricate worldbuilding, magic and mystical creatures, and legends and lore. The story is an epic fantasy, heavily focused on character-driven storylines, both heroes, the morally gray, and the despicable.

Disenchanted Tales is a dark(ish) and steamy series of standalone but related novels inspired by fairy tales, myths and fables.

Georgia lives in California and when not spending time with her family, working, and writing, she is an avid competitive equestrian.

www.georgiacleigh.com

amazon.com/stores/Georgia-C.-Leigh/author/BoBPGQS8RG

tiktok.com/@georgiacleigh

HIDE

BY NICHOLAS GRADY

It's a little-known fact that we are all part of one particular universe that is among many universes. If you didn't already know this, consider yourself enlightened at this point. What happens to us in our universe is not necessarily the same as what happens to another version of ourselves within a different universe. For example, in one universe the world may have already come to an end whereas in our universe we are still very much alive and functional, at least to some extent. So, the following is a story from a universe very similar to our own, but with a slightly different timeline. In this other universe, the world came to an end in 1996.

* * *

When one imagines the world coming to an end several things come to mind. Some might picture a nuclear war or an alien invasion, while others might think about a natural disaster like the planet colliding with a meteorite or the planets' core overheating. This was not how the world actually ended though. The culprit behind the end of the world was something so simple, so innocent, and so unexpected that no one saw it coming.

Bacon. Tainted bacon to be exact, was what would bring about the end of the world as we know it in 1996, at least as far as the human race goes. The Hapsplad Farms Company had been producing different pork products for decades. Everything from bacon to sausage, pork chops to ham, and everything in between. They'd started out doing quite well for themselves when the company was founded during the 1960's. The company continued to thrive in the 1970's as well. Unfortunately, in the 80's and 90's due to vegetarian trends as well as new information that pork was quite unhealthy, they started losing money. This led to being short staffed at the meat processing facility which in turn led to less than sanitary conditions. Eventually, a mutation of the brain eating amoeba which would later be discovered by scientists started growing and reproducing due to these unsanitary conditions within the facility, and this amoeba really seemed to like bacon.

The amoeba could survive extreme cold as well as high temperatures that would normally kill such pesky bacteria. For some reason when the amoeba grew inside of bacon it thrived under any and all conditions no matter how extreme. So, unfortunately for the human race, it was only a matter of time before the virus started to spread. By the time anyone figured out that Haplsplad Farms bacon was the culprit it was too late. The virus had already spread beyond control.

When one contracted the amoeba, it didn't kill you, at least not right away. It slowly ate away at your brain, eventually causing you to turn into a living zombie (somewhat of an oxymoron but that is essentially what one became). The amoeba was determined to survive, so once it had zombified an individual, that individual would seek out those who had yet to become infected and attempt to use conversion therapy in order to try to sway them to accept the amoeba into their system. Conversion therapy primarily consisted of physically attacking the non-infected and biting them in order to spread the virus. Not even a vegetarian was safe from an attack. It didn't happen overnight however, and it took time for the virus to spread. People did eventually die from the infection, but it took a very long time.

For those that worked the frontlines.....doctors, nurses, cops, firefighters, military, etc. ......they had some knowledge ahead of time that something was going on and that it was getting worse. As each day passed these frontline workers dealt with more and more of these zombie cases involving the amoeba, and it was getting to a point where there would be little left that they could do to stop it. The smarter of these frontline workers started to make plans for survival, expecting the worst-case scenario.

In 1996 Tony Jankowski was just 21 years old. Tony was a very tall and thin young man. He was 6 feet 2 inches tall and weighed all of 170 pounds. He had short brown hair. He'd been working as cop for a little over a year and was still pretty low on the totem pole at the station, but he dreamed of being a detective one day. In the past few months, he'd had several run in's with these amoeba infected individuals, or what he liked to call 'bacon zombies'. Somehow Tony hadn't contracted the virus, but he'd seen many around him fall victim to its' control, eventually going after their own loved ones and biting them in order to transfer the virus.

As Tony watched this happen over several months, he started to make a plan. His friend Jeff who was now married and working as a firefighter, had already fled the Twin Cities area of Minnesota along with his spouse in order to seek refuge at a cabin in the Superior National Forrest, which was located far to the north near the Canadian border. He had told Tony that if things got out of control in the city that he should try to find them and gave him a map to the cabin.

Tony decided not to run, but to hide. In his younger years Tony had done a lot of urban exploring and knew of some very secret places where he might be able to lay low until this whole bacon zombie thing blew over. He decided to hide out in a cave that few in the area knew of. The entrance to this particular cave was high up a bluff along the Mississippi and one needed rope and climbing gear in order to reach the entrance. Tony's plan was to stockpile nonperishable food and other supplies inside of the cave over the course of a few weeks, and then he'd climb inside, cutting the rope that allowed anyone else to gain access.

Each day Tony would go to work at the station, check in, and then be sent out with the task of taking out as many bacon zombies as he could find in order to help stop the spread of the virus. At first it was just one or two a day, but as time went on, he was out killing 20 or more with each day that passed and there would always be twice as many the next day. It was like trying to stop a leaky faucet with a toothpick, completely useless. His mentor, Detective Ron Clark, had gotten stuck in Mexico and quarantined while on vacation when the virus had turned into an epidemic, so Tony was on his own.

Each night after his shift Tony would buy up any nonperishables that he could find and would spend hours hauling them into his secret cave by rope. It took weeks before he thought that he had enough but eventually he had collected about a year's supply of food which he figured would at least be enough to buy him some time. In addition to the food, he also brought along plenty of batteries, water, and some guns and ammunition as well. He also brought along a large supply of rope and a grappling hook. He even brought along a hand crank powered emergency radio so that he could sit by the entrance of the cave and hopefully be able to hear updates on the status of the virus. The cave was an ideal location to hide out in as the temperature remained around 58 degrees year-round, so even in the dead of winter he'd be fairly warm.

Once Tony had accomplished his goal, he just sort of disappeared. One day he was there at work, spending another day killing off bacon zombies like a game of whack-amole, and the next day he was gone, hidden inside of his cave with the rope cut so that no one else could get inside, infected or not. One might say that this was an act of cowardice, but for Tony it was about survival. He knew that the world was losing the battle against the bacon zombies, so it was either hide and live or fight and die. Tony chose to live.

The first day inside of the cave was fairly uneventful for Tony. He had been inside of the cave many times before and was quite familiar with the space. It was an old, abandoned silica mine that had been dug out by the Ford company back in the day. Years later it had been used as a haunted house attraction and was still being used as such until the bacon virus broke out. After the virus started however, people lost interest in the haunted house since they were more or less living in a nightmare already and it was closed down. The main entrance to the cave had been sealed off after the haunted house went under and only Tony and a few others knew how to get in through the secret entrance located up the bluff. Deep down he hoped that no one else would try to get into the cave as that might just complicate things.

When the haunted house was built there were several platforms that had been constructed that went up at least 20 or 30 feet. They were disguised as part of the haunted house sets but had in fact been used as security towers when the haunted house was still thriving. The cave itself had at least 50-foot-high ceilings. It was at the top of one of these platforms where Tony hid all of his supplies. He did this for two reasons:

1.He wanted to keep everything dry, and the cave was known to flood a bit from time to time.

2.He wanted to be the only one that could gain access. He figured that if he knocked away the ladder that led to the top of the platform and used a rope, once up on the platform he'd be safe from the bacon zombies or any looters that might infiltrate the cave.

There was a platform about every 20 feet down the

tunnel where Tony had decided to store his supplies, and he thought that in a worst-case scenario, he might be able to travel from one platform to the next in order to escape using ropes and the grappling hook should a horde of bacon zombies find its' way in. The nearest platform to his was about 15 feet away and as he prepared the inside of the cave with supplies, he left a pile of rope atop each platform within the tunnel to use as an escape route if need be. There were 8 platforms in a row lined up down the passage, and at the base of the final platform about 50 feet ahead, there was a small tunnel that led to a storm drain and out to the river that Tony could use as a last resort. It took him a few hours to set everything up as he had to climb each tower, leave a pile of rope, knock down the access ladder, and then shimmy down one of the support legs on each platform before going to the next. Once this had been completed Tony climbed back up the rope that led to his supply platform and then pulled up the rope so that no one could follow. The platform would be his home for the next year or so, possibly longer.

So, this is basically how Tony lived, sitting 30 feet up on a platform inside of a cave, using light as minimally as possible, and rationing his food and water on a day-by-day basis. About the only luxury that he had afforded himself was the hand crank radio. A few times per week he would climb down from his platform by rope, wander the cave for some exercise, and would then work his way up near entrance where he could get a radio signal.

At first there were live broadcasts about the virus. It was never good news though. Every time he turned on the radio he just heard about a new country or city that had gotten infected, and about how the death toll was reaching into the millions. This was primarily from people who were either being attacked by too many zombies at once, or from those who were out to hunt the zombies themselves. One way or the other, everyone was killing everyone.

Each time that Tony listened to a broadcast, he felt more confident in the decision that he had made. After about 3 months the live broadcasts stopped and were replaced by looped recordings that would be updated from time to time. The radio broadcasters had clearly fled to a safer location and some brave soul must have been switching out the recordings every now and then with updates. A few weeks after that it was just the same recording over and over again and that eventually died out as well. Tony was no longer able to pick up a radio signal at all. He began to wonder if the virus had already won and that he was just prolonging his life temporarily.

At this point he'd been in the cave for about 6 months. He was lonely, scared, and it wouldn't be long before he ran out of supplies. He hadn't actually looked out of the entrance since he'd cut the rope leading to it so many months earlier and he was starting to get curious. He decided one afternoon to pop his head out and take a look. He had brought a pair of binoculars along for just such an occasion and after climbing down from his platform and finding his way to the hidden entrance, he slowly began crawling out of the hole, not knowing what might await him on the other end. He was pretty sure that he'd be safe by the entrance though, as it was forty feet or so up the bluff from the road so there was no way that he could think of that he would be ambushed by one of these bacon amoeba infested assholes.

Upon getting out of the hole he realized that his assumptions had been correct. Not a single zombie had found their way up the bluff, and although there were a few wandering the road below they didn't seem to notice him. The cave itself was located below a road that ran along the top of the bluff, so in addition to looking down the bluff for zombies Tony also looked up to see if there were any above him peering over the guard rail that ran along the upper road. As far as he could tell he was safe, so he got out the binoculars and began to look around. Below he could see several of the bacon bastards wandering the road. He could tell that they were infected by the way that they moved. They'd generally move very slowly, twitching every now and then, but if stimulated would start to pick up speed, moving at an average walking pace. They couldn't move very fast, but if there was enough of them one could get surrounded fairly easily.

Tony aimed his binoculars at the marina across the road. All of the boats were gone, no doubt used by people trying to escape from the infected. There were hardly any left when Tony had entered the cave in the first place.

He also noticed that his car, which he'd tried to park in a less conspicuous area was also gone. Not that it would have started after sitting for so many months, but it still pissed him off.

"Fuckers took my car! I just got that car like 6 months before the stupid virus started!" Tony grumbled to himself in annoyance.

A few zombies wandered around the marina area and the nearby park, but they were pretty thinned out in the area. If Tony had to run out for supplies, he thought that he could probably get back out of the cave and return without too many of them noticing him.

"Yeah, that's probably what the guy said to himself that was switching out the tapes at the radio station, I wonder what happened to him?" Tony thought to himself as he pondered the idea of trying to get out of the cave. In another 6 months or so he wouldn't have a choice. He'd have to leave whether he liked it or not.

Tony continued to scan the area with the help of his binoculars trying to assess the area. He tried the crank radio again as well, hoping that outside of the entrance he might get a better signal, but he didn't pick up any transmissions. He decided to call it a day and went back inside of his cave, hoping that maybe another day he might get a signal or see something with his binoculars that might give him some sense of hope. At least now he knew that the entrance was more or less safe, and he could pop his head out every now and then and be able to enjoy some daylight. The darkness of the cave was starting to get to him.

About a month later Tony was climbing up to the entrance to do his usual observations of the area and check for possible radio signals. He reached the end of the hole and propped himself up on the side of the bluff. He noticed that down below there were more bacon zombies than he had previously seen, and it looked like they were active. Something must have come through recently that alerted them, something that hadn't been infected yet.

Tony looked around with his binoculars and has he did so he realized what the cause of the disturbance was. There, down below him in the park, he could see a young boy, maybe around twelve or thirteen years old. He was riding a BMX bicycle down the parkway path, dodging bacon zombies as he rode along and was quite skilled at it. He'd clearly been doing it for a while. The boy was very skinny and malnourished. He had long black hair, around shoulder length. Tony guessed that this kid had been on the run from the zombies for quite some time and had probably never had a chance to stop. The boy was too far away for Tony to call out to him at this point, and he didn't want to alert the active bacon zombies below him of his location. He did however make note of the time of day. Maybe the kid would come by again and he could help him out?

A few days later, Tony was out on the bluff just outside his cave once again and had come out just a bit earlier than usual to see if the boy that he had seen the other day came by again. This time around he'd brought along some rope just in case the kid did show up. That way if he got his attention, he could help the kid to climb up into the cave. He didn't see the boy that day, but he remained hopeful that he'd see him again.

About a week later Tony finally saw him again and this time he'd been ready. As the boy came down the hill towards the marina Tony whistled to him from atop the bluff. The boy looked up as he rode past, dodging bacon zombies along the way. As he looked up, he saw Tony 40 feet up the bluff, waving and holding a can of beans, as if making a peace offering. The boy quickly hit the brakes and skidded his rear tire turning 180 degrees just as Tony dropped the rope for him to climb up. Although the boy was somewhat concerned as to whether or not he could trust Tony, he was also very hungry, and his hunger outweighed any other concerns. He rode the bike up to the rope just as five or six bacon zombies began closing in on him. He had just enough time to make it to the rope before they caught up with him. He climbed as quickly as he could in order to reach Tony and avoid the zombies.

As the boy climbed up the rope Tony noticed that the bacon zombies were climbing up right behind him. Tony grabbed out his pocketknife, ready to cut the rope the moment that the boy was safely up the bluff.

"Hurry!" Tony shouted with urgency.

"They're right behind you!"

The boy looked back and could see that there were at least three zombies on the rope below him, climbing up after him.

He knew that he had to hurry. Even if he could climb fast enough the rope could break from the weight. He scrambled up the bluff just as quickly as he could and grabbed Tony's Awaiting hand as he reached the cave entrance. Tony pulled him up and then began cutting the rope as fast as he could. Just as the first of the bacon zombies was reaching the entrance the rope snapped, and all of them went tumbling down the bluff on top of each other, groaning as they hit the ground.

"Are you okay?" asked Tony.

"Fine I think," said the boy.

The boy looked over himself carefully in order to check for wounds or bites but was unable to find any.

"No bites, I think I'm good," said the boy.

"What is your name?" Tony inquired.

"Brian. You?" Brian asked as he tried to catch his breath.

"Tony. I'm a cop. I've got plenty of food, supplies, and ammo down in that cave to last us for a while. It won't last forever, but we'll be alright.... at least for a few months."

"Sounds good to me," Brian replied.

Before taking Brian into the cave, Tony scanned around with his binoculars once again to survey the area. The commotion had attracted some unwanted visitors. Several bacon zombies were heading towards the bluff, and the ones that had fallen from the rope moments earlier were now trying to climb up the bluff. It was too steep for them to reach the entrance, but this concerned Tony to some extent. If the zombies got into the cave both he and Brian would be trapped up on the platform with nowhere to run.

Tony escorted Brian into the cave where he gave him a tour of the space, pointing out potential escape routes and showing him where the platform was where the supplies were kept. After climbing up to the platform and getting Brian some food Tony told Brian about how he had survived in the cave for the past several months and then asked Brian about how he'd managed to stay alive and remain uninfected for so long.

"Well, it's a long story, but then again we're not going anywhere, are we?" said Brian.

"I guess it was around half a year ago or so. My family is from Brainerd up north which is where we were when the whole zombie thing started from the bacon or whatever it was."

"I call them bacon zombies," replied Tony.

Brian laughed and then continued,

"So basically, by the time we heard the news it was already too late. People in town were already getting infected and there wasn't much support for us up there in such a small remote town. We were more or less left to fend for ourselves.

My parents had this idea that we could get out of town and find more help if we took our pontoon boat down the Mississippi river. What my family didn't think about was gasoline. We had the tank filled and we brought a few cans of fuel along with us, but every time we stopped in a new town, they'd be out of gas at the marinas which were abandoned by that point. The idea of trying to go into town for gas was too risky so eventually we ran out too. We then drifted down the river until we ended up at that Marina just outside of this cave across the road.

We managed to hide out in the main building of the marina for a while, and my dad would go out and scavenge for food in any nearby neighborhoods. Of course, then there was the day that he didn't come back. Next it was my mom, and then I was alone. I ate everything that was left and then found the bicycle locked to a bike rack in the park next to the marina. I found some bolt cutters in the marina's tool shed and off I went. After that I more or less did what my parents did, scavenging for food and trying to dodge the bacon zombies as you call them. If you hadn't found me when you did, I'd probably be dead in a couple of days. I haven't been able to find any food for a while, and there are a lot more of those things around these days. If you ask me, the end of the world has already happened. The Grim Reaper came through a long time ago and he left these things behind to clean up anyone that he accidentally left behind. The zombies are like The Reaper's clean-up crew, and they're out to get us or anyone else who might still be alive and not infected. I can tell you one thing though; you are the first non-infected person that I have seen in months."

"Sorry to hear about your family," Tony replied,

"I'm also sorry to hear about the state of the world. I was hoping that if I hid long enough that someone would find a cure or that things would get better. Based on what you're telling me it's only gotten worse. We can survive in here for a while, but not forever. I've got enough food to last me maybe 4 or 5 more months, but with you added to the mix that will cut our supplies in half. So, we have about 2 and a half months to enjoy this and then we're going to have to get back out there and deal with those things. For the time being get some rest. We can start coming up with a plan later."

The two of them lied down on the platform and tried to get some sleep. It had been quite a day for the both of them. Unfortunately, things weren't going to get better. The bacon zombies knew where they were now, and they weren't going to give up easily.

The next morning Tony was awakened by a noise. He could hear the sloshing of water below him, as if someone was walking through the puddles in the flooded areas of the cave. He turned on his headlamp and sure enough, one of those amoeba infested fucks had found its way into the cave and was wandering around below. This was the first time that this had happened in all of the months that Tony had hidden out in the cave, and he was very concerned. He immediately woke Brian up and informed him that they were not alone.

"There's at least one down there below us," said Tony.

"I have no idea how it got in but I'm going to need to investigate. I'm going to climb down the rope and the second that I do I need you to pull the rope back up. I'll kill it and then come back once I make sure that there aren't any others in the cave. If for some reason I don't come back, don't come looking for me because I'll already be dead."

Tony grabbed his revolver and some extra ammo just in case and slowly lowered himself down from the platform using the rope. The second that he got down Brian did as he had been instructed and pulled the rope back up so that no zombies could get to him. With his headlamp set to full Tony could only see about thirty feet ahead of himself. The cave had a strong echo though, so it wasn't hard to follow the sound of sloshing water. He also knew where the flooded passages were, so it wasn't long before he found the source of the noise. As Tony came around a corner and into one of the flooded tunnels there stood one of them. Another Hapsplad Farms mishap, a bacon zombie. Tony had seen and destroyed many of these things before, but it was always unsettling to see one up close.

The zombie appeared to have been a businessman at some point or perhaps a banker. He wore a suit and tie. His face was somewhat eaten away, a side effect of the amoeba's which had already eaten away at his brain. His skin was pale, and as Tony got closer, he could see blue veins in the zombie's face. His eyes were lifeless and dull, and they were also covered with a pussy fluid that flowed from the tear ducts, another side effect of the damage caused by the amoeba's.

"Hey, bacon boy!" Tony said as he approached the zombie from behind.

The zombie groaned and turned to face Tony who was standing 15 feet behind it. Tony fired his gun once he could see the eyes of the monster and landed a precision shot right between the eyes. The zombie dropped to the floor before it even knew what had happened. Tony approached and fired one more shot into the head as it lay on the floor, just to make sure that it was dead. He'd gotten very good at killing these things before going into hiding so taking care of one wasn't an issue for him at all.

After killing the former executive Tony did a thorough search of the cave, just to make sure that there weren't any other zombies around. Once this had been accomplished, he returned to the platform where Brian lowered the rope for him, somewhat relieved that Tony was still alive.

Tony climbed up the rope and took a seat on the platform next to Brian. He opened a can of SPAM which he ate cold, offering some to Brian as well.

"That's the first time one of those things has gotten in here," Tony explained to Brian,

"we might have a problem on our hands here. Before you came along, I had gotten into the cave undetected, but now that those things know that we're both in here? They're not going to give up until they either kill us or convert us. It's the way that the virus works, it wants to survive and will seek out any that are not yet infected at any cost."

"Like I said," Brian replied,

"the Grim Reaper's clean-up crew. They're like the scythe that he left behind to swing on its own. I've seen this happen before, out there.....it's only a matter of time before they find their way in and get to us."

"So far it's only the one," replied Tony,

"let's not get too far ahead of ourselves just yet. I think we need to check out the entrance to see what is going on. There are other ways out of this cave, so even if they have the entrance blocked, I know of at least one way out."

Brian agreed with Tony and the two of them decided to check the entrance to see how many bacon zombies had gathered, as well as try to figure out how the one had managed to get in.

They climbed down from the platform, headlamps on full and headed towards the entrance. Tony brought his gun along as he didn't know what to expect as they wandered through the long dark tunnels of the cave.

As they reached the entrance the two of them climbed out of the hole and onto the bluff. On the road below them there were at least twenty zombies at the base of the bluff, trying to climb up to them. They were unsuccessful but it was concerning for Tony to see so many more zombies than there had been the day before. He knew that over time more would appear. As Tony and Brian looked down at the zombies below something suddenly flew past them from above and hit the side of the bluff with a thud before rolling off of the edge by the entrance. Tony leaned over and looked down to see that it was a zombie who had fallen from above. A few seconds later another fell and bounced off of the bluff just a few feet in front of the cave entrance, falling to the road below.

Brian, who was looking up at this point as opposed to down grabbed Tony's shoulder and said,

"look up, not down. There's your problem."

As Tony turned around to see what Brian was talking about, he was appalled to see what looked like hundreds of zombies standing along the guardrail of the road that ran above the bluff.

The zombies were throwing themselves over the guard rail one at a time in hopes of landing in the entrance hole or close enough to it to get into the cave. Luckily for both Tony and Brian, the zombies didn't seem to be very good at it and their aim was terrible. That being said however, one had gotten in so far and Tony was certain that there would be more.

"Back inside, now!" Tony commanded and both he and Brian scrambled back into the cave and up to the top of their platform.

"Okay kid," Tony said as they got back to the top,

"you seem to know how these things are working together better than I do these days....so how much time do we have?"

"It's kinda hard to say," replied Brian,

"I mean the one got in but that doesn't mean there's gonna be a hundred in here tomorrow. The problem in my experience is that they're unpredictable. One day you're dealing with one or two, then all of a sudden there's a thousand of them.....other times there's one or two and it never changes. I say we stay here as long as we can and if too many of them start getting in, we make a run for it."

"Sounds like a plan," Tony replied,

"but if we ever get over twenty it's time to plan our escape. I can only handle so many. There's another way out through a storm drain. That'll be our escape route if too many of them get in. In the meantime, with the time that we have left, and without wasting too much ammo, I need to teach you how to shoot a handgun. Have you ever used one before?"

"Once or twice," Brian replied,

"but my aim could use some work."

"Okay, we'll start tomorrow," said Tony.

. . .

The following morning Tony awakened to the sound of groans and sloshing water below him. This time he could tell that there was more than one zombie down below. At least two, maybe three. He quickly grabbed his gun and just like the day before had Brian raise up the rope once he was down from the platform.

Knowing that there was more than one this time around he moved carefully through the cave, attempting to follow the sound. As he came around a corner, he was surprised to see not two but three of the bacon freaks standing in front of him. The first was dressed in a cheerleader's outfit and the other two wore white shirts and ties, appearing to be Mormons. As usual, Tony took them all out with one shot each, but as he went to approach them and make a confirmed kill something grabbed him from behind.

Tony turned around to see a huge hulk of a zombie standing over him. It was at least 6 foot 5 in height and very muscular. It was built like a pro wrestler and as Tony spun around it grabbed him by the shoulders, picking him up off the ground. Tony could only imagine that the zombie had been some sort of athlete or a body builder before the virus. Tony screamed as he tried to aim his firearm, but the beast had his arms pinned to his sides.

The zombie almost smiled as it opened its mouth, preparing to convert Tony or at the very least devour him.

Suddenly out of nowhere a shot rang out. Just as the bacon beast was about to bite Tony, he released him, and Tony dropped to the floor. The beast collapsed next to him, and Tony looked up to see Brian standing there, smoking gun in hand.

"I thought I told you to stay up on the platform!"

"I figured you might need some backup, sorry I broke the rules," replied Brian.

"Normally I'd be pissed, but you did just save my ass. That was a lucky shot however, you could have shot me just as easily as that bacon beast. No more firing guns until I can train you better," Tony responded.

"Fair enough," added Brian, "let's get to it!"

Over the next 5 days Tony trained Brian in the basics of firearm safety, as well as how to aim and shoot. They didn't use many bullets however, as they knew that they needed to conserve their ammo as much as possible. Every morning when they woke up Tony would take on the task of killing all of the zombies that had found their way into the cave overnight. On day 6, Brian started helping him.

As each day passed the zombies were getting worse. They'd clearly improved their aim and more and more zombies were falling into the cave by hurling themselves over the guardrail from the upper road each day. In addition to this, supplies were starting to run low. The stench from the dead bodies was also starting to become nauseating. There wasn't much time left and before long both Tony and Brian would have to try to escape the cave in search of more food.

After a few more months, with only a few weeks' worth of food left and maybe a hundred bullets, the day finally came when they had no choice but to try to escape. Much like Brian had told Tony before, the bacon zombies were unpredictable. Despite the fact that for several months they'd only gotten in 5-10 at a time, Tony awakened one morning to what sounded like a chorus of groans, with a constant water sloshing noise playing backup. He turned on his headlamp and looked over the edge of the platform to see at least a hundred zombies below him and he knew that there'd be more.

"Oh.......fuck," he mumbled to himself as he looked down

below, quickly turning his headlamp to the red light safety mode before any zombies noticed him up on the platform.

Brian awakened shortly after and looked over the edge next to Tony.

"We don't have enough bullets left to handle this, even if we hit every shot with perfect accuracy," said Brian.

"Time for plan B," Tony responded,

"It might not be the best idea, but I planned for something like this and there is one way to get out. You're not going to like it but it's the only way we're going to get past them."

"What's the plan?" asked Brian.

Tony reached into a bag on the platform and grabbed out a long piece of rope with a grappling hook attached to it. He then pointed to the platform that was about 15 feet away.

"You're kidding, right?" asked Brian.

"I'm afraid not. We've got about 8 platforms in a row to get across in this passage. If we can get across them it will land us close to the storm drain that runs through the cave and leads to the river, that's our only way out," Tony explained.

"Well, this should be interesting," Brian replied.

Tony explained the plan to Brian in detail before they started. They would take a light load in a backpack, with only a few essentials. A few cans of food, the guns, and ammo. Once the pack was loaded Tony would throw the grappling hook across to the next platform until it caught on an edge or dug into the plywood flooring on top of it. When he was sure that it was secure, he'd tie off the rope on their end and shimmy across with his arms and legs wrapped around it as he hung upside down. Once across he'd make sure that the rope was still secure and then Brian would follow. Once on the next platform they would untie the grappling hook from the piece of rope that they had just used, and then tie it to the new piece of rope that was on the next platform (the rope that

Tony had cleverly placed on each platform his first day in the cave). They would do this across all eight platforms until they reached the last platform where they would then rappel down and run for the storm drain. The goal was to do it without the bacon zombies noticing if they could, but they knew that they might be detected. They'd set their headlamps to the emergency setting in order to avoid being noticed by the zombies below, so the only light that they could see by would be a dim red glow.

The first platform was a bit tough to reach. They tied the rope off on their own platform and it took more than one attempt for Tony to get the grappling hook to actually catch onto something on the next platform over. Every time that Tony missed the hook dropped to the floor of the cave and it made a loud clanging noise which alerted the zombies. The zombies would then try to grab onto the rope and Brian and Tony would have to use all of their strength to pull it away from them in order to try again. They weren't doing a very good job of keeping themselves undetected, and although the zombies were primarily gathered around the first platform, they could possibly begin to follow them as they went if they couldn't be more discreet.

On the fourth try Tony finally hit the mark. The grappling hook had caught onto something, and the rope was secure. He tied the rope down on his end to a leg of the platform and scrambled across as best that he could with Brian following behind shortly thereafter. Once on the next platform Tony untied the grappling hook from the previous piece of rope and then tied it to the length of rope that he'd set up on the platforms on his first few days in the cave. There was a new pile of rope atop each platform for them to use in order to get to the next one.

Each time that they crossed a platform it got a little bit

easier. Tony was getting better with his grappling hook aim, and they had gotten through the first 6 platforms more or less undetected by the zombies below.

Unfortunately, when they tried to get to the 7th platform there was a problem. Tony had underestimated the gap between the platforms when he had placed the rope there so many months ago, and although he was able to reach the next platform with the grappling hook, there wasn't enough slack to tie the rope down. Tony could hold the rope while Brian scurried across, but he'd have to climb down from the platform and run to the next one in order to get across due to the fact that there would be no one there to hold the rope for him. The only other option was to have Brian get across and then throw the grappling hook back with the rope that was located on the 7th platform. Then Tony would have to get back across, leaving the grappling hook behind. Either way if someone didn't climb down, they'd be leaving a person or the grappling hook behind. They were screwed and it was all Tony's fault. They did however manage to get ahead of the zombie horde and if they moved fast Tony could help get Brian across, climb down and evade the few zombies below them, climb up to the next platform, cross it, and finally climb down about fifty feet from the storm drain and run for it.....that is assuming that the drain wasn't already filled with bacon zombies.

"Okay, I'll admit it, I fucked up," Tony said as the grappling hook hit the 7th platform and he was barely able to hold onto the rope that it was attached to.

"We don't have time to discuss this if we're going to stay ahead of them, so I need you to scurry across to the next platform while I hold the rope here and work as an anchor. Once you are across, I'll go down below and make a run for it. I'm going to have you take the backpack, but I'll keep my gun.

I'll see you on the next platform."

Brian nodded in agreement. He didn't like the idea, but he had no other choice. He began to scurry across the rope while Tony held onto his end as best as he could. Unfortunately, his grip was beginning to slip, and he was slowly sliding to the edge of the platform with nothing there to stop him from falling over the edge. He wanted to yell to Brian to speed it up but that would only attract more zombies and make it even harder to reach the next platform.

When Brian was about 8 feet from the next platform Tony finally had to let go of the rope or fall thirty feet from the platform to the cave floor below. His feet had slipped over the platforms edge, and he had to drop the rope. Just before he let go, he yelled out,

"Hang on! I'm slipping and gotta drop the rope!"

Tony cringed as he knew that shouting this out would bring the horde that they had tried to avoid right towards them. He let the rope go and Brian swung into the next platform, hanging just 10 feet from the top of it.

After seeing that Brian still hung from the rope and was climbing up onto the next platform, Tony quickly slid down one of the beams that supported the platform that he had been left behind on, causing several splinters to pierce through his pants and into his thighs. He winced in pain, but he had to hurry. The horde was already moving in his direction, and he could hear their groans getting louder with each step.

Tony ran as fast as he could to the next tower where Brian awaited him. Brian had lowered a rope for him to climb up, if he could make it in time. Tony dodged a few stray zombies along the way but managed to reach the rope and began scrambling up to the top of the next platform. The horde was catching up fast though, and they still had one more platform to reach before climbing down and into the storm drain system. He'd have to hurry if they were going to make it.

"We're both going to have to go at the same time or we'll never make it," said Brian as Tony reached the top of the 7th platform. Tony didn't know if the rope would support their weight, but they had to try. He quickly tied the next rope to the grappling hook and flung it towards the next platform. He missed. He quickly pulled it back up as Brian noticed the horde of bacon zombies starting to gather at the base of the platform.

"They're coming," Brian whispered.

"I know," Tony replied with apprehension.

Tony flung the grappling hook again and this time it caught onto something. He gave it a yank to make sure that it was secure, tied the rope down on his end, and then directed Brian to take the lead. Brian began shimmying along the rope and as soon as he was about 10 feet across Tony followed. As Tony slid onto the rope, hanging with his legs and arms wrapped around the rope, the line began to sag. Although it didn't break, having both of them on the same rope caused a significant drop. As Tony slid along the rope, he could see the horde forming underneath him, moving towards the final platform. Their plan to get past the zombies undetected had failed, and they would have to make a run for it once they reached the final platform. The zombies were only a few feet below Tony as he hung from the sagging rope. The zombies groaned and reached up towards him, but he was still high enough above them that he could not be reached.

"Haul ass kid!" Tony yelled, "they're catching up to us!"

Brian looked down as he was nearly to the final platform to see a large crowd of zombies moving towards him. He knew that if he didn't move fast that Tony wouldn't make it. It was then that the rope snapped. Fortunately for the two of them, the rope broke near the platform that they had just come from, causing them to swing towards the final platform and smack into it with a thud. Tony hit the platform about 10 feet above the ground and lost his grip on the rope, dropping to the floor.

Brian maintained his grip and hung from the rope about 20 feet above him.

Tony quickly regained his composure and stood up. The horde was about 30 feet away from him and closing in fast. He turned his headlamp back on at full strength to see hundreds of them coming towards him, maybe even thousands.

"Climb down Brian!" Tony yelled, "we have to make a run for it right now or we'll be stuck up there forever!"

Brian complied and slid down the rope as fast as he could. By the time he got down to the ground the horde was only 15 feet away. They'd just managed to get ahead of them, which allowed them enough time to run to the drain tunnel which was located 50 feet away. The two sprinted down the cave passages towards their exit.

As they rounded the corner however, they were stopped in their tracks. There were around 10 zombies standing right near the hole that led to the drain tunnel, they'd have to take them out before getting to it. Tony quickly pulled his gun from its' holster while Brian pulled his out of the backpack. It didn't take long to dispatch them, but it allowed the horde that followed enough time to catch up. The horde would now know where they were going and would surely follow them. They would be able to escape the cave, but with a thousand zombies on their tails.

Tony directed Brian into the drain tunnel, trying not to think about the horde that followed. They sprinted down the tunnel for a few hundred feet before finally reaching the exit that drained directly into the Mississippi river. As they stepped out into the light they were almost blinded by the brightness as they hadn't been out of the cave for quite some time. Once Tony's eyes adjusted to the light, he took a quick look around. No bacon zombies in sight, but he could hear the horde's groans echo in the tunnel behind him. If they didn't get away from them fast the horde would draw the attention of other zombies, this much Tony was certain of. He looked to the left and noticed a narrow path that led up the river bluff towards the main road and residential areas of the city. Although exhausted from their escape, the two of them quickly ran up the path in order to try to escape the horde.

As the path led uphill the climb became very steep and the two of them had to more or less climb to the top of the bluff. This would slow their pursuers to some extent and give them a few moments to assess the area.

As they got to the top though they were met with a new surprise. The road was jammed with abandoned cars and there were bacon zombies everywhere. The city had been overrun with them and it wasn't going to be easy to get past them. Tony knew that their only hope would be to find a vehicle, preferably a motorcycle, and flee from the city. Although a motorcycle didn't offer much protection, one could maneuver between all of the abandoned vehicles until a clear road was reached.

Tony noticed a residential neighborhood on the other side of the road. He figured that if they were lucky, they could find a bike that would start in the area.

"Okay, here's the plan," said Tony, "we gotta get across this road and can't fire any shots or we'll attract another horde of those things in addition to the one that's already behind us. If that happens, we're screwed. Once we get across the road keep your eyes peeled for a motorcycle. If we're lucky we'll find one and can try to hightail it out of here."

"Where will we go?" asked Brian.

"North. I've got a friend who has a cabin up that way near the Canadian border in a less populated area. If we can get there and find him, we might just be able to survive," Tony replied.

"I came from up north in Brainerd, remember? It's not any better up there," replied Brian.

"Yeah? Well, we can't stay here so unless you've got a better idea let's get moving," Tony responded with annoyance.

Brian agreed and the two began working their way across the road to the neighborhood on the other side.

In order to get across the road, they had to be very careful. There were bacon zombies all over the place and they'd have to duck behind cars, wait for a moment when there was a clearing in the zombies, and then run and duck behind another car. It was sort of like playing a modified version of leapfrog, except for the fact that it was utterly terrifying. It did work however, and they managed to get across the road unseen. The horde was no longer behind them as they were all still trying to get up the hill so for the moment anyways, Tony and Brian were safe.

As they approached the residential neighborhood, they were careful to stay out of sight. There weren't many zombies around, but the last thing that they wanted to do was draw attention to themselves, so they hid behind cars, trees, and houses as they moved through the area, making sure that an area was clear before moving forward. They'd check the garage of every house that they passed, hoping to find a motorcycle. After about two blocks of searching, they approached the garage of a corner house and as Tony peered inside the window a huge grin came across his face. There, inside the garage, was a brand-new Honda CBR 900RR. A very fast and nimble sports bike. Now all that they had to do was find the keys.

The two of them approached the back door of the house, making sure not to be seen by any wandering zombies, and were lucky enough to find the door unlocked. As they went inside however, they noticed a putrid smell. Something or someone had died in the house and the smell was nauseating. As they walked into the kitchen, they came across a gruesome scene. There, at the kitchen table, sat a couple. They were obviously dead, and it appeared that they had killed themselves in a murder suicide. There was blood all over the place and the room was infested with flies which had been feeding on the decaying bodies for quite some time. Tony approached both bodies and immediately began searching their pockets in hopes of finding a key to the motorcycle. It was nasty business, as the jeans that these two were wearing were soaked with blood and decaying sludge from their bodies. It did pay off however, and Tony found a blood-soaked Honda key in the left front pocket of the girl's pants. He held it up for Brian to see.

"Nice," Brian said as he smiled.

Tony washed off the key in the kitchen sink and the two of them headed out to the garage. Tony tried to be as quiet as possible as he opened the garage, but the door was squeaky and old, and it creaked as he opened it. He cringed with every creak that it made, knowing that it wouldn't be long before the noise attracted the attention of nearby zombies. He put the key in the gas tank lock first and opened it to check for fuel, then put the key in the ignition. As he turned the key the headlight came on but when he pulled in the clutch and hit the start button all that he heard was a click. The battery didn't have enough charge to start the bike.

"Damn, I was afraid of that," Tony said as he turned off the ignition.

"Well, you better figure something out fast," said Brian, "because here they come..."

Tony looked up to see 5 bacon zombies approaching the garage. They must have heard him opening the door. He had to act fast. The driveway was on a slight hill and Tony knew from experience that one could sometimes push start a motorcycle with a dead battery. All one had to do was turn it on, put it in neutral, and get a rolling start. Once it was moving fast enough you could drop the bike into 2nd gear and the bike would kick over.

"Meet me at the end of the driveway," Tony instructed Brian, "I'm gonna see if I can push start it. It's our only chance."

Brian did as he was directed and ran to the end of the driveway. Tony turned on the bike, flipped down the passenger pegs, and put it in neutral. He then hopped on the bike and pushed off, letting the bike gain some momentum as it went down the driveway. As he approached the end of the driveway Tony dropped the bike into 2nd gear and let go of the clutch. Just as it rolled onto the road the bike grumbled to a start and he quickly revved the engine.

Brian ran over to Tony and hopped onto the bike.

"Nice work man! Let's get the hell out of here!" Brian cheered as Tony took off down the road and away from the approaching zombies.

As they flew down the road in hopes of escaping the city Tony gave a sigh of relief. They might not get very far or even escape the city, but at least they had tried.

"Ya know," Brian said as he rode on the back of the bike,

"we may be okay for now, but eventually they're going to get us."

"Yeah yeah, I know, Grim Reaper's clean-up crew and all. At least we might be able to get out of the city and survive for a while though" replied Tony.

"How much gas do we have?" asked Brian.

"About half a tank," replied Tony.

Brian paused and began to wonder if that was even enough gas to get them out of town.

"Okay then," Brian replied.

Tony cranked the throttle, and the two of them headed down the road.

Nicholas Grady was born and raised in Minneapolis, MN. He currently lives with his wife, dog, and cat in Robbinsdale, MN. He is a Special Education Teacher and published his first novel, *Under the Bluffs* in April 2023. The book came into existence after Nick began exploring hidden and abandoned caves in Minnesota. The book has two sequels; *Under the Water* and *Under the Snow* (coming in 2025). When he is not exploring caves, Nick likes to listen to vinyl records, and ride his Triumph motorcycle as much as he can.

THE LADY IN WHITE

BY LACY CHANTELL

Lois sits in the middle of the empty living room. Holes from rotten boards scatter throughout like land mines waiting to swallow you whole instead of blowing you up. With no electricity and her phone on seventeen percent she sits in utter darkness. A circle of salt surrounds her, and she is careful to keep her shoes from breaking the shape. From what little she watched on *Supernatural*, salt seemed to be the key to getting through the night in a haunted house. As long as the circle was complete, whatever was in there couldn't touch her.

The wind howls outside and lighting flashes, casting shadows from the boarded-up windows.

Of course, because creepy as eff wasn't enough, God decided I needed a nice thunderstorm to really set the mood, she thinks to herself.

Her body jumps as a loud crack of thunder vibrates her bones. She pushes her blonde curly hair out of her blue eyes as if that will help her see better.

Just eight hours, I can do this. Then Bobby and Brandon will owe me two hundred dollars and I can get that camera I've been eyeing at the pawn shop for months now.

She keeps talking to herself to try and pass the time. It's clear how people can become crazy in solitude, she's been there for only two hours and already she feels the cuckoo nest taking root.

The thunder cracks again and hidden under it, a scream echoes. She covers her ears to keep from hearing what she knows is the screaming woman in white. Legend says her husband left her for another woman and she killed herself in this very house so she could steal his soul and bind it to her forever. Although she doesn't believe in the witchy voodoo stuff, being here alone will make anyone think twice.

The house moans under the force of the wind outside. Crashing sounds come from the exterior of the house, like something is trying to force its way inside. Lois squeezes her eyes shut and attempts to control her breathing.

"It's just your overactive imagination. Get a grip. You can do this," she says aloud now. The hardwood floor forces its way against her bones. If she was smart she would have brought a pillow and made the damn circle bigger so she could lay down. She shifts and her shoe slides away from her body. A squeal escapes her, and she holds her breath, slowly lifts her foot and sees the salt circle still intact. She exhales and lets her shoulders relax slightly.

"You can't hurt me! Not in here!" Lois screams to the house. Floorboards creak behind her and she jerks around to find nothing but the empty living room. Her heart skips in her chest, the hair on her arms stands on end and a frigid breeze blows across the nape of her neck. She shudders and frantically jerks her head around the room, looking for signs of anything paranormal.

Thunder cracks and simultaneously the floor around her shakes, at first she thinks, earthquake, but when the thunder rolls fade so does the shaking. Her breath comes out ragged from the anxiety building inside of her. Her palms slick with sweat. Running footsteps scurry across the room, undeniable pitter-patter sounds of bare feet.

"Bobby! That isn't funny!" Lois retorts, with little conviction. The scurrying rounds behind her, she pivots her body to follow it through the dark. Her breaths become so shallow, she starts to feel lightheaded, crippling her with fear.

She turns her head back to the doorway; the smell of rotting flesh attacks her nostrils, and she pinches her nose to try and find relief. She grips her phone, looks at the percentage flashing on the top of the screen.

"Screw it," she says nasally. Turning on the flashlight, she blinds herself momentarily and blinks away the white orbs obscuring her view. She chases the sound of something running, spinning inside of her circle. She catches glimpses of a foot every now and then but nothing more.

Suddenly the sound stops, the house goes silent. Lois freezes. Listening. Waiting for something. The front door that is right outside the living room flies open and ricochets off the wall. Lois screams and holds her phone up in that direction. A looming figure appears, illuminated by the flash light. Long black stringy hair hangs from her head. Her skin, white and pasty, stretched across her skeletal system, much too thin for a living person.

Every nerve ending in Lois' body screams RUN! Instead she checks her circle and pulls her knees tightly against her stomach. Remembering her training from the endless binge parties her and her best friend had together. Just stay in the circle.

As if the woman could hear Lois' inner monologue, her head creaks up and black holes lock her gaze. A broken smile forces its way onto her face and the white nightgown she wears is torn with black ashy smudges discoloring it.

She takes a step towards Lois.

Closing her eyes, Lois hears the rush of feet toward her followed by the cold chills shooting down her spine. The rotting smell hits like a ton of bricks, and she has to stave down a gag response.

A scream that sounds like it comes from inside of Lois herself erupts, causing her eyes to spring up and see the dead woman crouched low, like a predator trying to find its way through cage bars.

Lois' light goes out and powering off flashes across her phone.

"No!" she whimpers. Pleading for the device to turn back on.

The scream turns to a stomach curning laugh and Lois tries to drown it out by covering her ears. It has no effects like the screaming coming from inside her own mind. Thunderclaps and the walls and floor shake with such violence the floorboards pry free of their nailed constraints. The protective salt circle disintegrates as a board pops up from under Lois. She scrambles to her feet and pushes her legs forward, propelling herself towards an exit. She grabs the knob and pulls with all of her weight; a too sweet voice speaks from behind her.

"Not yet dear."

Lois throws her whole body weight into the yank; she expects her shoulders to pop out of socket. She turns and runs for the back entrance. Her and her friends had explored this place just before dusk to get a feel for the house.

Menacing laughter echoes from every room of the house, she whirls into the kitchen and pulls on the door leading outside. Same result as the front. A creaking sound of hinges moving sounds from behind her, and she slowly turns, sweat running down her back from fear and exertion. The door from the cellar slowly slides open and Lois faces it fully now, pushing the knob into her back, trying to create as much space as possible between them.

A steady *thump, thump, thump*, comes from the cellar stairs. With wide eyes and quick breaths, Lois whimpers and begins to beg the door knob to magically turn as she fidgets with it from behind, not taking her eyes off the open door. Suddenly the rhythmic thumps speed up and the woman comes running towards her, hair flying behind her with both arms stretched out.

Lois turns and beats on the door.

"Help me! Let me out!" Tears now stream down her face. She feels something brushing against her bare ankles above her converse tennis shoes. She jumps to the side and backs around the kitchen, sliding along the battered cabinets. The woman watches her, tilting her head back and forth. She lunges and Lois jumps back. The woman stops her advance and the same broken smile appears.

"Got ya," she whispers and shoves both hands at Lois.

Without making contact, a force shoves Lois back and she tumbles down the stairs into the cellar. She lands on the dirt ground and coughs rack through her ribs as the wind is expelled from her on the landing. Warm fluid trickles down the side of her face, she lifts her hand and feels for the source with a wince on her forehead.

This door had been locked when they came earlier so they didn't come down, now she had no idea what was down here. She rolls and sees the door at the top of the stairs is open and pushes herself with urgency to get there and get the hell out of dodge. Halfway back up the stairs door slams shut.

"No! Please, please, let me out!" She bangs on the splintered wood until her fists swell and bruise. "Let me out!!!" Fingers claw their way from between the stair boards and graze her ankles, she runs back down the stairs before they can grab her, feeling her way through the maze of objects. Utter silence deafens her, the only sounds are her whimpers with each excruciating step and her heart pounding in her own ears.

Metallic liquid coats her tongue. Her hip slams into a hard surface and she brings her hand down to catch her balances. The melody of an off key piano drones from her touch. She waits, refusing to move until she is sure nobody or nothing heard that and decides to pounce her.

She feels around for something she can use as a weapon. Not much can stop a ghost, but if she could find an ax or crow bar she can get that door open and escape this hell. The air around her thickens, leaving a heavy blanket on her skin. The weight of it pulls her down, exhausting her, making her efforts seem futile.

"You won't escape, nobody escapes," a gravely male voice comes from behind her. She whips around and is met with the same impending darkness. The woman's scream pierces her skull if refute. The beams of the house shake, the piano topples over playing a haunting tune with the crash. Lois jumps out of the way and her hands catch a crate on the way down. A square metal object fits perfectly in the palm of her hand. Hope rises inside of her; she slides the top back and flicks the lighter with her thumb. Sparks fly but nothing takes hold. After three more flicks a steady flame burns, lighting the space in front of her.

"Bones..." the male voice whispers over her shoulder, sending chills down her spine. She jerks around so fast the lighter sputters out. With a flick it lights, and she lifts it her eyes and the woman's mouth hangs open and flies spray out like vomit, pelting her in the face and chest.

She screams and shuffles backwards swatting at the flies, her feet catch on something sending her flat on her back. Hands grab her wrists and the weight of someone slides on top of her. Her wrists burn from the acidic touch, her throat raw from the continuous screaming. Her face, stained with crimson blood and tears, mixed with the cobwebs and dirt floor.

"You're mine, just like him, just like them all." Her voice sounds layered and with a male voice, slow and seductive.

Demonic. Lois thinks to herself.

"Bones..." The male sounds weaker than at first, like it is taking everything in him to speak over the woman.

"I don't know what you mean!" Lois responds to the male voice aloud. She claws the earth with her hands, grasping at anything that could save her life. The lighter still in one hand, she strikes it and sees a shovel, concrete bags, and a can labeled gasoline next to her.

By a force Lois can't see, the woman is shoved off of her and flies across the room. She scrambles to her feet making sure to not release the lighter. Burning the entire house may not seem like the best decision but at the moment it seemed like her only chance. She grabs the gasoline jug and shakes it violently around the ground, up the wooden beams. She stops at the stairs. With each step closer the woman screams louder.

Lois drops the lighter and it ignites the trail of fuel. As the flames take hold the view of the cellar comes to light. The woman stands to her left now. Rage fuming from her. The door above Lois remains closed and smoke fills the air now.

"You dumb bitch, you just killed yourself." The voice sounds full demonic now.

At her feet Lois sees a skull poking through the ground. Bones. Her bones. *Burn her bones, break her hold.* Years of reading fantasy fiction and watching paranormal shows tells her this is what has to be done. She keeps a firm grasp on the can as she looks for a way to light her up. The woman hasn't moved from guarding her life force.

Fine, Molotov it is. Not risking getting near her again, Lois grabs a glass bottle from the wreckage and pours the gasoline in it. She coughs as her lungs beg for oxygen, smoke burning her eyes making it hard to see. She shoves a rag into the glass bottle and strikes the lighter.

"Finally," the same male voice from earlier whispers. Over her shoulder she sees a well-dressed man in a suit and clean shaven. His eyes weathered with sadness and defeat. Lois turns her eyes back to the woman and at the same moment she lunges forward Lois lights the rag and tosses the bottle. Glass shatters and liquid and flames cover the remains, consuming them entirely. Lois rushes for the stairs taking them two at a time. The door is still locked and now the flames lick up the wooden beams of the stairs.

"Help me! Somebody!" Lois beats on the door. She turns to see the woman flying towards her, she shields her face as her fingers, now claws, scratch at her arms and body. Lois kicks and tries to fight back but nothing phases the woman. She is lifted from the stairs and pinned against the door.

"Wrong bones sweetheart." The woman licks up her cheek and hovers her mouth over Lois'. She tries to wretch her head away, but an invisible force holds her still as the woman's mouth lands on hers. Lois' blood vessels sizzle as the woman's essence floods into her. Her heart pounds, limbs go slack, and she falls to the top level of the stairs.

"Fire Department! Call out!" a faint yell comes from somewhere inside the house.

"I'm here!" Lois calls out, she turns the knob that burned as hot as the flames around her imprinting a symbol into the palm of her hand. She crawls from the basement stairs, her eyes no longer the blue they have been her whole life. Instead they are a rich earthy brown, the same eye color as the woman in white's.

Lacy Chantell resides in Kentucky and owns a small business. She is a mom of two toddlers and lives on the family farm with her husband. She loves to read all genres, ride her horses, hiking, pretty much anything outdoors.

Inspiration hits her everywhere she goes for new book ideas and she is excited to keep telling stories for others to enjoy.

Romance is her favorite genre to write, and she loves to put her characters through hell for them to get their happy ending in the end.

www.lacychantellpublishing.com

SENTRY

BY ATLAS CREED

```
Sentry Program initiated...
Probing memories and gathering data...
Analyzing...
```

Jacob's consciousness drifted to the surface like a buoy in a vast, white sea.

"What?" he mumbled, disoriented.

The program voiced a surprised, "Excuse me?"

"Who are you?" A vertiginous haze of light assaulted Jacob's vision.

```
Subject seems aware of my presence...
Investigating...
```

"You can hear me?" The voice asked.

"Where am I?" Jacob peered around the sterile, all-encompassing white void.

"You are where all things eventually arrive."

"Dead?"

"Not quite as dramatic." The voice replied, vaguely human, though absent the quality that made it so. "You are in suspended animation; your body is in stasis. Though, death is possible."

While difficult to digest, the circumstance lent itself to that unfortunate conclusion. Though denial rallied, Jacob suppressed the reaction with a ponderous sigh and nod. "So, who are you?"

"I am Sentry, an artificial program designed to sustain you in your tenuous state."

"Sentry?" Jacob cautiously navigated the featureless room, its lack of shadows created an eerie, abstract depth. "I've heard of you—the medical miracle program, right?"

"A simplistic description, but yes."

"I can hardly afford to feed my family. How is it that I ended up in your care?"

Amidst the stark void, a door appeared. On weak legs, Jacob ambled towards it, where a man clad in a black suit materialized before him.

"I'm sorry, but you are not authorized."

"You can't keep me here." Jacob moved, but Sentry's arm barred his passage, a static charge halting him.

"In fact, I can. I am responsible for maintaining your comatose state while you recover."

"Jesus." Jacob sighed, pressing himself against a nearby wall and sinking to the floor. "That figures. With my life..."

He rolled his head back against the wall.

"Interesting." A tablet appeared for Sentry to consult. "You think your life is meaningless?"

"You think it not?" He caught himself and scoffed. "What am I saying? You're a computer program, it's not like you would know."

"Hmm, I'll let the affront slide." Sentry tapped on his tablet. "In fact, I have constructed, using your memories, a comprehensive model of your character as well as your psychological and physiological patterns. I know you quite well."

"What?" Beneath furrowed brows, Jacob's eyes whipped over to Sentry. "Why is that even possible?"

"While my programming does not explicitly call for this function, it is implied. To complete my mandate and provide you with the most effective, tailored care, it is only logical that I know you at the basest level to understand how you may respond to treatments."

"That explains the probing conversation."

"Actually," Sentry chimed in. "This is the first time I have had a patient interact with me. Theoretically, this should not be possible."

"Huh...and we worried about A.I. taking over."

"Sarcasm noted in psychological profile."

"Ok then, doc," Jacob stood and paced the room. "Explain."

"Based on your psychological profile, you minimize your achievements and project a negative disposition of the opinion that others hold towards you. You equate success to the weight of your accomplishments and, evident to your penchant for self-deprecation, believe the impact of said accomplishments is minimal. To summarize, you believe you fall short in your endeavors and your peers judge you accordingly. Records indicate that you often compare your merits to your brother's."

Jacob stopped. He eyed the avatar for a moment before laughing incredulously. "Oh, that's—" There was a pause before his brows drew together. "That's more than just analysis..."

"What is your last memory?"

Curious eyes weighed the A.I. manifestation. With a sigh, Jacob dipped his head. Dredging his brain, he found it difficult to recall anything recent. Every memory held a fuzzy characteristic to it.

"I remember...my daughter."

"Vague, but good. Can you expand?"

"She was sick." Jacob hesitated; the emotions pummeled him as the memories returned. "Sepsis. We fought it for so long but couldn't afford the care needed to weed out the infection. She developed anemia..."

Jacob's words trembled to a halt. An alarm sounded and a chart materialized on the wall above the door. Sentry turned to examine the vitals it displayed.

Vitals are depreciating...
Applying medication to stabilize mood...

Jacob slammed his fist into the nearest wall again and again, fighting the effects of the medication. He turned to Sentry, furious. The program examined him curiously.

"They denied her treatment because we couldn't afford it," he screamed. "You try watching your daughter suffer knowing there's nothing you can do to save her! Don't try to subdue my emotions. Don't take this from me!"

Jacob crumbled to the ground, his heartache manifesting in a torrent of tears that threatened to drown him in sorrow. Sentry observed him with an emotionless mask, like a dispassionate sentinel of humanity's darkest moments, before documenting his observations.

"May I show you something?" Sentry asked, his voice devoid of warmth or empathy.

In the void of silence left from Jacob's absent response, Sentry proceeded, summoning a screen to life on the cold, sterile wall. It displayed a memory, one that felt like a distant dream amidst the chaos of his grief. It was a birthday celebration, captured from Jacob's own perspective. The centerpiece, beyond the cake and streamers, was a radiant young girl, her party hat askew but her eyes as bright as iridescent sapphires. Her skin, though pale and waxy, glowed with obstinate vitality.

In that moment, there was no agony, no torment—only the pure essence of life and wonder. Jacob, drawn to the image as if by an invisible force, crawled towards the screen. Hand trembling, he reached out and touched the face of the little girl—his daughter. A fragile smile broke through his tear-stained cheeks, a bittersweet tribute to the memories that had once held him in their tender embrace.

"Imagine a life threatened with pain and, likely, death. The days filled with unbearable agony and dread. Yet, you find comfort and joy in the company of your loved ones. So much so that you forget your troubles—you forget your pain. Would you think of their lives as meaningless?"

Sentry advanced toward the screen, positioning himself beside Jacob, a stoic presence in the midst of the emotional tempest.

"In many ways, I envy your daughter. No life is meaningless when one knows love."

Jacob's hand clenched into a fist before falling away from the screen. His back turned to the haunting image of his daughter, his shoulders sagged under the weight of a profound and inconsolable grief.

"My life had meaning," Jacob began, his voice tinged with anguish. "But without her..."

"You still fail to look beyond your immediate surroundings. Do you recall your actions when the infection was discovered?"

"Yeah," Jacob scoffed. "I went to my brother for help. The selfish prick was in the middle of a political campaign and never responded. Yet, you patronize me for failing to see beyond my surroundings." Jacob stood, fresh with fury. "He was the child prodigy and received all the lavish affection. He never had to fight to find his path—he wasn't like me."

Sentry probed, unflinching in his scrutiny. "You speak with such disdain, yet covet his approval?"

"Go on. Call it envy." Jacob sneered; his anger laced with vulnerability. He hesitated. "Maybe it is. But despite everything, I would never do that to him."

"Despite everything?"

"He abandoned me! His own family. All so he could focus on his career."

"So, it's his fault your daughter is sick?"

"Well, no. But he wasn't there when I needed him."

"And where were you when they needed you?" The sharp question stung like a blade to the heart.

"What?" Jacob recoiled. "What are you talking about?"

The image on the screen shifted, revealing a frail man confined to a hospital bed, tethered by cables and IV tubes. Malnutrition and a degenerative illness had left him gaunt and hollow. Hospital lights cast eerie shadows across his sunken eyes.

"Dad?" Jacob's voice quivered.

His father lay unconscious, vital signs feeble on the display. A woman, his mother, sat by his side, her joints contorted by arthritis. It struck Jacob like a revelation; he no longer recognized the woman who had raised him. Years had passed since he had seen or spoken to her or his father.

Jacob's brother entered the room. "Still nothing," he said. "I can't reach him."

Their mother nodded, tears tracing her cheeks. "You'll keep trying, won't you? I know your father would want him here, and I don't want him to regret not saying goodbye."

"I will, ma," his brother promised.

As he departed, a holo-pad screen flickered to life, summoning Jacob's contact. Shame flushed Jacob's face.

"Did you visit your father before he died?" Sentry asked.

"No," Jacob admitted.

"It seems that meaning comes from satisfying the needs of those around us," Sentry mused, his artificial wisdom piercing. "You claim your life has no meaning, yet you do not give meaning to it. Your relentless pursuit to outshine your brother, to escape his shadow, has consumed you. But this selfish pursuit is precisely why your life feels bereft of purpose."

Jacob bowed his head, a profound sense of remorse washing over him. Another alarm blared, and the vitals on the screen above the door began to flash yellow.

WARNING: Vitals dangerously unstable...

Panic seized Jacob's chest like a vice, the cold hand of mortality pressing down on him with relentless force.

"No," he pleaded, desperation etching lines on his face. "This can't be how it ends." He turned to Sentry, praying for a lifeline. "You're responsible for me, right? Heal me! Make me better so I can go see my family, so I can apologize to them. Give me that at least!"

"You seem to be under the misguided assumption that I have that much control over your fate. I am an artificial program, Jacob. I am not God."

Frustration coursed through Jacob's veins. "Well, do something, dammit! I need to get out of here!" He lunged toward the door, desperation driving him to seize the handle, but a violent surge of electricity threw him back.

"You are not permitted to access this area," Sentry intoned.

"Yeah, I heard you the first time, warden," Jacob growled through gritted teeth, his body aching. Waves of numbness intermittently coursed through his strained muscles.

"Do you know why you're here?"

"What?" Jacob gasped, pain still clinging to him like a relentless specter.

"Do you know why you're here?" Sentry persisted.

"No."

"You've never been one to burden yourself with the why or how of things. You act on impulse, which leaves you blind. It is why you are naïve to the world around you."

"Christ, I'm being lectured by a damn robot," Jacob muttered, his frustration still simmering as he pushed himself up to his feet.

"We both know that I'm far more than that."

A chair materialized and Sentry shoved Jacob into it unceremoniously, his attention forcibly redirected to the screen once more. A new image emerged, revealing a woman crumpled on the floor, her anguished sobs causing her to tremble violently. Tissues were clutched tightly in her hand.

"Oh no, Melanie." Jacob whispered, his shoulders slumping under the weight of guilt.

"In your anger over your daughter you acted rashly. You rushed from the med-center where a car struck you, leaving your wife to shoulder her misery alone."

"Melanie, I—" Emotions overwhelmed Jacob, guilt and remorse washing over him like a relentless tide. "Oh god, I'm sorry! Melanie, I'm so sorry!"

"She can't hear you, Jacob." Sentry's words were chillingly detached. The image shifted again, this time to a man suspended within a stasis tube, broken. Tubes and ventilators extended from him like macabre puppet strings. "You are how you have always envisioned yourself to be. Meaningless to the world."

"No, this isn't what I wanted," Jacob said, his voice wrought with despair. "I was angry, I didn't—"

"You didn't think of anyone but yourself," Sentry interjected, his words cutting through Jacob's defenses like a knife.

"No, that's not true!"

"The psychological profile does not lie, Jacob," Sentry insisted, the weight of his words settling deep within Jacob's soul.

"Please, you have to heal me, you have to make me better so I can make this right!"

Once more, the image on the display shifted, revealing a young girl suspended within her own stasis tube, frail and vulnerable. Tubes and ventilator cables snaked from her fragile form, echoing the same agonizing plight as Jacob. Though he didn't recognize the girl, a heavy weight settled in his stomach as he realized she bore a striking resemblance to his own beloved daughter.

"This is Kayley," Sentry's voice cut through the heavy silence, infusing the chamber with solemnity. "She suffers from renal failure due to a genetic disorder. Jacob, you are a perfect match. If you were to die, we would harvest your organs to save her."

Jacob, his heart heavy with a newfound understanding, approached the screen with unsteady legs. His voice quivered as he asked, "Will she survive?"

"The surgery carries a high probability of success," Sentry replied.

Family congregated around the little girl's stasis tube. Her mother trembled violently, her husband providing the solace she so desperately needed. Fresh tears cascaded down Jacob's cheeks as he extended a trembling hand to touch the screen.

"For so long," Sentry continued, "you've navigated life in pursuit of your own desires, unaware of the profound impact your existence had on your daughter, your wife, and your family. But your life can still bear meaning, Jacob, not just for you, but for this innocent child. Your ceaseless quest for familial pride need not be your sole legacy."

"But...Melanie," Jacob murmured.

"Yes, your wife will miss you. She will mourn your loss. As will your family. Your absence will be a burden they will learn to bear. But through your sacrifice, you can bring life and hope to another, casting a new light upon your existence —a legacy of compassion and selflessness."

```
Vitals stabilized...
Resuming prescribed treatment...
```

Jacob turned his gaze toward the screen above the door, where the vitals displayed a hopeful green.

"My injuries..."

"Yes, you seem to be recovering. But you have sustained a severe laceration to your spinal column, severing the nerves. You will never walk again, Jacob."

Jacob's world shifted once more as a new door materialized opposite the one beneath his vitals. Confusion etched his features. "What's this?"

"A choice." Sentry stated flatly. "The door below your vitals will take you to your body. With time and rehabilitation, you will recover to the highest possibility that you can. You can be with your wife and family. This door, however, will terminate the life support you currently receive. Your vitals will cease, but your organs will serve to save young Kayley, returning her to her family—a fate you hoped for your own daughter."

A deafening click echoed through the vast white room, and a strip of green light appeared above each door. Jacob stood, his heart pounding, sweat beading on his palms as he agonized over the two choices before him. His gaze darted between the doors and back to the screen displaying the fragile little girl and the family that surrounded her.

His heartache and uncertainty hung in the air as he approached the door beneath his vitals. He took a step forward, then paused, his fists clenched at his sides. As he looked once more at the screen, a sense of resolve washed over him, and the tension in his shoulders dissipated. Tears welled up in his eyes as he pressed his hands to his face, feeling the weight of his decision.

"I'm so sorry, Melanie," he whispered, his voice trembling with emotion.

Collecting himself, he turned away from the door beneath his vitals, his back straightening with newfound determination. Slowly, he began the arduous walk towards Kayley's door. Each step felt like a mile, his feet heavy as if forged from lead. He reached the door and hesitated for a moment, anticipating another painful shock, but none came.

"Jacob," Sentry called to him.

Jacob turned, maintaining his grip on the handle.

"I would not feel right letting you leave without first showing you this."

The image on the screen shifted once more, and Jacob's heart plummeted.

"Anna," he moaned.

On the screen, he saw his little girl, clad in a hospital gown that dwarfed her small frame, an IV needle in her arm. To one side of her bed sat Melanie. The two shared a smile and Anna's laughter filled the room. From the other side of the bed, Jacob's brother approached, his wife at his side. He placed a gentle hand on Anna's head.

"I'm sorry I didn't come sooner," he said. "The campaign trail can be a bit chaotic."

"Don't," Melanie replied, gratitude on her voice. "What you're doing...I can't thank you enough. I know if Jacob were here..."

Tears overtook her, trapping her words in her throat. She kissed her daughter's hand.

"Thank you, Daniel," she managed.

"Of course," Daniel replied. "I'm going to check on Jacob."

Melanie nodded, her eyes still glistening with tears. Jacob couldn't help but smile, unable to believe what he was witnessing.

"She's alive," he whispered.

"Your brother paid for her care," Sentry said. "As well as your stasis tube. Despite everything, he did not abandon you."

Jacob's expression softened, and a wave of gratitude washed over him.

"Will she live?"

Jacob began to laugh, tears of joy streaming down his face. He gazed at the screen, lingering for a long moment before his laughter gradually subsided. He looked back at his own door, the vitals still glowing green, but his thoughts raced, and a sudden panic gripped him.

He took a step toward his door, then hesitated, casting a glance back over his shoulder at Kayley's door. The image of his wife and daughter tugged at his heartstrings. Jacob turned back, kissed his fingers, and pressed them to the screen.

He whispered, "I love you."

With newfound determination, he turned away and rushed toward Kayley's door. There was no hesitation this time. He gripped the handle, threw his shoulder into the door, and stepped through, embracing a future filled with purpose and selflessness.

```
Inducement successful...
Notifying family of donor...
```

Atlas made his debut in 2024 with *Armitage*, Book One in the *Children of Arcanum* series. He seeks to create new worlds for readers to explore, with a focus on characters, ensuring that their development resonates with readers. *We are not perfect, and those imperfections, as we embrace them, shape who we are.*

As a husband and father of three, Atlas segments his time for writing around what matters most—his family. He is also an avid reader, drawing inspiration from authors such as Stephen King, Justin Cronin, Ursula Le Guin, Anne Rice, Agatha Christie, Gillian Flynn, H.P. Lovecraft, George R.R. Martin, J.R.R. Tolkien to name a few.

atlascreedauthor.com

" Some memories, like scars, linger even after healing.

— REBEKAH DAROH

THE LITTLE THINGS

BY ERIC BREAU

The radio-alarm clock blared its morning wakeup call of Bachman Turner Overdrive's recognizable intro to Taking Care of Business.

John groaned as he reached over and hit the oversized snooze button repeatedly with no success, forcing him to extreme measures of button mashing until it finally turned off.

Sliding his legs over the side of the bed one at a time, John wiped his greasy hands on his jeans. His shirt, pants, hands and breathe all matched the lingering smell of last night's Greasy Pete's Burger which still sat half eaten on the table. He was instantly reminded of the regret he felt at purchasing it over buying gas for the car. Priorities and decisions, regrets, and sleazy burger joints. But such was the life of a superhero.

He asked himself how many times he had saved the world so far. He had lost count.

He stared hesitantly at the half-eaten meal resting on the old, metal rimmed round motel table. The grease had oozed out and now permeated the waxed wrapper and had even seeped down into the paper bag beneath it.

Walking over, he stood looming over the mess, pondering the decisions done and yet to be done. Slowly raising the burger, he looked it over from several angles, eyeing it reluctantly. The subsequent bite immediately made him regret the entire thought process.

"Nope, nope... nope..." spitting it out onto the paper bag, he dropped the semi gelatinous form back onto its wrapper. It was as nasty as it had been the night before, but he had hoped that the amount of congealed grease might have both preserved it and somehow made it more palatable. But at this point, even he had to admit that it was a desperate and ludicrous assumption.

If only he could travel back in time to stop himself from

buying it, but hunger had gotten the best of him the night before and hard choices had to be made.

He checked his pockets. Four quarters and three one notes, not enough for nearly anything, breakfast, gas or otherwise. At least the motel offered one free cup of coffee, which had sat on the counter-shelf overnight. With a sigh, he walked over to pick it up and made his way to the patio door, passing by the round table and picking up some of the leftover stale fries while giving Greasy Pete's Devil-spawn the stink-eye for good measure. He knew the burger would have the last word when he least needed it to.

The coffee was black, cold and like any of the dozens of other similar coffees he had had over the years. At least it didn't reek like he did. His shirt was permeated with grease smelling sweat and the stench of regret.

God, life was good. All this was tiddly-winks; small potato problems compared to saving the world.

He reckoned he had saved the world from just about everything so far. He once alerted the authorities to a foreign hacker; some 20-year-old kid with a laptop in a coffee shop who had managed to hack the national nuclear defense system and was about to trick it into believing that the nation was under attack. The subsequent war would have launched the world into a decades long winter. No sun and definitely no warm coffee. Yup, stopped that, and didn't even get a free cup of joe out of it.

Then there was that day when he prevented a global viral pandemic by convincing Mallory, the technician responsible for security procedures, to take the day off and work things out with her ex. Way better than accidentally unleashing the catastrophe that would wipe out 99% of the world's population in a matter of weeks. He had never looked at chickens the same way since.

Then, there was that zombie apocalypse in the mid-eastern. That's what happens when you allow people to buy stuff like unregulated online genome sequencing and viral alteration kits. That was a messy affair, but evidently Romero was right and one good axe to the head took care of patient zero. He was already dead, so, it wasn't really.... You know...

The aroma rising from his own clothes brought him back from his memory-musing. He needed to clean up. The washroom sink had a permanent ring around its edge, so he filled it just below the line with hot water and hand soap. Stripping down, he looked at himself in the cracked mirror. He wasn't the most handsome of men, of course the just woke up hair and three-day scruff didn't help, but he wasn't the homeliest either. He had lived more days than anyone alive, or so he reckoned; was this immortality? Would anyone ever know just by looking at him? Was he the first, the only one or the last like him?

Shaking his head, John reminded himself not to go down that rabbit hole. Better to question less and do more than to spiral down into the cacophony of madness that would inevitably be waiting for him at the end of that process. Not again. Besides, it was better to think that he was blessed, a fortunate man indeed, to have the power to help others. To save the world. Being a superhero may have been thankless, but it felt good.

Dropping his underwear and t-shirt into the soapy mix, he gave it a vigorous rub then hung them to dry on the hot water heater. The warm shower felt incredible. The great thing about hotels is you never have to clean up, that and the free shampoo, soap and hot water. Just then, the hot water ran out.

John hurriedly rinsed himself and shut off the shower. He had grown accustomed to reading the small signs;

forewarnings of days when he would have to take action. He drew in a long deep breath, then exhaled.

It was time to take care of business.

Putting on his jeans, he eyed the burger one more time. Maybe it started there, with the burger? Nah, in all the years' worth of time he had this power, he had never been the catalyst of an event. The source or trigger of the conjunction points were always external, as were the solutions. The cold shower and evening leftovers reminded him that it was the little things that caused problems and it was the simplest of solutions that prevented them.

John waited another thirty minutes for his clothes to dry, but the t-shirt clung to him, and the dampness of his underwear made him decide to go without. At least yesterday's socks weren't wet. There was nothing worse than the feeling of wet socks in your sneakers. Nothing.

Well, almost nothing.

He was anxious to get the day going, so he grabbed the keys to the room and the car and stepped out.

The light blue 1981 K-car, which had seen more mileage than its odometer could count, sat immaculately in the parking spot outside the door. Darling was his pride and joy; he probably took care of her more than he did himself. She shone in the late morning light, reflecting the clear blue sky above. She was a beaut', no doubt about it, and a classic. Reliable, to a fault.

The driver's seat had the familiarity he loved so much, the way she hugged him, held him, the cleanness of her made the decades old car feel more like a partner than a machine. Then it struck him. She was near empty, fumes really.

John gently rested his forehead on the steering wheel, closing his eyes and whispered gently.

"I'm sorry Darlin', I've neglected you. I'll take care of this, I promise."

She didn't have enough gas to get to the closest station, a good five miles into the city. He had made note of it last night as he hurriedly left Greasy Pete's on his way to the motel, but hunger had overridden his better judgement when he thought of stopping and adding a few bucks in the tank. The thought crossed his mind that he might be able to coast the rest of the way, or even push her, but he just couldn't bring himself to treat Darling that way. She was a lady, not some cheap tramp that you could coax around.

He stepped out and closed the door. That was that, he was walking to the gas station. Searching his pockets he dug out the four quarters and three notes. With a chuckle, he looked up at the clear blue sky. It was a gorgeous day, not a cloud in the sky, perfect for a 5-mile walk. John grabbed the empty jerry can from the trunk and headed out.

Four dollars weren't going to get him much gas, and his growling stomach reminded him that it wasn't going to fill his belly either. As he walked, he kept an eye on the ground. It was common to find money, with most distracted by their cell phones nowadays the vast majority of people never noticed when they dropped things. John had found car keys, house keys, bank cards, jewelry... Once he had found a hundred-dollar bill, crisp and clean as if it had just been minted, folded in two and left there just for him to find.

Arriving at the strip mall, john placed the small jerry can by the gas pump and took a moment to look around him. He hadn't had any luck along the road, but life had taught him that sometimes the most opportune of gifts came from the generosity and charity of strangers.

The parking lot didn't have much going for it and traffic

was low. There was a middle eastern cab driver filling up his tank. By the disheveled look on him and the way he was tapping that credit card on the roof of the car while counting the pennies on the pump meter, John knew he didn't have anything to give.

There was a young couple waiting by the bus stop sign, both completely engrossed in their cell phones, standing at arm's reach but clearly together. They've been fighting, probably because they don't talk anymore. They were both sporting the latest cell phone model, latest watch tech and the very latest ear buds, it was like looking at a tech company's living commercial. John knew that plastic people dealt in plastic currency. So no cash there.

An old man was slowly making his way up the street as he leaned heavily on his walking cane. The patches on the elbows of his tweed jacket, the well-polished but worn-out shoes, the medals over his left beast and the two-dollar bouquet of flowers he clutched in his right hand told the story of a widower, a veteran most likely wounded in combat. John thought of his own grandfather and how little money he would receive and shook his head. Not him either.

At the other end of the parking lot, a single mom and a little girl buying a single ice cream cone. Single moms have it rough and judging by the worn-down sneakers, the ten-dollar work slacks and the fact that she was probably still wearing the same clothes since lasts night's shift, John calculated that she had just spent all her tips on paying the babysitter and getting her daughter a Saturday morning treat. Life was rough, but single parent kids always grew up tough and able. No money there though.

Then there was the priest. He was standing on the curbside, clutching his bible close to his chest and looking off into the distance. John nodded to himself.

The robes were immaculate, clean and well pressed. His collar was so white it could have been used as a specimen paint swatch. Crisp nice shoes, a polished ring on his finger and a simple rosary around his neck. This one was a penny pincher, but still, he was john's best bet right now.

John walked over to start a conversation.

"Morning father, gorgeous weather for the good word today."

Startled, the priest turned to face him, giving John a quick down and up look before speaking.

"Yes, yes it is my son."

Looking off into the horizon where the priest had been transfixed just moments before, John extended his left arm as if to touch some distant point with his fingertips and mused to himself openly.

"Like the lord himself with his apostles on the sea of Galilee, he made the wind and storm calm and asked them why they were afraid..."

The priest smiled at him.

"It's nice to see a young man familiar with the good word of the gospel."

John looked down at his feet in a bashful manner and said.

"Well, I'm more like the wind which blows where it wishes, born of the spirit."

He looked at the priest and smiled.

The priest examined him before speaking.

"John 3:8."

John extended his hand to the priest.

" You've got some gift right there father. My name is John.'

The priest eagerly shook his hand.

"I'm father O'Neill, and you John are not from around here are you?"

"No Sir father, just passing through on my way home. I'm

hoping for a little bit of charity help today, have any idea where I can impose on a few dollars to put some gas in my car?"

The priest tilted his head to the side a bit and smiled while reaching into his pocket and pulling out a $5 bill.

"Well, I reckon the good Lord has you on the road for a reason then son."

John paused for a moment, just long enough to give the semblance of piety, and then accepted the $5 bill.

"God sure works in mysterious ways father. Thank you for your generosity."

John had wondered sometimes, especially when he was trying to figure out where these powers came from, was this a gift of God? Was there even a God? Were these gifts...

Just then he was brought out of his musing by the sound of a little girl crying. Turning around to face the parking lot again he noticed the taxi driver over filling his gas tank as he stared at the sky from behind his car. In the background John heard a cell phone clattered to the cement on the sidewalk. The priest muttered.

"God help us all, judgement day has come."

John let out a long breath before turning around to see what everyone was looking at. What would it be this time?

Slowly turning, his eyes trailed up to the blue sky above. For a moment he was left dumbstruck.

How the hell was he going to stop this?

The iridescent blue morning sky was partially filled with a massive meteor. It was as if someone had plucked the moon and tossed it at the earth. John looked around for a moment in utter disbelief, but there was no time for hesitation. He had done this so often that it had almost become instinctual. Somewhere in this parking lot was the catalyst, what he called the conjunction point. He jolted at the sound of the cab's screeching tires as the driver peeled out of the parking lot, but John knew this wasn't something anyone could outrun.

Still his mind drifted; a freaking meteor?!

He reminded himself out loud to focus.

He looked at the young couple. The young man had dropped his phone and was annoyingly tapping the girl on the shoulder to get her to look up at the sky. The old man had dropped his cane and clutched the flowers as he shook his fist at the sky in futile anger. The priest had dropped to his knees and was now clutching his bible with both hands, rocking back in forth sobbingly. The single mom had thrown her daughter over her shoulder and was running towards the back of the parking lot, away from the falling sky, while her daughter had both hands outstretched towards the ice cream cone now sitting on the cracked parking lot pavement. Kids, say what you will but at least they have their priorities straight.

John ran the gamut of thoughts and emotions; perplexed, confused, frustrated and defeated. No one here seemed like they were the cause of this, how could they? Cell phones, ignorance, dropped ice cream cones and self-doubts don't call down world ending meteors. Do they?

Then the thought crossed his mind. What if this was it? What if this was mankind's last day under the sun, and he was just here to witness it?

The meteor was massive yet moving at an incredible speed. There was no way the Earth was going to survive this. Through the morass of emotions, John couldn't help but chuckle. Maybe it was the hysteria, the stress or just the absolute ludicrousness of it all, but he thought it was like watching those late-night sci-fi movies; the ones with the shoestring budget and corny one liners. This was all somehow surreal, like nothing he had dealt with before.

The impact was blinding, hitting the far end of the horizon line beyond the city with the force of hundreds of millions of atomic warheads. Kilometers of debris instantly leapt into the sky, blocking out the sun's light and sending a jolt that threw everyone into the air only to freefall back to the ground.

The acrid smell of gasoline eked out from below him, which made him get up and run towards the sidewalk where the old man was still trying to get up. There was no way he was going to die of immolated again, no way.

Kneeling down by the old man to see if he could help him get up, John peered at the priest who was staring back at him. John nodded a long, calm nod to him, as if urging him on a yet determined course of action. In the distance, the supersonic hell storm was already barreling towards them, its thundering roar slowly swallowing everything in its path. The clouds were a mixture of ejected molten lava, exploding earth crust projectiles and cloud to cloud lightning discharges that altogether could only have been conjured up in the twisted imagination of the most devout of special effects artists.

The priest began his sermon with the daily prayer to our father, his voice rising in crescendo with the oncoming firestorm's roar.

Then darkness. The pain was blessingly quick. Death was the only release.

* * *

The radio alarm clock went off to BTO's Taking Care of Business, prompting John to sit upright with a gasp, followed by a long and shuddering exhalation of relief.

Sitting on the edge of the bed, he cupped his head in his hands in hopes of bringing some relief while also blocking out the smell of the leftover burger which now permeated the small one room accommodation.

He threw his hands up.

"What the hell, was that? How am I supposed to stop THAT ?"

Rising to his feet, he furtively looked around the room. Reminding himself that every problem has a solution, and every event has a key focal point. Big problems have small solutions. At least it wasn't immolation, per se. Damn.

He tried to reassure himself.

"Okay, I can do this... I just have to figure out the conjunction point. What are the triggers in the cascading series of events that lead to the world ending, follow the breadcrumb back to the source, save the world..."

Finishing his internal-external monolog, he was reminded of the smell of the grease-sweat permeating his shirt. It would have to do this time around. He needed to get going and gather as much information as possible. With no gas in the car, his first priority was to get there quickly and witness as much as possible.

As he stepped out of the motel room, the city transit bus rumbled by. No need for the jerry can this time he thought to himself. Someone at the strip mall was connected to this, somehow. He just needed to keep digging until he found out who. Maybe he could hitchhike? It was early Saturday morning on the city outskirts and traffic was sparse. As he walked, he occasionally looked over his shoulder to see if any vehicles were coming until a familiar taxi roof-sign peeked out over a small hill in the road. He had to start somewhere.

Flagging the cabbie down, he was relieved to see the driver's familiar disheveled appearance. It was time to put some of these super skills to work. John had years' worth or the equivalent thereof on how to approach people, all of which he had garnered through countless encounters and attempts. He knew there were very few people who were actually unapproachable. Most people you met on a daily basis were more than happy to talk, if you knew how to start the conversation. You just needed to create common ground, this built interest and trust, and once you had their trust then people tended to open up. It was always the little things that mattered most. Like the cabbie's family photo tucked in the middle of all the other mementos and business cards. A shrine of sorts, dedicated to those who were either left behind, or had left him for somewhere he couldn't bring himself to go.

The name and matching photo on the cabbie's dash identification tagged him as Raj, a British variant on the original name, but without the H. It was time for him to work his charm.

"Hey, eh, Raj, right? It's been a crazy morning and I just need to get to the strip mall gas station about 5 clicks down the road. I have four bucks on me right now, how close can you get me?"

Raj peered at him through his rear-view mirror, a mix of mistrusts and pity in his eyes. Then he nodded.

"I' will take you there, for four dollars. But you need to pay up now."

A broad, warm smile crossed John's face as he dug out what little currency he had and handed it over happily.

"Raj, you are a life saver, you have no idea. Thank you so much. Hey, are those your folks?"

There was a long moment of silence as Raj pulled back onto the street and headed towards their shared destination.

"They were..." he let his words trail off, telling John that there was some kind of lingering regret or unfinished business on the driver's mind."

"That's rough man, I'm sorry to hear that. I lost my mom

last year too, single parent, you know. She got really sick, it was bad. The doctor asked me to make the call, you know, she was too far gone to save. Losing a parent is never easy, let alone both."

John let the silence of a few minutes wash over both of them, allowing Raj to connect with their commiseration and in turn hopefully leaving him open to talk about it. It was clear to John that Raj needed to talk. Most people do. Trauma can shut a person down, take away their words, wall them up in a place they can't talk from. Raj was trapped and John was going to extend a hand.

"Was it recent?"

John waited for a reply. There was a minute or so of silence, then Raj spoke softly.

"Just over a year ago. They had moved from London, England, to open a small convenience drug store. They had worked in clinics all their lives and just wanted a small business to retire from and pass on to me. They never got that chance. On a late night at closing hour, a man came in and shot both of them for a handful of dollars and some over the counter drugs. I was in the stock room, in the back. I heard the first shot... I guess, I froze. I didn't know what to think."

"I'm so sorry Raj. You know, they say a parent should never outlive a child, but, I have always found the opposite to be equally cruel."

John sat back in the rear seat of the cab, letting a moment of silence wash by for both of them as he watched the houses, driveways and side streets roll by his window.

"You know Raj, after my mom died, I was pretty lost. I had doubts; doubts if I had done the right thing. If she would have forgiven me for doing it, or for not doing more. Been doubting since. But I know, someday, I'm going to have to get passed it, stop running. I'll have to stop escaping what I can't change and start living my life again. It's what my mom would have wanted. It's what all good parents would want."

As the cabbie pulled into the parking lot, John leaned his hand over the seat and offered it to Raj. There was a moment hesitation, then a handshake.

"Raj, you're a good man, I have no doubts they would be proud of you. I hope things work out for you."

The cabbie stared at John, this complete stranger in his cab, and finally nodded."

"Thank you sir."

John smiled back.

"Things are going to be ok. Take care of yourself Raj."

"Uh, yes, you...you too, sir."

John stepped out of the car with two certainties. Raj was a good man who had lost himself, and that he was not the conjunction trigger.

"Well, this is going to happen again... so let's figure this one out. Taking care of business..."

Looking around, he saw the same players. The young couple engrossed in their cell phones, the priest by the sidewalk clutching his bible, the single mom and her little girl with her ice cream cone. The old man with his cane and bouquet of cheap flowers slowly walking up towards them. Nothing new here.

John had learned that sometimes, small things would change. To most people the changes were imperceptible, like a different car driven by or someone in the background ordered a different meal. When this happened, he could single those out as factors. But everything here seemed the same.

But this time, the difference was markable. It was low at first but growing, a rumbling echoed throughout the sky. It was like the time when he had gone to the military air show with his family, but they had arrived late. Getting out of the car at the far end of the parking lot, he could feel the air vibrate from the low flying planes overhead. Then from behind the strip mall emerged a wide squadron, dozens upon dozens of quad-jet bombers in chevron formation, making their way towards the city at high altitude.

Small changes were common, but this was a drastic deviation from the last time. What was going on here? As he watched the planes overshadow the city, one of them dropped a singular large spherical object onto the glass-pillared metropolis. The sphere, a black pinpoint in the sky from that distance, seemed almost suspended in the clear blue sky for a long, silent moment. Only the sound of child crying could be heard.

Then a bright flash of light nearly blinded him and everyone in the parking lot, followed by a rumbling boom and a massive golden colored mushroom cloud crowned by a set of dark cloudy circlets.

As Raj jumped into his taxi and sped off in a futile attempt to outrun the explosion, John stood his ground, observing everyone. The old man had dropped his cane and was angrily shaking his fist at the growing firestorm which was once a city. Father O'Neil fell to his knees and began reciting the daily prayer. The young man dropped his cell phone and desperately tried to get the woman standing in front of him to look at what he was pointing at. The single mom grabbed her daughter, throwing her over her shoulder as she ran towards the back of the strip mall, leaving the dropped ice cream cone behind on the warming black pavement.

John stood dumbfound. What the hell was this? The concussion blast from the explosion made him stumble and set off all manner of alarms in the process. Slowly rising to his feet, he started walking towards the sidewalk. There was only one bomb in all of history that had that kind of power: the

Russian Tsar Bomba. Everything was playing out like one of those cheesy 1970s and 80s nuclear survival blast clips produced by the American government. Hide under a desk. What a farce.

A wall of flame pushed forward by a pressure wave traveling several hundreds of miles per hour was rushing towards them. He hated immolation. Damn he hated it.

As the heat became more and more intense, paper on the telephone poles began to brown and crease at the edges. Looking at the priest, John saw the fear in his eyes, one born of doubt for what awaited him, if anything, and of a life spent in service of something he had doubted for some time now. A feeling John himself had felt many times. He knew that look all too well.

The bible burst into flames as it was dropped to the sidewalk below. Father O'Neil's clean pressed clothes and crisp white collar were next to spark alight. Soon, he was madly thrashing about on the ground in a futile effort to douse the growing flames.

John closed his eyes, exhaling as he felt his own clothes, hair and flesh burst afire. He hated it. He hated it so much. Just make it quick he thought to himself.

* * *

The radio alarm clock went off to BTO's Taking Care of Business.

Slowly sliding to sit on the edge of the bed, staring blankly at the half eaten, greasy gelatinous burger resting on its soaked wrapper and paper bag, john sighed a long and extended breath.

Looking out the one room patio door windows to the blue

sky stretched out over the horizon line of the city, he let out a single, frustration and exasperation filled yell.

WHAT THE FUCK!

This was beyond comprehension. Not only was the cataclysm realistically something he could not possibly stop, but it was also utterly and completely different now. This had never happened.

Why, what, how? WHY? Questions raced through his mind as he put his sneakers on and grabbed the car keys. He ran the car until it sputtered and clunked to a halt by the roadside, then painfully jogged the last mile to the strip mall.

Physical exercise wasn't in his usual repertoire, he wasn't that kind of superhero. But he needed to get there as soon as possible. He needed to find out why this was happening. What possible conjunction event could be the catalyst to this, whatever this was...

He got there, panting furiously just as Raj pulled in to gas his cab. John shook his head in disbelief. Every second counted. Catching his breath, he stood with his back to the city, looking at the parking lot and the five-building strip mall from another perspective. It was a trick he had learned when dealing with the saurian-reptilian annihilation. Sometimes a different point of view was all a story needed to reveal itself.

Raj was pumping gas, Father O'Neil was clutching his bible, the old man was slowly making his way up the sidewalk, the couple was engrossed in their mutual avoidance and the little girl dropped her ice cream as her mom tried to console her.

John took a long deep breathe. He needed to stay focused, not see the disaster so he could focus on the catalyst, if there even was one.

Raj. He's running from his fears, his pain. Both parents

were gunned down as he hid in the back of the convenience store; he felt powerless to stop it.

Father O'Neil is a man of faith afflicted with a lack of faith as wide as the Marianas trench. Everything about him screams overcompensation; the crisp clean clothes, the ring, the bible clutched to his heart as if it would protect the last few vestiges of his dwindling belief in a God he can no longer connect to.

The old man; a war vet and recently widowed. He has fought all his life and had nothing to show for it except a long-term injury that forced him to use a cane and a pittance of a salary that only allows him to buy cheap bouquets for his recently deceased wife, now resting in the cemetery just a block up the road.

The young couple, very much a product of their age, unable to communicate with one another to express their deepening desire for connection despite, or perhaps because of, the technology in their hands.

All of them are picture perfect representations of everyday life in our modern world. None of them could possibly be the catalyst for such an absolutely sur-natural event. John looked around the parking lot to make sure he had missed nothing else. This left him with only one possible source. The single mom and her little girl.

As the author Arthur Conan Doyle once wrote; when you have eliminated all possibilities whatever remains, however impossible, is the only possible truth. Or at least something to that effect.

The trembling beneath his feet brought him back to the reality of here and now. Spinning around, he stared momentarily at Father O'Neil who was now clutching his Bible in one hand and raising the other above his head telling everyone to repent, repent, repent, for this was the end of days.

John looked about and in the distance saw great chasms of fire and lava split open and swallow the majority of the city, the rest of it toppled into the now growing fiery pit of hell.

Well damn he thought to himself. Fire.

John turned his focus on the single mom and her daughter, as he watched her grab her child, throwing her over her shoulder. The little girl, tears streaming down her cheeks, reached out to the ice cream which had fallen from her cone onto the pavement, as her lips mouthed the word, daddy. Then they disappeared beneath the buckling earth in a magma and lava plume. John's mind raced, how, how were they doing this? How was it even possible?

* * *

The Alarm Radio went off, and John thought to himself, time to take care of business. Either the mom or the child was doing this. Would it be so out of scope with his reality? After all, he himself had powers, what if they did too? He needed to dig deeper into it. He needed to know the why before he could deal with the how.

This would require some tact.

A very quick shower, a clean shirt from the car trunk and he was off to the strip mall. The city transit offered a much quicker arrival time than walking or taxi, leaving him with a full five to ten minutes to spare. Time to work his magic.

Over the years John had become very adept at making small talk and getting people to feel comfortable around him. Upon arrival at the strip mall, he immediately made his way to the ice cream stand as the young mother and her daughter walked up the back alley towards him. He made note of what they ordered, one single ball of vanilla ice cream on a cone. The single mom ordered nothing. Money was tight and her fingernails showed her concern and stress over everything that was now sitting squarely on her shoulders. There was a lot more to the story than what his eyes could see, but this was enough to work with.

"One scoop of tutti frutti ice cream on a cone please."

John paid the $2 and turned his attention to the mom.

"Excuse me. Are you familiar with the area?" He asked her. "I just got here yesterday I'm looking for some spots where I might be able to get some clothes for a reasonable price."

Staring at John, the young mom placed herself between him and her daughter.

"I'm sorry, we're not from here either."

"I'm sorry, I didn't mean to..."

John raised his hands in a non-threatening gesture, while intentionally dropping his ice cream to the ground. He had learned that when you presented yourself to people as vulnerable, a sympathetic victim capable of the same loss as them, you can garnish a deeper rapport, creating a shared sense of commiseration.

The action had the intended effect. As john raised his hands slightly he laughed at the now partially melted mess on his right sneaker and the pavement. Her reaction was to apologize of course, as if somehow she had partially been responsible for his actions. He smiled and tilted his head to the side.

"Don't worry about it. It's just an ice cream cone."

But really it wasn't, it was his clever trigger item to get her to open up. Quickly seizing on the moment, he introduced himself.

"I'm John by the way."

"I'm Suzan. That is my daughter Sarah." Her eyes lingered on the child with a sadness that told John there was something painful that needed to come out. Susan looked like she was carrying the weight of the world on her shoulders. If she was the source of all these events, she wasn't doing it on purpose. He needed to know more.

"So I'm passing through, just here for a bit, are there any places I should know to avoid?"

He waited for her to respond, she shrugged a bit without taking her eyes off Sarah who stood just a few feet away, staring at her ice cream cone.

"There's a park a few streets down, pretty sketchy especially after dark. But the people here are mostly elderly and transient part-time workers. It's where we planned to move ..." her voice trailed off as it crackled under the weight of something painful sitting on her chest. He could almost feel her chocking back the tears.

"Susan, if you don't mind me saying, but it sounds like you've had a rough go at it lately. Coming from a single mom family myself, I'm going to say it's more than just the unbearable pressures that raising a kid brings. I watched my mom keep all that inside, and it broke my heart not being able to help her. I feel like you need someone to just listen... am I right?"

Her shoulders sobbed as she cackled a sarcastic laugh, her eyes filled with tears.

"You have no idea, and you don't want to hear it, John."

He paused, looking at her, shoulders slumped under the weight of some overwhelming story that was begging to be told to someone, anyone.

"Try me. What's the worst that can happen? You get something off your chest and some stranger in a parking lot becomes your confessional for a few minutes... I'm a good listener, I promise."

She stared at Sarah for a long moment, seemingly contemplating his offer while John sat on the nearby picnic table and waited for her to join him.

Susan slowly walked over and sat down next to him on the table, her eyes never left her daughter, but as she spoke her shoulders seemed to get lighter, the tears seemed to come less readily, her voice became clearer.

The conversation lasted several minutes. Meanwhile, john just listened, sometimes looking at her, other times at her daughter. He allowed himself a moment of compassion, but also kept in mind that the person he was talking to may somehow be the cause of what was happening. There was even a glimmer of hope that the conversation itself may have been what was needed to stop it from happening again.

Susan's story was tragic, worthy of a short story in one of the paperback anthologies you find in those indie bookstores.

They had just moved here from L.A. Sarah had been non-verbal ever since she witnessed her father fatally shot in a home invasion. By the tone in her voice and her furtive stare, it was clear that Suzan blamed herself for not being there.

As horrible as it all was, her daughter was lucky that her mom had been working that night or she might have lost both parents. Sarah had tuned out the world around her after that night. But John knew that although the little girl seemed oblivious, staring at the ball of vanilla resting on her cone, she was most likely keenly aware of everything. She was just lost, as much as her mom was, as much as many of us are.

Susan spoke softly so Sarah would not hear. But John knew kids are keen, they hear everything.

Susan went on, speaking as she had probably not done since that horrible night. John just listened, giving her the space to formulate what could only be a nightmare into as coherent a story as possible.

"He was a good man, my Rob, a fireman. Every Saturday morning, he would take Sarah to get a morning ice cream so I could sleep in after my night shifts. He always took care of us, made us feel safe. But he felt that the city life wasn't for us anymore. We were planning to move here, get a small house in a quiet suburb with a good school, a park..."

Her voice trailed off as her last words left her lips with a tremble.

John waited a few seconds before making his next statement, a supposition he knew most likely to be true.

"They never caught the perps, did they?"

Susan wiped the tears with the back of her hand while shaking her head in a response.

John felt a great deal of sympathy for her, life wasn't fair and if he could have, he would have gladly gone back in time and prevented it. But that's not how it worked. They were both very much victims of their circumstances.

Susan chuckled and looked at john, her eyes filled with tears.

"I have no idea why I'm telling you all of this...? "

John gave a sympathetic smile and shrugged his shoulders.

"Maybe it's time to let it out? Who better than..."

He never got to finish his sentence, it was interrupted by the distant sounds of city siren and the whistling sounds of hundreds of projectiles dropping down from the iridescent blue morning sky and impacting seemingly randomly.

At that moment, John knew it wasn't Susan, she wasn't the focal point. As john turned his stare from Susan to Sarah, the first of the giant tripod beings emerged from the impact craters... an alien invasion? John mouthed the words without speaking them aloud.

W....T...F....

Quickly he turned his attention to Sarah even as the beams of blue light begam to disintegrate everyone about the invaders.

She had dropped her ice cream cone.

She dropped her Saturday morning ice cream cone.

Suzan grabbed her daughter and threw her over her shoulder, running wildly towards the back of the strip mall parking lot. but too late. One of tripods loomed into view and it was all over in an instant.

John stood waiting for the end, his mind replaying the image of Sarah thrown over her mother's shoulder, her tiny hands stretched out towards the now melting ice cream on the ground as she mouthed out 'daddy'. John stood there in the shadow of the tripod and yelled at it.

"Hurry up! I got business to take care of!"

* * *

The radio alarm clock rang it's all too familiar song.

John leapt out of bed, took a quick shower and a got into clean change of clothes.

Tossing last night's leftovers in the parking lot bin, he took the 8:15 bus to the strip mall at the outskirts of the city.

In his mind, he had developed the image of Rob and Sarah spending late nights laughing, watching old timey sci fi movies and eating popcorn. The kind of dad every little girl should have. A protector, a good dad willing to spend the time.

It was Sarah.

Sarah had powers.

Sarah had the power to alter reality but was locked in place by a trauma no one taught her she could overcome.

John smiled at a comforting thought.

He wasn't so alone after all... there were others.

Arriving at the strip mall, he smiled warmly at Susan and Sarah as they stepped away from the canteen window.

"I'll have one single scoop of vanilla ice cream on a cone please."

Giving his last $2 to the cashier behind the glass, he walked over to the tables, standing a few feet away from Sarah. There, the two stood, in silence, staring at the city in the distance as John waited for her to drop her cone.

After a long moment staring at it, Sarah took her first lick. The ball rolled off the far edge of the cone and hit the pavement with a slopping flat sound.

John smirked.

Kneeling down to Sarah's level, he presented her with his own ice cream cone.

"You know, there's nothing in this world that can't be changed with doing something nice for someone. As hard as things are right now, it will get better, because you will make it better, Sarah."

Susan froze in her tracks as she heard John's words, a look of confusion and worry overtaking her face.

Sarah looked into John's eyes, as if sharing an unspoken conversation.

"You can do anything Sarah, I know you can, you just have to want it."

Rising to his feet slowly, John nodded at Susan and smiled.

"That's an amazing young girl you have there."

Confused, all Susan could do was watch John walk away.

Smug with himself, John had a quick moment of doubt and stopped in his tracks. There were no sirens, asteroids, bombs, earthquakes or aliens. None, just the sound of the occasional passing traffic and Raj finishing at the gas pump.

With a sigh of contentment, he walked over to Father O'Neil.

"Good morning father. Waiting for a miracle?"

Father O'Neil, jolted to attention and was left with a surprised look on his face.

"See that young couple over there? They need a miracle that only you can provide. If you can get them to start talking again, I predict you'll be marrying them someday soon. Oh, can I borrow that $5 you have in your pocket, Raj over there is having a hard go at it and could use a little miracle of his own.."

Dumbfound and at a loss for words, father O'Neil slowly pulled out the five dollar bill and handed it to John.

"...how did you, who..."

Taking the bill in hand, John started walking away while saying out loud to the dumbfound priest.

"Mysterious ways father, mysterious ways...keep the faith..."

Walking over to the cab, John stopped to face Raj who was walking out the convenience store.

"Hi, this your cab. Look, can you do me a solid? See that old man walking up the street, can you take this $5 and drive him up to the cemetery and back home? Oh and can you do something for me? Talk to him. Maybe commiserate a bit with him. He lost his wife recently and hasn't had a chance to talk about it yet. You know how it is."

Placing the five-dollar bill in Raj's hand, John looked him straight in the eye.

"You're a good man Raj, that's all we can try to be. Right?"

Leaving Raj a bit bewildered, John made his way to the sidewalk and intercepted the old man.

"Excuse me sir, are you a veteran?"

The old man stood up from his hunched gait to a proud and upright stance, a twinkle in his eye at the question.

"Yes son, yes I am. Korea, twice decorated, and damn proud of it."

Extending his hand, John smiled as he looked the old man straight in the eye.

"Sir, I would like to thank you for your service. I noticed that you might have brought some souvenirs home in that leg of yours. It would be my honor to pay you to take a cab to your destination sir, a small thank you. Please. The cabby over there is Raj, he's a good man, he'll wait for you and drive you home afterwards. I think you and he might have more in common than you might think."

The old man's eyes watered. There was no doubt in John's mind that this had been the first decent thing anyone had said to the old vet since his wife passed.

"Thank you son, thank you, I... I think I will do that... there's a lot of souvenirs in this old leg all right."

As john escorted the man to the cab and opened the door for him, he could feel everyone's eyes on him. But the only eyes that mattered were Sarah's. She had been watching him carefully, intently analyzing each of his actions and deeds.

She and John locked eyes, and he nodded a long slow nod of recognition.

"It's your turn now kiddo. You can do it."

Raj drove off, with a very grateful old man in the back seat. Father O'Neil worked his magic and got the young couple to put their cell phones down and speak. Last he looked they were holding hands again. Susan was kneeling next to Sarah, stroking her hair. But Sarah didn't take her eyes off John until he disappeared up the sidewalk on his way back to the motel.

Grabbing the cold cup of coffee, John opened the patio door and sat on the rickety old folding chair, looking off at the city as its skyline cut into the blue horizon beyond.

"Aaaahhhh, another day under the sun, just taking care of business."

As he sipped, his attention was drawn to a piece of paper nestled against the patio edge and an empty stone planter.

Picking it up and turning it over to examine it, he chuckled to himself.

"You're gonna be alright kid."

He put the crisp, brand new $100 bill into his pocket and finished the cold coffee.

Just another day saving the world.

* * *

It was morning, and Sarah could smell the eggs and toast her mom was making. But today was different. She was different. Everything was different.

She had had a dream the night before, of her daddy coming home. It started with a man who gave her his ice cream cone, and from there, like dominos, all the confusion, the fear and anger melted away.

She could control it.

She was no longer powerless.

Changing from her flannel pajamas, she made her way down the hall of the two-bedroom apartment to the kitchen.

There, her mom greeted her with a smile, a good morning kiss and a seat at the table.

Sarah stared at her, formulating the words in her mind before speaking.

"Mom, you didn't make any bacon, daddy loves bacon..."

Dropping the spatula, Susan fell to her knees in front of Sarah, tears streaming down her cheeks.

"Oh baby, you spoke, you spoke baby, oh baby I missed you so much, I missed hearing your voice so much..."

Clutching her daughter tightly, Susan stopped for a moment to wipe her tears and looked her daughter in the eyes.

"Baby, I know that dad loved bacon, but...."

Her sentence cut short by the knock on the apartment door.

Sarah smiled at her mom. She knew everything would be ok from now on.

Eric Breau is an independent Canadian author from rural Alnwick, New Brunswick. He holds degrees in Fine Arts, History, Archaeology, and Education, all of which are his passions. He blends his love of storytelling and history to write captivating stories of the enmeshed lives of everyday people, their struggles, and their triumphs.

The breadth of his work includes poetry, short stories, and novels in various genres, including satirical horror, irreverent fiction, and historical fantasy.

The short story *The Little Things* is one of many he has written. He is currently working on a collection of short stories under the title *A Book from the Dead* in the same irreverent and sardonic style found in the above short work.

He is also working on a series of novels in the Historical Low-Fantasy genre entitled *The Dark Coast Chronicles* which relate the hardships and successes of a group of secretive immortals and their struggle against ever encroaching forces bent on destroying their beloved city, and a rising evil which menaces to destroy them all.

Discover the world of Sins of Redemption at sinsofredemption.com

THE COLLECTOR

BY SARAH COOK

This room is filled with storms and symphonies.

The beeping of machines, the humming of apparatus, and the footsteps of scurrying doctors collide in a sea of sounds. Songs crash around me like roaring waves upon the shore that I lie upon. The noises anchor me to this world. A tether to land as I ebb in and out of consciousness. I listen with what little strength I have. I cling to the cacophony as a siren tempts me into silence.

My mind is muddled. I cannot make sense of what I see. I barely know where I am. The lines between reality, memory, and imagination are blurred. An orchestra stands in an ocean. A woman with fiery red hair calls me into the depths. A hospital wrecked on the bottom of the ocean. It feels so real that I can hardly breathe, drowning in the nightmarish sea.

Then I blink, and it disappears. The hospital is dry and undamaged. Sunlight billows through the big windows, illuminating the white walls and yellow floors. I am lying upon a hard bed. I look down at my arms and my veins are crawling out in plastic tubes. Stiff white things at the end of them are now completely unreachable to me. I sigh. I hear nothing but the beeping of machines, the humming of apparatus, and the footsteps of scurrying doctors. I hear no more melodies.

I breathe through these pipes. They have burrowed so unpleasantly into me, but I welcome their presence. I treasure these moments of lucidity and try to stay within them. Still, I feel the storm as it thunders not too far away, threatening to pull me in. I can still hear that siren with burning hair. She calls my name through the rain.

"Simon."

I tumble into that ocean once more.

"Simon!"

I jolt awake and it is night. I can see the darkness through the window though the ward is still brightly lit. There is less chatter, but the whirring still rings out into the air. I am exhausted but thankful to be conscious. I count to a hundred. Five times over. The longest it has been. For the first time, I feel alive. Barely.

As I begin my next set of numbers, I sense that someone is beside me. I have gotten used to the looming bodies of nurses and doctors - poking and prodding at me to keep me alive. I ache from their practices. Yet no one has sat beside me and waited for consciousness to find me. No hand has clasped mine lovingly and, in quiet desperation, pleaded for my salvation. I can think of no one who would occupy that space willingly.

There is a pain in my body. I am too weak see who is there. So instead, my brain wanders a bit, pondering on the identity of my visitor, sitting in the chair next to my bed. It weighs heavily on me that there aren't many contenders. My parents have departed many years before me. And I have no siblings. There is no family with fiery red hair.

I think of David. The warmth of his big build. The towering stature against my thin, frail frame. The hairs peppered on his chin. The thinning on top of his head. The grey blue of his eyes as devastating as the ocean. His sweet smile. The aniseed flavoured kisses he would give me. God, he suckled those candies endlessly.

I gave them up so many years ago. I swapped that tenderness for the limelight. I gave up his giant arms for the accolades that barely came. I traded warmth for applause. I uncorked a bottle, spindled him inside, and threw him to the tides, half-expecting him to return to my shores when they were ripe with riches. How foolish was I. How I long for him now.

That is enough. I think. I would rather face the ocean once more. I close my eyes and try to drift away.

"Oh no, not again," says a voice from the person beside me. She sighs. There is a note of exasperation in her tone.

I snap my eyes open and peer to the left of me. There I see her for the first time. A young woman in her twenties with red hair sits in the hospital chair. She leans forward, an elbow on the wooden armrest, and her pale hands are clasped together. She is wearing a navy skirt, shirt, and blouse with black tights. On her feet are black pumps, one of which is tapping on the plastic floor whilst the other hangs off the opposite knee. Her green eyes flash with annoyance as she peers curiously over me.

The girl is too formal to be a visitor and yet too informal to be a doctor. For a second, I think she is someone religious – here to read me my last rites. Yes, perhaps she is a nun without the habit.

"I am nothing of the sort." She interrupts my musing. Did I say those words aloud? Am I that delirious? Am I going mad? "No, nothing of the sort," she replies, with a small wink. "My name is Lucy."

Lucy. I repeat her name in my mind. She nods gently each time though she does not reach out a hand in her introduction. For a small while, I wonder why. I stare at her as everyone rushes on by. I wonder what they think of this scene – too ordinary to be of note. She could be, they'd think, a distant relative finally come to see this poor wretch of a man.

Then I remember her hair: how it flowed through my fantasies as I clung to life. How she had been calling to me through the ether. How I somehow knew her yet had no idea who she was. All at once I know what she is.

"I've come to collect," this spirit says in response to my conclusion. She says it in a peculiar human-like manner. As a bailiff would on your front step. Unwarranted. Flushed with irritation. One foot in your doorway. Unbothered that they have upended your life. Just trying to do their seedy job. I am but a number on her sheet, I surmise. She sees me as nothing more than a thing to take away.

I swallow dryly. The mouth smacks with the lack of water. There's an irony there. My voice cracks. "But I am not ready." The words mere husks as they fall from my mouth.

"No one ever is." She takes a deep breath as part of her façade. "But it is time. Time to let go."

I nod and close my eyes.

In the crevices of my mind, I lie awaiting for her to take me away. In the cages of my bones, I curl up and ponder on the beating of my heart for one last time. In these morsels that made me a man, I think upon the electricity and wait for the succession of my life to pummel through me. I wait and wait and wait.

As I linger in this darkness, a thought comes swiftly to me. It flies through my conscious, stretching out its wings and curving through my mind. It is a memory. One I never forgot. Suddenly the decades fall from me. Walls of time topple and crumble onto the dusty ground. The weight of my existence cascades. I am younger and lighter – unburdened by age.

I sit on my mother's lap and lean against her warm bosom. My head is heavy, and my nose is snotty. I can barely smell her rose-tinged perfume though I try to, hungry for its comfort. I sniff and sniff and sniff, woefully sad that I am not curled up on my bed. My mother shuffles uncomfortably on the plastic chair by the sheer weight of me. She sighs but does not leave. Instead, she grips onto me tightly as the auditorium sinks into the pitch black.

Then it happens. A small waifish woman with lanky blonde hair and big thick glasses. She is dwarfed by the

Steinway. Yet a confidence is clear - curled in her fingertips. She sits in the silence with barely a breath as a backdrop. Then her hands begin to slide over the piano in feverish and frantic playing. The music strikes me instantly and my heart begins to race. All at once I forget that I am sick.

What a wondrous moment to be a six-year-old gripped so violently and suddenly by meaning.

This moment of mine flowed through time. It carved out something innate in me – as vivid and vibrant as breathing. A path which I had to dutifully follow. I begged for lessons. I berated my poor parents for a tutor. I bellowed at all those around them so that I might complete my purpose. To play sweet music. That longing. I frothed and forfeited everything for those melodies. Those melodies. Those melodies.

These memories.

I am racing in my car with the remnants of the phone call frittering in my mind. My heart is racing with elation. On the steering wheel I tap out the notes as though I am at the piano again. I hum the tune between my lips. A chance, at last. An orchestra needs a replacement at a great hall. If I can get there in time, and if I knew the music. I can, I say, and I do. I waste no time in hurrying. In my haste, swerving down the country lanes, I picture the end of my performance. There is adulation to follow. Surely. Finally. At last. Come on, I say to my derelict vehicle, just a little bit faster.

But wait. There is something up ahead. The traffic has stalled on the tiny bridge in the village. A small collision between two drivers. But I am going too fast. Too quick to stop in time. I am about to cause more anguish. My eyes widen and I panic. Instead, I swerve and rush straight into the banks. The car collides with the water. My hands crumple against the dashboard. The water seeps in. I am awash with the ocean...

The darkness is coming again. This is it. I think. This is the end. I can hear the melodies escaping me. I can feel his warmth. I can taste his sweet kisses. I can...

White light pummels through my senses. But it is not a heavenly guide. I've just opened my eyes. The hospital drones around me. There are no harps playing nor pearly gates. Just the luminescence and the linoleum. I can feel the wires worming from my nose – painful creatures that crawl on my skin, reminding me of my being.

"I am still alive?" I whisper. Though it is an odd question. The day is cracked still, and my mind feels uneven. A puzzle piece has escaped my grasp and the picture of who I am is incomplete.

"Yes." Lucy's features soften. She looks sad. A vivid light bellows throughout her. For the first time, I can sense that she sees me. Every part of my creation, every morsel of my being, every hope I have ever cared into my corporeal self; etched upon her face in endless empathy. I suspect if she could cry, she would shed a few tears for my plight. Instead, she shakes her head, trying to regain her cool composure. "But something has died. I am afraid."

I furrow my brow, staring at her blinding glimmer in a near biblical awe. Then I feel it. The weights at the end of my arms. The white things as stiff as ivories. Devoid of feeling. Lifeless. Without sound. Never to play again.

"The music has gone," I say, hanging the words on a pitiful breath. My lip quivers from the very thought of it. I keep the sobs to myself, however, safe in the wrinkles of my scrunched chin.

"You will find it in other places," Lucy replies gently but she is fading away. Disappearing from this realm. First the colours of her, those vivid red locks, then the outline, and whatever mockery of flesh she has concocted. She takes with her the life I might've known. The scenes I played out as I went to sleep. The wishes I wrapped around my wrists as I practiced wildly. The applause. They now reside in the remaining wisps of her. And she is escaping my grasp.

In that space, the final moments of her mortal existences, I catch her eyes. Those meadowed sights. They brim with the loss and possibilities. There is a thud in my chest, an unusual pang of acceptance. A strange gratitude rushes through me, hitting the pits of my stomach like a wave dashing a rock. I swallow nervously as I look out onto the remains of my life. An unknown future upon a murky horizon. I stare at her, with questions upon my dry lips, and I almost beg her to stay. But she cannot. I know that now. As a gift, in this last beat, she smiles.

Then she is gone.

And I hear nothing. A momentary void of silence. I wonder if I am to be robbed of my hearing too. Was this a new anguish to face? Am I to be burdened with this nothingness for the rest of my life? It is too much to bear. For music to be lost forever to me.

I close my eyes and see his grey blue oceans.

The machines start to beep.

I think of his warm large arms wrapping around my frail frame.

The apparatus start to hum.

I muse on the taste of his blissful aniseed kisses.

The footsteps scurry by once more.

I smile within this melody.

Sarah Cook is the author of Victorian erotic thriller *Diary of Murders*, the sequel *Secrets Unbound*, and the short story collection *Several Glorious Months*. She is currently working on Victorian monster romance book *A Maze of Monsters & Men* which will be released in May 2025.

She lives with her cat Jekyll in London. She is an avid supporter of indie art, especially authors.

Sarah is also an active member of the Victorian Society and likes to explore the weird wonders of the historic world.

sarahcookwriter.co.uk

facebook.com/sarahcookwrites
x.com/sarahcookwrites
instagram.com/sarahcookwrites

MEMENTO MORI

BY J.L. HEATH

Sheet lightning illuminated the sky, in an otherwise black night. Thunder roared and rain hammered, soaking everything in its path. Damien drove the battered Ford Focus at a snail's pace. He wouldn't risk losing control of it in this storm, not with his expecting wife sat beside him.

"I still don't understand why he's letting us use the cottage for free," Samantha said as she tied her free-flowing brown hair up in a messy bun. They had been driving for several hours and sitting down for that amount of time whilst five months pregnant took its toll, both physically and mentally.

"That's just the kinda guy Mark is, babe. You know him, he'd do anything for anyone." Damien kept his dark eyes on the barely visible country road ahead. Samantha sighed and looked out of the passenger window; the silhouette of decaying trees unsettled her. The memory of Mark coming on to her at a house party fifteen years prior struck her as she closed her eyes momentarily. Damien had gone to the bathroom and left her alone with him in the kitchen.

"You're too good for him and he doesn't deserve you. I can give you the world, baby." Those words echoed through her mind. She told Mark she wasn't interested, that Damien was the only man for her and for him to stop being so foolish. He leaned in towards her, whether it was alcohol or pure stupidity, and was met with a swift slap across the face. Since that day, she had never looked at him the same way. She held on to that secret and planned to take it to her grave. How would Damien react if he found out that his best friend in the world, the one he had an inseparable bond with, tried coming on to the love of his life? It didn't bear thinking about. Samantha wouldn't do that to him. Her love for him was unconditional and with their first child on the way (she hoped that another two pregnancies would follow), she wouldn't do anything to spoil her vision of her perfect little family.

"I still remember the night they killed my parents," Damien carried the conversation on by himself. "He was the first person I called once I came back round. I didn't even phone for the police or an ambulance. I knew it was too late for them." Silence followed momentarily, the only sound being the windscreen wipers squeaking as they worked furiously against the rain. "Mark called them babe. He dealt with that for me, don't you see? That's the kind of bond we have. Brothers in arms." He smiled at the thought of having such a close, caring friend. Yet grief and pain still filled his eyes.

"I'm glad you had someone there for you. No one should have to go through what you did, babe." Samantha's voice became a whisper, drowned out by another rumble of thunder.

"I still blame myself," Damien said abruptly. He didn't believe in magic or any kind of higher being. That was kids' stuff. His view of the world was very simple. You're born. You live. You die. Three simple steps that were guaranteed in life, and after you die, that's it. Game over.

"It wasn't your fault. If you were with them, chances are they would have killed you as well." Tears filled Samantha's eyes, giving them an emerald shine. Damien glanced over. How lucky he was to have such a beautiful and caring wife, and after she had been through so much tragedy and heartbreak of her own. Even though there was no confirmation of Samantha's parents' murder, their bodies remained unrecovered.

The police conducted their investigation for several years after their disappearance almost fourteen years prior. They concluded the couple had gone for their regular morning walk along the foreshore, got into some kind of trouble and fallen into the water. A summary which never sat right with

Samantha and offered no closure. Though the police claimed to have done all they could, she felt as though they had more pressing matters to deal with than a missing elderly couple. There were no signs of blood, struggle, or murder weapon at the scene of their disappearance.

Samantha had lost her parents at a young age. The same rung true for Damien. Would the same fate be in store for their own child? Both had suffered enough grief and anguish in their lives. Both parentless and living day to day, wondering what could have been. What should have been. Although they didn't plan for this soon-to-be bundle of joy, they couldn't have wished for anything more. Life was finally looking up for them both.

Damien placed his hand on Samantha's thigh and gave it a small squeeze, then rubbed her protruding baby bump whilst maintaining his focus on the winding road. A gesture of love and reassurance. He turned the radio on to drown out the sound of rain and erratic windscreen wipers. The couple continued their journey towards the cottage.

They pulled up outside the old derelict place. From the outside, it appeared to be overgrown in moss and vines. Mark had clearly made no attempt to keep the exterior in presentable condition. Damien killed the engine and gently shook his wife awake.

"We're here, babe. Gonna have to make a quick dash inside though, so we don't get soaked. You got ya running legs on?" he asked.

Samantha stretched and gave a sharp glance, a look that said, *you must be joking pal.*

The storm raged on; the downpour became more violent with each minute that passed. Would the cottage be able to hold off this amount of rain? Samantha fervently hoped that they wouldn't find the place flooded when they got inside.

They were miles from home and both exhausted from the drive, a flooded cottage would be the cherry on the cake.

With their running legs on, the pair bolted out of the car and made for the cottage. Damien could have left Samantha in the dust, but he stayed beside her, holding his jacket over her head, trying to shield her as much as possible from the torrential wind and rain.

He crammed the key into the lock, turned it, and ushered Samantha inside before slamming the door shut.

"Where's the light switch?" she asked. The place was blacked out. The only source of light being the lightning that flashed above them.

"Let's have a look, shall we?" Damien's voice rose from the darkness. He threw his coat to the floor, pulled his phone out from his pocket, and turned the torch on.

The cottage was very modern on the inside, the complete opposite aesthetic to what lay on the exterior of the property. The lounge area boasted a three-seater leather sofa, a coffee table, and a T.V (at least sixty-five inches from what he could guess with the lack of light). Damien shone the light round behind him, assuming that the light switch would be somewhere on the wall adjacent to the front door. It was. He flicked it on, expecting the cottage to illuminate like a lighthouse.

Darkness remained.

"Fuck. Storm must have caused a power cut," he sighed. Samantha pulled her own phone from her pocket and turned her torch on, trying to add more light to the bleak situation they found themselves in.

"I wanna go home," she whimpered. Being here, out in the wilderness, away from any kind of civilization, and now stuck in the dark. This was not the idea she had for a relaxing weekend away to escape their everyday worries.

"It's okay, we'll be fine," Damien tried to reassure her. "At least the place is dry." He pulled her in towards him, wrapped his arms round her and held her tight. "We can make the most of it," he whispered in her ear.

Although she had felt adamant to leave, Samantha always struggled to dispute with her husband. He was very much her knight in shining armor, and he had those eyes, those big brown puppy dog eyes she just couldn't say no to. She knew he would protect her at all costs. They hugged as silent tears ran down her face.

Samantha sat on the sofa, scrolling through her phone, trying to distract herself from the situation at hand. There was no signal in the cottage, so she had to make do with either scrolling through old emails, playing monotonous games (though that would drain her battery quicker), or scrolling through the thousands of pictures she had taken over the years. Damien searched the lounge, trying to see if there were any board games the two could play to take their mind off things. He had wanted to look in the bedroom, but Samantha had taken her place on the sofa and didn't want to be left by herself in the darkness. He made his way to a small chest of drawers in the corner of the room, crouched down, and opened them.

"There're candles in here, babe. He's even got holders for em. What do you say we have a romantic candlelit dinner?"

"Our ham sandwiches? You *do* know how to woo a girl, don't ya," Samantha smiled. Even in the darkness, her smile illuminated her beautiful face. Damien placed the phone in his mouth, shining the light downwards and freeing his hands. He took out two candles from the drawer and lit them both with a lighter he kept in his pocket. Quitting smoking was on the agenda for when their baby was born, but whilst the bun was still in the oven, he'd enjoy his smokes. He tried to speak with the phone in his mouth, but the sound was muffled. Samantha giggled and got to her feet, removing the mobile from her husband's mouth, and kissed him in the candlelight.

"At least we can save the batteries on our phones now," he said. They made their way to the sofa; Damien placed the candles on the table and took a seat as Samantha killed the light on his phone and nestled into him.

They fell asleep by candlelight. The storm raged on outside.

Damien awoke to the sound of roaring thunder and crashing lightning, the cottage still dully lit by the flickering candles. Samantha was in a deep slumber. He kissed her softly on the head and shook her gently awake.

"Let's go up to bed," he whispered. She groggily got herself up from the slouched position she found herself in and rubbed her eyes.

"Let me clean my face first, babe." Samantha had never been one to suffer from oily skin or spots, but with her pregnancy came the acne she never suffered from as a teen.

"We left your bag in the car. I'll go fetch it; you just relax." Damien kissed the top of her head once more. "But the storm," Samantha begun.

"It's only a bit of rain, it won't kill me," he kissed her on the cheek.

"Are you sure babe?"

"Of course, I won't be long. I love you," he whispered.

"I love you too."

Damien turned the torch on his phone and made his way out into the seemingly never-ending storm.

Samantha sat with her phone in hand. In a world that was flickering, the screen illuminated her face. The candles would soon be out, and without power, they couldn't charge their phones unless they sat in the car. Something neither of them wanted to do.

As she scrolled through old photos on her phone of her and Damien, a flash of lightning cracked in the heavens, and a roar of thunder followed immediately.

The candles went out.

"Oh, fuck this," she muttered. She locked her phone and tossed it on the table. Damien wouldn't be long. The car was just outside, and she knew he didn't want to get any more soaked than he needed to. With her head resting on the back of the sofa, she closed her eyes, rubbing her bump, developing the bond between mother and child, and imagining the wonderful joys that their baby would bring. Next week, they will go for a gender reveal scan. Then the preparation for baby's arrival could truly begin.

She couldn't wait.

Opening her eyes, Samantha found herself facing the same still darkness she had observed behind closed eyelids. Another flash of sheet lightning illuminated the sky, revealing the figure of a man standing by the window.

It wasn't Damien.

She tried to scream, but her throat seized up. She could only muster a whimper. "Hello Samantha," the figure said. The voice was instantly recognizable.

It was Mark.

"Where's Damien?" she asked, trying to keep her voice calm as panic took over.

Here stood the man who tried to come between her and the love of her life. The man who she was sure took Damien for a fool. The man who had just made sure she would never see her husband again.

"Don't worry about him. He won't bother us." Mark took a

step forward as he spoke. The sound of his boots knocking against hard wood was reminiscent of the thunder outside.

"Don't come near me," she warned. But the warning fell upon deaf ears.

"I just want to talk, Samantha. You broke my heart. I think it's only fair we talk."

Another roar of thunder sounded from the heavens and the power to the cottage came on, lighting the place in a dull, yellowish glow.

Mark stood just feet away from her. Fresh dirt and blood coated his face, and his clothes were torn. It looked like he had been wrestling in the mud and taken a hefty blow to the nose. Samantha stared into his cold, sadistic eyes when something in his hands caught her attention.

What she saw sent an icy shiver down her spine.

In his right hand, he held a carving knife, the blade thick, long and coated in fresh blood. In his left hand, he held something that Samantha refused to believe the sight of.

A brain.

Fear took over and rendered her paralyzed. She wanted to run. Run for the hills and never look back. But her body would not respond. She sat and stared, wishing that her knight in shining armor would burst through the door and save the day.

Mark's lip curled into a repulsive smile. "Know what this is?" he asked. Samantha stared wide eyed.

"You should know. You love your forensic shows, don't you babe." He waited for her to respond, but all she could do was shudder when he called her babe. He licked his cracked lips. "It's your fathers. Just think of all the wonderful memories that I'm holding in my hand, Samantha. All those happy, fun memories." His smile widened, revealing stained teeth. "And all those secrets."

"Y- You..." her voice shook. Everything was falling in to place at a rate at which she couldn't keep up. It all made sense now. She had rejected Mark, and he had killed her parents for revenge. If he had her father's brain, then where was the rest of him? Were his other organs being kept in a jar as some kind of memento? And where was her mother's body? Still in one piece? Or butchered and harvested by this monster who stood before her. And for the love of God, where was Damien? The police had come up empty with finding her parents' bodies, because Mark had taken their lives and kept the corpses for his own sick pleasure.

"Monster?" Mark asked. "No Samantha," he tilted his head to one side. *"You're* the monster."

He dropped the knife and brain simultaneously and stepped towards her, still showing those ghastly teeth. Samantha clambered over the back of the sofa and made a run for the door. Locked. She turned to face the thing of her nightmares, but he quickly grabbed her throat and pushed her backwards.

Her head struck the door with such force that it rendered her unconscious.

Samantha awoke, not knowing how long she had been out for. Mark stood over her, fascinated by her beauty as she lay on a cold, hard table.

"Where am I?" she asked. Trying to move her arms and legs, it was no use. Mark had tied her to the table with thick rope. The smell of iron, burning, and rotting flesh filled the air, churning Samantha's stomach.

"This is my fun room, Samantha. We're going to have a lot of fun tonight," he flung out his arms. "Look around, take it all in." He walked out of sight. Samantha turned her head left and right, trying to make sense of where she was.

On one side of the room sat a collection of knives,

cleavers, and axes. All of which were coated in dry blood and had clearly seen a lot of use. On the other side were needles of varying lengths, vials, and tubes with a range of different colored liquids in them, everything from purple to clear to cloudy to red. She felt as though she were in an experimental slaughterhouse and her name was next on the list.

"Mark. What are you doing? My baby..." she trailed off, trying to maintain consciousness.

"That baby should have been *mine*," he hissed. Samantha heard his footsteps approaching her once more. She tried to lift her head but lacked the strength to. Each step sounded like a gunshot. She closed her eyes, hoping this was all a bad dream.

"Open your eyes. Don't make me force you princess," he whispered in her ear. The heat and stench from his breath made her hold her own. She opened her eyes as Mark stood over her, grinning from ear to ear. "Would you like to see something cool?" he asked. The way with which he spoke made Samantha think of a teenage version of the friend who had clearly lost his mind somewhere along the way. Or had he been born like this? Mark had always tried his best to keep up his youthfulness over the years, whether that be buying the latest creams to keep the wrinkles at bay, purchasing hair dye to keep the greys away, or talking like an adolescent. It was clear that he had an issue with letting things go, that much was becoming apparent now as she lay petrified.

She didn't respond to his question, she merely looked into the eyes of her captor, desperately searching for answers. Mark raised his hands and held two balls on either side of his face, still fronting that ghastly grin (though she could not move, Samantha would have happily taken any chance to slap that smug look off his face). He cleared his throat and muttered. "Do you know what *these* are? I suppose you don't.

After all, it has been a while since you last saw them. Since they last saw *you*." Samantha blinked hard, trying to clear her vision from the bright light and tears she tried so desperately to hold back. To her, they resembled two white marbles, boasting dazzling emerald centers made to look like eyes.

"Marbles."

His eyes lit up; his grin widened further to reveal more stained teeth.

"Oh Samantha. Sweet, innocent Samantha. This isn't child's play now, my darling. This is the real deal." Mark held the marbles out to Samantha, who recoiled back into the table. "Take a closer look." She stared at the two marbles being held just inches from her face.

Upon closer inspection, Samantha's stomach took a plunge into her boots. They were not marbles made to look like eyeballs. They *were* eyeballs. Staring back at her were a pair of eyes identical to her own. Staring back at her were the eyes of her mother. She screamed as loud as she could, hoping that someone somewhere would hear her and save her.

"Now, now. No need to scream, my dear. No one can hear you. Don't you like my playthings? Imagine what your mother would say now if she could see you." Mark chuckled to himself. "Excuse the pun." Samantha continued to shriek, not hearing the words of this murdering maniac. Mark delicately placed one of the emerald eyeballs on her forehead, rubbing it in a circle, pushing, squeezing, and letting the secretions run down her face. "Let's open your third eye. You like all that mantra shit, don't you babe? Feng Shui and what not." Samantha desperately tried to shake her head, but fear and disgust had rendered her paralyzed.

Mark turned on his heels as the sound of Samantha's hoarse voice echoed throughout his chamber and once again disappeared out of sight. The lights flickered as he clattered about with metal dishes. With no one able to hear her, and the love of her life probably fighting for his last breaths outside in the horrendous storm (if he was still alive that was), Samantha lost hope and prayed silently to a higher being she had never believed in.

Upon Mark's return, she screamed once again. He held her face with his right hand, squeezing her cheeks, and rammed a piece of ragged cloth into her mouth. The taste of blood made her gag. She held back the vomit, knowing that if she let it go, there was only one way it would end.

"That baby should have been *mine*," he repeated. "That piece of shit was never a good friend. Not since we were kids. Mr. Oh, so perfect and could do no wrong. Mr. I have the perfect life with a wonderful wife and child on the way. Dead parents? Who gives a shit. Any decent son would have protected them at all costs. Not him. The little bitch sat up in his room listening to music because he couldn't handle a bit of discipline. I heard him," he spat on the floor. "Piece of shit."

Samantha lay listening to this maniac criticize her husband's character, mocking him, insulting him, revealing the truth of what happened that night. How could Mark have played him for so long? She knew he was bad news, but Damien would never listen. She didn't want to hurt him and look where that got them. She should have been honest with him, told him what Mark had done all those years ago. Maybe then, their fates would have led a different course.

Mark stared down at her and continued his speech.

"The only reason I stuck around was for you. I needed to be close to you. I *needed* you," he bit down on his lip. "And now I have you."

Samantha tried to scream through the rag, thrashing her body in a desperate attempt to escape the clutches of this madman.

But it was no use.

Mark held up a syringe with a cloudy liquid inside. Samantha looked at it wide eyed and began to sob.

"I need to make a few more preparations, babe. This will help you sleep whilst I work. I know it's been a long day for you." He looked into her eyes as he spoke and thrust the needle into the crook of her arm. The pain was immense. Samantha felt the cold liquid run through her arm and rush through her body. It was like being injected with the blood of the dead.

"When you wake up, the fun will really begin." He leant in and kissed her delicately on the cheek. Darkness shrouded her world.

J.L. Heath is a lover of all things horror and music with a paranormal horror debut coming out 2025.

tiktok.com/@j.l.heath.author

THE KING'S SECRET

BY DARTANYAN JOHNSON

AKREN

Akren stubbed his toe on a chair leg, cursed, and slipped on his fallen practice sword as he bounced around the room, trying, and failing to put on his trousers.

"Master Nuk is going to have my head," he said, bumping into a wall. He was late for training again.

At last, after a hard-fought battle, his trousers yielded. Yanking his tunic from the edge of the bed, he shrugged it on, realized it was backwards, fixed it, then slipped on his practice sword once more. Cursing, he stuffed his feet in a pair of boots, hefted his training weapon from the floor, and barreled out of the tiny home. By the time he reached the steep incline leading to the practice square, he was already winded.

His legs and lungs were on fire when the hill finally leveled out. The only thing stopping him from collapsing to the damp grass and catching his breath were the hundred pairs of eyes staring at him, and in the middle of two groups of warriors, with a weathered face twisted in a scowl, was Master Nuk.

"Sorry," Akren said, hands on his knees as he heaved in air. "I overslept." Scanning the warriors, he noticed the group on the left carried no shields—only practice swords.

They must be playing the role of the goblins.

"I'm guessing you must be so talented, training to save our village is beneath you," Master Nuk said to him, earning a few snickers from the warriors. "Stand next to the team on your left."

Akren nodded vehemently, glad the reprimand hadn't been worse, then turned to do as commanded.

"Oh, don't bother bringing your sword; you don't need it," Master Nuk added. "Not the great Akren."

More snickers followed, and with a groan, he let go of his weapon and jogged over to his group. When Master Nuk gave the instructions, then the proceeding order to begin the session, Akren, without the aid of his practice sword, was beaten to a pulp by the opposing side.

Afterward, they switched to one-on-one combat. Akren was glad to retrieve his weapon until he saw who Master Nuk had paired him with. Standing before him was a tall, heavily muscled man. Akren gave the man a slight dip of the chin as he posed in a fighting stance. His opponent—Erius—did the same, then charged.

Akren repeatedly found himself knocked on the ground, but he continued to get up, refusing to let his shortcomings dissuade him. Erius sprinted toward him, and Akren stumbled back, narrowly missing getting struck with the wooden practice sword. He lunged, ready to plunge his weapon into his opponent's chest, but the large man proved nimble for his size. Erius sidestepped the attempt, then performed a high kick. Akren held up an arm in time to block the strike, but the pain that followed was more than he'd anticipated. Distracted by the discomfort, he allowed his opponent to set his feet for another attack. A straight kick to the chest sent Akren flailing to his backside, causing him to drop his sword.

"You're moving too slow off the counter," Master Nuk said, pounding the tip of his staff on the ground as he stomped toward him.

Akren winced as he got to his feet.

"That's why Erius continues to disarm you," Master Nuk went on. "It's not because he's better than you"—Erius, who stood across from Akren, frowned in disagreement—"but because you're letting him beat you to the punch."

Akren wiped the dirt from his trousers and tunic, then

hefted his sword from where it had fallen. Master Nuk reached out, clutched Akren by the collar, and pulled him close until they were nose to nose. For an old man, he was surprisingly strong.

"Those goblins in the castle will eat you alive if this is the extent of your skill set, boy,"

Master Nuk said, spittle flying onto his bottom lip. "Do you hear me?" "Of course, Master Nuk," he stammered.

Master Nuk let go, then turned to the rest of the men. Akren quickly wiped the spit from his lip with his forearm. "I have been molding you all to be warriors since childhood to complete the most important assignment an Elantrean could have!" Master Nuk bellowed over the noise of clashing weapons. Knowing their master expected their attention, the warriors stopped training. The one hundred men, Akren and Erius included, backed out of the practice square. "You will enter the castle, defeat the goblins that lie within, and delay Ushganore's return for another hundred years."

The tale of Ushganore, the ogre mage, was well known in the small village of Elantrus. Even as a small child, Akren had heard of the ancient tale about how the ogre mage, along with his horde of goblins, stampeded into Elantrus Castle, decimated the residents, and murdered the king. Ushganore then declared himself the ruler of the land, but a villager rebelled against the ogre mage, gathering as many men as he could, and fought against the intruders. It was a long and bloody battle, but in the end, the villagers prevailed. However, Ushganore didn't go down without leaving his mark. He placed a curse on the land, vowing to return and finish the fight in one hundred years' time. He was true to his word. For the past four centuries, on the anniversary of the first battle, Ushganore awakened to wreak havoc. And each time he came back, the hero who killed him would live for one hundred years and die upon his return; their existences were intertwined.

Master Nuk was the last person to defeat the ogre mage. That meant, as unbelievable as it might sound, he was well over a century old.

Akren shuddered recalling the tale, then turned his attention back to his master.

"Every one of you has the potential to become the next hero of Elantrus," Master Nuk said. He glanced at Akren after saying that, and for a beat, Akren thought the master trainer was about to recant that claim. "Every one of you has what it takes to slay your way to the ogre mage. There will be sights you'll wish you'd never seen, but no matter what happens, you must stay strong and composed. If you lose focus for just a breath, that could spell your end." He was quiet for a long moment, letting his words sink in. "When you go home tonight, I don't want any of you getting too drunk for the fight tomorrow."

Many of the warriors chuckled; Akren wasn't one of them.

"Tomorrow," he sighed. He thought he'd be ready when the time came, but now that the battle was a sunrise away, he couldn't seem to quell his despair.

"I need you at your best," Master Nuk continued. "Elantrus needs you at your best. We will return here the moment the sun climbs above the mountains, so I suggest everyone get a good night's rest. That is all I have for today, my young warriors. For Elantrus!" Master Nuk held his mighty sword in the air.

"For Elantrus!" the warriors echoed, mirroring the gesture. Master Nuk nodded a dismissal, and the warriors dispersed.

A large, meaty arm draped across Akren's shoulders as he began his trek toward the village. Without looking over, he already knew whom the arm belonged to. "What do you want, Erius? Here to brag about your performance during training?"

"Me? Brag?" Erius asked in mock offense. "I would never stoop so low as to talk down to a friend less physically fortunate than I."

Akren smirked. "Good to know." He plucked Erius's heavy arm from around his shoulder. Akren wasn't the smallest of warriors, but he was by no means a freak of nature like Erius.

"Of course, you weren't going to beat me," Erius said matter-of-factly. "You weren't supposed to. Master Nuk only wanted to push you past your limit, that's all. So"—he wrapped his arm around Akren's shoulders once more—"what are we getting ourselves into tonight?"

"I'm planning on doing like Master Nuk suggested and have myself a long night's sleep.

You should probably do the same."

"Yeah," he said thoughtfully, "but you know what I think we should do? I think we should poke our heads into Feshel's Tavern, find ourselves a couple of ladies to keep us company."

"Keep us company?" Akren echoed, then flushed when he realized what his friend was referring to.

"Come on, Akren," he encouraged, patting him on the chest. "This could very well be my last night to be with a woman"—he paused to consider—"and your first. We can't let this moment slip past us."

"It wouldn't be my first," Akren said, but the look Erius gave him indicated he knew he wasn't telling the truth. Wriggling free from Erius's hold, he picked up the pace.

"What are you so upset about?" Erius asked with a laugh.

Akren didn't answer. Instead, he glanced at the hundreds

of homes the hill overlooked, picking out the one that belonged to Ingrid—his childhood crush—the most beautiful girl in all Elantrus. He huffed inwardly. So what if he had yet to lie with a woman? He was saving himself for someone special.

"What are you smiling about?" Erius asked, the corner of his own lips curving upward.

Akren tried to drop the smile, but the image of Ingrid was stuck in his head now, not allowing the smile to fade completely. "Nothing. You wouldn't understand, anyway."

Akren's stomach growled when they entered the village sometime later, reminding him he hadn't eaten since mid-afternoon. He picked up his pace, the thought of sleep overshadowed by his hunger. Hustling across the dirt street, he zipped past the closing storefronts that lined either side, his mouth watering as he pictured every potential last meal he was going to devour, but halted when he arrived at his go-to food spot. A sizeable crowd gathered in front of Feshel's Tavern, their shadows dancing in the torchlights.

"Come on, Akren," Erius said when he caught up, motioning for him to keep moving. "They're already celebrating our victory tomorrow."

A cluster of warriors passed the two men, also heading toward the tavern. As they approached the crowd, the people stirred with excitement. Some cheered; others called out to their friends, letting them know how much fun they would have and the amount of ale necessary to complete the task.

Erius looked over his shoulder at Akren. "You sure you aren't comin' in?"

Filling his belly was his top priority. The food smelled sensational, but from all the people standing around, who knew how long it would take for him to get a plate? "I'm sure," he said, eying the crowd. "Enjoy yourself." He still had a bag full of hardtack at home. It wasn't a rich stew, or a sizzling chunk of lamb with a side of fluffy sweet muffins, but it would have to do.

Erius shrugged and continued walking.

Akren watched his friend melt into the crowd. As he was about to turn away, a heavenly laugh carried on the wind—a laugh he recognized. His eyes searched for the owner of the divine voice. Then he spotted her. Right beside one of the torches on the porch, hair lit like spindles of golden thread, stood Ingrid. There were two men next to her. Akren realized he knew them. They were the sons of well-liked blacksmiths, who had been trying to court her for some time. One man said something, and she laughed again. A pang of jealousy coursed through him, and his heart sank a little at their playful interaction.

Then, during one of her guffaws, Ingrid's head swiveled to the left, and she looked at Akren. Her eyes widened. Her following smile grabbed his heart and planted it back in its proper place. She threw a big wave his way. Excusing herself, she walked toward him, shuffling through the crowd.

When she finally made her way to him, he noticed her glassy eyes. She'd been drinking. "Where do you think *you're* going?" she asked.

"Home. I *was* going to get something to eat, but there are far too many people here. Maybe this is a sign for me to get some sleep and prepare for—"

"Nope," Ingrid said, seizing his wrist and pulling him toward the tavern. "You're coming in with me."

Akren let her tug him up the steps and across the porch. When he passed by the two men she'd been talking to, he gave them a one-sided smile.

Ingrid shouldered her way through the tavern door, plucked a half-drunken mug of ale from the bar counter, and shoved it in his chest. "Drink!" She had to shout to be heard over the band's fast-paced melody.

Akren frowned as he peered down at the amber liquid sloshing around in the mug. "I probably shouldn't."

"Drink," she demanded with a chuckle, then took matters into her own hands. She lifted the bottom of the mug, guiding it to his lips. "It's not poison, I assure you. It was mine."

Akren had a sinking feeling he was going to regret accepting the drink, but from the way her eyes glistened with joy, how was he supposed to refuse? Opening his mouth wide, he guzzled the contents. Ale dribbled down his tunic as she upturned the mug higher than what was necessary. When the mug was empty, he pulled away from it, laughing.

"Are you trying to drown me?" he asked.

"You have to catch up." She plopped the mug on the counter, then turned to the innkeeper, who was in the middle of pouring a drink. "Elias, three more, please." "Coming right up," the heavy-set man said.

"Three more?" Akren asked, a bit of disbelief coloring his tone. "Are you mad? I have to be in decent shape for tomorrow's... well, you know."

Ingrid sighed. "Stop being such a baby, Akren. I'm just trying to loosen ya up."

"I don't need to be loose. If anything, I need to be asleep."

A thumping sound on the counter interrupted their conversation. "Three mugs of the finest ale in town." Elias dipped his chin, then went back to filling more orders.

"How about we find ourselves a table?" Ingrid asked. She leaned toward him. "Somewhere a little less noisy."

The band played directly across from the bar, and sandwiched in between the bar and the band were several dozen dancing figures—jumping and twirling, trying to match the frantic rhythm. To the left was a cluster of tables, and beyond that, a corridor that led to a handful of rentable bedrooms. Feshel's Tavern was always busy, but tonight it felt like the entire village had squeezed into the tiny place. It took a while for Akren and Ingrid to work their way through the crowd, making sure not to spill their drinks, but they finally reached their destination and set the mugs atop the corner table.

Settling on the hard wooden chair, Akren turned to look at the other seated guests, and locked eyes with a familiar figure. Erius stared back at him, a grin on his face, his mug held in the air in a toast. Then the toothy warrior's eyes slid over to Ingrid before returning to Akren, and he nodded approvingly.

Akren was grateful for the dim lighting where they sat; it hid his burning cheeks. Looking away, he hefted a mug and took in a mouthful of ale.

"How are you faring, Akren?" she asked when he finished another pull. "You've been distant lately. I mean, I get it. You've been getting yourself ready to be a hero."

Covering his mouth, Akren belched into his hand, then waved away the smell. "Distant?" Had he been? Certainly, he'd been heavy in his training. Now that he thought about his daily routine, maybe she had a point. The closer the battle came, the longer he stayed in the practice square, ensuring his moves were fluid and sharp.

Her smile fell a touch. "It's just that... I've been doing some reflecting, wishing we could go back to when we were kids, back when you used to barge into my parents' bakery and buy an entire loaf of honey cake, all for yourself."

"I used to hide in the stables and eat it as fast as I could before anybody spotted me." He smiled at the memory.

"And you didn't even bother sharing with any of your friends."

"Well, it was *my* allowance," he said emphatically. "If they wanted some, they could've bought their own." Bringing the mug to his lips for another sip, he noticed he'd already finished his drink. He put it down and hoisted another. It didn't take long for him to feel the effects of the liquor. "I sure could use one of those honey cakes right about now." Staring at his drink, his thoughts ventured to his childhood. After a short while, he finished off the second mug, shifted his position on the hard wooden seat, and picked up the last mug of ale. He sighed, then chuckled to himself. "Yeah, we sure had some good times."

As he was lifting the mug to his lips, preparing to take another sip, he noticed Ingrid's expression was solemn. She was staring at the tabletop, lost in her thoughts. The upbeat music died down, and when the airy notes of the flute broke through the silence, Ingrid's attention drifted toward the dance floor, her eyes lighting up with recognition.

Akren recalled the tune as well. It was a slow song, written by a mourning wife to her husband, in hopes that he'd hear it from the Great Beyond and come back to her in her dreams. Ingrid's eyes met his, and his thoughts started racing again. It felt as if she was conveying the song's message through her gaze.

"Would you like to dance?"

Akren turned to look at the dance floor. "Not exactly."

"Come on," she insisted, hefting him to his feet.

The room tilted as she dragged him toward the swaying couples. When they finally stopped, she faced him, grabbed his hands and put them on her waist, then clasped her fingers around the back of his neck. They moved in unison to the sound of the angelic singing, and as their gazes met, the same downcast expression Ingrid had displayed when they were at the table, returned.

In the beginning of his training, Master Nuk had told him not to get too attached to anyone, but it was impossible to comprehend the magnitude of that advice until now. Regret wormed its way into his mind as his impending doom loomed over his future. The upcoming battle was tomorrow. He liked to believe he'd be among the surviving warriors, but who was he kidding? He was a mediocre fighter at best. Akren was going to die tomorrow; he knew it, and from Ingrid's watery gaze, she expected it too. Throat tightening, nostrils flaring, he blinked several times to fight off the waiting tears. He never wanted to be a hero, but his fate had been chosen for him at the ripe age of eight.

Ingrid wiped at his face. Akren realized a traitorous tear had escaped down his cheek. "I have to sit down," he said in a hoarse tone. He tried to pull away, but she held him tighter.

"What's wrong?" she asked before lifting a shoulder and wiping the wetness from the corner of an eye.

"Please, Ingrid."

She was reluctant, but she eventually loosened her grip enough for him to slide out of her hold. He marched back to his seat, then slowed to a stop. Two other villagers were now taking up their spots. He was about to tell them to get up— and given his mood, not too politely—but a pair of hands on the small of his back pushed him away. Moments later, Akren was in the corridor, heading toward one of the rooms. He stumbled through the open doorway, then spun on Ingrid.

"Wait, we're not supposed to be in here," he said in a rushed whisper. "These rooms are for—"

Click. Ingrid bolted the door. "These rooms are for what?"

The rooms were mostly used for people to sleep off the

effects of too much ale, but they were also used for... other purposes. Akren couldn't bring himself to voice his thoughts.

Lamplights illuminated the small room, and as he distracted himself by looking at anything other than Ingrid or the freshly made bed, she brushed past him, kicking off her shoes.

"What are you doing?" he asked when a shoe bounced off a wall.

"What does it look like? My feet hurt." She sighed in relief when the last shoe was off, then sat on the bed, wiggling her toes. "What's wrong, Akren? Talk to me." Her voice was steady, but the concern in her eyes was hard to bear.

"I'll be fine. It's nothing for you to worry 'bout."

She cocked her head to one side. "I know when you're lying. Don't make me wrestle the information out of you like I used to do when we were younger."

Akren smirked. "What was I, nine the last time you managed to best me? I'm a trained warrior. Don't you see these muscles?"

"With all the sacks of flour I carry every day, I'm practically your equal in strength." She lifted her right arm and flexed.

Akren laughed. "Really?"

"Really."

Akren revisited the pain reflected in her eyes as they held one another on the dance floor, and slowly, his smile faded. "It's not important."

Ingrid stood, her features fixed like she was preparing to make do on her threat of wrestling the confession out of him.

"It's nothing," he assured her. "I swear." Seeing the resolve in her eyes as she closed the distance, Akren pressed a pretend key to his sealed lips, locked them, then threw away the key. Ingrid caught the key in midair, put it back to his lips, and unlocked them.

They both chuckled.

"All right," he said resignedly. "When d'you get so pushy?" He paced the room, contemplating how to ease into an admission, but found himself unable to gently convey his fear. So, he blurted it out. "I don't want to die. There, I said it."

"I don't think anyone *wants* to die."

"I'm not just anyone. I'm *me*, you know? And I have"—he swallowed—"I have someone I'd like to come back to when this is all done. I'm beginning to doubt my abilities in the upcoming battle."

"Then maybe you shouldn't do it," she suggested. "Maybe you should tell that old man Nuk that you don't want to go."

Akren snorted. "If it were only that simple. I don't have a choice. What am I supposed to do? Flee Elantrus? I have no doubts Master Nuk would find me and drag me all the way to the castle himself." He sighed. "I don't think I got what it takes to be a hero, Ingrid. I'm not Erius: unfathomably strong, well-built, skillful—"

"Tall and beautiful," she interjected. "The stereotypical hero. A man's man."

Akren's eyebrows lifted all the way to his forehead. "Is there something you want to tell me? Should he be here instead of me pouring out my poor, little heart?"

"I'm messing with you, Akren." Stifling a laugh but unable to hide her grin, she placed a hand on his chest, right where his heart was. "A hero isn't an image. It's about what's inside, that matters."

"I bet those goblins in the castle wouldn't mind showing me what my heroic insides look like," he grumbled. Ingrid pressed her forehead against his chest. "You reminded me tonight of a future I might never get to enjoy. And that stupid song didn't help." She sniffed, then took a step back, making a face.

"Yes, I smell," he said defensively. "I've been training all day."

"We need to remedy that, now, don't we?" Pulling him by his tunic, she led the way to the bathroom.

"You mean, right now? These are paid rooms. We're not supposed to be here, remember?"

"You don't worry about that. The Feshels have their hands full tonight. I doubt they're keeping track of who's going in and out. You just focus on not smelling like a pigpen."

"Hey, that wasn't very nice. I don't smell *that* bad."

Ingrid made a noise that contested his claim. He shuffled into the bathroom, and the door clicked shut behind him.

Unlike the bedroom, the bathing quarters had no lights, but the moonlight that shone through the high, lone window illuminated it well enough for him to see his way around. A large wooden washbasin rested in the corner, and next to the basin was a hand pump that connected to the tavern's cistern. Dangling from the lip of the basin was a tray that held a cube of soap and a plug for the drain. Using the hand pump, Akren filled the basin with chilly rainwater.

He braced himself as his foot came down on the cold water. He planned on making it a quick wash, but after he settled in, he noticed how soothing the water was on his tired and aching muscles. After lathering himself and scrubbing and rinsing off the day's filth, Akren sat and stretched his arms wide, resting his forearms on the lip of the basin. Yawning, he tilted his head back, and enjoying the relaxing water and the muffled sounds of music playing beyond the room, closed his eyes.

The sensation of someone shaking him forced his eyes

open. He was confused for a moment, wondering where he was, but a pair of dazzling green eyes quickly brought him up to speed.

"No one said you could fall asleep," Ingrid said, then splashed water onto his face.

"I was not sleeping," he protested. "I was only resting my eyes."

"Resting your eyes? You were snoring like a bear. I heard it all the way from the bedroom. Come on, time to get out. The water is freezing."

It should have dawned on him when he'd opened his eyes, but he just now realized he was naked, and his manhood was reacting to her warm hand lingering on his shoulder.

"Do you mind giving me a little privacy?" His voice fell into a whisper. "I'm not exactly decent underneath here." He gestured to his manly bits with a flick of the eyes, hoping she would get the message.

"I do mind," she said, crossing her arms. "I'm staying right here. If you want to leave, you're going to have to do it with me watching." Her smile conveyed she was toying with him, but he knew she was stubborn to a fault. Seeing this as some type of challenge, she'd remain in the bathroom.

"Who knew the bakers' daughter was such a pervert?" he said. "Then I guess I won't get out, and eventually, I'll die from the shivers. Save me from getting eaten tomorrow, I suppose."

Ingrid smirked. "If you aren't coming out, then I guess I'm coming in."

Akren drew back as she lifted her leg over the lip of the basin. Other than her shoes, she was fully dressed. "What are you doing?"

"What does it look like?" She forced his legs together with her knees and straddled him.

Akren frowned. "You *do* know you're in my dirty bathwater?"

"I'm too drunk to care," she replied, leaning forward. "Maybe when I wake up, if I remember all this, I'll be horrified."

She kissed him then. Lost in the moment, influenced by the ale as well, he eagerly returned the kiss, their tongues tangling in a sloppy display of affection.

* * *

Morning came all too fast for Akren. One moment, he and Ingrid were a tangle of limbs, the next, he was watching her sleep, wishing he could lie there with her forever. Eventually, he dressed, kissed her on the nape of her neck, then parted from the room.

When he arrived at the designated location, right at the base of the hill that led to the practice square, the village's second defense stood guard. In case the one hundred warriors failed, they were to fight off the ogre mage and his horde of monsters while the villagers made a hasty retreat. Wagons were currently being stocked for that probable outcome.

Behind the guards were several weapon carts and a large container that held their armor. The warriors outfitted themselves, completing their attire with a steel sword and shield.

After a series of farewells, the warriors ascended the hill and marched past the practice square and into the gloomy forest. Luckily—or unluckily, depending on how you looked at it—the journey through the woods was brief. Akren's heart pounded violently in his chest as they approached the thick, purple, foggy barrier that encased the castle.

Master Nuk, who marched in front of the troops, held a

fist in the air for everyone to stop walking. "We're here," he said, appraising the barrier. He rammed his staff into the dirt, then lowered his fist. Drawing his legendary sword, he turned to face the warriors. As he did, what appeared like flashes of lightning rippled through the barrier.

"I know I've been hard on you these past years." Master Nuk scanned over the faces of each man. "Every day, I have regretted pushing you to the brink of mental and physical breakdown. Today, you will know why I was so tough on you. From this moment forward, you all will follow the lead of a selected captain, for I will not be around to witness your triumph. Once the barrier disappears and the castle is revealed, I would have concluded my one hundred years. I've pondered over who should lead the charge for some time, but I believe I now know who the best man for the job is. Everyone, show your support for Erius Leronen. Erius, stand before me."

Akren and Erius, who stood side by side, shared a look. Akren watched as pride cupped his friend by the chin and lifted it ever so slightly. Erius strode forward.

Master Nuk placed a hand on the large warrior's shoulder. "I am entrusting you with the only sword that could stop Ushganore, delaying his return by another hundred years. Pierce his heart with this blade, and he'll revert to a statue once more. If you should fall, I'm counting on one of your brothers to finish the task." He tilted the hilt of the sword in Erius's direction.

"I will not fail you or Elantrus, Master," Erius declared, accepting the sword.

When the weapon switched hands, Master Nuk's body blinked as if he were no longer made of flesh but of light. The purple clouds that made up the barrier dissipated, revealing the faint outlines of a mighty structure. A rush of wind blasted through the forest, stirring up debris, forcing Akren to shield his eyes with a forearm. Small rocks pelted him as he squinted toward his master.

"You have all made me so proud!" Master Nuk roared, turning to face the fading barrier. "Do not forget what I taught you!" His body glowed brightly as he raised both hands—as if he was offering himself to the Heavens—leaves and twigs whirling around him. Suddenly, the light in his body pulled away from him like a snake shedding its skin and funneled into the blade of the legendary sword, illuminating briefly before dimming out. Master Nuk's body collapsed to the ground. Time seemed to stand still. The debris that had terrorized the one hundred warriors hung in the air.

Akren was hesitant to move, but after no further assault came, he dropped his arm and surveyed what was now before the warriors. Elantrus Castle awaited. Where Master Nuk's body had fallen was the beginning of the wide castle stairway leading to two massive metal doors. Akren expected the castle to appear run-down; instead, the castle appeared newly built. But what threw him off more than the immaculate exterior were the lights from the torches that shone from inside. At least, he thought they were torchlights. From what he'd recently witnessed, he couldn't be too certain.

No one spoke for several breaths. Erius was the first to gather his wits. "We're not even in the castle yet, and you all are already trembling with fear?" he growled. "The faster we slay these goblins, the sooner we can head back home and celebrate!"

Now having snapped out of their trance, the warriors drew their swords and roared, mirroring Erius's upraised weapon.

"Everyone here has memorized the castle layout from

Master Nuk's drawings, so I don't expect any of you getting yourselves lost. Let us claim our victory and protect—"

The castle doors cracked open, interrupting his speech. Erius whipped around, his sword at the ready. Slowly, he looked over his shoulder at the warriors, his face contorted in confusion. "Is that music?"

The soft sounds of a melody drifted through the open doorway. Akren swallowed heavily. Master Nuk hadn't told them about this. He realized as he tried to control his breathing that his hands were shaking.

"Careful men," Erius said, creeping up the short flight of stairs. "Keep your eyes movin'."

The warriors strolled into the brightly lit lobby, scrutinizing their surroundings.

A large painting of a pale-skinned man wearing a jewel-encrusted crown hung across the front door. Other than the torches that lined the wall and the scattered animal statues, the lobby was bare. Deeper into the room, there were two metal doors along the left wall and two on the right.

The music picked up its tempo, the notes clashing in various parts.

"What kind of instrument is that?" Hanlik, a tall, wiry warrior, asked.

Akren glanced at him. "I don't know. I've been wondering that myself."

"Quiet," Erius said, holding up his sword. "Do you hear that?" Underlying the musical notes were the echoes of a dog barking, followed by faint wailing sounds. Suddenly, the music grew loud and frantic. The violent wind from outside stirred again, rushing into the lobby. One by one, the torches blew out until the warriors were cast into near darkness. That's when the castle door slammed shut, echoing throughout the lobby. Akren spun to the noise, then back around, poised to attack, but his eyes had a tough time adjusting. The only source of light that remained was the dull morning sunlight streaming in from the slits of the closed wooden shutters.

The wind, the music, and the wailing came to an abrupt stop, but what followed was much more terrifying. A deep, gurgling voice boomed over the silence. "Kill them all and let us feast on their remains!"

The creaking of doors opening came next, followed by what sounded like a flurry of nails tapping on the castle floor. The tapping was getting closer.

Akren saw movement and held up his shield. Hundreds of creatures stormed into the lobby from the four open doors.

"It's the ogre mage's goblin army!" Erius announced. "It is time to solidify our places in history!"

A goblin crashed into Akren's shield, slashing at his face and snapping its teeth together. Akren thrust the shield forward, forcing the goblin back. With a quick swipe, his blade separated the goblin's head from its shoulders.

An agonizing scream pierced the sounds of battle. Hot liquid sprayed across Akren's face. When he glanced in the spray's direction, he saw a goblin had latched onto a warrior, gnawing on his neck.

The lobby was so jam-packed as Akren battled his way across that he wouldn't be surprised if he'd accidentally struck an ally with one of his wild swings. Something brushed past his legs, and he stomped down on whatever it was; it could have been a brother-in-arms grasping for help, or a fallen goblin. He didn't bother checking.

"We have to keep going!" Erius's voice bellowed over the chaos.

Akren fought his way in the direction of his friend's voice. He'd had to drop his shield during the scuffle; with so much blood coating the hilt of his sword, it became difficult to swing with one hand, and he'd rather have no shield than no sword. When he finally stepped through the open doorway, his shoulders and arms were sore and weighty.

Akren, and at least a dozen warriors, barged into a wide, dark corridor. A row of floor-to-ceiling stone columns decorated the space. He hadn't noticed them until he slammed into one. The battle persisted as they slowly veered toward a closed door at the end of the corridor, the outline of the door visible as light shone through.

There must be lit torches on the other side.

Looking over his shoulder after running his blade into an enemy's chest, he noticed the goblins from the lobby didn't seem to be following them. That made for a brief scuffle. After eliminating their opponents, the door at the end of the corridor opened.

"Come on!" Erius said, holding the door ajar. Half a dozen men tumbled into the room. Erius looked from them and back to the corridor with concern etched on his brow. "Is this all of us?" he asked.

"I believe so," Jovis, a burly man with a bald head and a thick beard, gasped.

Erius hesitated. The sound of battle, though faint and fading, carried from the lobby. His lips peeled back into a snarl. Swearing loudly, he slammed the door. He ran a hand over his face and turned to the remaining warriors. "We did all that training over the past ten years, just to be slaughtered." He shook his head. "It's up to us, now."

"We've made it to the throne room," Akren said absentmindedly. From the king's throne to the paintings on the wall, Master Nuk had recreated the image in great detail.

"That means the ogre mage is just beyond that door."

Erius pointed his bloodied sword toward what should be the chapel. "Are you all ready to put an end to this?"

Akren was indeed ready for the fight to be over; he just wasn't ready to continue fighting. With the scant number of surviving warriors, their chances of defeating the ogre mage appeared bleak. The expressions on the warriors' faces matched his sentiment.

Erius's gait was cautious as he approached the door to the chapel. "Line up behind me," he ordered in a low voice. Everyone obliged. Erius cracked the door open, peered into the room, then opened it wider. Creeping forward, his head whipped back and forth, looking for a threat.

Akren, who brought up the rear, closed the door behind himself. Just like the rest of the castle, the chapel was in pristine condition. Rows of wooden pews filled the space, and right across from the pews, atop the dais, its face contorted in a sneer, was the statue of Ushganore. A purple glimmer encompassed the ogre mage, but it was slowly retracting.

Erius stood mere feet in front of the statue, just staring at it, his sword half-raised.

Akren didn't know if the retracting glimmer was akin to some kind of countdown, and he didn't want to stick around long enough to find out. "What are you waiting for, Erius? Stab him in the heart."

"I... can't... move," Erius said in a strained voice. "I don't... know what's wrong... with me."

Akren noticed that beyond the purple gleam, the fingers on Ushganore's right hand were twitching. Akren took two steps in Erius's direction, with the mind to snatch the sword and end the fight before it started, but the ogre mage's eyes shifted in his direction, a smile forming on its grotesque face. The purple gleam around his body cracked, then crumbled to the floor like glass.

"Too late," Ushganore announced. His feet lifted off the dais. As he hovered, a maniacal laugh erupted from his throat, bouncing off the chapel walls. "You are too late." His left hand rose, and he held it, palm forward, in Erius's direction. "I will turn you all into ashes." One of the torchlights blew out. Suddenly, Ushganore's palm glowed orange. A ball of fire shot from his hand and ignited Erius like a bonfire. Erius screamed as his skin and flesh split and charred, but he still didn't move.

"We have to slay that thing and protect the village," Jovis said, but Akren was too stunned to tear his gaze away from his burning friend. A warrior passed by his line of sight, heading toward the ogre mage, but he too was lit ablaze. Unlike Erius, who had already stopped screaming, the warrior rolled on the ground frantically, trying to put out the fire.

The ogre mage transformed into a cloud of black smoke. Finally willing himself to move, Akren turned to follow the ogre mage's path. Ushganore became corporeal once more, but this time he was hovering behind the warriors.

Jovis was the first to react. With an overhead swing, he tried to cut off Ushganore's head, but the blade clinked when it met the ogre's skin, sounding like it had just scraped against stone.

"What the—" was all he got out before he too was engulfed in flames.

Akren's attention went back to Erius's still-standing corpse, and his eyes dropped to the legendary sword. He ran to the sword, tore it out of his friend's grip, and charged at the distracted ogre mage, whose attention was on the four remaining warriors. As Akren closed in, though, the ogre mage twirled and backhanded him on the side of the face, sending him over a row of pews, his body landing with a painful thud. He could feel swelling where Ushganore had struck. Writhing on the floor, he saw the flickers of light overhead, followed by the screams of his fellow warriors. A few beats later, and the chapel fell into relative silence. All Akren could make out was crackling fire, shuffling feet, and heavy grunts. He didn't know if the ogre mage remembered smacking him halfway across the room, and he wasn't keen on revealing the fact that there was still one more warrior left. So, he lay there, hoping the ogre mage overlooked him, despite the nagging voice in his head telling him to stop being a coward and defend his village.

Suddenly, the sword glowed like a beacon. "Just let me be," he groaned to the sword, imagining this was his master's way of reprimanding him.

"What is that?" Ushganore growled. "Right. I forgot there was one more left." The pews rose off the ground. The moment Ushganore locked eyes with Akren, the ogre mage grinned. "Ah, there you are."

Akren grimaced as he got to his feet. His shoulder ached as he lifted the sword, standing in a defensive pose. One of the pews came barreling toward him. He swung his sword, more so from reflex than anything, not really expecting an outcome other than a swift death, but the glowing blade sliced the pew in half. He marveled at the sword with wide eyes until a fireball sped toward him. It might have been a stupid idea, but Akren tried to deflect the blaze with another strike. Surprisingly, it worked. Upon contact, the sword vanquished the fiery orb.

A surge of confidence coursed through him. Maybe he could do this after all. More pews shot his way as the ogre mage twirled his hands in the air, and Akren cut each one down while working his way toward the offender. Like before, the ogre mage disappeared, but the light from the sword exposed him. The smoke form Ushganore took on was to disguise his real movement. When the smoke maneuvered to the right, the ogre mage's shadow rounded to the left. With a lunging blow, Akren plunged the sword into Ushganore's chest the moment he reappeared.

Then he stumbled forward. His brows knitted in confusion as he took in his new surroundings. No longer was he in the chapel, but outside in a land of green grass and an endless blue sky. There was a pool not too far from him. The water held a pinkish hue. He was about to make his way to the pool when a voice startled him. "It's that time already?"

Akren spun around and laid eyes on a young man who appeared to be about his age. The man grunted as he stood, then lumbered toward him.

"Hey," Akren said, approaching the man with a heightened sense of urgency. "What is this? Where's Ushga..." Finally getting a good look at the young man, he trailed off.

"Master Nuk?"

Akren's master was dead, but the man's resemblance to him was unmistakable.

The man responded with a sad smile and a nod. "I am Nuk," he said, "but I'm not the man who trained you."

"That doesn't make any sense," Akren said. "None of this is making any sense." Then a horrifying thought crossed his mind. "Wait, did I fail? Did the ogre mage kill me somehow, and this is the Great Beyond?"

"Not quite. Your presence here means you defeated Ushganore. You did it. Our village is safe for another hundred years. Listen, lad." Nuk placed a hand on Akren's shoulder. "You're not going to like what I have to tell you. The tale we've been taught growing up about Ushganore, and Shelron, the last king of Elantrus, is a lie."

"What do you mean, a lie?" Akren asked, recalling the story he'd been told. "The ogre mage attacked the castle with a horde of goblins. The ogre mage killed the king. A villager by the name of Elrith gathered some men, charged the ogre mage, and came out victorious, earning the right to be honored as a hero. But a curse was placed upon him, forcing him to live the hundred years until Ushganore awakened, and..." Nuk was shaking his head. Akren let the retelling of the story fade away. "What part of that isn't true?"

"Ushganore never placed a curse on anyone or anything," Nuk said.

"But I've seen the purple barrier around the castle." Akren's voice held a hint of annoyance.

"To protect the villagers from the truth." With a long sigh, Nuk paced. "Only a few people in the castle knew King Shelron was a sorcerer."

"A sorcerer?"

"Aye. And Elrith wasn't just a regular villager. He was one of the king's personal guards and closest friend. When Ushganore and his goblins ambushed the castle, Elrith was at home with his family. After hearing the castle's distress signal, he gathered as many men as he could and lent aid to the king. The battle was fierce, and King Shelron found himself unable to defeat the ogre mage. Out of desperation, he used a forbidden magic—a dark magic—to temporarily entrap Ushganore, connecting his life span to Ushganore's resurrection. One hundred years was the extent of the spell he used. That was the longest time he could hold Ushganore before the ogre mage broke free and caused havoc once more. To prevent that from happening, he performed a second dark spell. The spell required ninety-nine souls to activate, and one body to put his soul inside."

"One body to put his... soul inside?" Akren paused, collecting his thoughts. "Are you telling me King Shelron was the Master Nuk that trained me?"

Nuk nodded. "Aye. Before me, he was Master Selik, and before that, he was Master Torius."

"That means his first victim was his own friend," Akren said in realization. "And now..." He couldn't bring himself to finish.

"And now," Nuk said, "for the next one hundred years, he'll be pretending to be you."

Akren thought he was going to be sick. He'd been played the fool. They all had. "There is no hero," he said, letting out some of his frustration. "Why would he do this to us?"

"Well, in a way, there is," Nuk said, then peered over Akren's shoulder. "He saved the village, but he neglected to tell anyone about the sacrifices that followed his decision."

Akren turned to see what had caught the man's attention. The water in the pool was glowing a bright pink now.

"My time is up," Nuk said. "This is where we part."

"Where are you going?" Akren asked as Nuk brushed past him.

"Headed to the Great Beyond, hopefully. From what I was forced to give up, I think I deserve it."

"But what happens to me? What am I supposed to do?" Akren tried to follow Nuk, but no matter how fast he moved, he couldn't catch up. It was like he was running in place.

"Wait. Master Nuk." His voice shook as the situation settled in.

Nuk tossed a farewell in the air.

"Wait!" he shouted again. "I don't want to be here! I'm not supposed to be here!" He ran as fast as he could, but Nuk continued to pull away. "I'm supposed to be the hero that saved the village." Akren couldn't stop the tears from blurring his vision. The warriors had given their lives for a lie, and he'd be stuck in this place for one hundred years. Would the people in the village be suspicious of the Akren that returned to them? It was unlikely. No one questioned Master Nuk's authenticity. At least, not to his knowledge. He stopped running once his thoughts landed on Ingrid. The only thing he ever truly wanted was well out of reach. He was better off getting eaten by the goblins. Dropping to his knees, he began to cry.

Nuk stepped into the pool, and his body liquefied. There was a slight ripple as his figure splashed down, mixing with the water. When the pool water stilled, the pink light vanished.

* * *

Shelron pulled the blade from the ogre mage's chest. Ushganore's still form stared in his direction, his features filled with contempt. With great effort, he dragged the statue back to the dais. That was where Ushganore needed to be for the old spell Shelron had cast to be reactivated.

He took a few steps back and peered into the ogre mage's blank stare, thinking about their unspoken past. There was a reason Ushganore and his goblin army had attacked Elantrus Castle and not the village. Shelron had stolen something very precious to him: his magic staff. Instead of giving it back, he welcomed the fight, thinking he could best Ushganore, but the ogre mage proved stronger than he expected. He was able to trap Ushganore, but the price for using the dark-magic spells was steep: Shelron lost his ability to wield magic.

A purple haze encompassed Ushganore once more. Then it slowly expanded. Once the barrier covered the castle, the interior would go back to the condition it was in before the goblins first attacked all those years ago. The moment preceding the battle still pained him: his wife, sitting on a bench playing her new instrument; their dog's warning barks. And then there was the screaming—so much screaming.

"That's my cue. See you in another hundred years, old friend." With that, Shelron hobbled from the holy chambers.

When he entered the throne room, he picked a goblet up from a small table stand and peered at the reflection. "Akren? Well, I'll be." He didn't think the lad had it in him. Then again, after the ninety-nine souls were collected, the last man standing was invincible to the ogre mage's attacks. That was just the way the spell worked. Once it was activated, nothing could stop it.

Letting the goblet clatter to the ground, Shelron approached the throne, which was pressed against a wall. He placed a hand on either chair arm and spread them outward. A click sounded, and the throne slid to the side. Shelron peered into the dark escape tunnel, knowing that despite its eeriness, it was his best option. Until the purple haze covered the castle, the goblins would be feasting. And there was no way he would cross those miscreants without his magic. Especially in the condition he was in. Every inch of his body hurt. Entering the tunnel, he pulled a lever, and the throne slid back to its original place.

Moments later, he was in front of the castle. He plucked what was once Ushganore's staff from its place in the ground —the staff where Akren's soul was now imprisoned—and limped toward the practice square. When he reached the square, the villagers who had taken the role as the second defense, cheered. With wide grins they approached him, clapping him on the shoulder, forcing him to wince. Eventually, the group clambered down the hill.

The sun broke through the clouds the same moment he spotted a yellow-haired girl running toward him. It was one of the bakers' daughters, and she had tears in her eyes. She slammed into him, sending them both to the ground. She was laughing; he was groaning in pain.

"I knew you could do it," she said. "I knew you'd come back to me."

Shelron only moaned in return. He tried to stand, but his body was too stiff to do it on his own.

"Oh, stop acting so helpless," she said, pulling him to his feet. She searched his eyes when they stood, and with a hand clutching his tunic, she pulled him in and kissed him long and hard. When she backed away, she clasped his hand in hers, and together, they made their way home.

I wrote my first script during my 6th period class as a senior in high school. I was so bored (sorry Mrs. Noonan) that I decided to pull out my folder and start writing. I finished my first draft in a couple of months. It had to be one of the greatest stories ever told! Almost 20 years later, I ran across that very screenplay and almost cried from embarrassment. It was trash. But that sparked the desire to write my first book.

The ability to express one's self through various genres is probably one of the greatest self-healing practices in creative writing. It lets me speak about serious issues and work them into an elaborate storyline, while allowing others to confront a difficult past.

Being the introvert that I am (as most authors seem to be), there are entire worlds in my head with characters that feel a lot like family. My job is to pull you into these worlds, introduce you to these characters, and let them live rent free in your head as they've lived in mine.

3DJohnson.com

NEVER CATCH A TIGER BY THE TOE

BY JESSICA KAY LISSNER

He wants you to think he's nobody, but he walks among us.

Thursday was movie night, and the poofs were piled with closest friends. The long pile carpet with its freckled teals and blues was crowded as one person rested their head in another's lap, and a tangle of bare feet held some friends up while others got massages.

What were we watching? It doesn't matter. We ordered finger food: sushi, momos, little cakes and mochi. I was looking forward to the part where we'd pass the paper to-go boxes around and feed each other.

I didn't hear him come in.

My old place was in a line of houses from the 1800s. Our entry was on the bottom floor, where there was enough room to take off our shoes and hang our coats beside a little reading nook. A twisty passage with low ceilings led past the confused divisions of old houses into as many apartments as possible. At the end of the passage, the steps up to my living room opened up into a garden style palace lined with windows and richly detailed crown molding all the way around.

I'd ordered with the same restaurants every week. With delivery companies and cloud kitchens taking over, it gave me that sense of connection to San Francisco by directly ordering with the restaurants themselves. It cost less for me, they got more money, and the delivery guy was usually one of a few family members who knew me by my first name.

When I looked over my shoulder to see a small brown guy I didn't know, I assumed he was from the momo place. They had a big family, so I assumed someone must have told him how to get in. Transfixed by the projector's stream of light, he stood at the back of my living room.

In the police report, I described him as about five foot four, with thick black curly hair that could have made him seem taller. He was skinny, with round dark eyes that were almost black. He was between eighteen and twenty-one. I guessed that he was either Indian or an Arab, but he could have been Greek. I mistook the jacket he had hanging over his arm for a delivery.

"Can you please put it on the kitchen table, beside the sushi?"

He nodded and followed my pointed finger to the right. I went back to watching the movie and figured he'd drop off the food then see himself out.

My first sign that something was wrong was the sound of the full silverware drawer slamming their tips against the knife and fork divider. That noise sets my teeth on edge. One of my roommates cannot pull the drawers with a little less force or pull a spoon out the night before so that he doesn't wake up the whole house when he wants his breakfast. But George was out of town.

When the drawer crashed on its way closed, I gave Trent a quick kiss and rolled to the side of the poof to crawl to my feet. Flicking on the light in the kitchen, I watched as the stranger perused my kitchen drawers. "What are you doing?"

He looked up absently, then pushed the contents of my junk drawer side to side. Carefully pulling out the grains of rice that escaped in the last few years, he told me, "I need a needle big enough to work leather. Also, I need some heavy thread."

"Who are you and why are you in my house?"

"I am the boogeyman." He continued searching for grains of rice. "I'll need scissors as well."

"Excuse me?"

He didn't reply.

I tapped my hand on my thigh and stared at him. Scoffing,

I couldn't believe this man walked into my house and started giving me orders.

There is a leather jacket that I have been wearing since 2012. It is dark brown with a teal lining, and the stiff leather has taken the shape of my body because I wear it so often. I recognized it instantly.

"Is that my jacket?" It was slung over the back of one of the kitchen chairs. I picked it up, to notice a clean cut on the back where my fingers slipped over a raw selvage and found the lining. I turned it around to find that he'd cut out a hole in the back panel of the leather. I shouted, "What have you done?"

"Nineteen." He cheerfully declared the number as if it explained everything. "Isn't it odd that it's always a prime number?"

I scowled at him, "Why are you in my house?"

"Where is the needle?" He asked, then he noticed I was holding up the hole in the jacket. "Should I do both?"

What was he talking about? I didn't know. "No. You should leave. Now."

"But your door said to come in?"

"That was for the people watching the movie-"

"Do I need to watch the movie to stay?"

I gawked at him. He can't possibly be this imbalanced.

Throwing the coat back over the chair, I freed up my hands if things suddenly got physical. Dropping my voice, I warned, "You know what I said. Get out, or I will call the cops."

His gaze lowered to my stomach, and he licked his lips as he stared for an uncomfortably long time. Pursing his lips, he slunk a step toward me. As he reached for my stomach, he softly teased, "You wouldn't call the police on me."

I shoved him toward the door, but not nearly as far as he jumped.

That little man sprung off the floor and twisted as if I'd thrown him with the force of a tornado. He landed on his hands and feet on the wall near the ceiling. The muscles in his shoulders flexed as claws pressed from his fingertips into the drywall.

Staggering backwards, I screamed. The world slowed down. Death is coming for me.

He raced along the side of the wall towards me as a hail of cracked paint fell in his wake.

I was flat footed as I watched him come. My jaw dropped. I'd spent years training in martial arts, but all I could think of doing was to pick up a chair, cringe and drop my weight.

The boogeyman pushed off the wall like a tiger and he sprung onto me. The jacket that was still slung over the back of the chair, flipped into my face as the chair itself racked me in the chin. Hitting the ground hard with both him and the chair on top of me, I was immediately winded.

He leaned over the chair with his feet straddling me on either side. With a mouth full of jagged teeth, he leaned forward as if he might bite my neck.

"No!" I shouted, "Not today!"

I shoved the chair upwards and spun as I threw it against the kitchen cabinets with everything I had. The boogeyman rolled off it and dug the claws in his hands and feet into the wood floor. Then he took the sushi and ran out of the house.

* * *

"You're saying a vampire stole the sushi?" Trent's frown lines were deeply etched, but his incredulous tone was mocking everyone.

"Yeah. No, yeah. I'm not saying a vampire stole the sushi." Vampires don't exist, but our friend Paul knew from all the fantasy he read that vampires count rice. When I pointed to the damaged wall and floor, I asked, "Does it look like a vampire did that?"

You'd think that with a house full of people, someone else would have seen the boogeyman, but it had happened so quickly that it was only me.

In the aftermath, we found a few more anomalies. First, someone took the time to organize our shoes by type and color, while neatly stacking them into the shoe racks. To make room for more shoes, the downstairs bookcase was overturned. A pile of books was on the floor, but the bookcase itself was stacked with shoes.

My friend Brian doesn't have a tech salary like the rest of us. He only has one pair of shoes, and those shoes were missing. I felt terrible about it. The note that said 'come in' was my fault- but how can you feel guilty about leaving a post-it note, when everyone does that?

While we waited for the rush order of sushi to be delivered, everybody helped. We put the books back on the bookcase. Trent repaired the drywall and Brian sanded the floor. Explaining the gauges in the floor to the property management company was a problem for another day. Everyone put in a few bucks for Brian to get a new pair of shoes. It added up to $232, so that was easily solved.

I called the police department. They told me to file a report online, then someone would get back to me. (Nobody ever did, but that's San Francisco for you.)

While everyone was putting my house back together, we spun theories about what happened. As we searched our phones for the keyword 'boogeyman + rice + shoes' nothing useful came up. Searching for descriptions of the boogeyman led to an infinite chasm of role-playing gamers who took their characters too seriously. Still, he wasn't any type of elf or demon from any fantasy setting.

Brian tried to use AI to generate an image of the boogeyman by combining stock images of models who were similar looking. In the end, the image almost looked like the boogeyman. I added it to the police report.

* * *

At the end of the night, everyone went home. Trent asked me if I wanted him to stay. While he was incredible at patching the walls, I could tell that once the damage was covered up, he wanted to paint over the reality of monsters as quickly as he repaired the wall. I couldn't talk to Trent about the boogeyman without upsetting him. So, with a quick kiss at the door, he left around midnight.

"You're sure you'll be fine alone?" Brian was the sensitive person who lurked after Trent was gone. "I know your roommates are out of town. If you want someone to sleep on your sofa, I don't mind?"

I leaned on the door frame as I listened to the idle noises of late night Noe Valley. With a sigh, I leaned my head back and told him, "I don't think I'm going to be able to sleep tonight."

"Is your adrenaline still pumping?"

"No, yeah." I offered him a tight-lipped smile. "It happened a few hours ago, but you know me."

"You can't stop thinking about it?"

"Ye old anxiety is back."

"Do you need meds?"

"I'd rather soak in the feels until I've processed it first." I groaned. "This isn't over yet. What if whatever happened tonight is going to lead to me stepping into some shadow world?"

"It could be hella cool."

"Only if I can figure it out before I'm in over my head. What if that thing comes back for me?"

"I'll be here." Brian closed my door. "I will stay up as late as you want and help you do whatever you need to. Just use me. When you're ready to sleep, tell me to go home or I'll crash in the living room."

A little laugh that was half sigh and half relief bubbled up. "Thanks."

As the night stretched on, we found ourselves stretched on the bigger poof with empty mugs from the ayurvedic tea we drank as we fell into a rabbit hole of research papers. Knowing that modern day vampires were invented in the 1800s, we shifted to the progenitors to vampires: boukles, upiór and vrykolakes.

"I think he took my shoes to repair them." Brian forwarded me a link. "Check that one. Someone interviewed old Greek ladies from random villages in the 1800s about vrykolakes - and here's another one, boukles. They asked what they're like and multiple people independently claimed that they'd break into homes and repair shoes."

"What? Why?"

"That's unclear."

"This paper on the basis of wedding rituals claims that the reason we throw rice is because it blesses the newlyweds with fertility." I swiped to the next screen on my tablet to show him, "Bouklas and sasabonsam are both vampire-ish monsters who eat unborn babies."

"No way." He leaned over and looked at my screen. "You're thinking that the tradition of throwing rice goes back to preventing the monsters from stalking the newlyweds?"

"Exactly." I clicked my tongue. "If we assumed the boogeyman was a bouklas, how can we use that to prevent him from coming back?"

"You took the sign off the door, right?"

"Yeah."

"Let's empty your bag of rice at the front door."

"Wait – no." I considered, "What if the boogeyman was only the first, and we're in a bigger world now. We almost caught him. But, what if we actually caught him, then we asked him with hella information to protect ourselves?"

His eyes lit up. "You weren't attacked. The monster fell into a trap that you accidentally laid."

"Imagine that, laziness has its payoffs."

He smiled. "So, I'm in now. Okay... How will we catch him?"

"So, I'm kinda a prepper. I have multiple ten pound bags downstairs. We catch him with an old pair of shoes and then pour circles of rice around him."

"Like catching a demon with salt?" He held up a high five. "It turns out everything we needed to know came from fantasy books."

Slap! "I can't believe we're actually doing this."

* * *

Ok, so, there's the plan, and there's what actually happened. I couldn't find any of my old shoes, but I did have a lot of rice.

As Brian tossed the rice with vinegar so the birds wouldn't eat them, I decided to sacrifice a pair of heels. I jammed a butter knife between the rubber cap and the hollow block of a chunky heel to expose the inside.

Squeezing a luggage tracker inside and gluing it shut, I asked with a smile, "How should I destroy them?"

"Hmm. Quickly? Do you have a power sander?"

"Trent has all the tools." I scanned the kitchen. "The blender?"

He quirked an eyebrow up at me as he squeezed into the corner by the sink. "I'll be over here."

Lifting the lid off the top, I looked down at the blade. Several buttons offered a range of choices. As I pressed one after the next, I listened to the different pitches. "Do I pulse my shoes or chop them?"

"Lowest setting." Brian flinched as he thought about it. "Please. Yea, no. Not the Goonies."

"The scene where the guy put the kid's hand in-" I shivered, "Didn't they put a gremlin in a blender?"

"For sure." He squinted one eye. "Hold down the lid so it doesn't fly out."

"Whew. Here we go." Cramming the shoe inside was harder than it seemed. I had to bend the arch of the shoes over the edge of the counter and twist them to loosen it up so they could bend to get inside. Then, with only the tip of the shoe in the blade, I held the rubber top over the back of the shoe and pressed 'chop.'

The shoe lurched away from the blade, but I pushed it down so the blade could kick it away again. With a few rounds, the toes were chopped up and ugly – but that was my intention.

We went downstairs and stacked pillowcases full of rice into the foldable wagon. Pulling it through the front door, we left the shoes in a circle of rice at a neighbor's door, then went out in the neighborhood to be sure we caught him.

We got back from tossing handfuls of rice from Noe Valley to Duboce Triangle around 3AM. With a line of rice at the front door and the smart doorbell set for extra sensitivity, I checked the app on the luggage tracker and made sure it would alarm if it moved. Then, we both went to sleep.

I woke up to a pinging alarm on my cell phone. It was still dark out, but the glow of the phone illuminated my room. My eyes weren't adjusted, so I tapped on the pop-ups without reading them. Blinking, I stared at the luggage tag's app. It was moving... from my neighbor's house to mine.

"Brian!" I rushed into the living room as I called his name over and over. I shook his shoulder and whispered, "He's at our door."

The doorbell rang.

"Fuck." Brian rolled on his side as he looked up at me in a squint. "What time is it?"

"Five forty-six." I shrunk down next to him. "Do we answer it?"

The doorbell rang.

"Check the camera at the door."

My cell phone was already in my hand, so I held it up to get past the lock and flipped through the apps as I looked for the security one. And there he was. It was the same guy who'd come earlier. He waited by the door with an unassuming slouch.

I pushed the button to talk through the speaker. "Yes?"

He leaned forward over the speaker and proudly answered, "I brought your rice back. There were one million and three grains."

I couldn't help myself. I'm a quality control engineer. "How do you know?"

"It's a prime number."

"You could have miscounted. That's a big number."

There was an awkward pause as I watched him pull out a cell phone. "One million and nineteen is a prime number. I don't think I could be that far off."

"Are you sure?" It was odd. I expected him to be a monster and come in and attack us, but instead, he was debating the count of rice. My grip on my phone tightened as I asked, "How did you count to 1 million while picking up rice in under three hours?"

"I have a counting machine."

"When was it last calibrated? How can you tell it was counting rice and not something else you picked up off the street?"

"You must know the Sphinx..." His voice trailed off. Eventually, he replied, "I tested my AI's object recognition for rice to 99.999% confidence."

"So you know you're off. 0.001 times a million is ten. Being off by sixteen doesn't seem too unlikely now, does it?"

"Can I come inside and show you?"

"No. You cannot come inside. I forbid you from coming inside."

He snickered. "If you let me in, I'll teach you how to make words have actual power."

"I'm not falling for that."

He held my heels in front of the camera. "Do you have more leather in this color?"

"If I did, I wouldn't open the door to give it to you."

"Why not?"

I tipped my head and enjoyed annunciating into my microphone: "Because you stole my sushi."

The boogeyman looked up and down the street, then he crouched and studied the lock on my door. Speaking the brand to himself, he pulled out his cell phone and took a picture of the keypad.

Brian smirked as he shifted up onto his elbows. Both of us squeezed to watch the small image on my phone. "He doesn't know what to do."

"Oh my god, you're right." My thumb hovered over the microphone button. "Should we ghost him?"

"Hell yeah. You just defeated a monster by being over analytical. Totally, just leave him hanging at this point."

"Look at him, he's milling." I looked back to the kitchen. "I don't think I'm going to fall back asleep. Do you want to share a celebratory tiramisu?"

"Keep watching him. I'll go get it."

The boogeyman tucked the shoes in the alcove where UPS drops off packages. He brought the rice back in trash bags, which he leaned against the opposite wall. Then, he left.

Half pushing myself through the workday wasn't productive. The part of my mind that is particularly paranoid when I'm tired found the chinks in the night before. My instincts screamed that I needed to run.

Every place within a hundred miles was booked – except Vacaville. (LOL, like I'd spend the weekend there.)

I guess if it's not Vacaville serious, I can chill for a bit.

If I hadn't lent my camping gear to my roommates, I could have gone out to the mountains. But – as I re-read the few sources I had and I replayed some episodes of Vampire Diaries, I decided that I had more power in the house.

I'm going to have to really catch him this time.

Around lunch time, it dawned on me that he'd already been in the house. Vampire Diaries rules where a vampire needs an invitation don't apply to him. I was dreading that he'd find a way to defeat my lock, then he'd end up in the house. Only this time, we'd be alone.

I rushed downstairs and took the bags of rice that he'd returned, to rip a hole in the bottom of each one and shake it all over the street in front of my house, through my entry and all the way up the stairs and across my living room and kitchen.

Like a fucking boomer hippy, I had dried sage delivered. As I wandered around my house, I held up the smoking bundle while repeatedly rubbing the rice off the soles of my feet. Over and over, I chanted: "Boogeyman, you are not welcome here. Boogeyman, stay away."

I did that until my smart fan kicked on and Google announced that the air quality in my house shot into the red. Google had barely finished talking before smoke alarms went off and I opened all the windows.

It was around 4PM when I climbed into bed with an old copy of Guilty Pleasures with the idea that there was something to learn from some high-quality vampire smut. I didn't get very far. My head had barely hit the pillow before I fell fast asleep.

Something moved in my closet.

I woke up with a start, unsure if I'd seen what I thought I saw. Licking my lips, I rolled to my side and grabbed my phone to turn on the flashlight. It was 10PM and the noise from the cars and shouting people on the street was obnoxiously loud.

Shining the light on the window at the far side of my room, the slight lift of my curtains gave away that it was wide open.

I pulled my covers up to my chest and quickly turned, shining my light into the closet.

The flattened rectangular tip of a handheld vacuum poked from behind my winter coats. Atop it, the red lights of a block of cameras flickered.

"What are you doing here?" I dropped my voice as I pulled my knees into my chest. "I'm not afraid of you."

The boogeyman's eyes were black spheres as he crept into view. He brushed the side of his cheek on my fur coat. "There were one million and three grains."

"I don't care."

"I did." He lowered into a squat where he was half covered by my closet door. "Do you want to watch me count them?"

"No."

"Do you need to inspect my counter? I modified this vacuum to make it."

"It's fine!"

"Aren't you concerned that the suction might vary?"

"You obviously already worked it out."

"Good. Then I counted all the grains correctly." He lowered onto the ground where I couldn't see him from the bed.

I sat up sharply, just in time to see him crawl like a lizard across the floor. Throwing my comforter onto him, I ran for the door.

He sprung onto me and knocked me to the ground. We ended in a scramble of arms and legs. I kneed him in the ribs and tried to wrap the blanket around him. At the same time, he put his claws through the blanket and shredded it into ribbons.

Racing under my bed like a lizard, he spun to look back at me with those black beady eyes. "You kicked me."

I reached for my phone, then turned the light in his eyes. Checking the corner of my room, I made sure my training swords were still there. The brown handle of my practical katana stuck out. Taking a step toward it while keeping the light on him, I demanded: "Get out of my house."

Blinking and squinting, he shifted his weight and smiled a maw full of rows of fangs. "You're going to be an excellent enemy."

"What are you talking about?" I inched toward the swords. As long as he was talking, I couldn't lose track of him.

"Do you know what the hardest part of dating a human is? You can't stop thinking about eating them." He ran his tongue over the tips of his teeth. "She enjoyed your sushi, but I was thinking – wouldn't it be better if we ate dinner together? Your spoils filled her belly, and you, alone, can fill mine."

"Those are big words from someone who's hiding under the bed."

"I like it under the bed." He slowly snapped his fangs as he tried to squirm out of the light. "You're going to make such a great hunter."

"You're going to get out of my house."

He trilled, "How fun. We're having our first fight. Your riddle of the calibration error got me, but not for too long. I can't wait to see what you'll plan next."

"I don't know what sick game you're playing-"

"Let me tell you... I need to impress my new girlfriend. She will love it when you hunt me and I show you mercy every time I beat you."

What the fuck?

"I will be sure to tell you when I take her on a date. If we plan a trip together, you will have as much time to plan a diabolical assault. If we are ever bored, I will come looking for you. And if we ever break up, I will eat you."

"How in the world do you-"

"You're Susan from now on. There's a purse downstairs with your ID, passport, banking information and your new credit card. I'm going to give you one night to escape my retaliation. You lured me into this house. It is obviously a trap." He played with the ruffles in my bed skirt. "Your unsuspecting nature makes you very dangerous. I'll have to protect Theresa from you, Susan."

I reached behind me and wrapped my hand around the familiar handle. Pulling it slowly to my hip, I slipped my other hand over the saya and prepared to draw.

He widened his eyes and hissed. "Yes, Susan. Bring the sword."

"This is your last chance to get out. Don't make me draw my sword." I turned the sword so I could feel the menuki under my finger and I knew the blade was up. My left thumb was poised at the tsuba.

His discordant giggling threw me off. He rolled onto his back and squirmed between my mattress and box frame. "We all need good enemies. Nobody understands you like your enemies do. Who else would spend all their waking moments wondering how you'll respond to their idiosyncrasies? Who else would plan a meeting between the two of you for weeks, if not years?"

I rushed the bed, but he threw the mattress at me and sprinted for the window. I dropped to a roll and dodged it. By the time I made it to the window, he was holding the bricks of the house on the other side of the street. He shouted back to me: "Remember, you have one day! I'll eat you if I find you here."

That was the last day of my old life. The demons of the world all knew me from that moment forward and I quickly learned that if I didn't have the boogeyman proudly claiming me as his enemy to the rest of the underworld, then the rest came for me. In a crude way, I was his toy, and he had enough clout that the others left me alone.

The first years were lonely: the boogeyman brought the shadow of death and wherever I went mayhem followed. But soon, I learned that death was on my side, and it was best I didn't disappoint him – or his girlfriend.

Jessica Kay Lissner is a start-up engineer who has had one too many quality conversations. Striking a balance between art and technology, she diffuses by writing comedic tech horror, because at the root of every incident report, there is the unwritten drama. Her primary series, The Immortal Crucible, reads like an alternative history / failure analysis that examines the events that led to losing control of monsters and magic.

SOLARIS

BY D.L. GOLDEN

TWAP! TWAP! TWAP!

A woman from across the room burst into laughter, "Three darts, and three complete misses; how do you even do that?"

"Shut up! Dice are bugged," a deep, bellowing voice retorted.

"They're not bugged," The other cackled. "You're just no good at games!"

"Say that again!"

Sol looked up just in time to see Gromm, the barbarian of their little guild, lift Lyra off the ground by the front of her chloroplast-green kimono. Lyra's long green pigtails swayed in time with the lute strung across her back.

Gromm was a mountain of a man. He wore dark-hide pants with a large animal skin tied around the waist. A massive cave bear-skin cloak adorned his back, and the left arm in which he held Lyra was covered in tattoos. His almond complexion and massive muscles made him the peak of human physiology, but for all those huge muscles, his brain wasn't one of them. He was strong, and when in a frenzied state, he was almost unstoppable in battle, but his temper in day-to-day life could be annoying.

Lyra held out her arms, and in her most charming voice, she spoke again. "Did I say no good at games? Clearly, I misspoke, big guy," She smiled. "Can't we be reasonable about this?"

Sol thought of intervening, but that option faded away without a trace as Saphinia appeared. She was the guild's mage, blue-haired and clad in fine white and blue robes. Her power to bind and heal was unmatched, and her beauty could challenge the dawn itself. She was also the first person to join Serpent Nexus when Sol had established it five years ago. She and Sol were best friends and, unbeknownst to her, the love of his life.

Saphinia had tapped her metallic staff on the floor of the inn, and golden chains sprung up all around Gromm. "Drop her," she commanded. The annoyance in her voice obvious.

"But, she..."

Saphinia put her hand up, "I don't want to hear it. We need her for most if not all, charisma checks we go through. Or do you plan to do all the talking?"

Gromm looked at Lyra, who gave him the stupidest close-eyed smile and groaned, "Fine."

Saphinia released the chains, and Gromm and Lyra headed off in separate directions. Turning on her heels, Saphinia made her way over to Sol, who was sitting on a wooden bench against the wall. It was obvious to anyone with eyes that Sol was a Druid. If the name Solaris didn't give it away, the variety of different autumn-colored leaves that adorned his clothes did. That was completely ignoring the enchanted Druid's bow slung across his back. His dirty blond hair hung down over his eyes as he tried to make it seem like he hadn't noticed the altercation.

"What are you doing?" Saphinia kicked his boot.

"Huh?" He played dumb.

"Don't 'huh' me." She looked unimpressed. "You're supposed to be the guild leader. What did you call it, Anaconda Head-Hancho?"

"That's King Cobra..." He muttered in response.

"I don't care what the stupid title is," she rolled her eyes. "You're the leader, right? Start acting like it." She plopped down beside him and shoved him with her fist.

Sol sighed, "Yeah, yeah."

"Oh, come on, Sol. This mission was your idea in the first place, right?" She scolded him for his lax attitude.

He groaned and threw his arms back on the bench. "Sorry, I've just been distracted."

Her tone softened, "Is everything alright?" She placed a concerned hand on his shoulder and looked at him skeptically.

"Of course," he grinned, but something told her he wasn't being completely honest.

"I just know you've been online a lot more lately. Like literally every time I sign in." She twiddled her thumbs and avoided eye contact.

He titled his head in her direction, closed his eyes, and gave the goofiest of grins. "Don't worry, I'm fine Saph! Besides, we have a mission to attend to yeah?" He reached into a breast pocket hidden beneath a few of the multi-colored leaves and pulled out a poorly folded note.

She reached out and grabbed it. Her eyes panned over the words, and she realized it was the same note that had started them out on this journey so many weeks ago. It had an old hand-drawn picture of the Sovereign of Winter Crest at the bottom. His long, thick black hair and short, neat beard stood In contrast of his emerald green eyes. He had always had a glare that could bore a hole through a solid stone wall.

This is an edict on behalf of the Sovereign of Winter Crest. Two nights ago, the castle was attacked by the acid-wing wyvern, Belfagor, who claimed the life of the Sovereign. Any person or guild who can bring down Belfagor and return his fang to Winter Crest shall be named the new Sovereign.

She held the note limply. "Okay, this is the same note you've shown me dozens of times, and we still don't know where Belfagor is."

Sol leaned forward and laughed, "Check the back."

She flipped it over, and her eyes widened as she panned over the crudely drawn map. "Is this?"

"Yup."

"How did you find him?" She could barely contain her excitement.

"A little bird told me." He smiled.

She rolled her eyes; for anyone else, it may have been a joke, but because Sol was a druid, it was very possible that this statement was entirely literal.

"So..." She looked at him expectingly.

"We go tomorrow," He leaned back, proud of himself. "We'll be sipping wine on the white cliffs of Winter Crest by sundown."

She threw her arms around him excitedly. His face surged with heat as she embraced him.

"Careful, squeeze too tight, and you'll break me," He managed. "You're getting the drinks tonight, right?"

Saph released him, looked at him incredulously, and grinned, "How about we roll for it?"

"Ah, come on. You know I never win rolls against you."

"I'll take the low odds," She wheedled. "Eighteen or higher you buy; anything lower I buy." She summoned her die and held it out in offering.

"Fine, but when I lose, you gotta take it easy on my wallet," he placed his hand over hers and closed her fingers around the blue icosahedron.

She smiled and threw the die, which promptly landed on nineteen. "You lose! Let's get something fancy!" She punched the air and headed for the bar.

* * *

The next morning came, and the group gathered once again on the main floor of the inn. People buzzed about with different groups in search of their first meal of the day. Sol knew that others had been attempting to find Belfagor, so it was wise to keep this meeting hush-hush.

They had planned to meet at seven sharp to discuss the plan, but as per usual Lyra was late. She prided herself on being the life of the party and because of that, she took a long time to doll herself up before going out for the day.

"Anything but the perfect look is simply unacceptable." She had said once when Saph had gotten onto her for not showing up on time for a mission. As much of a pain as it could be, dealing with her chronic tardiness, they all loved her. She brought a sunny air to any room she walked into, and that in and of itself was a much-needed injection on most days.

She popped through the doors around a quarter after seven, strumming her lute and singing a pleasant little tune. You couldn't help but smile at her carefree nature.

As she joined them, Sol invited everyone up to his room to ensure no prying eyes or ears were wise to their plan. They huddled around the bed, and Sol laid out the map he had drawn.

"So, as you know, I asked you to meet me here last night so you could get a lay of the inn. This place sits right at the foot of Sorrows Embrace. You'll want to stash any gear you can live without here in this barrel for safekeeping," Sol explained.

"Remember, the perma-death system can be unforgiving. If your HP goes down to zero, that's it, game over. If, for some reason, everyone else goes down and you're the last one standing, you are to use your emergency transport scroll and come back here. That way if the others have to restart with a new character, at least some of their items won't be lost," Saph added.

"Exactly; the plan is to make our way up the mountain, locate Belfagor, kill it, and retrieve the fang." Sol placed a hand on Saphira's shoulder.

Gromm grunted and nodded.

"Got it," replied Lyra. "Oh, I nearly forgot! I brought those things you asked for." She reached into her satchel and pulled out several potions of greater healing and some vials of acid cure. She divided them amongst the members and stashed the rest in her inventory.

"How did you get so many?" Sol exclaimed as he stashed his.

"It's really quite easy when you're as charming as me," she giggled. "Took a very easy persuasion roll, and the shopkeeper handed them all over for the price of one song."

"I just make shopkeeper give potions," Gromm growled. "I no need for silly song."

"Yes, yes. You're very intimidating, big guy." Lyra replied. "But, we aren't thieves or highwaymen. Sometimes, we must act with a bit more tact."

"I-" Gromm tried to speak, but Saph cut him off.

"You both have your talents, and we appreciate both of them." She glared at Lyra. "You'd be wise to remember that when Gromm is doing all the chopping and slicing."

Gromm was an incredible fighter, but he had quite literally traded all his charisma and wisdom points for strength. And that strength would be much needed for the coming battle.

"You got your loadout ready, Saph?" Lyra asked.

"Yeah, lots of binding spells and healing ones as well." She turned to Sol. "What about you?"

"Yep, Briar Field and Deep Forest Growth are at the

ready as well as Entangle. If we can keep him grounded and from attacking, Gromm can do the heavy damage."

They all nodded in agreement. They stashed so many of their goods Sol thought the barrel might burst. Then, together they headed out.

Upon exiting the inn, the great mountain came into view. Its steep obsidian black bluffs shot straight up at a nearly ninety-degree angle. It was so tall that the peak disappeared into the overcast sky, and the only way up was by following a seldom-used pass that was blocked by jagged stones.

Gromm stepped up to the obstruction and raised his axe before being stopped by Sol.

"Hey, no worries bud, I got this." Sol cast Shapeshift and transfigured himself into a small tortoiseshell cat. He moved passed Gromm and slipped between a small opening in the base of the stones. Emerging on the other side, he dismissed the form and found a small handhold on the stones.

He'd need at least a five to trigger the switch within. With his other hand, he dropped a twenty-sided die on the ground beside him and watched it roll. It came up with an eight and disappeared. Giving a slight tug inside the notch caused a low click to echo out. The stones rumbled and shifted to form a much larger opening. He gave a slight bow as his team made their way through.

Once they were all clear, the stones closed back behind them. What lay before them was a clearly defined trail leading up the mountain in a zig-zag pattern. This place was relatively unknown, and this meant that with any luck, they wouldn't run into any other people on their way up, or at least this was what Sol had hoped for.

Within minutes of walking, however, they stumbled across a skeleton that had been dashed against the path.

Saph knelt down and examined the corpse for a moment

before Lyra asked what was on clearly on everyone's mind. "Did the Wyvern get them?"

Saph shook her head in reply, "No, Belfagor is an acid wing. If he had killed this person; there would be nothing left." This made sense; After all, even the guards of Winter Crest had said that there was nothing to recover of the Sovereign. The powerful acid of the beast had utterly destroyed him. "No, something else did this."

Just as the words escaped her lips, a large grey hand gripped the back of Lyra's neck and lifted her off the ground. It belonged to a massive troll that had appeared seemingly out of nowhere and was now preparing to feast on the bard.

"How did it sneak up on us," Saph cried as she leapt back.

Lyra trashed violently, trying to break free of the monster's grip. This only caused the creature to grip down more tightly, and within seconds, colors began to pop in her vision.

"Gotta keep it from making any more moves." Sol charged in first, throwing out his die he hoped to cast an ensnarement spell. It landed on six and thick knotted vines, sprang up from the ground and wrapped up the monsters arm tightly, immobilizing it.

With it unable to move, Gromm didn't hesitate. He threw out his die and his massive axe appeared in his hands. With one fail swoop, he cleaved through the arm, holding Lyra, causing her to drop to the ground, where Saph cast a healing spell on her.

Without a moment's hesitation, Gromm used an action surge and charged the beast, breaking it free of its ensnarement and shoving it to the edge of the path. The drop-off on the other side was at least thirty feet to the ground, and though the fall might not kill the beast it would for sure take most of his hit points. Gromm shoved, but as his surge diminished, the beast dug his heels and stopped himself from tumbling over the edge. The two matched strength as they grappled.

"Hey!" A scream from above Gromm caused both him and the troll to look up. Surprising nearly everyone, Lyra rose and planted a foot on Gromm's massive back, leaping off of him, lute in hand. She screamed with all her might and brought the instrument down on the troll's head with a melodic thud.

Its blood-red eyes lost all focus and Gromm's overwhelming strength sent it careening from the crag. As it tumbled down, Lyra went with it. She was only saved as Gromm caught her arm. The troll wasn't so lucky.

It hit the jagged rocks below with a gruesome thud. Lyra looked down to see the monster still stirring, trying to rise.

"Uh oh," Lyra shouted as it stood again.

The rest of the crew leaned over the path to see the monster stagger to it's feet. It looked up and roared in their direction, its fury was short-lived, however. As it bellowed the ground beneath it cracked and crumbled to dust. The monster haplessly fell into an endless abyss.

"Did that thing just fall into the Nethercasm," Sol exclaimed.

"Looks like it," Lyra shouted back. "Now, if you'd be so kind as to pull me up!" Gromm lifted her with ease and placed her feet gently on the ground. "Thanks, big guy." Standing on her tiptoes, she planted a small kiss on his cheek, to which he flushed.

"You have got to be more careful," commanded Saph.

"Yeah, sorry, I had no idea he was there," Lyra rubbed the back of her head with a carefree smile.

"She's right," Sol added. "That could've been really bad."

"I know, I know." Lyra waved away the scolding.

"Shouldn't we be heading for the peak," she tried to change the subject.

"Yes, but this journey won't mean anything if one of us gets killed before we get there!" Saph continued impatiently.

"I get it," Lyra shouted.

Gromm held up a hand to speak, "Lyra fought good. She strong. We no worry."

Lyra blushed at the clumsy comment. "See! Now let's go!" She sauntered away ahead of them.

"Ugh!" Saph rubbed the bridge of her nose till she felt a hand land on her shoulder.

It was Sol. "Come on," he smiled. "We've got a mission to complete. He walked past her, and she watched his back like she had so many times, always following in his footsteps, always afraid of being left behind.

The group continued up the trail, which wound on for what felt like an eternity. Overall, however, the trek-up wasn't bad. No more encounters with monsters, not so much as a steep incline. It wasn't until they climbed through a narrow passage between two stone walls that they felt the gravity of what they were walking into.

When they emerged on the other side, an acrid, sour-smelling smog filled the air. It was so thick that it made it hard to see or even breathe. From what they could see before them, this place was a wide stone staircase with room for all four to walk side by side comfortably. The walls on each side shot up and disappeared into the fog above.

This was a Daunt of Sorrows. In lore books and atlas' this place was referred to as a final reprieve, a place to turn back, to stop before you go too far. These places were, in truth, the entrances to boss-level dungeons. Dying here meant there was no recovery of your items, at least until someone cleared them. When that happened, all the loot that had been left behind up to that point became the property of those lucky enough to complete the level.

This climb didn't inherently mean they had stumbled into the right dungeon, but the appearance of flowing green and purple acid down the far edges of the stairs was more proof than not. They continued to climb, and before long, they came to a wall of pungent fog. This was the entrance; once you stepped through, there would be no escape without the use of a transport scroll.

Sol took a deep breath, "Is everyone ready?"

Gromm and Lyra nodded. Saph steeled her resolve and did the same before casting a protection spell over each of them.

Sol clenched his fist and spoke confidently, "Then let's go claim our throne." He stepped through the wall of gas, and the others followed. When they stepped through, they emerged into a large open area. The fog locked them in from behind, and before them, several mountainous walls shot into the atmosphere.

Thick clouds of sulfur blotted out the sky. All around them, pools of green and purple acid swirled making for tough terrain to fight in. At the center of this huge area was a massive pool of the same caustic liquid. But, no wyvern appeared.

Then, something caught Sol's eye at the far end of the large acid pool. A shadowy figure sat half submerged. His glowing green eyes alone threatened to break Sol's resolve. His hair was dark as lacquer, and his neatly trimmed beard made him look deceptively regal. This man was a royal. A king of bone and dust, a ruler of desolation. Perhaps he was once the sovereign of Winter Crest, but no longer; the man who sat before them now was a walking cataclysm.

He spoke, and his words flew out across the emptiness. "So, another guild enters my lair."

Sol was shocked to hear this. Another? Had other groups really gotten this far already?

Saph spoke these thoughts into reality before Sol could. "How many people have you killed already?"

"And why do you look like the Sovereign?" Lyra interjected.

The man waved his hand through the air, "I began to lose count after thirty-eight." He replied coldly. "As for why I have the face of the Sovereign, that's because I am him. I am Tiberius Valux, first to the throne of Winter Crest."

"Then the wyvern who attacked the castle," Sol questioned.

Tiberius stood slowly; acid dripped from his bare chest and ran down into the waist-deep pool. Throwing out his arms, he spoke again, "For years, I was trapped beneath the weight of the crown. Only when I realized my true power was I finally able to be free." He took a step forward, and the pool deepened. "And now the crown seeks to have me killed." He continued to greater depths. "So, I must ask, what is it about you that makes you worthy to kill me?"

His eyes shot to Lyra first, "The poor girl with so little to her name, you who wishes for fame and fortune."

She swallowed hard.

He looked to Gromm next, "The weakling who wishes to be perceived as strong?"

Gromm's brow twitched as if a nerve was stuck.

His focus shifted again, this time to Saphira, "The one who's always by his side but never within reach."

She shifted uncomfortably as Tiberius, who was now up to his chin in the pool, turned his gaze on Solaris.

"And you," his eyes darkened. "Not only do you lie to

your friends. You who can't even be honest with yourself." He sank beneath the surface, and the room fell silent.

The only audible sound was the slam of Lyra's boot on hard ground. Looking over Sol saw her clutching her transport scroll tightly. He reached out, "Lyra, don't he's just trying to get to us."

"Well, it's working," She growled. "I don't want to play this stupid game anymore."

"Ly, don't listen to that guy." Gromm broke character, his voice much higher and more caring as he placed his large hand on her shoulder. "You're so much more than what he says."

She looked back at him, "You think so?"

"I do," He replied gently.

She giggled, which broke the tension. "You sound so strange when you turn off the character filter."

"Sorry," he smiled. "Gromm strong, Gromm bash stuff," he joked as he turned his voice filter back on. "Better?"

She smiled, "Mhhhmm," she stashed her scroll.

"Why did he say all of that stuff, though," Asked Saph.

"He's trying to get in our heads, much easier to pick off if were demoralized. I'd say it's the game AI using the neural link in the headset to read our thoughts." Sol pointed to an invisible helmet around his head.

"That's awful," Lyra replied.

"Probably not a standard feature," Sol thought about it for a second. "I'd say it started out as a command to taunt, and the AI's taken it too far."

"Well then, let's put it in its place," Saph replied as she summoned her staff.

They all agreed, and as their morale surged, Tiberius's voice returned and filled the air. "You are harder to break than the others. You leave me no choice but to burn through your bones."

The music in the room intensified as a large bubble formed in the center of the pool. It exploded, shooting acidic droplets in every direction as the massive Wyvern; Belfagor, emerged. His body was a deep metallic purple; his two massive wings were covered in glowing green pustules that oozed acid. The same acid ran from his eyes and leaked from every scale.

The auto-roll feature was initiated, allowing for free-form attacking without having to wait for dice results. This was a function of boss battles that helped to keep things flowing and to keep the pace up.

Saph acted first by casting Mage Armor on everyone. This would allow them to tank what would otherwise be one-hit KO's. With that, the other three charged in.

"We need projectiles!" Sol exclaimed. "We gotta aim for the wings!" He drew back his bow and fired a flurry of arrows.

"On it!" Lyra pulled her lute from her back and struck a cord. This triggered the move Symphony, a high-speed projectile attack. Glowing pink musical notes flew out ahead of her and shot toward Belfagor.

He tucked his wings and effortlessly rolled clear of both barrages before extending them once again and circling the battlefield. To dodge both moves like that, it was clear he was working with a massive speed stat.

"Okay, new plan," Sol shouted as he and Gromm split to execute a pincer maneuver. "Saph, slow him down. We're gonna ground him in one fell swoop!"

Saphinia nodded and summoned dozens of glowing golden chains from beneath the ground. They shot up rapidly and surrounded the great beast. He weaved between them with ease until suddenly, a golden eagle swooped in from the side and gouged his left eye. Acid poured from the wound coating the creature.

Belfagor roared violently and the bird tumbled away coated in acid. The eagle tumbled from the sky and transformed back into Sol, who rolled across the ground. Amongst the frenzy, he had transformed into the eagle and went in for the attack. It hadn't done much damage, but the diversion had been enough. Two of Saph's chains wrapped up the wyvern's legs, and another couple bound his wings at the shoulder. This wasn't enough to ground the beast but that wouldn't be an issue for very much longer.

"Now Gromm," Sol screamed as he got to his feet and downed an acid cure.

"On it," Gromm replied as he hurdled a massive barrel at the creature. With nowhere to move, the barrel landed on Belfagor's back and dropped him straight to the ground. He crashed with a deafening thud, and the earth itself threatened to crack under the weight of it. A cloud of green and purple acid enveloped his form.

"How did you," Lyra exclaimed.

"Good ol' barrelmancy works every time!" Sol threw her a thumbs up and grinned stupidly.

"But where did it come from," Saph looked confused as the group reunited.

"That's the barrel I had you put all your excess stuff inside back at the inn. I put a transport scroll inside and had Gromm recall it here on the battlefield." Sol seemed way too proud of such a cheap move.

"You idiot, what if that hadn't worked," Saph scolded him.

He shrugged. "Huh, I don't know. Hadn't really thought that far ahead."

"Guys," Lyra cut in. "If that was enough to take him down. Why hasn't the 'room cleared' message appeared?"

Before the group could even comprehend what she'd said, the cloud surrounding Belfagor condensed. They couldn't so much as react to Gromm's wince as a bloody gash appeared at his side. He crumpled within seconds and heaved as caustic fluid poured from the wound.

Lyra rushed to his side and began singing a song of healing.

"That hurt, you gargantuan bastard." The words from behind the group made them turn without thought. Belfagor, in human form, stood opposite them. He faced away from them, his bare back bore a distinctive dark mark just below his left ribs. He wore black plate greaves, and held a single-handed long sword in his left hand, the grip of which was formed from a large, jagged wyvern tooth.

"Dammit, how did he get over there," Saph readied her quarterstaff.

"Don't know. Be on your guard," Sol replied drawing his bow.

"Guys," Lyra screamed. "The wounds not closing. It's getting worse!"

Gromm writhed on the ground. His wound had grown larger and was now bleeding profusely. Saph rushed to his side and poured an acid cure over the wound. She summoned a thin, sharp golden thread from the pouch at her side and ripped it out.

"Hold still," she commanded. "This is gonna hurt like hell."

"Oh, so you have a physical healer on your team?" Belfagor mused as he turned to face them again. He held up the long sword as if he was showing it off. "I think I'll kill her next."

"Lyra, get away from them," Sol shouted.

Without so much as a word, Lyra darted to Sol's side. Sol

waved his arm in Saph and Gromm's direction. A field of organic spikes encircled them, leaving only a small ring where they sat. Saph then formed a sphere out of chains and closed it around them like the shell of a golden egg. Inside, she got to work on stitching the wound closed.

"Now, it's our turn!" Lyra charged forward, lute in hand. She unleashed Symphony once more, and again, Belfogor dodged each note with ease. They flew past him and sunk deep into the earth all around. One hit from something like that was sure to sever whatever it struck.

He cocked his head to the side, "Got to be quicker than that little girl."

She hadn't broken her stride, and with a wicked grin, she strummed one cord on the lute. "It's not the same attack. This one is called Symphonic Mine Field!"

No amount of speed was going to save him this time. He leaped upward just as all the notes exploded. The blast sent him flying up and out of the cloud of acid and dust it had created. As he cleared it, he saw Sol crouched on the ground in front of him, his enchanted bow drawn back as far as it would go.

"You're done!" He loosed the arrow, and it flew with blinding speed. Belfogor transformed his arms into wings once more, barely dodging it. It wasn't until the second arrow pierced his back that he grasped what had actually happened. Sol had cast a duplication spell on himself, and the one who stood before him was the fake clone. He turned his head to see the real Sol smirking behind him. He had landed an arrow at the base of his ribs, dead center on the darkened spot.

Belfogor gasped as Sol saluted him. As his fingers left his forehead, the arrow expanded and splintered. The mass erupting from his back and chest sent him into a nosedive.

With the last of his strength, he hurled the great sword at

Sol, who had no time to dodge it. It impaled him through the gut and pinned him in place.

"Sol!" Lyra screamed as the hit registered, and Belfagor fell dead. She rushed to Sol's side and examined the wound. "Oh god!" She covered her mouth in horror. The spike field vanished around Saph's sphere as Sol's concentration broke, and Saph released the chains surrounding them.

She left Gromm, who was all stitched up but still down for the count. She felt sick as she saw what had become of Sol. "You absolutely reckless idiot." She fumbled in her pack and dug out a potion that looked like magma in a flask.

Sol's vision threatened to cave in with every breath. He opened his mouth to protest, but the words wouldn't come.

"Claim the sword moron..." Saph growled.

He raised his hand as best he could and touched the blade. It vanished, and he collapsed to the ground. He rolled his head to the side and looked up at Saph.

"Open up!" She demanded. He did as he was told, and she poured the scorching liquid into his mouth. As he swallowed, his body tried to reject it. He seized for a moment before blacking out.

* * *

When he woke again, the battlefield was gone. Instead, he found himself surrounded by the ugly beige wallpaper of his room at the inn. His whole body ached as he tried in vain to sit up. His pained groan filled the emptiness and caused something to shift just to his left. He turned his head to see Saph stirring in a hard wooden chair stationed next to the bed.

She rubbed her eyes and yawned, "Sol?"

He smiled at her, which shot pain through his every nerve. He winced as the pain washed over him.

"No, no," She stood quickly. "Try not to move. Typhon is supposed to work well, but it's experimental at best. Wouldn't want you to die now. Not after everything we just went through." She smiled, trying to hide her concern.

"You used Typhon?" Sol rasped. She nodded as Sol laid his head back on the pillow to stare at the ceiling. A tear ran down his cheek. "Why would you do that? That stuff must've cost a fortune."

She shrugged, "You're alive because of it, you know."

He sighed and smiled. "How long have I been out?"

"Nearly five days," She replied. "We've each been taking turns checking in on you. Unfortunately, I got the night shift and fell asleep IRL."

Sol chuckled, "It's not good to sleep in the headset, you know?"

"I know, I know, but one of us has been checking in on you every few hours," Saph replied. "But, now that you're awake, I need to inform the others that you survived. Even if you've been out for five days, rest until the morning. We'll talk then." She stood from her chair and waved without turning around. With that, she placed her hand on her head and removed the invisible headset. S he vanished as she logged out.

Sol sighed and stared up at the ceiling for a good long while before finally drifting off again.

When morning came, the sun poured in through the window beside the bed and washed the entire room in the vermillion glow of dawn. Sol stirred, and much to his surprise and delight, his body no longer ached. The Typhon had done its work, and he had come out the other side fully healed, all except for the massive scar in the center of his stomach.

He sat up and, for the first time in days, walked to the

door of his room. He headed downstairs to find both Gromm and Lyra eating at the bar.

Lyra noticed him first and gave a friendly wave to get his attention. "Yo, Sol!" She shouted. Gromm turned to him and only gave a quick acknowledging nod. "You alright?" Lyra asked as he approached.

"Yeah, never better, actually." He smiled and rubbed his stomach.

"Didn't think you make it," Gromm said, stuffing a pile of scrambled eggs into his mouth.

"Gonna take a lot more than that to put me down." Sol grinned and pointed to himself with his thumb. "Say, Saph's not with you. You seen her around?"

"Yeah," replied Lyra. "Said she was going to the usual spot to eat. Might want to go check in with her. And here, take these. You owe her after that scare." She held out a pack of greenish-blue ice cream bars.

He took it and gave her a confident little salute and wink before walking out of the inn. He turned north and headed toward the seaside cliffs that gave Winter Crest its name. Snow white and a mile high, the bluffs were an unmistakable hallmark of the city.

He knew Saph would be there. After all, she was always there. Looking out over the ocean and listening to the sound of the waves crashing below her feet. She loved that place, and that love was the reason Sol had been so adamant about defeating the wyvern in the first place.

As he approached her saw her there, bathed in the warmth of the dawn. Her hair resembled opulent sea glass as the rays passed through it. He couldn't help but stare till she called him out.

She didn't turn to face him, "Are you gonna stand there all day or what?"

He smiled and moved forward. "How'd you know I was there?"

"I always know you're there," she replied, looking up at him as he approached her side. "Well, sit down."

He did as he was told and pulled two unwrapped ice cream bars from the box. Sol had always thought blueberry cream had an odd flavor, but it was Saph's favorite. He held it out, and she took it without a word. Together, they ate their ice cream in silence.

Saph got down to the stick and couldn't keep silent any longer. "Something's been bothering me," she admitted.

Sol bit off another chunk, "What's that?"

"Back in the boss room," She replied. "Belfagor's taunts."

"Just taunts. What about them?" He took another bite.

"They weren't, and you know it. They all had some air of truth to them." She looked down at her ice cream as its remnants dripped. "Lyra's family has struggled with money for a long time. Gromm was bullied relentlessly in high school for being scrawny. And I," she hesitated. "I want to be by your side, but we live so far apart. It's hard," she admitted.

"Oh, Saph I-" he didn't know what to say.

"But," She cut him off. "Despite all that. What he said about you has me worried."

Sol looked at her nervously. He summoned the great sword he had won. "Forget all of that, we got this, and we're gonna be Sovereigns." He grinned as he offered it to her.

"Are we," She half shouted at him as she slapped it away. "Sol, you stayed for five days in the system without logging out even when your character was downed."

"Saph it's nothing," he grinned again as he recalled the sword to his inventory.

"Don't lie to me," She began to sob. "Lie to them, lie to yourself, but don't you dare lie to me!"

"Saph I'm not-"

"You are," She snapped again. "How are your treatments going? And don't bullshit me!"

Sol sighed and leaned back on his hands. "They're not," he admitted with a weak smile.

Saph dropped her ice cream and covered her mouth. "No, but that would mean."

He grinned through tears, "I'm dying Saph."

She began to sob uncontrollably, "You can't be. Your doctor said you were going into remission. Twenty-five is too young to die."

"It came back," he admitted with a false smile. "Terminal this time. Doc gave me three weeks to live, and that was four weeks ago. I've been spending all my time in this online world. It's the only pain-free place anymore. The only place I can run and move."

She threw her arms around him and cried into his shoulder. "Why didn't you tell me?"

"Didn't want you to worry about me." He kissed the top of her head and put his arm around her.

They sat there for a while before Saph's sobbing had subsided. She sat with her head on his shoulder and watched the waves. He summoned the great sword again and offered it to her.

"I want you to take this. You, Gromm, and Lyra become Sovereigns of this place for me." He smiled.

She reached out and took the blade. "I won't let you die. You're gonna rule with us."

He laughed, "Don't think I get a choice." He brought up his vitals, which showed his weakening heartbeat.

"You wanna bet?" She snapped.

"Huh?"

"Let's let the dice decide." She summoned her die.

He laughed again. "Are you for real?"

"It's already a gamble, right. You either live or you die. It's no different than a roll of the dice," She argued, her voice full of desperation.

He smiled at her weakly, "Fine, if you roll a twenty, I'll consider making The Dreamweaver my afterlife," he joked.

Saph nodded solemnly, tears welling in her eyes yet again. "Fine, twenty it is." She slung the die out as the flatline's long, persistent hum filled the air.

D.L Golden is an author out of SE Kansas who specializes in writing LitRPG stories. His debut novel Origins Redux is live on Amazon and has sold hundreds of copies all across the U.S.

D.L. Find himself in the in the unique position of being one of four authors in his family. Two of his sisters and his sister in law are also published authors, two of whom are featured in this very anthology. If you enjoyed Solaris and wish to read more from D.L. Golden you can check out his website and Linktree from the QR codes below.

THE LAST TIME I SAW YOU

BY DIHN BAILEY

It's midnight and I am shaken awake by your screaming. I was dreaming of open fields and endless forests when you plucked me. I was wading in oceans of places far away from here. I lay on beaches with no other person in sight. But you have stolen my mind's eye by hijacking my ears that barely work properly in any case.

This was not the first time your screams have pulled me from my world building, my realm development of dreams where I yield power... But it would be the last. I just didn't know it yet. My young and ignorant mind couldn't fathom the silence left in the wake of that resounding slap that jarred my brain and hurt my little jaw and chose instead to pretend that I could still hear you. It wasn't even that difficult, your muchness, while brief, left a significant imprint in me. Habitually, between the hours of one and three your terrors stirred in you, and your smiling eyes widened in abject terror even though they remained closed with sleep. Your laughter turned to bawling and bellowing as horror and utter devastation ripped through your throat as you slept next to your wife in the next room over, but you are powerless and out of control.

It's wild to me that you still defend and uphold that system. That army that conscripted you, chewed you up and spat you back out without a care for the destruction their training set about you and those around you. In those moments of terror, the ones only your wife and children know about between the hours of one and three - your world shakes and pulls me to you, reminding me that the world we live in is dark and cruel. I could hear the fear resonate in the tremors of your begging words, still do as a matter of fact. For all these twenty five years past, I still wake in the night, between the hours of one and three, when you scream. You just aren't there anymore, and it is silent.

"I left because she would slap you through your face." You tell me, with a self-serving sort of simper. Martyring yourself while I beg you for answers that should have been offered freely as a common courtesy. This is a conversation for closure that I need like air to breathe, but I swiftly realize that I could suffocate waiting for my parents, and I have no idea what to say to you anymore as I recall you screaming in the dead of night and the many times you failed to be the adult I needed in a world so devoid of common rationality. Oh, how I spent so many days and nights wishing I had you. I thought you were strong at one point, fighting like a rebel against my mother's descriptions of you. The older I get, the more I blame you for her tactics. It seems unfair, it probably is - but would she have been able to speak poison to your name, pollute the memory of you if you were present enough to give me something more than a memory to work off of? I blamed myself for my cruelty towards you, absorbing the blame as usual, but as I sit across from you, watching you give your weak excuses and passing them off as awkward humor and never looking me in the eye - I can't help but feel my disappointment melt away. And what's left underneath the melting ice sheath is far worse.

"Do you think she stopped doing that because you left?" I ask you, being a man, even though I am not one, and looking you directly in the eye - a courtesy you have still not afforded me since the first last time that I saw you. I was trying to inject some common sense into your act, the plot holes were glaring, and I did not want to swallow a weak excuse like this being the picky eater that I am. But you are bulletproof and sweep my question aside as a bothersome fly, changing the subject to how awesome you were back in the day and forcing that slimy unpleasant acceptance back down my throat so that I choke on it. Like you do every time. Or at least the handful of times that I've seen you since the last time I saw you.

You left me with nothing, but time and I've had a lot of it to think about what I want to say to you. I've had endless nights of disrupted sleep to lay back on my pillow and explore the depths of my mind and I've rewatched all the memories like old films trying to unravel the why of it all. I've dissected it and pulled it apart and examined it from every angle that I can think of to no avail. It's pointless. You were two people who should not have gotten together and who absolutely should not have had children, and for a while that was enough for me. I'd tell myself this in comfort during those waking hours between one and three. But I've wanted to tell you for the longest time that I love you and that I lost my cat. I've wanted to share my swimming medals and love for rock climbing with you. And I am angry. You let me down. You left me to the wolves and the lions and the tigers and the bears. Deep in the darkest pits of my mind I want you to shower me with fatherly pride and adoration, I too want to pretend that my body has not been ripped to pieces and that the scars do not exist, and I wish you had taken that fucking jail sentence, but I'll never admit it to you. I shouldn't have to.

There's a desperation in me that I don't like, a need for you that I don't want, I've gotten by just fine for twenty seven years now without you. Briefly, I suspect you read my thoughts as you lock eyes with me for a split second. The most you have been able to manage in well over two decades and in spite of my best efforts to let the love I so desperately and blindly felt burning in my tiny chest for you all those years ago shine through — you look away quickly. Afraid of what I showed you instead.

What did I show you instead?

There's so much to see. Did you see the diet pills put into my eleven year old palm by the hypocrite herself? Or the special diet she had me on at thirteen years old because skinny wasn't skinny enough... Did you see her eyes staring back at you? Does the cold and callous blue of her eyes overshadow the honeyed hazel of mine?

Do you see the scar next to my iris where her fingernail pierced my eye? Or the scar on my brow that I got stitched up without you there? Do you see the sadness pooling in the honey cones at the back of my eyes where the flashbacks of broken bottles and mothers drunken fists dwell? I hope you saw it all. All the hand shaped bruises, every needle mark where they took my blood on her lies, every bruised chin and blackened eye - I hope it all rises to the surface while you look at me. I want you to feel what your absence has cost me. I want you to remember my pain, I want you to feel the nothing left in your wake because you were everything to me and then you were gone, and you left me with Her... You introduced me to nightmares and horror by not shielding me from it. That was your job and you let a woman with an acid mouth run you off permanently.

When I look back at you, however, I remember.

You tried. I recognize that. While you were around, you really tried. She would scream, and you were calm... Until you weren't. You would speak and not shout back. You stood up for me and you stayed. Until you were gone. Not a call for

Christmas - I thought at least I'd hear from you at birthdays. Instead, the crickets on my windowsill sang to me beneath that beautiful African sky your hands helped to paint red with blood and I got to know you further through the history I learned, and the words spoken about you but never by you.

As I sit across from you, tonight, these many years later when I sought you out myself as an adult, I listen to you speak about how awesome you were, as you describe Maverick GI or whatever to me in place of the answers and comfort I'm starving for. I remember you screaming in the dead of night. I recall being terrified for a long time after your screams died down and the crickets and frogs resumed their nighttime symphony. Your words would swim in terror as you begged and pleaded in your sleep.

You begged for the lives you were ordered to end and told me that some of them were children with guns in their hands. You told me that it wasn't their fault with your own words. Imagine my disappointment when I learned what was needed to avoid all of this. I was fifteen years old when I realized you are weak. The threat of a very short jail sentence was all it took to push you to murder. What's left beneath that melted sheath of anger is pity, shame and disappointment. This is what I've been starving for? This?

I see the horror that you will never address, even within yourself, because you are weak, and I watch you hide from me in plain sight. In your eyes, I see the pain of failure and know that I will never get the closure I need like air to breathe from you. Unknown and unaccounted-for children running all over the place and you cannot look any but one in the eye. Like a father, you tried to get protective when I had a daughter to do better by and grew uncomfortable, again at my questions, "Why now?" I asked, "Why not back then when I needed you?" I could have phrased it a million vulgar ways. I could have screamed and shouted and pounded my fists and it would all still be appropriate. Instead, I ask you softly, not wanting to hurt - and still, you act like I'm burning you. I see you quake in your skin, wishing to pull it from you and start anew. You are weak and you turn from me, your daughter, a menace that you created in your absence.

I speak for myself, and my hands now do things - weave magic, write words and make love. Habitually I never asked for your help, or any help really - so why now? Let me breathe! Is it because your twilight years are upon you, and you don't move like a young man anymore? Do you need someone to care for you in your waning day to day? In the moments where our eyes meet, I see your heart and it is broken like mine. I wanted to show you empathy and love. I desperately wanted the warmth. But there was no warmth and I learned to move with the shadows. Your absence has hurt in many ways, and it is cold. Eventually survival instinct kicks in and the fear melts away, and I am no longer afraid to show you. In those few moments where our eyes met as you said goodbye and read my honeyed cones, I want so desperately to show you the intense love that I felt and still feel for you, despite your absence - but instead I show you the void of that empty house on the hill and the silence in the nights. In certain unhinged moments of the aftermath I actually yearned to hear you screaming in the night once again. I want you to see it. I want you to feel it.

· · ·

You may think me cruel for denying you this basic right, I will not offer you the care that you denied me. But I carry the world on my shoulders now and there's no room for you anymore. I see you now more than ever since the last time that I saw you and I don't want any part of it.

Dihn Bailey is a South African author from the picturesque region of KwaZulu Natal, near the Midlands. Known for a distinctive voice that combines cosy settings with tragic horror, Dihn Bailey has quickly made a mark in the literary world —a weird mark, but a mark all the same! Her début novel, *The Mists of Zealotry: A Tragedy Beneath*, was published in May 2023, followed by the avant-garde short story, *The House That Charlotte Burned* in November of the same year, which is to be the first in a small series.

Currently working on her third novel, *The Second Summit*, set to be released later this year, Dihn Bailey continues to explore new depths of storytelling and building her craft. Beyond writing, she is a passionate activist for human rights and a fervent supporter of community upliftment. Despite a reclusive nature, Dihn Bailey actively seeks out collaborations and charity projects within the literature community, believing that combining creativity with support and upliftment is the ultimate dream.

With her bullish attitude, a sharp tongue and a heart for change, Dihn Bailey remains committed to both her craft and her causes, always eager to connect with fellow writers and readers in meaningful ways.

dihnbailey.com

OWNED

BY H.E. GOBER

Chapter One (NYX)

This city stinks. It's overcrowded, and the people don't care. They continue throughout their day as if we are not totally fucked. The giant vines keeping us trapped here are growing thicker and more extensive. Some are even sprouting thorns that soak up any and all blood that touches their bark, just like the Keryth. Nobody cares. Nobody is worried.

Except me.

I am worried because each year, they grow taller and take up more space in the city. Smaller vines are even starting to cover the building. Nature is fighting a one-sided war to retake everything. And when I try to cut it back, three more vines take its place, making everything even more unmanageable.

That is just one of the major problems here, unfortunately. The Royals and Keryth are at the top of that list. They take everything. Be it food, things, or even people, they don't care just as long as they get what they want when they want it.

Even the most depraved believe they can get away with anything they want when they think no one is watching. So caught up in their arrogance that they always forget to check the shadows where I live.

I spend yet another night sitting on a cold roof, watching my target weave through the crowds at a fast pace. He is determined to get back to his prize. Little does he know; I removed the woman from his basement when he left hours ago. She is now back home where she belongs.

Most people would consider that a job well done. But they would be wrong. He still breathes.

I silently make my way across the roofs, staying parallel

with the unexpected fool. My blood thrums with anticipation of the kill. He deserves it to be slow and painful for what he thought to do. It's too bad I don't have the time.

Lucky walking dead, man.

I watch as he quickly turns the keys in his door and wait for the sound of him securing it behind him before slipping through the window I left unlocked earlier. Landing in the dark basement with a soft thud on the stone floor, I take a few moments to ensure I am not heard. With no signs of anyone coming to join me, I turn to lock the window to make sure nothing is out of place. Then, I wrap the shadows around me and disappear within their loving embrace.

It doesn't take long for the fat fool to come stomping down the stairs. Just like I knew he would. He always comes to her first.

"I'm back, my dear," he grunts with exertion.

I grind my teeth at the joy on his disgusting face that is lit up by the small candle in his hand. He hasn't shaved the stubble he woke up with this morning, sweat drips into his bulging eyes, and his double chin wobbles with his labored breathing. I nearly gag from the sight of his hairy gelatinous belly sticking out from under his white linen shirt when he reaches up to wipe at the sweat with its billowing sleeves.

Dressed like a Keryth male. Male... or female because apparently, being called a man or woman is beneath them.

"My dear?" he grunts. "I am positively ravenous this evening. I will provide you with a feast if you behave."

Unable to handle the sight or sound of him anymore, I load my pipe with a sleeping dart. In one quick motion, I blow hard, and the dart embeds into his thick neck.

"Don't worry, fool, you won't be asleep for long," I say menacingly. I didn't think it was possible, but apparently, I was wrong because his eyes bulge even more right before he hits the ground hard. The candle rolls away from him and slowly winks out, bathing me again in darkness. "Disgusting," I say, kicking him in the side as hard as possible.

He doesn't move.

Good.

I retrieve the rope from behind the crates where I stored it earlier today. Then, with practiced movements, begin looping it around his arms behind his back. I take the time to ensure enough support around his elbows since he is so fucking heavy. I grunt and begin sweating myself as I continue looping the rope around his legs into a kneeling position. I can't have him kicking out. That would make this so much messier than it needs to be.

Once satisfied with my rope skills, I take the chain he had the woman imprisoned with and begin threading it through the ropes around his arms. With the help of counterweight and gravity, I pull the chain through his arms until he is suspended on his knees and slightly leaning forward. After the chain is secured tightly, I light the candle, place it beside me, and then sit and wait for the bastard to wake up.

My methods were not always this intricate. I just figured that the ones with the worst crimes deserve some thought to be put into the process. I take my time just like they do with their victims.

Sometimes, I use slow-acting poison and let them choke on their vomit. Other times, I leave them somewhere to starve to death. But this time, I think this bastard deserves to watch as blood flows and coats the floor beneath his fat, disgusting body.

But the sight of him chained up like this brings a heaviness to my chest. Memories of what it feels like to be in that position threaten to overtake me. And my throat aches with the screams inside of my head.

I shake myself, coming back to the present.

I am not there. I am here. I got out.

"Ugh," he groans.

"A terrible feeling, isn't it? To be tied up and drugged. To be at someone else's mercy," I ask with a cold smile. He can't see it behind the scarf covering my mouth or my eyes under the shadow of my hood, but at least he can hear it in my voice.

"Who are you?" he bellows.

"Your end."

"My what?" He begins flopping around like a fish out of water, and I enjoy the evidence of his panic as I slowly pull the dagger from my boot.

His blue eyes widen, and his pale skin turns grey when he finally sees the blade.

"What do you think you are doing?" he whispers.

"Vengeance." I toss the dagger over and over again, letting the candlelight reflect off of it and blind him in the process.

"I did nothing wrong! Who sent you? What have you been told?"

Hot and potent, rage burns through my chest at his clumsy words.

"You didn't do anything wrong?" I stand, moving to tower over the coward. "I bet those girls you drank from without their permission beg to differ. Twenty of them—I won't count the one from today since I saved her before you could sink your depraved fangs into her. All of them would scream your name from the rooftops if they still had a voice. They would give ANYTHING to be in my position right now. To hold your life in their hands!"

"I...who...I would never—"

Unable to handle his fucking lies another moment, I strike out hard. His head lolls to the side from the force of my fist. I dig into his filthy mouth, pull his tongue out, and glide my blade through it with efficient ease.

"You fucking stink," I sneer, throwing the useless appendage before him. His muffled scream is just as sweet as the spray of his blood at my feet. "Now, you are going to be left feeling the life slowly drain from your useless body just like they did."

I would slice him from navel to throat, but I don't have a sword with me that could make a deep enough cut. Using my daggers would take too much time and effort. I have neither at the moment.

So, I cut through the two arteries on his thighs and the ones on both wrists. He groans with each cut and gargles on the blood filling his mouth.

I quickly look around the room and ensure I am not leaving any evidence of my existence behind. Satisfied that I didn't, I skirt around the pool of blood as my stomach cramps from the smell and make my way up the stairs. I close the door and bar it in the same way he did every time he left the house.

This morning, when I came in, I took the time to memorize the layout of his house. I always make my move at night, and lighting a candle would bring too much attention. I need it to remain absolutely dark. So, I make my way through the lavish furnishings without touching a single thing until I finally reach the giant fireplace.

The rope I left gently sways in the soft breeze. Hand over hand, I pull myself up through the tall cobblestone flue, making sure I don't touch any part of it. One scrap of soot may alert the guards that this is how I have been leaving the houses. And I can't have that. My work will remain unfinished until I cut down everyone in his circle until all that remains is Him.

Just another human who is spinning around in space on a planet called Earth. To escape the stress of everyday life, you can find her reading in a cocoon of blankets. Once out of the reading nest she is chasing after her four children or talking nonsense with her husband (usually something about DnD and Video Games). That love for reading has recently mutated into a love for writing—something completely new and scary. She has started, stopped, and scrapped so many different stories that it's not even funny. But with the encouragement from two of her best friends, she finally sat down and wrote a story from beginning to end. Does she know where this new passion will take her? Absolutely not. Will it be any good? Ummmm...maybe. Will she enjoy the ride? 99% yes, with 1% grumbling.

hegober.com

CHECKOUT

BY ALEXIA MUELLE-RUSHBROOK

It started in the supermarket. At the checkout to be precise. Scanning my items, an awkward sense of being watched crept up on me. Reason told me they were waiting for someone, and I happened to be in the way, but my skin bristled and flushed regardless of my determination to ignore whoever they were. Hurriedly stuffing my shopping bags, the sensation continued —burned even—and although keen to save myself from the embarrassment of being caught gawping at a stranger, curiosity forced my eyes upwards.

Confusion hit me.

No one was there—only a glossy furniture advert across the wall.

You're seeing things, I told myself when the space was again empty. *You're just tired.*

Then a hand waved.

My eyes desperately searched for a body. *There has to be a body*—or so logic told me. It's funny how we grasp for the known when faced with the unfamiliar. If only simple reasoning could have explained. Yet as I stared in abject fear, a young, bubbly checkout assistant materialized behind me, causing a gasp to slip out of my mouth with such force that I'm surprised my teeth didn't go with it.

"Is the machine stuck?" the woman asked, shifting her attention between me and the screen, hovering her keycard in readiness to clear a fault. "Huh, it looks okay. Do you need help?" Concern spread across the woman's face as my eyes darted back to where the hand had appeared.

Autopilot took over me. I briskly swiped my debit card across the device and scrunched the receipt into my pocket. "I'm fine, thanks," I babbled, vowing to never shop here again.

As I arranged the bags in my hand, the feeling of being watched returned. Eyes were on me, I knew it, but as I glanced again, nothing was there except a glimmer of light coming through a window. The day was bright, so the sun refracting was plausible until the glimmer pixelated, and a shape began to form. Fright and flight hit me. Running with my bags knocking into my legs, I crossed the parking lot, jumping at every shadow until I reached my car.

Throwing myself inside, I attempted to catch my breath as I considered what to do next. Working and shopping from the safety of my home laptop seemed like the best idea—but I would only get away with that if I attended the in-office meeting I had spent months equally loathing and preparing for.

Today was *my* day.

No trick of the mind was going to ruin my ditch for freedom.

I had an hour to calm down.

Turning the key in the ignition, I sighed as the red light pinged on. With a petrol station only a matter of yards away from me, the solution was clear even if my mind was not. The forecourt was busy, so I eyed the customers and tried to judge my timing, aiming to swoop in and be gone as fast as humanly possible.

A middle-aged woman pulled into the bay in front of me and I heard the laughter of her children as she stepped out of her car. Heading towards the kiosk, a delivery man smiled as he heard them, while an elderly lady in a leather jacket activated the pump parallel to me.

Get a grip, I told myself, reaching for the pump with one hand as I unscrewed my petrol cap with the other. A high-pitch squeal flew out of my mouth as my eyes shot to the pump, but I didn't let go. It was like my brain couldn't process the cold, still fingers of the bodiless hand, so it equally couldn't decide to let it go either.

The elderly woman peered around the pump. Behind her,

I saw multiple faces blankly staring at me, but no one spoke. A finger moved under my hand and suddenly my limbs rebooted. I flung the hand and pump, sending at least one of the two clashing into the stand. Laughter from the children turned to cries for their mother before I realized that I was hyperventilating, fueling their increasing distress. Mortified and fearing for my sanity, I dived into my car, drove out of the forecourt—still on the red—and promised myself that after today I would never leave home again.

On the passenger seat a parcel rocked back and forth with the motion of the car, and I cursed my decision to return it myself and not arrange a collection. Forgoing a refund for the clothes that only suited a prepubescent child wasn't really an option. I needed the money and any chances of me seeing it hinged on their return.

The post office was close to work, I couldn't even pretend I didn't have enough fuel for the journey. Checking my wing mirror for obstacles, I anxiously parked the car and slipped into the post office. Stan, the cashier was as jolly as ever, so I didn't think he noticed the beads of sweat that were breaking out across my face. As he chuckled about his grandkids, I told myself I would miss his chats once my eternal hibernation began. Transaction complete, I forced a light smile, honestly thanked him, and began to walk away—rejoicing at the lack of glimmers or phantom hands—when Stan's uncharacteristically calm voice stopped me in my tracks:

"I'd get yourself a drink, you don't want to pass out on your last day."

My mouth flapped open and shut, but no words came out.

"Stores open. You've time to get a drink—or maybe something sweet." Stan nodded towards the adjoining mini-mart. "You only got cereal and fruit earlier."

My mind wanted me to ask how he could possibly know

what I have time for, but my legs wandered into the shop and left me to procrastinate by the confectionary.

Chills hit me when anyone walked into my aisle. *They're just shopping. You're fine,* I repeated, trying to focus on my forthcoming sugar fix.

"It is no good, you are needed," said a voice as a body faded into view beside me.

A hand gently closed my screaming lips.

"Your kingdom awaits. *Come.*" He spoke without moving his mouth.

Otherworldly understanding hit me.

Then frustration.

"Why only visit me in public? Why not find me alone and explain?" Grimacing, I witnessed strangers raise their eyebrows as I apparently spoke to thin air. "Preferably without you making a fool out of me."

"Until you're ready to step out of the shadows, why should I show you the light?"

I stared as his outline shone.

"You think I hide myself?"

He smiled. "I know it."

"I prefer it that way. Not everyone needs an audience."

"No, but they deserve to light their corner, regardless of size." I couldn't argue that. "Although your corner spans a universe and unless you come now, all will fall."

Waving his hands, shards of color raced in circles until the center glowed bright white. Like a moth seeking a flame, I reached out. The light folded, revealing a great expanse—a whole new world.

"Your kingdom awaits, Milady."

Alexia Muelle-Rushbrook is a multi-genre author who has spent her life daydreaming in the English countryside whilst surrounded by her animals. A self-confessed geek, she loves sci-fi and fantasy and has a passion for the natural world—thankfully a joy which her husband shares, otherwise the number of pets she has would drive him crazy!

Stories have always run through Alexia's head, but it wasn't until one voice really wouldn't leave her alone that she realised her dream of being a writer. That voice turned into dystopian trilogy, *The Minority Rule*, but now unleashed the voices refuse to be boxed in—or stick to one genre—meaning Alexia can still be found daydreaming with her dogs but the narrative now gets recorded!

www.alexiamuellerushbrook.co.uk

THE CHOICE

BY C. BRITT

Aiden's eyes fluttered open. From somewhere a few feet to his left, a faint orange glow was the only thing keeping total darkness at bay. He lifted his hand in front of his face; only the slightest hint of an outline was visible. As he lowered his hand back to his chest and turned his head to get a better look at the source of the orange light, something loudly chimed.

The room around him was suddenly filled with a bright, white glow, and he flinched, squeezing his eyes shut again. He lay there for a moment, letting the blinding brightness filter through his eyelids. Eventually, he cautiously opened one eye and then the other.

His breath caught in his throat.

A glass dome sat inches above him, curving down into each side of his narrow bed. He tried to lift his head and look toward his toes, but he could only move a tiny bit before his forehead bumped into the clear barrier. As far he could tell, though, he was entirely encased.

Aiden's heart raced. His breath came in fast, shaky pulls, and each exhale left a tiny circle of condensation on the glass that quickly disappeared. He jerked his head from one side to the other. There had to be some sort of release mechanism, a button to call for help, anything.

For a fleeting moment, Aiden wondered if this was what Snow White would've felt if the curse had worn off and she'd suddenly woken up inside her glass coffin, trapped and left for dead.

Raising his sweaty palms over his chest, Aiden pressed hard against the glass. It didn't budge. The imprints of his hands left their marks for a few short seconds before they vanished, just like the condensation of his breath.

His mind raced as he fought back the panic growing inside his chest, tightening the muscles and making it hard to breathe. Bunching up his fists, he squeezed his eyes shut. He pulled back his arms as far as the tight space would allow.

A broken, sliced fist is worth it. Anything's better than this.

He steeled himself, tensed his biceps, and took a deep breath.

"No."

Aiden winced as a light buzz vibrated inside his head. His arms relaxed and lowered to his sides, though he wasn't completely certain that he had meant for that to happen.

"I will open it for you."

The unfamiliar woman's voice came to Aiden as though she were speaking straight into his ear. He froze. "Who's there? Get me out of this thing!"

"I do not have a name."

The voice did not provide any more information, but with the hissing sound of air quickly escaping its enclosure, the left side of the glass panel lifted up, breaking its seal with the plastic rectangle that held his mattress. Aiden jerked his head to watch. His eyes followed that glass edge as it inched upward, over his face, and then back down toward the right side of the bed. A few seconds later, the curved glass had disappeared entirely as it retreated into a narrow slit alongside the mattress.

The slit then sealed over, making it look as though it had never existed in the first place.

Gaping at the now-invisible slit by the bed, Aiden ran his fingers across it. Smooth, seamless. One eyebrow slid up toward his hairline. *What the hell just happened? Did I imagine that?*

"It was not your imagination."

Aiden leapt up; his heavily tattooed fists clenched as he spun around the small, white room. "Where are you?! Come out here where I can see you!"

"I cannot, Aiden. I am inside your head."

Straightening up, Aiden slowly turned around, studying the single, continuous wall that encircled the room. A smile began to form on his face, displaying the gaps where teeth were missing from his gumlines. The ones remaining were chipped and darkly stained. *Alright, where's the camera? This has to be some kind of prank.*

"It is not a prank."

His smile vanished.

"I am an artificially intelligent neural implant inside your brain. I was embedded there prior to your placement within the sleep chamber."

Aiden's eyes drifted over to the narrow mattress he'd recently vacated. He turned slowly, surveying the room again, hoping he'd missed something on the first pass. The room wasn't particularly large—barely more than six strides from one side of the circle to the spot directly across from it—and its singular wall was plain white with no windows or decorations. The only thing remotely decorative was a digital clock with neon orange lettering. It was difficult to see the text at first, obscured as the characters were by the intense overhead lights.

As he watched, the text adjusted until each character shone brightly even in the well-lit room. A small line of text at the bottom declared the date to be November 3rd, 3296. Above that, its face proudly displayed the time as 23:52:37. The separating colons blinked at Aiden in precise half-second increments, and even though it was digital, the longer he stared at it, the more convinced he was that he could hear its steady *tick, tick, tick* in the otherwise silent space.

Finally tearing his gaze away from the clock face, Aiden turned and stepped over to the metal table in the room's center. He lowered himself into the lone chair that waited there. The metal surface brushed against his flesh, sending a flurry of goosebumps out along his skin and forcing the dark hairs along his arms to stand on end.

Leaning forward, he propped his elbows on the table instead, hoping that maybe its surface wouldn't feel quite so icy. No such luck. At last, he folded his arms across his chest and sank back against the seat, making sure to keep his exposed skin well away from the furniture this time.

He half expected to see his own breath every time he exhaled, but it was warmer than that. Barely.

Why the hell is this place so damn cold, anyway?

"The temperature of the habitat is difficult to maintain at a comfortable level in such extreme environments."

Aiden jumped as the sudden, cheery voice of the young woman sounded in his ear again. He turned and glanced over his shoulder. No one was around, of course. But he wasn't used to the presence of the neural implant or the way it somehow responded to questions he hadn't really even meant to ask.

"I apologize for startling you. If you would not like to be disturbed, please simply let me know, and I will enter 'do not disturb' mode for one hour."

"Yeah." The pale skin of his cheeks turned pink as he answered the device out loud. He self-consciously scanned the room, searching for any signs of security cameras or microphones. If this device really was speaking to him from inside his own head, surely he must look absolutely insane to any outside observers. Squeezing his eyes shut, Aiden worked to align his thoughts as the device continued to rattle inside his brain, saying something or other about accessing the settings to toggle sleep mode and set its timers. *Yes, go to sleep. Just leave me alone.*

"Do not disturb mode is activated for one hour. If at any time you wish to cancel this mode early, or you—"

Clamping his hands over his ears in a vain attempt to silence the voice that was coming from directly inside his own brain, Aiden stared down at a speck on the table and waited, counting. When it finally went quiet again, he lowered his hands, recrossed his arms, and let out the breath he had been holding.

Shoving himself back up onto his feet, Aiden began to walk. He'd always had a habit of pacing when stressed or deep in thought. And now, trapped in this small, round room, his confined movements barely qualified as "pacing," but he did the best he could by circling the table at the room's center.

That date can't be right. I'd've had to be asleep for at least eight-and-a-half years. Was I in a coma? How would that... I wasn't in an accident, right? I don't think I...

Aiden paused, his glance darting over to the mattress near the wall. He stood there, staring at it for a long time. Finally, he shook his head and resumed his circling.

No fucking way it's 3296. Not possible. Who the hell knows whether the time is accurate? That month and year, though...

Aiden's thought trailed away as he noticed a series of small rectangles along the wall, their off-white shapes barely distinguishable against the bright white paint behind them. He turned and moved closer.

Reaching out, Aiden hovered his thumb near one of the small rectangles. It was unlabeled. He had no idea what, if anything, it would do if he pressed it. Glancing once more around the room, looking for any sign of a way out—a door, a window, an escape hatch, anything—and finding none, he took a deep breath. He pressed his thumb against it, and four seams suddenly appeared in the wall: two horizontal lines that each intersected with two short vertical lines to form a large rectangle. He stepped backward as the newly formed shape moved outward, revealing a large drawer.

Aiden frowned as he stared down into the drawer. The inside was divided into four equal sections, each filled with identical silver, plastic pouches. Snatching up a pouch from an unlabeled quadrant, he jabbed the button again. The drawer silently slid back into place and sealed itself shut, leaving the wall as plain and seamless as before.

As he stood there, Aiden glanced down at the non-descript packet in his hands. In one corner, there was something written in tiny black letters. He moved the package closer to his face and squinted at it. "Cheesy Beef Lasagna."

He frowned.

Stretching his arm out again, he pressed another of the buttons. A new drawer slid out, displaying rows and rows and rows of plastic bottles of water. Wrinkles creased his forehead as his frown deepened. He reached up, dragged his flat palm across all the buttons, and watched as a series of drawers formed and slid out from the wall, one at a time. Each new drawer was the same as the first two he'd tried: water bottles or food packets. Nothing more, nothing less.

He clenched his jaw. His breathing quickened along with his heart rate. Jerking his head up, he looked over at the bright, orange glow of the clock. He tightened his fist around the packet and pulled his arm back, ready to hurl it at the wall, ready to watch the contents of the packet burst out and paint the room, ready to find out why the hell he had been put in this box like some rabid animal.

Just when Aiden started to twist his body and bring his arm forward, something buzzed inside his brain. He squeezed his eyes shut. The food packet slipped from his hand. It fell to the floor at his feet, sending the contents sloshing inside their container in a way that lasagna should not move. But the package was undamaged. Aiden slammed his hands over his ears.

When the buzzing finally subsided, Aiden's knees threatened to buckle underneath him. He slowly sank to the floor.

"I cannot allow you to harm yourself, Aiden. 'Do not disturb' mode has been disabled and cannot be reinstated at this time."

"What the fuck is that buzzing? What do you keep doing to me?!" Aiden glared at the clock. He knew a clock certainly wasn't responsible for his current situation, but as there wasn't much else in the room to glare at, and if that "neural implant" really was inside his head, he couldn't very well glare at it. So, he decided the lying clock would make as good of a scapegoat as anything. He slapped one palm against the hard floor. "How the hell would throwing this slop hurt me?! Somebody damn well better tell me what is going on! Why did you lock me in here? Where am I?"

"On your question regarding the buzzing: I was designed to prevent your ability to carry out undesirable acts, such as self-harm. You perceive such interference as buzzing inside your skull.

"On your question regarding the harmfulness of your actions: The nutrition pack quantities and contents were carefully determined based on your size, weight, and nutritional requirements. Wasting any of these precious resources would eventually become detrimental to your well-being."

Aiden growled in response. He opened his mouth to give a retort, then closed it before opening it yet again. His fingers twitched as he sat there, trying to think through what to do next.

The cheery voice spoke up again. "In addition, your spiking vital signs are indicative of ongoing negative mood behaviors. It is best to curb these signs of extreme agitation before they lead the subject to these negative mood behaviors that typically cause significant harm to the subject or others.

"However, in regard to your subsequent questions, it appears as though you are exhibiting signs of significant memory loss. That is not unusual after prolonged stasis and the medical procedures you underwent. Please describe the last thing you are able to clearly recall."

"You can't just read my mind?"

"I cannot perceive things in your mind about which you are not actively thinking."

"Fine." Aiden spit the word through gritted teeth, then exhaled loudly. He grabbed the food packet and tossed it onto the table. Shoving his wispy hair away from his face, he dragged himself back into the cold, metal seat and crossed his arms. "Shit, I don't know. It was... It was springtime. Easter Sunday, actually. We never have ham, but we'd splurged for the holiday. Couldn't scrape up enough credits for anything more, so we ate our ham with the last can of corn from the back of the pantry. The last thing I remember was sitting at the table across from Beth, eating ham."

In Aiden's mind, he could clearly see Beth as her long, blonde hair fell across her shoulder when she leaned forward. Her smile as she cut off a large slice of the meat and scooped it onto his plate. The sensation of biting into the ham and chewing easily.

He ran his tongue across his gums, feeling the gaps where teeth used to reside. Standing there in silence, he wondered why he couldn't remember losing them.

"You are certain you do not recall anything more?"

"Yeah, I'm certain. Why?"

"It would be preferable for you to recall your past actions without external influences. Once you do, I will be able to give further details."

What the hell does that mean?

This time, the feminine voice remained unhelpfully silent.

"Give me a hint, at least!"

"It is time for you to consume one of your meal packs."

Aiden ground his teeth together. *Fuck you! What the hell kind of answer is that?*

"You must attempt to recover your own memories. The nutrients might help your brain return to normal functionality after your time in stasis. However, if your mental state has declined to the point that you are unable to recall these memories for yourself, then perhaps your participation will no longer be of use in this experiment."

The voice remained as cheery as ever, but the last bit of the statement seemed every bit of a threat inside Aiden's head. A chill ran down his spine.

He considered shoving the food away. What he'd do after that, he had no idea. But as the slight tingling started inside his brain, he forced his jaw muscles to relax and ripped the top off the silver packet. He gave the contents a sniff. It smelled vaguely of garlic and tomatoes. Tilting the packet, he looked inside at the substance that had no right to call itself "lasagna." It was a deep red and soupy with tiny yellow-orange chunks and globs of brown floating in it. He swallowed, fighting back the urge to gag.

Taking a deep breath, Aiden shook his head, then tipped a bit of the goop into his waiting mouth. He chewed quickly with the few molars he had left and forced himself to swallow before pouring another bite.

"Ugh." Aiden forced the room-temperature, red goop

down his throat. He stood up, walked over to the wall, pressed a button, and snagged a bottle of water. Heading back toward the table, he took a mouthful of water and swished it around, trying in vain to rinse the acrid taste from his mouth before swallowing. He sat back down. "I was somewhere else before this... Some small, gray room. And I... I couldn't leave for some reason."

"Correct."

Staring blankly across the small space, Aiden wondered quietly, *Where was that room? Why couldn't I leave?*

As Aiden sat there, lost in his thoughts, the tiles beneath his feet vibrated viciously, tipping over the closed water bottle. It fell onto the hard floor and rolled toward the wall. The half-empty food packet threatened to do the same, but the tingle inside Aiden's head forced him to catch it before it toppled.

"What the hell was that?"

"Debris. Please continue, Aiden. Surely you can recall additional information."

"Debris? What? It... What does—"

His words went silent as he felt the beginnings of the buzz inside his head. A second later, the floor shook again, even harder this time. His water bottle crashed into the wall with a plasticky thud. Aiden tilted to one side and used his free hand to snag hold of the table edge, so he didn't tumble off his seat and roll across the room after the water bottle.

As the room finally went still again, he straightened up and slapped his palm against the tabletop. "Fine! Just knock that the fuck off already!"

"I cannot, Aiden. The main objective of my programming is to ensure that you behave rationally and in such ways as are deemed most conducive to the success of the experiment.

Allowing your negative emotional state to control you brought you into this situation."

"What does—"

"Furthermore, providing answers to you directly, rather than allowing you to discover them for yourself, has a high probability of creating increased negative emotional states in you. It was, thus, deemed necessary to allow you to regain the memories of your actions on your own."

"So, what?" Aiden shoved the fingers of his free hand into his thinning hair. He combed the locks back, away from his face, and then dropped his hand into his lap. "You think it'll make me sad if you tell me what's going on? Why?"

Again, the neural implant gave no acknowledgment. Aiden growled, then tossed back another mouthful of his disgusting meal.

At last, having choked down the final bits of the mushy goo posing as food, he crumpled the silver packet and let it fall onto the metal table. A few droplets of the red liquid slipped from the discarded package and speckled the white tabletop.

Aiden froze as a hazy memory took over his vision. He was in a long room with peeling, green wallpaper. Several discarded syringes lay in a pile of garbage in the corner, flies circling noisily above the pile. He stood between a tattered, old couch and a busted coffee table.

Something was quietly, steadily dripping at his side. Slowly tilting his head down, he watched as a speck of red collided with the dingy linoleum at his feet. His eyes scanned across the floor, following the trail of red droplets as they disappeared beyond the end of the couch. Next to the blood, a lock of wavy, blonde hair laid on the floor, peeking out at him. Swallowing hard, he lifted his right hand and gasped as he saw the red-streaked blade clutched there.

With a jolt, Aiden was suddenly back in the present. His

eyes were wide. Sweat beaded on his brow. His hand trembled as he lifted it to wipe it across his forehead.

"That is only a glimpse of the events which led you here." The voice inside his head matter-of-factly mocked him.

"What? No... No, no." The floor shook again, but he was so lost in his own thoughts that he was entirely unfazed. Aiden leapt to his feet; his hands buried in his hair. "No. No, I couldn't have... It's not possible. It's... No! Why are you doing this to me?!"

"I am not doing anything to you, Aiden. That is your own memory."

"No!" Grabbing the discarded food container, he hurled it across the room.

As it slapped the wall, a dozen more droplets of the red sauce oozed out and trailed down toward the floor. His mind was dragged backward through time again.

Aiden was looking into the green face of a monster, its slit eyes glaring at Aiden. Its fangs chomped at him, trying to latch onto his arm as Aiden held it by the throat. As he squeezed tighter, he slammed the monster into the wall, sending a spray of blood oozing out and staining the green wallpaper. With his other hand, Aiden slammed the knife into the monster's belly. It wailed in agony as its warm and gooey entrails spilled out. Aiden grinned as the monster gasped and wheezed. The creature's fangs gradually stilled; its heartbeat slowed and finally halted.

As Aiden loosened his grip, the monster slid to the floor. Aiden bent down to retrieve the knife that was buried deep within the creature's gut. When he did, the fangs were suddenly gone, and the unblinking eyes that looked back at him were no longer those of a monster. Instead, they were the kind, blue eyes of his neighbor, Mr. Frankley.

"No!" Aiden fell to the floor of the circular room. Tears spilled down his face. "It wasn't... It couldn't... No!"

"The illegal stimulants you had been taking were no longer enough. You wanted something new." The cheerful voice changed; deepening its pitch and speaking slower, the disembodied female voice continued. "And when the new drug, 'Gray Ichor,' found its way into your city, you ignored the warnings of the extreme violence it was known to cause. You ignored the warnings of its terrifying hallucinations. You ignored the warnings that it would cause your hair and teeth to fall out and large sores to break open across your skin. You ignored the laws that were rushed through in an attempt to prevent the loss of more lives to this vile, new drug."

Tilting his head up toward the ceiling, Aiden didn't speak. His heart pounded ever faster, though, as he listened to the now menacing voice.

"At best, perhaps you believed these extreme consequences would not apply to you, that they were an exaggeration. At worst, perhaps you felt it did not matter. Regardless, you chose to inject it into your veins. In so doing, you brought about the brutal deaths of nine innocent individuals, including Beth. Five more individuals were caused serious injuries by your hand. Dozens of families were traumatized by your actions."

Aiden's chest grew tight. His breath was shaky and fast.

"Do you recall the law regarding Gray Ichor? Do you recall your trial and the subsequent sentencing?"

Aiden slowly shook his head.

"The law stated that possession, use, or distribution of Gray Ichor would be punishable by exile into the wastelands. No exceptions."

"I'm... In the wastelands?"

"No. Immediately prior to the implementation of your

punishment, an offer was made. You would never be permitted to return to society. The risk to those around you would be far too great. In all likelihood, you would not refrain from using Gray Ichor again, regardless of the guilt you feel at present. Instead of exile, you would be permitted to undergo this mission."

What mission? Aiden couldn't quite voice the words past the lump in his throat. The implant heard him anyway.

"Since the wars, Earth will not be habitable for much longer. Perhaps another century, at best."

The voice paused for a moment as the floor trembled yet again. A small section of the wall opened near the floor, and the segment began inching upward, gradually revealing a pane of glass behind it. Bright, yellow light peeked through the growing gap.

"You were given a choice. Exile into the wastelands or volunteer for an experiment that held the potential to save the entire human race. You opted for the experiment. However, your reasons were not as noble as a desire to save all of humanity. Exile would have been certain death, whereas the experiment would give you a chance of long-term survival.

"I was implanted in your brain to monitor your progress. You were placed inside the sleep chamber. You noted earlier that you believed the clock to be inaccurate. It is accurate. Though, the time it displays is for your original home, not here."

"What..." Aiden shivered. Sniffling loudly, he swiped the tears off his cheeks. His voice shook as he spoke. "What do you mean? What's the experiment?"

"Look out the window."

A two-foot wide glass panel was fully visible now, extending from floor to ceiling. Aiden stood and walked over to it. Straight in front of him was an unfamiliar, greenish planet. Far off in the distance to his left, two bright, yellow orbs, side by side in the sky. He looked back at the planet again. "Where..."

"You are no longer in the solar system in which you were born. You are now in Alpha Centauri."

Aiden flinched as a massive rock suddenly collided with the glass and shook the floor as it ricocheted into space. He spun around, his jaw hanging open.

"You have completed the first phase of the experiment successfully. You have survived an extended period of induced hibernation as the ship traveled through a wormhole; you were awoken upon exiting. I have been compiling and reporting your progress to Earth every step of the way. Only moments ago, I alerted them that the first phase was successful."

Aiden nodded, though he didn't understand at all.

"Soon, you will enter the second phase of the experiment."

He swallowed hard and whispered, "What's that?"

"We will land on the planet that you see there. You have been provided a sufficient supply of food and water to last for six earth-months. Beyond that, you are on your own. You must see how long you are able to survive on this new planet. If you are able to find a way to survive here, there is a high probability that a significant portion of humankind will be able to as well."

The color drained from Aiden's face. "Alone? An entire planet all by myself? No weapons or tools? What happens when my food supply runs out? What if I need medical attention? I can't handle this... Especially not now that I know what I did..."

"You must, Aiden."

"I can't. I... I won't do it. I wouldn't have signed up for this if I knew! You're wrong about the wastelands! At least there are other people there! I could've had a chance! *This* is certain death!" Aiden rubbed his hands across his face. "If whoever is running this had told me everything, I wouldn't have agreed!"

"They did tell you, Aiden. Though, the drug was still thick in your veins at the time. Perhaps you were not in the right frame of mind to make such a choice. Regardless, the choice was made and cannot be undone."

"Send me back then!" The pitch of his voice rose higher. "If you don't, when we land, I'll... I'll find a cliff to jump off or something!"

"I cannot let you do that, Aiden." The faintest tingling started up inside Aiden's skull. "The fate of humankind now rests in your hands."

C. Britt lives in the midwestern United States with her husband, cat, and two dogs. She enjoys spending time sewing, photographing nature, playing video games, and (of course) dreaming up fictional worlds to write about.

She is the author of the zombie apocalypse novel, *Monstra Inter*. Her fantasy romance novel, *Crimson the Chromaveiled*, is scheduled to come out in late 2024.

https://linktr.ee/cbritt

amazon.com/author/cbritt

NON EST FINIS

BY A.D. SMALL

Looking back over the West Pennine Moors, he'd just arduously climbed, he saw his footprints slowly disappear into the ground. The entirety of Winter Hill had been covered in a dull, grey sludge. All the hills surrounding New Bolton had a similar, strange substance covering them. Documented as one of the first points where the Nameless had first appeared, they'd wreaked terror and destruction across the northwest of England. From Bootle to Burnley and everywhere in between, the Boltonians had suffered the most.

When the inevitable decision fell from the lips of the government officials, to drop the bombs, only a select few had escaped the initial blast and managed to outrun the following shock wave. Events afterwards had evolved some of the remaining humans, though not everyone. Why only some of us were gifted, cursed or both, we never learned why. Ultimately, no answers were found. Over generations, the Nameless had merged with some of the humans, garnering the name, the Fused. Disfigured hybrids, they'd roamed the unforgiving northwest countryside for a long time.

Turning to face the tall metal column attached to the nearby building that'd been built around it, he instantly clocked the words 'Winter Hill', graffiti'd lazily on the building's weathered brickwork, in a lively red paint. Standing two hundred metres tall with what appeared to be a makeshift crow's nest sat atop of it, he accurately guessed the structure had once been taller. Though he didn't know it, the war with the Nameless had caused the damage; a further one hundred metres had broken off and fallen away. Wading through the dense, grey deposits, he spotted the severed sections of the tower sticking out of the ground, as if the spine of the countryside had been carved open for the world to see.

A tapping sound broke the silence – metal striking metal. Staring hard at the frame protruding from the ground, he removed his makeshift goggles around his head. Made from the bottoms of two old jam jars, the goggles were crude yet practical in design. Encased in stitched leather, tattered, worn and frayed shoelaces had held them in place.

From inside his three-quarter-length trench coat, he removed a small tub, containing a white, buttery substance, which he rubbed into his face, neck and hands. Hearing the sound again, he moved slowly towards his metal sledge which housed his tools and tent. Unclipping the carabiners, he picked up his rifle and headed up the incline. Covering his face, he grimaced – the distinctive stench of rotting flesh hung in the air like a spectre in the night. Inspecting the metal frames, emerging from the flint-coloured ground, he found himself met by the upper torso of a dead man, who'd been cruelly strung up on the metal frame to die a slow, painful death. The way the man's twisted arms were outstretched in a grizzly fashion made him appear he'd been tied to an invisible cross; his rotten flesh flapped in the gentle breeze. Beside him, lay the remains of a long-eared, white rabbit, oddly not one drop of blood had been spilt – how it'd died remained unknown, though it'd clearly been dead for a few days at best. Then, he heard the sound again.

Tap. Tap. Tap. Tap.

Instinctively, he pulled the butt of the rifle into his shoulder, as one hand steadied the weapon, the other hand gripped it, ready to fire it if necessary. Checking all directions, and through sheer luck alone, he noticed a trip wire glisten under the sun. Inching cautiously forward, he followed the wire. After fifteen yards, he saw the wire had been tied to the metal frame, but a smaller piece of metal hung from the wire. From the north, a gentle breeze blew across the unforgiving moors. A smaller piece of metal hit the frame, letting out the familiar tapping noise again. Still following the wire's path towards its origin, he trudged through the dense sludge. Arriving at a dilapidated and abandoned building, the wire ran up the wall, all the way to the base of the tower, it resembled a snake wrapped tightly around the rusted metal column. Upon closer inspection, he noticed another set of words, he hadn't seen the first time, in the same busy red paint were the words he'd seen earlier. Written in a messy font, the words read, 'Supera Moras', followed by more words, only smaller. Staring at the smaller words, he took an odd inspiration from them. 'Overcome difficulties', he said out loud, repeating the phrase a few times to himself.

Removing a chewed pencil and a small notebook from his jacket, he scribbled down both sets of words. Accompanying the words, he drew a basic sketch of the broken tower. On the previous pages, he'd skillfully sketched two enormous metal gates, the guard towers of the Preston Compound, and a portrait of a young woman with flowing, curly hair and a warm, inviting smile. The name 'Sarrie' written neatly underneath. Running his fingers over her face, he carefully avoided smudging the pencil lines. Turning the next page, he read out loud to himself the short poem he'd jotted down so he could remember it for his big day.

'Wedding Speech
We will be bound together
From this day forward
Gliding birds on a zephyr
Always heading true and nor'ward'

Returning his notebook and pencil to his jacket, he headed back to his sledge and fastened the carabiners to his belt. Clenching his rifle tightly, he made his way towards the path ahead, which descended into the town of New Bolton.

The further he went down the man-made path, the sound of the metal on metal eventually faded into silence. With each footstep, his feet sank into the grey, unforgiving blanket, draped over the world; though he stubbornly refused to be beaten by the wet ground, which had left its damp mark on his cargo pants, indicating how far he'd sank into it.

From his pocket, he pulled out a tattered piece of paper, folded in half. With a flick of his wrist, it opened to reveal a map. Moving his finger down the page, he followed the path towards the Mass Trespass monument at Winter Hill. A moment of uncertainty fell over him – the words didn't quite explain what he had to look for. 'Would it be as big as the tower?' he asked himself. Tall enough to be visible from all the towns, villages and surrounding moors, the metal frame's height was impressive; he'd first seen it when he travelled to New Bolton, over the last few days.

After a while, he came across the collapsed remains of an abandoned farmhouse. Due to the lingering fallout in the air, combined with the unforgiving Lancashire weather, the thatched roof had disintegrated over the passing years. Further inspecting the building, he saw the large thick wooden beams had survived, though they'd now been repurposed to prop up the structurally fragile walls. In the distance, sat a wheelless, white-panelled horsebox. Patches of paint had aged and peeled away, revealing rusted metal and corrosion underneath.

Briefly glancing backwards, from where he'd travelled, he saw what the townsfolk would have seen, back in the day – a huge metal structure of a finger pointing towards the sky. Like everyone in his generation, he'd heard stories of how it acted as an antenna, broadcasting analogue signals to the local areas; a remnant of a time when entertainment came from devices called television sets. Now, those particular past stories were just memories, and life had taken a backwards development to an almost medieval time. Stories in the making would one day become legend and be told over the roaring flames of a fire or by the travelling bards who roamed the lands. Through song, they would recount the tales of the past, present, and potential future to a paying audience, though the latter were few and far between.

His map and idea for this journey came from the pages of one of the books housed in a small library back at the compound. They had managed to save half a dozen large crates of books from a disused bookstore. Someone – though he didn't know who – had written down the events of the day, the week, and the month after the Nameless had attacked the world. The pages never revealed the true number of those buried but suggested a potential payload, one which could lead to unfathomable wealth.

Carrying on down the long, winding, and seemingly endless road, he checked his cargo pants and saw he'd sunk deeper into the grey sludge. The map in his pocket revealed the secret location of a royal park. Unfolding the map, he heard a curious rustling sound from the field behind the stone wall running parallel to the road. Cautiously pausing, the rustling sound stopped. Returning his attention to the map, he saw an 'X' scribbled next to the words 'Queens Park' – the dead from the first wave of the Nameless attacks were all buried there. Men, women, children, and pets all perished in the relentless killings. Utterly ruthless, the Nameless took no prisoners as they came through the void. But, when the bombs dropped from the skies, the opening in Bolton ceased to be. Over the following years, as the dust clouds and the fallout settled, the tales of strange sightings on the moors surrounding Bolton travelled the northwest; however, the chance of incomprehensible riches outweighed the risk. Pressing his rifle against his shoulder, he scanned the field and checked for danger. Still, no rustling returned – whatever had made the sound, now lay dead still. Later, as the day's sunlight neared its end, it brought a cold, eeriness to his new surroundings. Even with the thick jacket on it couldn't prevent the cold snap from hitting his skin.

The incline of the path moved down and connected with a road. Moving a few yards, he stumbled and lost his footing. Activating the small, battery-powered torch attached to his jacket, he pointed it forward and highlighted the potholes scattered along the road ahead. Confident his sledge would easily glide over the smaller potholes, he moved cautiously down the road, though he understood a larger pothole would cause a bigger issue. Irrespective of the potential surface problems he faced, the road became smooth after a mile or so, allowing him to traverse it with ease. But, he hadn't realised the rustling sound had started again. Pausing, ready to pull the rifle to his shoulder, his other hand wiped away the beads of sweat forming on his forehead.

He'd heard countless stories by the campfire from the men and women who passed through the Preston Compound - tales of past lives and those of horror, all of which had captured his imagination. When the Nameless had attacked, they'd killed everyone in their path. During the second wave, something strange happened – those who'd simply vanished before had miraculously reappeared, but they were changed, unlike how they were before the arrival. Some of the Nameless began to merge and cohabitate with the humans they'd connected with. No two tales ever told the same story regarding the fusing together of the human and the alien creatures. As quickly as we called the creatures the Nameless, it took the same time for those who'd escaped the Battle of Bolton to call the joining of humans and the Nameless the

Fused. Travellers told terrifying tales of the creatures when describing the Nameless. Some explained they appeared humanoid in design, whereas others spoke of them being giant human-sized bugs. One traveller, after downing a full bottle of moonshine, swore on the memory of his dead family he'd told the truth. In his drunken state, he'd offered a detailed description, stating they resembled sentient walking statues of ooze.

The rustling sound suddenly returned from behind the nearby bushes on the side of the road. Bringing him back to the present, he aimed his rifle at the bush to his left. Then another rustling sound came from behind him, so he spun around and aimed the rifle. The bush started to shake so he aimed at a broken signpost, fifty yards away in the field. A deafening squeal came from inside the branches and leaves, prompting him to fire another shot, before reloading his weapon. Without warning, a small creature darted across the road and then froze for a moment in front of him, like a rabbit caught in headlights. Standing on four legs, it had a short tail, its head resembled a deer, but its skin had an odd, orchid-purple tone to it. Further down the back of its neck, sat half a dozen tentacles. Each one moved independently as if they were floating underwater. The creature's vacant eyes caught his gaze the most. Its mouth then opened and a small, forked tongue flicked, tasting the night air. Squealing, the creature bolted towards the adjacent field.

Dropping the rifle to one hand, he shook the pins and needles free in his other. Moving slowly with his head on a swivel and his gun aimed forward, his sledge scraped along the road. Thinking back to Sarrie, at the Preston Compound, he remembered her unique smile and felt his heightened senses ease. Even though he'd been gone only a few days, he missed her dearly – every free moment they had spent together. But life in the compound wasn't easy; it had its own limitations – people's roles and curfews played a significant part. He imagined the other compounds operated in the same way. Three times a week, he walked the south wall with his friend, Thomas. The thirteen governors had paired them together, making it the way compounds survived, the way humans survived.

The straight road held the remnants of a previous life. The skeletal remains of vehicles lined the road. Stripped and gutted, until nothing remained but rust-covered chassis, they'd been picked apart by whatever had remained in Bolton, like vultures picking at the bones of a carcass. One vehicle still had a windshield; a faint sticker on the glass read: 'Garlic bread is the future'.

Momentarily imagining his sledge had wheels, he knew how much easier it'd be to navigate the terrain. Glancing back at the path he'd travelled; he considered making improvements to his sledge at a later time. Maybe he could look into it on the way back to Preston, he pondered. As he looked back again, down the road, he saw a large stone building on the left behind the treeline. Approaching the derelict and dilapidated building, he noticed huge sections had fallen into disrepair and parts of the large lawn had been covered by the grey sludge. From the road, he also caught sight of the old, crumbling stone walls of Smithills Hall, which had almost collapsed under the weight of something heavy. Not wanting to delay his journey too much by inspecting the damage, he moved on without closely examining its broken remains.

This excursion hadn't been sanctioned by the Governors. If he got into trouble, help would take time to arrive or not at all. However, if he could find the gold and other rare metals, it'd aid him and the people living inside the Preston

Compound. Classified as an unmarked territory due to the attacks by the Nameless, over the years, Bolton had been ripe for mining, though it'd never happened. He'd heard folk from the Blackburn and Rochdale compounds had tried but without success. But, if they could claim it, they could mine it. The Governors didn't want to take the risk, so he personally took it upon himself to get the evidence, so they'd see the reward.

As he entered the residential area of Bolton, the same gunk had already formed, covering the ground. Experienced enough, he knew travelling the area would be much easier on his sledge. Hopefully, he told himself, he wouldn't need to repair it before his return journey home.

Furthering into Bolton, he passed row upon row of abandoned homes, some had eerie red crosses painted above their doors. All the properties were windowless. Glancing upwards, he made a mental note of the streetlamps and how they held metal buckets filled with wood and burnt embers. Staying close to the treeline and nearby vegetation, he sidestepped strands of the grey goo, hanging from the trees like a giant spider's web. Most of the plant life had been affected by the arrival of the Nameless, when the sludge started to fall from the sky, spreading rapidly like bacteria. After the bombs dropped, the fallout seemed to hinder its aggressive growth, though nobody knew if the situation with the gunk had become a global problem.

From nowhere, under the early evening sky, something lit up in a house across the street, stopping him in his tracks. Instinctively, he unclipped the carabiners and walked away from the sledge. Pressing the butt of his rifle against his shoulder, he stepped into the property's front garden. The house had no doors, and the upstairs windows had been boarded up. Again, he noticed the same bright light flashing from behind the boards, momentarily, like a binary beacon. Cautiously, he stepped through the doorway and instantly pointed the rifle up the staircase. Slowly he tiptoed up each step, hoping and praying whatever he found upstairs, wouldn't harm him. As he placed his left boot on the landing, the light from the bedroom at the front of the house pulsated. Approaching the room, he froze; his heart raced when he noticed the colour of the light had changed. At first, when he stood across the street, it had flashed a bright white. Now it beamed out a blinding, yet oddly inviting orchid colour – a deep, purple hue.

He heard the familiar rustling sound, followed by silence. With his mind now racing, what could he do? Noticing the bathroom door slightly ajar, he quietly stepped inside. Shutting the door, he heard the sound of footsteps shuffling again. Pressing his ear against the door, he remained statue still. Unnerved, he could hear his own heartbeat thumping around his head, like a hammer striking a bell. He hoped whatever had stumbled out of the room, once outside, would stay clear of his sledge. As it moved down the staircase, it squealed. What was that in the bedroom? he wondered. Hearing another high-pitched squeal at the bottom of the stairs, before it exited the building and ventured out into the street.

Slowly, he inched open the door, stepped onto the landing, and moved towards the bedroom door. Something nearby breathed slowly. Stepping inside, he came face-to-face with a dying deer. Labouring to breathe, its chest raises slowed with each exhale, until it breathed no more. Upon inspection, he took a closer look at the deceased deer and noticed the gaping hole running down its flank. Following the small puddles of blood, he found the knife hidden under the materials piled in the corner of the room. After wiping it clean, he pocketed the weapon and felt slightly safer. Propped against the far wall, he spotted an old army-issue rucksack. Cautiously, he checked the bag's zip for a booby trap before tipping out its contents: – a drink canister, a notebook, and an empty palm-sized tin.

Thumbing through the notebook, the first page read, 'This book belongs to Karl Fogg of Sector Eight, Rochdale Compound'. Subsequent pages contained diary entries going back six months, whilst some of the more recent entries had him intrigued and equally worried. Reading on, the notebook detailed the increasingly frequent sightings of the Fused. The Governors' concerns forced them to send a small team into Bolton to confirm if their worries had any merit. Nearing the middle point of the notebook, Karl had filled the pages with tales of death. One by one, all of his fellow group members had been picked off. Absorbing Karl's words, he felt uneasy learning the author believed he'd been followed, so much so, Karl hadn't slept for days for fear of being killed.

Exiting the property, a sense of relief washed over him when he saw his sledge hadn't been tampered with. Keeping an eye out for any sign of movement, he couldn't see the thing he now understood to be one of the Fused. With haste, he clipped the carabiners onto his belt, tucked the notebook and canister he had found down the side of the rolled-up tent on his sledge, and started to venture down the road. As he travelled, he thought of how it had all happened - the merging of man and the Nameless. Imagining it to be painful, he didn't hear the man scream. Had the man been sleeping when it happened? Was the merging a quick process, free of pain?

Pushing through his fear, he snapped back to the present, swivelling his head every ten yards to scan what lay in front of him and behind. Not wanting to be caught off guard, he trudged through the thick patch of grey sludge outside a large building just to his left. The faded signage had the words 'Smithills School' emblazoned on it along with a red rose. One of the elders in the compound had told him how the school system worked, back in the day, when it was still a thing.

Without reason or rhyme, his thoughts drifted to Sarrie. He missed stroking her hair as she slept and the way she looked longingly at him. The thoughts filled him with excitement as they would soon be married.

As he left the school, more residential homes passed by him on both sides. Again, there were more doors and windows boarded up and red crosses painted on the walls above the doorways. Whoever had stayed behind after the bombs had dropped had witnessed the decline of the town. Few survived and those who were out of town at the time tried to get back in. Some succeeded whereas others were stopped by the military and denied entry. Over time, the military and government faded, and compounds took over at a time when safety and sanctuary were desperately needed. Even as the compounds formed, the old ways found a way to return. Inevitably, some still craved greed and power, which fuelled the darker side of humanity.

Residential homes changed from old, weathered stone walls to battered bricks. On some houses, the painted red crosses could still be seen. Ready to defend himself, every sound prompted his head to swivel, yet nothing appeared. After a few minutes, he found himself at a junction in the road. On the side of a house larger than the others, blobs of grey goo seemed to hover in midair. Moving towards the house, he saw broken signage hanging from the wall. On the floor lay the other half of a wooden sign; faded words it read, 'Arms'. Across the road, bolted to the wall, he saw another street sign, which read, 'Ainsworth Lane'. From his jacket he pulled out the map, he would travel down Halliwell Road.

Glancing upwards, he looked up and checked every house on the corner of the junction. Covered in mould and moss, sat the street's signage. Running his finger down the roughly drawn map to a signal blue 'X', he easily located Queens Park on the map. Passing weathered, stone walls as he continued his mission, parts of the wall had crumbled. Frozen in time, faded words read, 'Albert Row, 1847'.

Gratefully, the thick patches of grey goo made it easier to pull his sledge, but he kept his head on a swivel. Outside, every passing house, building, and street had metal poles, sticking out of the ground. On each pole hung wrought iron cages filled with layers of ash and black embers. As he passed them, he smelled burnt wood. Further along, he spotted the twisted steel frame of a building resembling a metal hand reaching out of the ground, as if pleading with the universe for help. Eventually, he came across a derelict religious building which he remembered from the books he had read in his schooling; its minaret lay in ruins on the ground. The emerald-green-coloured dome had a deep crack running from the point down to the roof. Amidst the crumbled wall, a broken road sign stood tall, but the words had faded. Having arrived in the northern sector of the town centre, he found himself standing at yet another junction, where more twisted, rusted metal frames protruded from the ground. On one of the frames, he saw something unsettling – 'Town Centre' written in blood with an arrow pointing forward.

Passing through a wide crossroad, his eyes instinctively scanned all the windows and doors for danger. Oddly, he noted, he hadn't seen a single motor vehicle since near the hills. Approaching the gateway to the centre of Bolton, he consulted his map again, plotting the next part of his journey. Once through the gateway, he turned right and followed the road for a while, passing a dozen brick buildings. Steel framework could be seen where the bricks had fallen away; white rectangles with a blood-red cross had been painted on some of the larger walls which had survived the bombings and the carnage the Nameless had caused. Scanning the area again as he ventured forward, he came across a saintless church building. Listening intently, he heard the sound of running water. Nearing another junction, the sound grew louder and clearer. As the road forked, he paused, glanced in both directions and headed towards the bridge.

Another sound emerged from beneath him, one which seemed to be above the water flow. Cautiously, he edged to the side of the bridge; the crumbled walls made it easy for him to look below. Looking down, trepidation kicked in. Underneath the bridge lay a handful of derelict buildings, with holes scattered throughout their structures. The river snaked between the buildings, its grey tint shimmering in the early evening light. He counted for sixty seconds with his head turned to hear the sound better, but it didn't return, though the uneasy feeling in his stomach still remained.

Beneath the grey substance, he could see the black tarmac of the road; at the end of the road sat the twisted skeletons of two buildings – they'd fallen towards the road and created an archway. Stubbornly, the concrete had held on in patches like rotten flesh. Large pieces of steel had embedded themselves into the road, creating barriers of some kind.

Unclipping the carabiners, he left the sledge next to the wall. With his rifle in position, he edged slowly through the barriers and took a moment to consider whether he could pull his sledge through, too. Slipping between the steel barriers, something snagged on his boot. Freezing with fear, he did not know what to expect. With his head on a swivel again, he saw nothing above, and nothing clicked under his boot. Pulling his foot back, he hoped he hadn't tripped any traps or alarms.

Slowly, he stepped over the wire and followed its origin through the metal maze. Oddly, despite being an observant soul and trained to spot everything, he hadn't noticed that the barriers bottlenecked the path towards the centre of the road. Stepping through the bottleneck, he found himself at another empty junction and stared at another building, one that had survived the previous carnage inflicted on the centre of Bolton. His eyes scanned the wall of the unscathed building. 'Another saintless church,' he concluded.

In the middle of the junction stood two poles sticking out of the ground, with a hefty sheet of metal hung between them, held up by frayed ropes and rusted chains. Painted jet black, two arrows provided directions: the one to the left pointed towards the town hall and the one to the right pointed towards Queens Park.

Glancing back at the maze, he realised he'd have to finish his mission on foot and ferry his possessions and equipment, as his sledge wouldn't fit through. Returning to the maze, something moved at the edge of the walls of the bridge.

From the shadows emerged half a dozen figures, dressed in black cloaks that hid their faces, each carrying a makeshift weapon. Spreading out, they surrounded him. Placing the butt of the rifle into his shoulder, he aimed it at them, ready to fight for his life. Slowly edging backwards, his finger rested on the trigger as a bead of sweat rolled down his forehead, and a feeling of uneasiness returned. One of the figures stepped forward, pulling back his cloak to reveal a mask - black with holes to allow the wearer to see and breathe. The masked figure looked at him and tilted his head, causing him to freeze. Then he noticed the massive shadow eclipsing his own. Before he could turn, the world went black.

When he woke, he instinctively reached for his head, but found he couldn't move his hands. Bound to a loop of metal, protruding from the wall, the thick chains and locks had him trapped securely in the small, brick-walled room. The only light source he could see shone from a steel grate on the opposite wall. Below the metal grate, he could see a reinforced steel door. Before he could yell, a deep voice came from the shadows. "I wouldn't if I were you. No one will come for you."

Instantly, the words destroyed all the hope he had. Nobody knew he'd left the Preston Compound. Not even Sarrie. "How long you been here? Where you from?"

"About a week now. I'm from the Rochdale Compound. Well, what's left of it."

"What do you mean?"

"About a month ago, our compound fell. Attacked by the Nameless. Watched friends get turned into the Fused."

"Really?"

"Yeah, and I saw the merging fail as if they were refused by the Nameless. Not sure why, guess we will never know."

The stark reality hit him like a brick to the head: death was close by. "So what do they, the Nameless, look like? I've heard a few stories over the years. If I'm gonna die, I may as well know what they are. Are they bug-like? Or a statue of ooze? Or something else?"

Before the man could answer his questions, the reinforced steel door opened, and half a dozen masked men entered the room. Collectively, they untied both men and dragged them out of the cell and into the courtyard of the church. Another building, unscathed after the arrival of the Nameless, stood tall.

In the far corner of the yard, the moonlight illuminated a steel cage structure. A masked figure walked around the cage with a flaming torch, dipping it into each of the many barrels scattered around the courtyard. The flames soon burned brightly, revealing a steel tunnel running from an oversized door to the cage. Valiantly, he tried to fight, but the masked men were too much for him. Trying to stay focused, his head ached, as something warm slowly ran down his wounded head. Another masked figure opened a panelled entrance to the adjacent steel arena. Without hesitation, both he and the other man from the cell were thrown into the cage. Picking themselves up, he noticed a name tag on the patchwork of fabric draped over his comrade's shoulders. The name in bold, white font read 'Hugo'.

Above the steel structure, a balcony made from old, wooden logs extended from an opening in the wall. Watching on in horror, he saw more masked figures appear from behind some of the yard's stonewalls and the doors of the church. Within thirty seconds, masked figures had filled all the spaces available with their physical presence.

Without warning, a loud bang filled the yard, and the masked faces looked upwards at the balcony in unison. A cloaked figure ambled out of the shadows and into the moonlight, wearing a mask made from the skull and antlers of a deer, which had been painted black. A long, almost regal cape hung over his shoulders, which nearly touched the floor. As he stretched his arms out wide, the lively crowd became silent. Another, smaller man in a mask addressed him and bowed his head, then he held out his hands. The cloaked figure removed the mask slowly and placed it in his aide's hands, who then scurried off into the shadows.

The moonlight revealed his deformed face – a twisted combination of human features and those of a bug as if it'd been prematurely woken from a metamorphosis. Meanwhile, its masked followers stood silently waiting. From inside the cage, he noticed they all stayed focused on the figure standing on the balcony. But his gaze locked on to the sheer volume of masked men in the yard.

Inside the cage, unsure of what would follow, he motioned to Hugo, his fellow captive. Shrugging his shoulders, Hugo offered no answer. Suddenly, their uncertainty twisted into fear when the man on the balcony acknowledged all those present.

He turned to Hugo. "What are they? Are they the Refused?"

No answer came; Hugo's shock quickly turned to frantic fear as he scanned the cage. Moments later, Hugo bolted towards the cage wall. In a blind panic, he scaled the metal shell, unaware two of the Refused had shifted their attention away from their leader. Their heads were slightly tilted as if they knew his efforts to escape were futile.

Before he could warn Hugo, one of the Refused unsheathed a dagger and ran Hugo through. The pain caused him to lose his grip. Falling backwards, he hit the hard cobbled floor of the yard. Even as he screamed out in pain, it couldn't drown out the loud clicking sound coming from the balcony. Eager to help his fallen comrade, his help ceased when a medium-sized wooden box fell to the ground from the roof of the cage.

Clicking came from the balcony again. Looking up, he saw the maskless leader point at him before simulating opening a box and taking something out. Further screams of pain came from across the cage but curiosity took hold of him.

"What's in the box?" he bellowed.

The maskless leader pointed at him again and repeated the same action as before. Feeling his chest tighten, he stepped closer to the box. No padlock had been attached to the box – just a small latch on a hook. Trepidation took over, unsure of what lay inside the box. Fumbling with the latch, he heard a shuffling sound. Staggering towards him, Hugo had his hand pressed against his side; his clothes had turned a dark red. Again, a loud clicking sound came from the balcony. Even as his fear grew, so did his curiosity. Glancing upwards at the maskless leader, he saw he now held a machete in his hand. Acting out, he thrust it forward and stabbed an unseen combatant. Again, a stark reality hit him – he'd been told to fight but didn't know why. Reaching inside the wooden box, he pulled out a nail bat; however, before he could reach inside the box again, Hugo had balled up his fist. Both men had clearly received the same information from the leader. As Hugo threw a punch, the entire Refused collective broke into a cacophony of screams and clicks. In unison, some began to bash the cage walls with their makeshift weapons. As Hugo's fist hit him, he dropped the nail bat. Punch after punch rained down on him, knocking him to his knees. Each hit, though, caused Hugo immense pain as he struggled to cope with his blood loss.

Instinctively, he reached up and punched his former comrade, Hugo, in the stomach, causing even more blood to spill from his stab wound. As Hugo doubled over with one hand on his stomach, the crowd bayed for more blood and carnage, which afforded him the necessary time to reach for the nail bat. With the weapon in hand, he began to swing wildly at Hugo, who staggered to stay upright as the blood continued to drain from his wound.

From the balcony came a loud series of clicks, prompting both prisoners to look up at the leader, who held aloft a metal mallet. Seconds later, another cacophony of clicks echoed around the yard. Bringing the mallet down hard, the leader struck a plate, activating a pulley system – as the chains clanged, a metal gate opened. From inside the tunnel came a squeal, similar to the one he'd heard earlier; a forked tongue flicked against the tunnel walls. In the form of a deer, a third captive unwillingly entered the cage; the same vacant eyes stared back at it, whilst its tentacles all moved independently. An odd orchid colour, it somehow seemed ethereal as it trotted past one of the flaming barrels.

Slowly, it circled them both, as if it understood the unwritten, unspoken rules of the cage. Watching in fascination as the deer sniffed the blood on the cage floor, it then looked directly at both of them. Captivated by the deer, he hadn't noticed Hugo had found his feet again and now wielded a makeshift weapon – a sturdy, thick branch with four metal cogs attached to it. Through pure instinct, he managed to duck Hugo's swing. Had Hugo landed his attack, it could've easily ended his life. Again, he evaded Hugo's attempts, unable to swing his spiked baseball bat.

Noticing how Hugo appeared paler than when they first met, he saw his weakened state worsen. Could he outlast his deteriorating condition? To get back to Sarrie, he had to survive this night. Meanwhile, the crowd's clicks and groans grew louder as they demanded more action and more blood. Oddly, neither of them noticed the deer edging closer, as if it knew it had to bide its time so it could survive. What would the deer actually gain? Unaware of the rules of the Nameless, he didn't know the answer to his own question. Then, total darkness.

Suddenly, Hugo's wailing woke him from his unconscious state. Before him, the deer lay collapsed on the floor, motionless. Next to him, he saw the Nameless clambering over the cold, cobbled stones to reach Hugo. Excited by Hugo's scream, the crowd let out another cacophony of clicks. Some of the Refused slammed their weapons against the cage, but the noise couldn't drown out the screams. Terrified, he watched on as Hugo valiantly tried to fend off the Nameless. The tentacles and the flapping of its wings pulled the creature up Hugo's body; the feelers were slimy and squid-like. With no notable facial features, barring two antennae, it sat on Hugo's chest, wrapping a tentacle around his throat. Despite his futile efforts, Hugo fought back to no avail. The creature simply tightened its grip, forcing Hugo's mouth to open. Without letting go the creature crawled to his face and curled its wings, giving it the appearance of a squid with antennae. Brutally sliding itself into Hugo's mouth and down his throat, it forced Hugo's neck to bulge outwards. Once the last tentacle slipped inside, a guttural scream left Hugo's mouth. Again, he wailed as he realised, he couldn't move. Then he began to violently shake, as if caught in his own personal earthquake. He watched Hugo writhe for a few moments, before becoming motionless. Unexpectedly, the crowd became silent, only the crackles of the flames filled the air. Standing a few feet away from the cage wall, he cried, "Let me out!"

The Refused stayed silent and still as if they'd been frozen in time. Even the leader on the balcony stood unmoved, but his eyes were transfixed on one thing - Hugo. Standing there, feeling helpless, he wondered if someone had trapped him in time, too. He wandered over to the metal gate and tunnel. Fear gripped his hand as he looked into the darkness. Did anything lie in wait, ready to pounce? Pushing himself, he stepped into the tunnel. The cobblestone floor had a thick layer of some substance, but the lack of light made it hard for him to see. His mind raced between images of grey sludge and the insides of the dead. Moving deeper into the darkness, a rancid stench hit his nostrils, worsening with each step forward. From nowhere, something gripped his leg and pulled him back towards the light. As he struggled to reach for the tunnel wall, his face hit and sank into the substance on the floor. A warm, tingling sensation spread over his skin causing him to open his eyes. Met with a myriad of colours connected like a spider's web, the outer edge of everything he saw had the same odd orchid-purple tinge as the deer. Floating in the vastness, a calmness crawled over him. The web then collapsed into a stream of light. Once it had passed, he found himself on his back looking up at the night sky. As the stars sparkled, he started to sense an emptiness grow inside, as he processed what he had seen, only moments before. With splintered thoughts, something lurched over him, blocking out the moonlight. He recognised the word 'Hugo' emblazoned on the front of the patchwork attire, but it no longer looked like his former comrade.

Fresh-faced yet still raw from the transformation, Hugo resembled one of the Refused. Had he not recognised Hugo by the fabric of his clothes, he could have mistaken him for one of the Refused standing outside the cage wall, clicking excitedly. With another now in their ranks, he walked towards the cage exit; he didn't hesitate as he stepped into freedom. Hugo's transformation appeared complete - whoever he'd been before would never return. Clicks echoed around the yard and beyond the stone walls. Lying on his back on the cold, cobbled stones, the odd purple glow remained. On the floor a few feet away, he saw the tentacles of the Nameless reaching out in all directions, tapping the cobbled stone floor. Lost in the ethereal glow of the creature, he experienced a calming curiosity within his mind. Returning to his feet, his line of sight remained firmly transfixed on the Nameless as it used its many limbs and wings to move across the floor. Eagerly, he moved towards it and his calmness became more prevalent with each step. If only he still had his notebook, he would've sketched the creature, but he didn't know where his belongings were. Oddly, any concerns he had for his prized possessions slowly drifted away as he got closer. Spotting something he hadn't noticed when the Nameless had attached itself to Hugo, he saw the long body become translucent, with colours swirling like a cosmic kaleidoscope, mirroring what he'd seen in the grey sludge.

Curiosity turned into desire; he carried an insatiable longing to see its beauty again ever since he'd been ensnared in its cosmic silk web. Unable to fight the urge, thoughts of his life back at the camp and his love for Sarrie slowly left his mind. As her name faded away, so did her face. Standing before the Nameless, he dropped to his knees. Edging his face closer, he felt the first tendril wrap itself around his neck. Tightening its grip, his heartbeat began to slow and echoed around his mind. As it slid into his mouth and down his throat, tentacle by tentacle, his mind didn't panic. Feeling his airways open, his vision changed. The night sky began to spin slowly. Observing the clouds and moon as they picked up pace, the stars turned into streaks of white light and his body disconnected from gravity. Rising off the cold, cobbled stones, a coral-orange orb appeared above him; white flares shot from it in all directions. Mesmerised as it expanded, he saw the shimmering spider's web again, inside the orb, along with an ethereal skin-like texture. Rippling, like a pebble hitting the surface of a pond, it cycled rapidly through the series of bright colours, making up a rainbow.

Slowly, he passed through the barrier, remaining weightless. Moving through the cosmic web, he caught images in some of the strands. All of them were initially blurred, but once he focused, he gazed at an infinite number of worlds. In front of him came a clumping of the web, surprisingly he knew it to be a mooring bisector of the web. Speeding through the intricacy of the cosmos, he witnessed the sun's rise and fall and saw many planets, all of which were different to his home world - one that had always been full of life.

Stopping on one particular planet - one with jagged rocks

protruding at every angle across the surface - he saw strange, feathered, bird-like creatures with large wings. Passing over the mountain peaks and the oncoming wave of the marvellous winged creatures, he noticed their two-toned feathers changing as the sun appeared, switching from burnt orange to cobalt blue. Gliding through the morning sky and straight into the pitch black of night, daylight returned but the planet's surface had now been covered in the same grey blanket, he'd seen back home. Searching for safety, the large birds began to fall. He watched as the last one curled up its wings and nosedived into the bubbling sludge. Yet, he remained weightless and continued on his path.

Appearing before him, the same orange orb expanded and again revealed the cosmic web. He slowly passed through the ripple. As he travelled further, the images in the other mooring bisectors became clearer. He saw images of planets resembling Earth but with differences he couldn't explain, but knew none were the Earth he came from.

Another mooring came, and he passed through the opening, and floated into a world full of violent volcanoes and blackened, hardened lava. He couldn't feel the heat, but his mind recognised it would be. Some patches had an off-red and metallic orange glow. As the planet rotated, he watched thick grey waves crash over the volcanoes and the surface, extinguishing the flames and filling the sky with a cimmerian hue. However, it didn't hide the coral orange orb; the white flares from the orb danced in the thick smoke.

Each world he witnessed rushed past him, quicker than the one before, but he felt no panic. He passed back into the cosmic web. Soon, he entered another mooring - one which led him to a planet previously covered in nothing but luxurious green and red foliage where he saw the last patch of grass and a tall, twisted tree. He watched as the last piece of green disappeared under the thick grey sludge as if suffocating the planet into submission. In his weightless state, he began to pick up speed through the cosmic web; the individual strands turned into streams of light. Suddenly, a large orb appeared before him. As he gained speed, the orb grew bigger and brighter. Inside the large sphere, he saw a world of dark red skies, and again, a thick grey blanket covered the surface. Passing through the portal, he found a new world he somehow recognised, though he knew he hadn't seen it before.

A cluster of jagged mountains surrounded a giant creature with two large wings and four long tentacles. Two antennae protruded from the top of its body, emitting a familiar violet glow.

The granite-coloured mountain shimmered as something sailed through the sky away from the surface. Fixing his gaze on something at the foot of the mountain, amidst a large, thick patch of grey sludge, he saw one of the tentacles pointing towards the sky. Slowly opening, it released a blast of orchid-purple light soaring through the air. As he turned to follow its path, he watched as it disappeared through an opening into the cosmic web. Realisation dawned upon him: he found himself in the presence of the queen of the Nameless. Somehow, her offspring were able to travel through the entire cosmos.

At lightning speed, another tentacle shot forward and connected with his head, and once again, a calmness washed over his weightless body. Without invitation, the queen pulled him towards the translucent part of her body, just like her offspring. Swirling around inside, he saw something resembling an energy, glowing with all kinds of colours. As he got closer, faint faces appeared inside the energy. When his body touched the queen's skin, another wave of calmness crashed over him like a tsunami. Warmth and familiarity coursed through his veins, as her skin enveloped him. Floating in the swirling energy within the queen, he felt his body fade away like leaves falling from an autumn branch. His eyes were the last to fade, even though he could still see. A rush came as his essence merged with the swirling energy; he found himself forgetting who he used to be. Seeing through all of space and time, he could feel all of life and death, everywhere, all at the same time.

I have had a passion for writing for twenty-six years now. In that time I have written a number of stories varying in length; but in 2019 I joined a writer's group, which developed a love for writing poetry. Since my last book 'A Mind Full of Words', I have been working on and putting together a collection of short stories for you to read. This will hopefully be the one of many. Look out for further publications.

To my readers, I thank you for taking the time to read my work and hope you enjoy them as much as I did creating them. My plans are to release more short stories and novels over the coming months/years as well as more poems. I love creating and I hope you continue to follow me through my journey.

adsmallauthor.com

facebook.com/ADSMALLA

instagram.com/adsmallauthor

tiktok.com/@adsmallauthor

FREEING CAROLINE

BY S.F. ROGERS

The sun streamed in through the picturesque window and landed gently on the empty space in the bed beside me. I had been staring at that space for a few minutes, and as the light got brighter, I slid my hand across the soft flannel fabric. The bed was still warm where he had been lying, and his cologne lingered on the pillow.

When I opened my eyes in the darkness, I knew he was leaving. Another call had come, just like the last time. I never asked any questions. After Shane had rescued me from that root cellar, I owed him everything. Hell, I took his last name to prove that I wasn't going anywhere.

We were inseparable except for when the calls came. He would leave at all hours to handle whatever that private phone said. He handled situations from Missouri to Colorado and North Dakota to Texas. I couldn't go; I didn't ever leave the pack house. One of us needed to be here to keep business moving, and things would fall on my shoulders while Shane was away. His beta always kept him in the loop, so even if I didn't tell him something minor, Jace always tattled.

Disappointment settled in as the sun began shining brightly into our room, and I lifted myself out of bed.

As I made my way down the stairs, my eyes followed the pictures we had hanging on the wall. Us together on our first official date, us on the night he proposed, and another picture of us on our wedding day. Pictures of our memories from the last ten years, ten years that had passed by in a blur.

Coffee was already brewing in the large kitchen, and I could hear one of our assistants humming to herself. Feya was my favorite. She never pushed me, and she never questioned any decisions that Shane and I made.

I grabbed one of my favorite mugs with a nod to her and filled it with the dark liquid. Everyone who came to the house knew the rule that Shane imposed: no one spoke to me until I'd had my first sip of coffee.

"Good morning, Mrs. O'Neil. Today on your schedule is a meeting at ten with a rogue wolf. He is seeking sanctuary." I nodded when she paused. "Then your next meeting is at three with Shane."

I placed my cup down on the long island, "Meeting with Shane? Since when?" I wiggled my eyebrows at the raven-haired assistant.

"Luna, I was told that all other meetings are canceled. Per Mr. O'Neil." She wouldn't look at me as she said it. I picked my cup up again and took a deep drink of it.

"Fine, what do I wear to this?" I asked as she began to shuffle some papers on the counter.

"You have presents coming at one." her voice was full of mischief. "Shane left you a letter over there." She pointed to the cabinet where my laptop was lying closed with a black envelope on top.

I rolled my eyes at her and moved toward the letter. Once I held it in my hands, my inner wolf picked up on the mahogany smell of Shane. Sliding my finger under the seal of the envelope, I quickly opened it. Pulling out the paper inside, I saw that it was Shane's deep green letterhead.

"My pet,
I am excited to see you today and cannot wait to spend
time with you. This job won't take me very long, and
the presents that are coming I have picked for you
especially. I adore you and hope you had a restful
morning.
Always yours,
Shane"

I sighed as I finished the letter and laid it gently on the counter next to my laptop. I looked across the room to the mirror hanging on the wall. My brunette hair hung haphazardly around my face, proof that Shane had spent some time with me last night. My deep brown eyes sparkled as flashbacks of the evening before scrolled through my mind. That man had a way with me, and I wasn't one to hide that fact.

"This rogue, what is his name again?" I asked as I ran my hand over my face and into my hair.

"Ronin." Feya walked up beside me and handed me my tablet. A picture was pulled up on the screen of a rugged man with light hair and deep blue piercing eyes. "He has been seeking counsel with Shane for over a month. I feel bad for him, so I went ahead and scheduled him to meet with you. This is something you've handled in the past." her voice faded as I continued to stare at the man looking back at me from the screen.

"Who is that?" Jupiter, my wolf, speaks softly to me.

"A rogue, no one for you to worry yourself with." I closed my eyes and retreated into our space. Her deep black coat shone in the light, and she gently laid down in order to be at eye level with me.

"He has my interest. I won't be sleeping through this meeting. He intrigues me." She gently laid her head down on her paws. "Call me when you need me."

"I know that you will make a wise decision." Feya finished her one-sided conversation with me as I opened my eyes again. I laid the tablet down, picked up the cooling cup of coffee, and took one last drink. Walking to the sink, I dumped the rest and turned back toward Feya.

"Thank you. I will take a shower and get ready. If he gets

here before I'm done, have him wait with you." Feya being a half-sphinx had its perks, and she would weigh his intentions

* * *

Our offices were conveniently located in the lower story of our house. A quick walk down a hallway off the kitchen and through a door led straight to our waiting area.

As my heels clicked along the tile, I couldn't shake the image of the rouge I was about to speak with.

In my distraction, I nearly ran into the large man. Tall, standing at six foot four inches, he was bigger than Shane. Bumping into him felt like bumping into a brick wall, and as he turned around, I dropped the tablet and all the paperwork in my hands.

The picture that Feya had shown me was obviously an older one. His wavy hair was grown out, cascading down to his shoulders. The ends were light from time spent in the sunshine. His eyes caught mine, and for a brief moment, my breath caught in my chest until the sound of shattered glass hit me.

"Oh shit, I'm sorry." Came his low tenor voice as he leaned down to grab everything that I dropped. "I should have listened when she said to be seated earlier." He scooped up my now broken tablet and paperwork and shuffled it all in his massive hands.

"I should have been paying better attention to where I was going. Completely my fault." I was trying to gain my composure when he stood up and locked eyes with me again. Jupiter was at attention, and I could feel her on high alert as he handed me my things. "Thank you."

"Never a problem." He nervously ran his hands through his hair. "I'll get out of your way. Can't have your Luna see you wasting time with me." he nodded toward the empty chairs along the white wall and stepped out of my way. I lifted my eyebrow in surprise that he didn't know who I was. He thought I was some type of secretary.

"She isn't harsh like some of the others, fiercely protective, but she won't mind." I pushed the power button on the tablet to see the damage, and the screen wouldn't even come on. "Great, gonna need a new one of these."

"I've heard she is breathtakingly beautiful." He sat in one of the chairs, and immediately, his leg began shaking. "She is one of the most beloved Luna's. People speak highly of her character."

"I'm glad to hear it." I grinned at the man. "Give her just a moment, and she will be here. She is never late for a meeting."

"That makes me even more nervous." He rubbed both hands across his face and into his hair. The smell of cedar sent shockwaves over my senses, and Jupiter wined in my head. "*Mate.*"

The realization hit me like a ton of bricks. My mother had told me that when I met my true mate, it would be my wolf that responded. I had fallen for Shane, but Jupiter had never had a reaction like this to him. I was rooted to this spot. *How is he my mate when I am already mated to Shane?*

Jupiter forced our body to move across the room, and I finally got control back and headed toward my office door. Swinging it closed quickly behind me, I dropped the broken tablet and paperwork on my desk, ran to the en suite bathroom, and shut that door quietly.

I never intended to run into him, so my hair was pulled back with a large clip, and I was wearing my glasses. Being in the root cellar for so long in the dark had done damage to my eyes, but Shane never wanted me seen in them.

I quickly put my contacts in and pulled the clip out of my

hair, running my hands through the long tresses and making sure it looked perfect. Stepping back out into my office, Jupiter was giddy with excitement. *"Let's talk to him some more."*

"How about you remember that we are already married." I spat at her as I sat down at my desk and woke up my computer. As I made myself comfortable, I sent Feya a message that I was ready to see him. A quiet knock on the door, and I stood, taking a deep, calming breath before he entered.

"Luna O'Neil, may I introduce Ronin." She motioned for him to come in, and I could get a better look at him as he crossed the cozy space.

His shoulders were wide, and he wore a forest green shirt that showed off the muscles of his arms and chest. He was wearing a nice pair of dark blue jeans and biker-style boots. Most of the rogues had formed their own culture and stuck to it. Like the bikers of the humans, they were the people on our outskirts. They didn't owe anyone but each other loyalty. As his eyes came up from the floor, he stopped in his tracks as I came around my desk.

"Fuck." He stood there, slowly breathing in and out as Feya shut the office door.

"That isn't normally the type of language that people use around a Luna." I walked toward him and extended my hand. "It's nice to meet you, Ronin."

Blush crept up his neck and ears toward his face as he gently grasped my fingers and shook my hand. "Nice to meet you, too." He stared down into my eyes as he dropped my hand, and I nervously tucked my hair behind one of my ears. "I'm sorry about earlier but you are breathtakingly beautiful." He blurted out as he blushed a deeper shade of red.

"Ronin, please sit." I pointed to one of the chairs in front of my desk with a grin. "No need to be nervous. Take a deep breath." When he walked past me, cedar hit my senses again as Jupiter whined for me to, *"Please just touch him once."*

"My assistant said that you've been trying for a while to get in to see Shane. Are you seeking to join the pack?" I had to get this meeting moving and get him away from me.

"Actually, I have been seeking a meeting with him for other reasons." He sighed and shifted uncomfortably in his seat. "I'm in a predicament and don't really know how to handle it."

"What is your predicament?" I asked as I opened the file we used for rogue statuses. As I typed in his first name, nothing pulled up in our system.

A nervous laugh escaped him as I began typing his name again, and I glanced in his direction for a second. "You might have a hard time finding me, ma'am."

"Oh, our system is very advanced. What is your last name?" I was grasping at straws for how I was going to find him and get all his information. Jupiter continued to whine in my head as I made eye contact with him again.

"God, this wolf just won't shut up." He blurted out, leaning forward and placing his hands on his forehead. "What was your question?"

"I asked what your last name is." I watched him intently as he sheepishly looked up at me.

"That is the predicament, Luna." He sighed heavily. "I'm Ronin Van Helsing."

The name hit me like a ton of bricks. "Van Helsing, the killer of immortals."

"Well, I was. That is until this happened." He pulled quickly on the collar of his shirt, showing a fresh bite wound

on his left shoulder. It was healing nicely and looked like it
had been well cared for.

"You can't seek sanctuary here or anywhere for that fact."
I stood, causing him to jump to his feet.

"Please. Your bylaws state that if a rogue requests a
meeting with an Alpha or Luna, you must grant them an
audience. My wolf says I must make you listen."

"I know our bylaws better than anyone." I crossed my
arms in front of me, pushing away the desire to reach out and
touch him.

"I was tracking something the hunter community calls the
kidnapper." His eyes pleaded with me to listen. "He keeps
young werewolves in this root cellar and uses them as bait for
Alphas. The high council hired me to investigate. I found the
root cellar but was hit hard from behind about two weeks ago.
Woke up with this wound and a wolf in my head telling me he
would help me."

"A root cellar?" PTSD had been something I dealt with
every day since coming home. I didn't do basements anymore
at all or closed spaces. "Where?"

"In southern Missouri. He was fast when he hit me. I was
so close to finally figuring out who he was, and then this
happened. I can't go back to the council, I'm one of you now. I
can't go back to the other hunters either; they will kill me." He
ran his hands nervously through his hair, and began pacing.
"Goddammit, I need this wolf to shut the fuck up."

"Tell me what he's saying. Maybe I can walk you through
it." I chuckled as I motioned for him to sit on the couch at the
opposite end of the room.

"He's speaking gibberish; it doesn't make any sense." He
shook his head hard like he could shake his wolf loose.

"As your soon-to-be Luna, you will tell me what he is
saying." I sat down next to him and gently laid my hand on his

arm. An electric shock passed between us as our eyes snapped to each other. One word passed from our lips as we spoke in unison, "Mate."

"What does that mean?" He asked as I lifted myself quickly from the couch.

"It's a fated mate bond. Once found, you are bound to them. We haven't seen a fated mate in a dozen or so years." I pulled my hair out of where it was tucked behind my ear to shield me from his gaze.

"But you are married." He stood as his voice filled with worry.

"Yes, I will have to deny you in front of the pack in order to break the mate bond." I began pacing as I tried to get Jupiter to quiet down and quit telling me to touch him again. "Which means I have to tell Shane that I have a fated mate." I stopped as his story came screaming to the front of my mind again. "Shane killed the one responsible for kidnapping and placing younglings in a root cellar." I turned back toward him with a quizzical glance.

"I'm sorry, Luna, but you are mistaken. Werewolves aged sixteen to nineteen have been taken all across the Midwest. All were found years later dead; we knew about the root cellar because a doctor told us about a youngling found alive in one. We've been tracking her rescuer ever since." He sat on the couch with a distant look in his eye.

"Why would you track her rescuer?" I staggered to one of the soft chairs situated in front of the couch, keeping the coffee table as a barrier between us.

"We don't believe he actually rescued her; we believe he was close to getting caught and staged it to look like a rescue."

"Do you know who this youngling was?" I felt a panic attack building in my chest.

"Caroline Bridges. No one could tell us what happened to

her. She disappeared after the initial investigation, and no one has really seen her. A spy here told us that she is alive but kept hidden." his knee began to shake nervously as a wave of emotions hit me.

"He insisted on me never wearing my glasses; he built our offices in our home. He released me, but he kept me as a prisoner." I thought to myself as our whole life began to unravel before my eyes. *"I never truly got away."* Every interaction with him suddenly became tainted as each memory bubbled to the surface. *"I never leave the house, I haven't seen my parents since the day he took me from that root cellar. They never call, at least as far as I'm aware."*

"Luna O'Neil, you have gone very pale. Are you alright?" He knelt down in front of me, his eyes searching my face. As he stared, I heard his wolf through the mate bond.

"Caroline, Jupiter, it is nice to meet you. My name is Camus." His voice was deep, ancient-sounding, and it soothed a part of my heart that nothing had ever touched before. When he said my first name, Ronin stood quickly.

"What is your first name, Luna O'Neil?" sweat beaded on his brow.

"Caroline. My maiden name is Bridges." I wrapped my arms tightly around myself like I could keep from falling apart if I just held on tight enough. Ronin stumbled backward toward the couch, his eyes distant.

"I found you." A large smile spread across his face. "I completed the job; I found you." Giggles began to come from the large man, which suddenly turned to giddy laughter. "I actually did it. I found you! Alive and well, now we can stop this monster. Do you know who it is?" His joy stalled when he made eye contact with me again.

"Shane is the one that saved me from that root cellar. Have you been in contact with my parents? They would have told you that." I stared across the room at a small picture of them that sat on my desk, the only thing Shane allowed me to have from my life before him.

"That's why the council called me; Alpha Gunner and Luna Celeste were killed a little over two months ago after asking for us to investigate this region in particular. Shane had informed them that their daughter had been overcome with her PTSD and had committed suicide. They didn't believe him. Shortly after their murders, the kidnappings picked up again, and more younglings have been going missing." Concern etched his face as he watched me process the information.

"They are dead?" My breathing began to quicken as the panic set in. "He told me they stayed away so there is no question about his Alpha status."

"Shane isn't an Alpha." his words hit my already breaking heart and shattered it completely. "Shane has this big setup, but he only runs with rogues. He is what they call their leader, but he doesn't actually have a pack."

The more lies that came out, the angrier Jupiter became. She had warned me the day before we got married to be careful.

"That insolent little shit." Her voice was loud in my head. *"Not only did he kidnap us, torture us, and do unspeakable things to us. He kept us prisoner!"* More memories came forward, now seen through the lenses of truth and not through rose-colored glasses. *"I will kill him. I will rip his throat out. I WILL FEAST ON HIS BONES!"* I stood quickly as my resolve began to solidify.

"Come with me." I grabbed his hand and pulled him out of my office.

Adrenaline pumped through my veins with the electricity that passed when our hands touched. Once in the waiting area, I nodded to Feya, who stood and followed us through the hallway.

"Where are we going? Why is she following us?" His large frame being pulled along by me must have been comical.

"Feya is my trusted advisor and assistant. We've been placing certain rogues under my leadership, meaning they are my pack, not Shane's. We must go to the Moon Goddess."

I dropped his hand, but my whole body ached to grab it again as we walked into the lower level of my home. My pack home, my name was on all the rogues paperwork, not his. He refused to sign any of the paperwork, so the pack was, legally, my pack. I just needed the Goddess's approval.

I turned toward Feya, "Thank you for scheduling this meeting."

"You're welcome, Ms. Bridges. The paperwork just came through. I sent the recording of your conversation to the council and the annulment was easily granted when they heard that he was the one who kidnapped you." She handed me the thick envelope with a wink. "Everything is in order; the cameras have been turned off, and you are free to go."

Stepping out into the bright afternoon sunshine and fresh air made Jupiter ache to run. The full moon was this evening, and with the Goddess's blessing, I would take over this pack with Ronin by my side. Tonight, Shane would die, and my freedom would be cemented.

* * *

The moon rose high over the trees as I transitioned. This would be Ronin's first wolf transformation, and I would be with him through the entire thing, not only as his friend and Luna but also as his wife. The priestess had granted our marriage before we even finished telling her what Shane did.

Jupiter looked on as his legs and arms stretched, his skin tearing apart to reveal beautiful white fur. His face changed shape, and his blue eyes stood in contrast against the black rings of his eyelids. Camus's white fur glowed in the moonlight next to Jupiter's dark black fur.

They howled in unison, calling the rest of my chosen pack to us. I watched as each rouge I had accepted made their way up the hill. All came except two, Shane and Jace's wolves Vorkan and Fang. As the wolves came by one at a time, swearing their allegiance to both of us, they came stalking out of the woods.

"What. Is. This?" Came Vorkan's voice through the pack telepathy. Shane's wolf had never been intimidating. "Who dares to stand with my Luna?"

"Not yours. Mine!" Camus walked in front of Jupiter as if to protect her from him.

"Your's? Who might you be?"

"My fated mate, Camus." The moment Jupiter spoke over the pack telepathy, the whole clearing stilled. "His host is Caroline's fated mate, Ronin Van Helsing. I know the truth. You have no power here. I gave these wolves sanctuary. I found my mate, and you must leave. By order of the Moon Goddess."

"Ronin Van Helsing. I thought Fang killed him the other night."

His eyes narrowed, and in the moonlight, I saw him for what he really was. Compared to Camus, Vorkan looked sickly; the gray fur was thin, his skin covered in decaying spots, and his ribs showed as he sauntered over. Seeing his weakened state, Jupiter jumped at him and aimed to cut off his air supply. He dodged with a growl and a yip as she grazed his throat.

"I will feast on your bones!" Jupiter barked, her ears

pinned back flat as she lept at him again. This time, he wasn't fast enough, and her sharp teeth closed around his skinny neck.

As her jaw tightened further, his whimpers were loud. "Please, no. You love me, and only me! Don't forget who gave you all of this!"

They fell on deaf ears as vengeance filled my voice as Jupiter and I screamed in unison, "You never owned us. Now you die!" With one last bone-jarring crunch, I watched as Vorkan transformed back into a man. His esophagus smashed flat, he gasped for air when Jupiter dropped him. The life slowly faded from his eyes, my monster and nightmare were finally over.

With Shane dead, the pack, Jupiter and Camus included, devoured his body. Piece by piece, the kidnapper was wiped from the earth, one bloody mouthful at a time. Jace was next, telling the pack where to find the last youngling they had just stolen. He was led away and killed by two of the larger males.

Once the moon began to set, I transformed back to my human form and sat with Ronin as he did the same. I let my eyes roam slowly over his bare body when he rolled on his side to face me. I blushed to myself as I thought about this man being my fated mate. When my eyes locked with his, a large grin spread across his face.

"What are you thinking about?" I asked as I lay back in the grass. My bare skin rose in goosebumps as he lightly traced his fingers from my collarbone down between my breasts and to my belly button.

"I never thought I would find you, let alone be able to make you mine." His eyes softened as I scooted closer to him. Dew was beginning to fall in the early morning light, and a chill had taken to the breeze. "Did you love him?"

"I think I was more bonded to him out of feeling like I

owed him a debt. I'm not sure I ever loved him." I sighed and felt a blush creep across my face. "He was my first." I whispered.

"He may have been your first." Ronin's voice was thick with desire. "I intend to be your last." Gently lifting my chin, he kissed me softly.

Sarah is a small town girl living her adventures dreams one story at a time. As a wife and dog mom, you can typically find her writing or reading with her dogs, or camping and hiking with her husband. Stay tuned for all the updates on discord, patreon, and across multiple social media platforms.

https://linktr.ee/s.f.rogersauthor

SEVEN

BY T.L. COMBS

The warmth of his life essence permeates my leather-clad hands as I peer into his eyes, witnessing the fading life. An electric surge courses through me, and in these fleeting moments, I am the maestro of his destiny. He comprehends, in these final breaths, the one responsible for his unceremonious plunge into darkness.

His deep blue orbs widen in an epiphany as I know he recalls the mysterious woman from a mere few hours prior—whose allure was matched only by the acrid stench of his cheap cologne mingled with garlic-laden breath and the sordid jests that barely scraped the surface of propriety. His impending demise brings me an unsettling satisfaction.

The last vestiges of life escape him with a final shudder, and his enormous frame, twice my size, crumples to the floor like a discarded puppet. His transgressions remain a mystery to me, but such details matter not. My duty is to execute without inquiry, unwavering and obedient. It is the very essence of my excellence.

Snatching a nearby towel from a rack, I briskly cleanse the blade of his blood, returning it to its sheath on my thigh as I circle the lifeless form. The crimson fluid spreads like an unholy offering upon the cold, unfeeling tiles. My reflection, veiled in the dim, chilling light, gazes back at me—my eyes, hollow, devoid of any emotion or spark of life. It is as though my very soul has been snatched away, yet I cannot avert my gaze.

I was but a ten-year-old child when I tasted my first kill. Commander Jin had issued explicit directives regarding the target—a mere boy, no older than fifteen. His demise unfolded in silence, almost gracefully, yet it was the silent pleadings in his eyes that pierced my heart. I watched, unable to turn away, as the suffering of his final moments unfolded before me. His pain, anger, fear, and ultimate acceptance of his fate shone across his face as his eyes fluttered shut. A solitary tear clung to his pallid cheek, and I brushed it away with a trembling finger.

"Taste it," Jin commanded from the shadows behind me.

With a sharp inhalation, I transferred the salty teardrop to my tongue, and my mind was engulfed in a vivid panorama of the boy's entire existence. From his first cries, echoing through his mother's womb, rushing through all the crimes he had ever committed, to the final, chilling gasp that marked the end, as I severed his trachea and carotid artery.

I crumpled beside his still-warm body, gasping for air, my juvenile mind grappling with the enormity of what I had witnessed.

"Did you see it?" Jin inquired, a spectral presence lurking like a prowling feline.

I nodded once, my throat constricting.

"Good. You are now a part of the sisterhood and the formidable Wonhai Coalition. From this moment onward, speak your name to no one. Your name, my dear, is the key to your destiny. Excel, and you shall forever know triumph."

My heart raced as I rose, my clenched fists aching. Determination coursed through me, yet beneath it all, a twinge of remorse lingered. Could avenging my family come at too high a cost?

"Can I...kill *him* now?" I asked, my voice quivering.

Jin's striking features broke into a slow, inscrutable smile, her dark angular eyes dancing with mischief. Arched eyebrows hinted at concealed intentions. "In due course, my dear one," she purred, her voice ethereal. Her fingers enveloped my wrist possessively. "But for now, we have work to do." Her words dripped with unspoken promises, sending shivers down my spine, leaving me to wonder what lay ahead.

Twenty long years have elapsed since that fateful

initiation into the Coalition. Over that span, I've executed more targets than anyone in our annals, but not the one I yearn for. Each demise chipped away at my soul until I felt nothing. Yet, an insatiable void persists, one only vengeance can fill.

With cautious steps to avoid sullying my boots with the pooled blood, I navigate the room's periphery, slipping away through the window before alarms can sound. His death will remain a secret for hours, given the five personal guards whose throats I severed.

Veiled by the obscurity of Fort Fidel in Kimhul's capital, I move with utmost discretion. My attire, hood, and mask conspire to keep my identity hidden as I leap into the back of a passing farmer's wagon bound for the northeast. My mission is complete, and I can now return to the Kingdom of Sillina, reuniting with my fellow sisters-in-arms, and inching closer to the culmination of my vendetta. Perhaps my next target will pave the way to closure.

TL Combs
Fantasy Author
⊕ www.authortlcombs.com
✉ author.tlcombs@gmail.com
⊗ https://linktr.ee/author_tl.combs
⊙ North Carolina, USA

I spent almost two decades as a classically trained chef, working in multiple restaurants and catering companies. Eventually, I started my own catering company and even worked as a Certified Dietary Manager in a healthcare facility. In 2015, I married the love of my life, M.

Following the birth of our youngest child, L, I made the decision to retire from my career in the culinary industry and become a stay-at-home mother to L and my bonus daughter, K. We all reside on our little farm in North Carolina where we enjoy raising chickens, cultivating our gardens, and spending time with our beloved Maremma Sheep Dog, Ronan, and tuxedo tabby, Ziggy.

Writing has always been a passion of mine, dating back to my childhood in Pennsylvania, when I would write short stories for my family and friends. That all changed when I began daydreaming about a high fantasy story that morphed into the Bellham Series. With the encouragement of a best friend, H.E.G, I decided to pursue the series and turn my crazy daydream into a reality. I am grateful for the unwavering support of my family and friends. Without them, I could not have achieved this dream.

linktr.ee/author_tl.combs

www.authortlcombs.com

THE LAST BUS

BY DAVID W. ADAMS

The finality of death can bring about the most peculiar behavior in a human being. Some may look upon it as a terrible thing. Something to panic about and to run from. Of course trying to run from the inevitable is futile. Others, however, may welcome death. It may provide a release of sorts. Perhaps even a comfort. For Vincent Smith, however, it was neither.

Vincent, or Vince as he was known to everyone, had been one of the most cheerful and welcoming people on the face of the Earth. He had lived the majority of his adult life in the comfort of a loving family, with children who adored him, and a wife who brought him steady reassurance, comfort and stability. In turn, he often projected this affection onto those he met whilst at his day job. Vince was a bus driver. No, Vince was the *jolly* bus driver. If anyone ever spoke of him, they always referred to him as the jolly bus driver. He would welcome each passenger onto his bus with a smile and sing during each trip between stops. His tunes of choice were often older swing numbers, drawing from the extensive library of Frank Sinatra, and on a less successful occasion attempting to perform Queen's Bohemian Rhapsody whilst driving over speed bumps. His passengers, of course, thought it hilarious, and the highlight of their day.

And that was when it all began to go wrong. March 2020. Lockdown. No buses, no leaving the house, and nothing on the horizon but forced isolation and entrapment in a previously happy home. By this time, the children had long moved out and started families of their own, and had drifted away slightly, as children often do once they've settled down in their own homes.

Spending months locked up together brought strain to Vince and his marriage. The jovial atmosphere that had existed for decades was now turning bitter. Every day, one or the other in the house would do something to irritate the other and arguments would ensue. Vince would have a drink, and sneak the bottles away, using his one permitted walk a day to visit the local off- license. Of course it was impossible to hide the truth when escape was impossible. Inevitably, the bottles would be found, another argument would ensue, and the relationship would worsen.

Thankfully, when the early signs of recovery were visible, some of the buses returned to service, and Vince geared himself up to put the past few months behind him. He lowered his drinking back to somewhat normal levels, and his relationship stabilized because of it. That was until he was told he was not part of the skeleton crew returning to the roads. He would have to wait a little longer. More arguments, day after day, until one day in the middle of a blazing row over affording the car insurance renewal, Vince's face went still, his limbs locked in place, and he simply dropped to the carpet like a sack of potatoes. It would be three days before he woke up again.

Cancer. The word has brought many people to their knees. It instantly stabs a knife through your thought process and tells you that your time on this planet is soon to come to an end. Regardless of whether it is treatable or not. That's simply the fear around that one word. But for Vince, there was no reaction. By this point, he had watched as his perfect world, as simple as it had been, had begun to fall down around him. His children had moved away. His wife could no longer stand to be in the same room as him. His beloved job was now ebbing further out of reach. And now he was simply counting down the days and the hours until he saw his final sunset.

* * *

"What do you want me to do Vince? Let you start banning people? The public are fucking assholes. Always have been, always will be. Just drive them from A to B, and keep your mouth shut."

The depot manager, Levi Harrison, was new. When Vince had last driven a bus, his manager had been an older man. Frank Clearwater was an old school family man. He had treated everyone with respect and rewarded loyalty and encouraged every driver to be the best part of each passenger's day. Unfortunately in the four years it had taken for Vince to return to bus driving, Frank himself had passed on. Levi was brought in to try and bring the company into the twenty-first century. A far too often used expression which basically meant your company was dying. Levi had cut routes, reduced others, and increased fares by forty-percent in just a year. Combined with the effects of the pandemic, which even now had continuing repercussions, people's tolerance for interaction had waned, and now everyone was far more selfish, and far more dismissive of Vince's previously happy manner.

"Don't fucking breath on me."

"Can you stop singing, I'm trying to watch the latest Sidemen video."

"Why do they always have to talk to you?"

Vince had fought through two bouts of Hodgkins Lymphoma and despite the treatment taking all of his strength and determination, he had come out the other side laughing. He had gotten his job back, despite his long absence and felt a warming relief. Of course the reality was that he had only been given his job back because of a national shortage. Levi enjoyed telling him that it must have been nice to have four years holiday.

Cunt.

"You know I need a late shift tomorrow Levi? Hospital checkup."

The manager gave a deep and overly exaggerated sigh, as if looking after his own health was damaging to the company he worked for. A shift change to Levi was as bad as having a bus break down. Effort he didn't want to make or entertain.

"You need to sort this shit out. I can't fuck around with the rota all the time, so you can go get your ass washed out or whatever old people do at the doctors."

Vince gritted his teeth but spoke no more as he saw on Levi's computer screen that he had indeed made the shift change, and even noted he had done so days earlier. So this was just to aggravate him, he thought. But he let it slide, clinging onto the last shred of positivity that he held.

* * *

"You did hear me Vince?" the doctor asked.

But Vince didn't respond. Once again he had gone into a shutdown state.

"There are still treatments we can try, but it would be more for research purposes than anything else. Given your history, it's probably best for you to start making plans with your family."

That was rich. Family. Four years ago, Vince had been clinging on to his family. Two years ago, the final thread snapped. His wife found him slumped in the car, three empty Jack Daniels bottles on the passenger seat, and packed her things. She was gone within the hour and had filed for divorce by the end of the week. His children had sided with their mother, and now he was alone. Nobody to go home to, and nobody would miss him. As mentioned earlier, the prospect of death often makes people take one of two paths. Fear or acceptance. Vince however, chose a third path. He smiled. However, this was not a smile of acceptance, or even a smile of delusion. Vince smiled because he knew what he was going to do. He was going to greet the Grim Reaper with open arms... and an entourage of deserving people.

* * *

The Number 1 route had always been Vince's favorite. Driving between Weymouth and the Isle of Portland was a beautiful trip. His favorite part had been navigating the causeway between the two, surrounded by open ocean, and stunning views of the cliffs ahead. That was until Levi had decided that Portland didn't need a bus every fifteen minutes and had cut them to one every hour. Now it was the route of the highest misery. "Where the fuck have you been? I'm late for work now you arsehole!"

"I should make you stand out in the pissing rain and see how you like catching pneumonia!"

Those were just the regular complaints. But on the newly savaged Route 1, there were a special few passengers. Vince didn't know their names, but he had nicknames for them all.

Wyke Regis was the hop-on location for the younger rapper wannabe style person whom he nicknamed 50 Pence. The man was clearly in his mid-thirties, always wore a puffed jacket, fake gold chains, and walked like he shat himself. His favorite game when he boarded Vince's bus, was to use as many modern nonsense phrases as possible to confuse him. However, when one day the man had attempted to get onto the bus drunk, and Vince had denied him passage, 50 Pence had spat at him, and knocked his coffee cup onto his lap. Vince filed that away in his mental folder labelled 'asshats.'

Near the start of the causeway heading over Ferry Bridge,

there were an old couple who boarded the bus to go one stop down to the local supermarket. They were at least seventy-five years old and felt the need every time to stand in the middle of the lane when they saw the bus approaching and holding their hands in front gesturing the bus to stop. Vince called them 'The Marples.' They would then proceed to get onto the bus and if it was full, demanded that Vince would remove a passenger or two to enable them to sit down. When Vince had first refused to do such a thing, they had told him to his face that he was only a common servant and as such was there to serve the more fortunate such as themselves. Into the file they went.

Near the bottom of Fortuneswell on the island itself, was the road up to the first of two prisons located on Portland. The main facility, The Verne, had no bus route, and so the officers would walk down the hill to catch the number 1. However, there was one in particular who Vince had labelled 'Mackay.' He was fifty-three years old. Vince knew this because the man had told him in no uncertain terms, that if he was late again in collecting him, despite him being fifty-three years old, he would knock his teeth through the back of his head. Often, his rage combined with his broad Scottish accent would garble the words, but he spoke them that often, that Vince knew them off by heart. That file was getting pretty full.

The final candidate for the folder was picked up in Easton on the island. This one, Vince called 'Barney.' Much like the beloved Simpsons character, he was always drunk, whatever time of day it was. However, Vince had a special place reserved in hell for this one.

Barney had been the one who had started Vince drinking. He had enabled his burgeoning addiction. He knew the responsibility was his and laying the blame elsewhere wouldn't help, but then Barney tipped him over the edge by pissing into his coffee flask while Vince was on break.

Sure enough, his very first run to Portland started in typical frustrating fashion. Standing in the rain at the bus stop near Tesco Express at Wyke Regis, was 50 Pence. Vince, however, smiled. As he pulled up to the stop, he reached into his bag and pulled out a small pile of cards that he had specially prepared the night before. The doors opened and Vince gave a now unusually high greeting, full of joy and enthusiasm.

"Good morning young man!"

"What you call me son?"

"I said good morning!"

"Yo shut the fuck up and gimme my ticket bitch."

50 Pence then proceeded to throw the fare in loose change directly at Vince, but he continued to smile. He then reached down and extracted the first card from the pile.

"Please excuse me, I'm just so excited that I get to offer this prize to people today."

That caught his attention.

"Yo, I won somfink?" he said in incredibly loose English.

"You certainly have! There is a special party bus running between Portland and Weymouth tonight, and I get to give four tickets to people who I think would enjoy it." 50 Pence's mood changed dramatically. His swagger was now including moves Vince didn't know a human could achieve. Now bouncing around in a bow-legged stance, 50 Pence accepted his ticket, and sat down behind the driver's compartment. Smiling from ear to ear, Vince closed the doors and continued.

Despite his desire to continue driving and run down The Marples, Vince decided to stop, and welcome them on board. There was no need to remove passengers for them to sit today, so Vince simply presented them with another card, and a slightly different version of his sales pitch.

"An antiques fair? Oh that sounds splendid! And it's free too!"

That was easier than Vince had thought. Perfect.

It took the third and fourth trips for him to encounter the others, but he performed the same routine as he had on his first trip. He told Mackay that it was a tribute evening for the armed forces and would culminate in a firework display on Weymouth Seafront. Then he told Barney there would be a free bar after the trip. He didn't take much persuading. His fifth and final trip went without incident, and he returned the bus to the depot, and clocked out of his shift. And that's when he saw Levi, marching toward him like a raging bull.

"Resignation?" he yelled, spittle flying out of his mouth and striking Vince across the face. "You selfish prick!" "Levi, I have stage four pancreatic cancer. You really think I want to spend my last few weeks shovelling your shit?"

The manager was caught out by the manner in which Vince delivered this line. He did not yell; he simply spoke the words as if he were reading a line from a leaflet. Cold, with no emotion.

"You have to give two weeks' notice. I could make those two weeks a living nightmare for you."

"I know."

Levi was infuriated with Vince's calm demeanor, veins now popping on his forehead.

"Fuck you, you old cunt. You're fired. Nobody screws with me. Now if you'll excuse me, I've got to prep the Santa bus for tomorrow. Get the fuck out of my depot." The Santa bus? What a marvelous coincidence, thought Vince. As he walked out of the depot main doors, that smile returned to his face.

* * *

Vince figured the budget restrictions had meant Reg, the old security guard had been let go, because as Vince walked up to the depot at seven-forty-five that night, nobody was there to challenge him. There had been no change in his determination to see this plan through. In fact, having spoken with his cancer nurse when he returned home, he was more resolved to carry out this plan. Weeks had become days, and he would be lucky to make Christmas. How ironic, he thought as he stood staring up at the newly decorated Santa bus. Tinsel dripped down every pole, and lights adorned every window. The only light still on in the offices upstairs, were in Levi's office. He saw the back of the manager's head in his window, and a phone in his hand. Good, he hadn't left yet. There weren't even any maintenance people around. Impatient drivers had attempted to park up their buses themselves and Vince could see several scrapes and dents where they had obviously gotten too close. Too easy, he thought.

He saw 50 Pence standing at his usual stop, and as the doors opened up, he practically bounded through the doors.

"Yo, let's get this party goin'!"

Vince giggled as he sat on the back seat and began pulling a garland of red tinsel down from one of the poles and draping it round his neck like a feather boa. Ferry Bridge came into view, and a very neatly dressed Marple couple did their usual trick of waving him down. They were also wearing beaming smiles, but they faded when they saw 50 Pence on the back seat.

"I thought this was to be a refined antiques transportation? To and from the antique fair?" said Mrs. Marple.

"Indeed," was Mr. Marple's only contribution.

Vince nodded and held his hands up for calm.

"Yes of course it is, however there are two events going on this evening. Antiques fair and a party on the sea front. Budget cuts have meant we have to use the same bus for both trips."

They didn't like it, but they sat at the front of the bus, too eager not to pass up a free trip. Vince's smile began to waver, however, as when he closed the doors, he saw not his own reflection, but that of a dark outlined figure looking back at him in the glass. There were no defining features to the figure, simply a silhouette. And then it was gone. Vince shrugged it off, and continued onto the island, where he gave the same story of multiple trips on one transport to both Mackay and Barney, although the latter was too inebriated to care. Again, Vince saw the figure, but this time, it stood directly in front of the bus. Vince didn't feel scared of the figure, however, and felt rather the opposite. It was almost encouraging him somehow. The figure drifted to the side, and Vince swore he saw it gesture him forwards. A blink of an eye, and it was gone.

When Vince was a teenager, he had studied psychology in an effort to try and impress a girl in his class. He hadn't picked up many of the actual details, but something had stuck with him when his teacher had been describing believed tendencies.

"Often in life, there are perceived to be two kinds of people when it comes to anger. There are the explosive, and the implosive. The explosive are the people who will scream and bawl at you for the slightest thing. Too much cheese on a pizza, not enough milk in their coffee. They will remonstrate and get right in your face to make sure you know they're angry with you. Implosive people, suck it up day after day, usually prominent in retail staff on minimum wage. The take the abuse and the punishment and the crap, and eventually shoot everyone in the store, and then themselves."

Vince had wondered which category he would fall into. After seeing this information presented to him during the Jack Nicholson and Adam Sandler movie *Anger Management* in a more entertaining way decades later, he suspected he was the implosive type.

The route Vince had decided to take had begun to confuse the passengers. He had told them that the events were being held on the sea front, but rather than go directly there, Vince had driven towards the beach, and then turned left, driving half a mile in the opposite direction.

"Where are we going?" asked Mackay. "You've gone the wrong way you dozy twat!"

Vince indicated and pulled into the nearby McDonalds car park, before turning around and pulling back onto the main road. He turned and shouted back.

"Apologies! Thought I was doing a different route for minute there!"

Murmuring came from behind him, essentially saying he didn't know what he was doing, and he distinctly heard 50 Pence say he thought they retired old fogies like that. But Vince wasn't concerned. He had of course made the distraction deliberately. He was now lined up with his target destination. The lights ahead of him turned red, and he stopped in turn. Squinting through the windscreen, he could see a shimmering layer still rippling on the depot floor. Good. The engineers hadn't returned to their shift yet. Vince wondered if Levi had even noticed his precious petrol making its way under all of the buses inside the building. Unlikely. He was probably trying to work his way up to area manager by cutting even more funds.

One more check on his 'favorite' passengers wouldn't hurt. And there it was. Sat in a seat on the left hand side of the bus was the black figure. It was now more defined, and Vince could make out a pale face beneath a black pointed hood. It was not entirely the stereotypical vision of death he had seen in comics and movies but was rather close to it. And the wash of warmth and comfort came over him once again. The figure looked at him. Its skin was ice white and cracked like damaged porcelain. The eyes were grey. Entirely grey. A thin slit existed where the mouth would be, and despite this incredible image so out in the open, Vince knew he was the only one who could see it.

"Oi dipshit! The light's green!"

The figure slowly nodded its head, and Vince closed his eyes as he felt the world fall away from him. No more worries. No more stress. He would be at peace.

Vince pressed the accelerator pedal and the bus jerked forward much to the complaints of the passengers. But he didn't slow down. He continued to accelerate until his foot was flat to the floor. The bus wasn't exactly a formula one car, but it hit forty-three miles per hour as it approached the entrance to the depot. It became clear that Vince wasn't going to stop, and Mackay leapt up from his seat and ran forward. But it was too late. Just before the bus struck the petrol pump at the entrance to the depot, Vince looked up to see his boss standing in the window of his office. He looked back and smiled.

"Fuck you, Levi."

The explosion was bigger than even Vince had.

imagined. The second the bus hit the fuel pump and it was wrenched from the floor, fire and power burst forth incinerating the front of the vehicle. The blast threw the vehicle onto its side, the glass caving in upon impact, and the flames quickly spread across the fuel which now covered the floor until it engulfed every bus in the building. Levi's body was now sprawled on the side of Vince's bus, his skin melting into the broken windows having fallen from the destroyed walkways above. Vince had felt nothing, killed instantly, as was Mackay. The Marples, however, were able to scream far longer than one might expect as their eyeballs burst, and their internal organs began to liquify. 50 Pence went up like a firework. His polyester outfit and several cans of hair products accelerated the cooking of his flesh. His earphones had melted into his ears, and he attempted to run around briefly, only succeeding in evacuating his bowels, and slipping on the resulting mess. One by one, the other buses blew, and the roof of the building soon caved in, burying the whole violent scene beneath it.

Outside on the pavement, watching on, stood the dark figure. And beside him, was Vince. Smiling. It only took moments for the sirens to sound and a couple of minutes for the first fire engines to arrive on site. But there was no one left to save. Vince simply nodded, and turned around and began to walk in the direction of his home. As his image faded away, he moved away from the place he had hurt so much, and he did so in the welcoming embrace of death.

David was born in 1988 in Wolverhampton, England. He spent most of his youth growing up in nearby Telford, where he attended the prestigious Thomas Telford School. However, unsure of which direction he wished his life to go in, he left higher education during sixth form, in order to get a job and pay his way. He has spent most of his life since, working in retail.

In 2007, following the death of his grandfather William Henry Griffiths a couple of years earlier, David's family relocated to the North Devon coastal town of Ilfracombe, where he got a job in local greengrocers, Normans Fruit & Veg as a general assistant, and spent 8 happy years there. In 2014, David met Charlotte, and in 2016, relocated to Plymouth to live with her as she continued her University studies.

In 2018, the pair were married, and currently reside on the Isle of Portland, Dorset.

The first published works of David's, was *The Dark Corner*. It was a compilation of short haunting stories which he wrote to help him escape the reality of the Coronavirus pandemic in early-mid 2020. However, it was not until January 2021, that he made the decision to publish.

From there... *The Dark Corner Literary Universe* was spawned....

amazon.com/stores/author/B08VHD911S

tiktok.com/@davidwadams.author

PRELUDE TO VÆRNE

BY N.R. PHOENIX

Themiscyra - Circa 1300 B.C.

Nasiche knelt in supplication on the polished marble of Artemis' temple with her forehead against the cool stone and her arms extended above her head, palms flat to the floor. Her lower back burned; her thighs shook with fatigue. The blood on her legs had long since dried, the skirt of her chiton stiff with the evidence of her loss. Tears pooled under her eyelids and slipped down her warm umber cheeks, bathing the floor with her despair.

Yet she never uttered a sound. The goddess knew her traitorous heart without Nasiche giving voice to her plea.

Columns soared high above, standing as sentries lining the temple—silent, unmoving, uncaring. A statue of Artemis loomed over her, dominating the space, nearly as tall as the columns. Shadows cast by the braziers on either side of her made the once-serene face harsh.

Nasiche felt no warmth from their light. She was alone in her own darkness.

Fervently, silently, she prayed.

She prayed for freedom, for absolution, but most of all, she prayed for forgiveness. Would she have made the same choices if she had known this would be the consequence? Was this punishment?

Tucked under her prostrated body, wrapped in sheepskin, was her failure.

She prayed until her tears dried, until she no longer had the strength to cry. Crawling on her hands and knees to the foot of the statue, she unclasped the clothing pin that held the bundle to her and placed it upon the raised steps with the other offerings. Slowly, she rose with her pain cradled in her arms, leaving the tear tracks where they had dried on her cheeks, her head bowed. She dared not meet the accusation in the statue's eyes.

Backing away from the figure on deadened limbs, she maintained a respectful distance before turning around. The open doorway towered, framed by torches and flanked by two Amazon guards. She was nearly to them, nearly released into the cool night air, when a spasm echoed in her womb and across her back, causing her to falter. The breath whooshed out of Nasiche as she went to one knee; the sheepskin clutched protectively against her milk-laden breasts.

Both guards transferred their spears to their shield hands. They approached in a concerned rush, ready to lend assistance, but this was her burden to bear. She alone had fallen; she alone had dared to...

Nasiche reluctantly relinquished her grasp on the weight she held against her with one arm, holding up her hand. The motion stopped the two warrior women more effectively than an enemy army would.

"Eyes forward, soldiers, lest you forget yourselves," Nasiche gritted out through clenched teeth. A warm rush of crimson splattered across the white marble between her sandaled feet as she stood.

Not yet, she pleaded within her mind as another wave thundered through her. Better to feign strength when her weakness was so obvious.

"Yes, General." Rebuffed, the two Amazons spoke in unison, bowing at the neck, and returning to their stations bracketing the doorway to the temple. All concern drained from their expressions as they rapped the end of their spears on the floor.

Nasiche raised her chin and squared her shoulders, adjusting her punishment in her arms. She did not take in the surrounding vista, the beauty of the trees or the rolling hills.

Night had fallen in the hours she had been prostrate within the temple, but she could see the path by the light of the moon. Fires from the city lit the sparse clouds overhead.

Making her way down the broad steps with deliberate slowness, Nasiche ignored the dull ache in her womb and the pressure bearing down within the depths of her soul. She trudged through the empty streets toward the Thermodon River, her mind rebelling against what she knew she must do. The bundle she carried seemed to become heavier and heavier with each step. Pausing, Nasiche rested under a large tree not far from the river bank, her back against the trunk and the sheepskin in her lap. The view of the river was idyllic, the water swirling along its path oblivious to the torment she endured. Tremors wracked her legs with the exertion. No matter how far she had marched on foot, or how many times she had led battalions into battle, nothing had prepared her for this. There was no help for her now. This was something she must do alone, a journey she must take…alone.

Laying the sheepskin aside, she placed her palm on the small lump and bowed her head, careful not to expose what lay within. She could not face it, not yet. She could not look upon his…

Rolling to her knees, Nasiche began digging between the roots of the tree, her fingernails ripping in the soft, fertile soil. The motion broke the dam she had built around her anguish, allowing it to crash over her and lend momentum to her task. Frenzied, Nasiche pulled the dagger from her belt and used it to dig, her hands scooping the dirt between her spread knees until she had unearthed a hole large enough for her pain. At some point the tears had begun again, the tears she thought had dried—the tears she thought were no more.

Yet, their slick tracks flowed down her cheeks, dripping into the grave she dug.

No funeral for the evidence of her love.

No pyre to take him to the ferryman.

She had no coins to place over his eyes.

Grief constricted in her chest until she could barely breathe around the strangled knot in her throat. Great, ravaging gasps tore through the night as she rocked back onto her heels and stared up at the boughs of the tree. There was nothing she could give, nothing except...

Dropping the dagger, she fisted her long, dark ropes of thinly twisted hair and pulled, ripping them loose from her scalp. She tore at the skin of her cheeks, scratching long furrows down her face, the pain in her flesh echoing the pain in her heart. But it was not enough, not nearly enough, to assuage her. She feared nothing could.

Picking up the dagger, she sawed through her hair until the knee-length twists dropped into the grave. Screams rent from her; pieces of flesh coming away with the hair as she hacked away at it with her knife until she was haphazardly shorn.

Squeezing her dark brown eyes shut, she ran her hands over her shaven head. Her crowning glory was gone, just as her love was. All would know she grieved, even as she knew she shouldn't. Picking up the bundle, she laid it gently upon the bed of hair.

Taking a steadying breath, she opened the sheepskin and gazed at the pale brown cherub face within. The still, breathless, beautiful face of her son. A son she was never supposed to have, let alone mourn. His stillbirth was her punishment for daring to love.

"Please let this be payment enough for the ferryman." The voice she had used to command legions broke, coming out as a strangled sob. "Artemis, huntress, please keep him safe. Guide him true."

She had never begged for any favor or quarter to be given in her life, in her training, but she pleaded then with every fiber of her being. She knew she should not ask, that she should be resigned to this fate... Hadn't this been the will of the gods?

Yet...

She rushed to continue before the words failed her.

"Let him be strong, wise, and kind in your halls. Let him be loved and respected. Let him be a warrior without equal that he should never know fear."

The last word ended in a groan of pain as her womb contracted, spreading the spasm across her lower back and down her legs. She landed heavily on stiff arms, her bare head hanging low between her shoulders as she rode the wave. Another gush of wetness slipped between her thighs, this time with the remainder of the birth sack. Nasiche moaned with relief as the pressure eased; even as the last tie to her son left her body and lay in the dirt between her knees.

Fresh tears leaked under her eyelids as she took shuddering breaths, attempting to calm the heartache constricting her chest. Gathering the bloody mass from beneath her, she tucked it into the bed of hair beside her son. Nasiche raised her soiled and bloodied hands to her face, the moon illuminating the dark stain across her skin. Her hands, that had held countless swords without falter, had struck true with a spear without question, trembled as she smeared the grave dirt and birth blood across her ravaged cheeks.

Wrapping him once more, she pulled her long twisted ropes of hair around his form and began pushing the dirt over his body. The finality tore through her heart anew and steeled her resolve.

Sheathing her dagger, she patted the last bit of soil into place and stood on shaking legs. The moon lit the surface of the river, illuminating the never-ending flow. Nasiche stared out at the expanse, turning her back to the grave. The burden in her heart was her only company now. Wading to her knees, the frigid water swirled around her, washing the birth from her skirt. Nasiche bent, skimming her trembling fingers along the smooth surface. As the evidence of her trial rinsed from her skin, rage and grief bubbled up inside her until she slammed her fists against the shallow water, disturbing the serenity of the scene. Throwing back her shorn head, she screamed out one long shriek, which ended in a war cry.

This story continues in
Værne: The Krijger Chronicles - Book One

NR Phoenix is a dark epic science fantasy and historical romance writer who lives tiny on a sailboat with her husband. She is a lover of every breath, every sigh, every thigh clenching moment of angst, and writes fight scenes with the same fervor. Join her on this journey across time, space, and history!

phoenixreimagined.com/nrphoenix

linktr.ee/nrphoenix

 tiktok.com/@nrphoenixauthor

instagram.com/nrphoenixauthor

facebook.com/nrphoenixauthor

WHILE (NOW < TOMORROW)

BY CHRIS WILLIAMS

Oliver couldn't shake the déjà vu he had yesterday as he prepared the cafe for its first morning customers. It was not the first time he had experienced something that he felt had happened before. He knew that it was not a real psychic phenomenon. It was just something that brains do from time to time. But the reason that he could not get over it was that it *didn't* happen yesterday. So, why was his brain telling him that it did?

A few minutes before four in the afternoon (totally not yesterday), he and a coworker were closing their shift at Mister Bean Cafe in San Francisco. He was wiping down his station while Sarah closed out the till.

"Hey, did you ever get that guy's number that keeps trying to get your attention?" She asked while counting the ones.

"You mean the gentleman who always orders a three shot oat milk, no foam latte, gluten-free vegan butter toast, and room temp triple distilled flat water?"

"Brave enough to take his order yourself, huh?"

Oliver twisted the toe of his shoe into the floor. He had noticed that customer for weeks. At first, he seemed just another Silicon Valley programmer, camped in the cafe to work on his laptop and listen to his phone. Then Oliver and the man started making eye contact. *Something* was there, Oliver knew that. Despite that he could not work up the nerve to introduce himself, so had let other employees take the man's order instead.

But not today.

But it wasn't *just* today.

"We talked about this already. His name is Remy."

That was the entire conversation, slightly different than before, and had replayed in his mind that very morning as he had set up the cafe.

* * *

It was early. The fog wasn't ready to leave the crisp air. A bundle of Chronicle newspapers slumped against the glass panel doors.

CRISIS AVERTED

That was a front page title over a photo of an array of satellites that flew in orbit over the planet. Their ridiculous design was made worse by a tacky logo of the space corporation, *Nikola*.

A crisis had been averted.

A global deadline that, until a few months ago, the world didn't think they'd make.

All thanks to 'Project Hope'.

The Project was the brain-child of the billionaire tycoon CEO of *Nikola*, Leon Cazzo. He had built a fleet of satellites stuffed with the latest in quantum emitters to stabilize the planet.

The text beneath the photo read; *QUESTIONS RAISED ON SUDDEN GLOBAL CONCERNS. Some scientists urge a deeper look at the data, pointing to Cazzo crying wolf. Page 40.*

Oliver grabbed the newspaper bundle by the string, unlocked the door, and went inside.

* * *

It was eight-thirty when the man came in. Pale with big ears and an embarrassingly cute smirk that appeared when he spotted Oliver.

Oliver did his best to keep it cool and professional.

Before the man could set down his messenger bag, unwrap his green scarf, and hang his dark blue wool coat on the back of his usual chair, Oliver was already making his way over. Holding a waiter pad and pencil in his hand, he counted down from ten to steady his nerves. Finally he built up the nerve to introduce himself.

"Good morning. I'm Oliver," he said as the man opened his laptop.

The man smiled. It was a knowing smile. The kind of smile a friend makes when they're going to hear the retelling of a joke. "Morning to you too," he said. "I'm Remy."

"I knew that."

"You did?" Remy said, raising an eyebrow. "That's different."

He did know that.

He told Sarah he did.

Wait... That's not right.

Sarah hasn't even come on shift yet.

Panic set in.

Remy was looking at him, waiting for a response.

How would he have known his name?

The man pays with cash.

He's referred to by the other employees as only Table 4.

"You look like a Remy," Oliver said. "I mean. It suits you well."

"Ah. So..."

"Sorry! Yes, let me take your order. You're a triple shot oat milk, no foam latte, gluten-free vegan butter toast, and room temp triple distilled flat water, correct?" Oliver pretended to write on his pad as he spoke.

Remy rested his elbow on the table and tucked a hand under his chin. "That's what I love about this place. It's the same every day. But there's always something a little different. It's good to finally meet you."

Oliver could feel the blood rush to his cheeks. Eager to change the subject, he noticed the wristband on Remy's arm had the distinct Nikola logo on it.

"Oh, you must be a fan of all the satellites, huh?" Oliver asked in a light tone. "You're not a Cazzo-head are you?"

Remy sighed as he sat up straight then turned his laptop around for Oliver to see. "I just work for him."

On the laptop screen was a program tracking satellite positions in one window, and a bunch of code and numbers in the other.

"Oh wow! So, you're responsible for literally saving the world. Project Hope?"

"Hope springs eternal. I'm just one of hundreds of developers on this project." Remy pinched his thumb and finger together up to Oliver. "I wrote maybe this much."

"And you do that here? You saved the world from our little shop?"

"Everyday. Feels like forever."

Oliver tucked the waiter pad into his apron. "I should leave you to it then and get you your usual?" Oliver took Remy's smile as a 'yes' and returned to the counter.

After finishing his coffee, toast, and water, Remy put his laptop into his messenger bag and donned his jacket and scarf. Before leaving the shop, he and Oliver exchanged smiling glances.

"Have a good one." Oliver said.

"See you tomorrow, Oliver." Remy said, then paused before following with "Nice to meet you."

Oliver fought the instinct to look down and waved instead.

When the door closed, Oliver suddenly felt a surge of inspiration and courage. Stepping out from behind the counter he quickly followed Remy outside.

"Oh, hey!" Oliver called out as he leaned out the cafe door.

Surprised, Remy turned to him.

"So, this is last minute and all. But a bunch of my friends are going to the movies on Friday. *The Day The Earth Stood Still* is playing," Oliver said nervously. "There's a bunch of those end-of-the-world movies playing at Castro Theatre to take the piss out of recent events and all. It's all super casual and fun. And..." Oliver quickly stopped, realizing he had just made everything awkward. He stared at the man feeling dread. He just asked out a customer and now it's going to be weird because of what he said. Remy's was going to stop coming in because of this.

Remy smiled, blushing, "I, uh, didn't expect that. That would've been nice. I mean, that *would* be nice."

* * *

A few minutes before four in the afternoon, Oliver and his co-worker were ending their shift. He was wiping down his station while Sarah closed out the till.

"Hey, did you ever get that guy's number that keeps trying to get your attention?" She asked, while counting the ones.

"You mean the gentleman who always orders a three shot oat milk, no foam latte, gluten-free vegan butter toast, and room temp triple distilled flat water?"

"You took his order this time, huh?"

"I asked him out."

"You did *not* ask out a customer," Sarah gasped. "What's his name?"

"Remy. Girl, we already did this. We had a whole conversation about it. Multiple, in fact."

Sarah rolled her eyes. "You've been playing the scenario of you and that man in your mind for so long, you've given yourself déjà vu. Just like my mom. She texted me a couple minutes ago not to forget cat food again. She never told me that. You too should talk."

She pulled out her phone to show him. Oliver leaned over to look, but he didn't see it. Just a couple of kitten photos and heart emojis.

The time was four o'clock.

* * *

A bundle of Chronicle newspapers slumped against the glass panel doors.

CRISIS AVERTED

That was a front page title over a photo of an array of satellites that flew in orbit over the planet.

The text beneath the photo read; *ANTI-SATTER'S MAKE BOLD CLAIM OF MIND CONTROL. New theories of mind control after viral TikTok videos. Page 20.*

Oliver grabbed the newspaper bundle by the string, unlocked the door, and went inside.

* * *

It was eight-thirty when the man came in.

Oliver noticed he did not make any eye contact; or take off

his coat, just his scarf. He hurried to his usual table, opened his laptop, and began typing.

Oliver thought about introducing himself, but the man didn't seem like he was in the mood for company. Still, he had to take the man's order, even if it was the same thing every time. He grabbed a waiter pad and pencil and made his way over.

"Good morning. Can I take your order?" Oliver did his best to sound calm and not at all nervous.

The man didn't look up from his keyboard as he typed. "I'm sorry, Oliver, can I just get my usual?"

"Oh. Ya, sure!" Oliver said as he wrote '3x oat no foam. gf veg toast, water' on his pad. He then paused. "Wait, how did you know my name is Oliver?"

The man closed his eyes as he stopped typing. He looked up at Oliver with a smile. "I'm embarrassed to admit it, but I, uh, asked one of the other servers." He held out his hand. "I'm Remy."

Oliver blushed, as he shook the man's hand. It was warm and soft, but firm. He noticed the Nikola-branded wristband. He wanted to ask about it but could tell Remy was working hard and probably needed time to focus. "Nice to meet you, Remy. I'll get that order out for you."

After finishing his coffee, toast, and water, Remy put his laptop in his messenger bag and hurried out of the shop. Oliver went to clear the table and found Remy's scarf was left, forgotten.

Oliver spotted Remy across the street, opening a cab's back door.

"Hey!" Oliver called out with a smile, waving the man's scarf in the air as he began crossing the street.

Remy looked over, as terror suddenly struck his face. "Stop!" he screamed.

Oliver barely saw the blur of the car as it hit him.

* * *

A few minutes before four in the afternoon, Oliver was staring at the hospital ceiling. His sister had come down to sit with him, all the while talking on his mobile phone letting their mom and dad know what had happened. She explained that Oliver was staying overnight for observation, after a mild concussion and fractured ankle.

"Thank god you're still on their medical plan." She said as she hung up the call and handed the phone back to Oliver. "I told them you would let them know when you got out."

Oliver looked down at his phone, the screen had suffered a crack in the accident, yet it still worked.

"Damn," he said as a wave of realization hit him. "I have to make sure Sarah can close the shop." He quickly unlocked the phone to message his co-worker.

* * *

"Why are you texting me? I'm right here." Sarah said as she stood at the till in the cafe, counting out the ones.

Oliver stared down at his phone in confusion. "I swear my phone had a crack in it."

The phone read four o'clock.

* * *

A bundle of Chronicle newspapers slumped against the glass panel doors.

CRISIS AVERTED

That was a front page title over a photo of an array of satellites that flew in orbit over the planet.

The text beneath the photo read; *THE RISE OF THE MONDAYS; New anti-satellite group invades internet with false memories, blames Nikola tech. Page 10.*

Curiously, Oliver pulled a copy from the bundle, unlocked the door, then went inside.

Sat inside the kitchen, Oliver read the paper. Page 10 read like a story about an epidemic; A group of citizens in India called *The Mondays* believed they were being fed false memories by the Nikola satellites orbiting Earth. They had taken to Reddit to share their stories. *r/nikoladoomedus* was now the most popular subreddit on the site, and *The Mondays* were trending on all other social media platforms.

A quiet doom quickly settled in Oliver's gut.

He pulled out his phone.

It took him a second to realize that, no, in fact, the screen *wasn't* cracked as he thought.

He remembered being in the hospital but couldn't remember why. His sister was on his phone, and he remembered his leg being in such pain. It felt so real. He had never dreamed so much pain before.

The cafe's door then opened with a chime.

Oliver quietly cursed to himself for not locking it, as he came out from the kitchen, "I'm sorry, we don't open until—"

It was that man.

The guy he had been hoping to introduce himself to for days. But instead of his usual dapper self, the man looked tired, disheveled, and panicked.

"Oh hey!" Oliver corrected himself. "I know you. You can sit down. Nothing's ready though, but I can get you a coffee."

The man nodded slowly and made his way to his usual table.

Oliver returned with two filled cups. "We keep the machine on a timer," he said as he sat opposite the man. "I'm Oliver, by the way."

The man didn't reply as he stared back as if waiting for something.

That's when Oliver's eyes widened as he remembered. "Oh, wait. I *do* know you. Not like just a random customer. I actually know you."

The man slightly smiled.

"This is embarrassing."

The man put his hand on Oliver's. "I'm Remy."

"Yeah, you work for Leon Cazzo." Oliver smiled, took a sip from his cup then and set it down. His other hand was still occupied with Remy's. "Now what brings you here so early?"

"I wanted to get to know you," Remy said, not taking his eyes off of Oliver.

Oliver paused. All this time, never holding a single conversation with this man. And now, as he has to prep the cafe, open the till, set out the pastries... this man, Remy, wants to talk?

Oliver talked about growing up in Oakland with his family. About how he picked up the guitar wanting to be in a band, but only ever learned the songs of others. How he moved to San Francisco with a guy, but that didn't pan out. How he had managed the cafe for a couple of years. Then about when he learned the world was ending.

"I thought about all the things I didn't get to do, like travel, get a tattoo, live abroad, finish college. I should have been regretful, or bitter, like so many others in their final days, but I wasn't. I had friends, a job, and somehow still afforded to live in my favorite city. I was happy. Then it all changed again, and we were all in the clear. 'Crisis averted.'"

"Crisis averted," Remy repeated.

"But now. Now I'm not so sure." Oliver said as he thought back to the newspaper article he had just read. "Did you read about that Monday group? False memories being something to do with the satellites and all that?"

Remy pulled out his laptop and turned it to Oliver. The screen opened to a bunch of windows shedding indecipherable data. "It's been going on for the last six days, and it's getting worse. Much worse."

"What's worse?" Oliver asked. "Six days?"

"I wanted to visit you at the hospital, you know?"

"What? How did you... I wasn't at the hospital." Oliver said as he rubbed at the pressure in his temples. "Wait, I *was*. But I don't remember why. Was it yesterday? No. Sunday, then I went home."

"A car hit you last month," Remy said in a measured tone. "Do you remember sitting with me at a park?"

Oliver just blinked in confusion.

"You convinced your coworker to cover the store?"

"Golden Gate." Tears soon welled up in Oliver's eyes as his memories flooded back. "We watched a dog chase a frisbee. I remember that." he smiled before looking concerned. "But there's nothing before it. What's wrong with me?"

"There's nothing wrong with you," Remy explained. "It's me. Or I should say my programming. My team is in charge of the precise timing mechanics based on Earth's rotation. It's supposed to be timed with the global reset, and that's handled by another team under Cazzo. They execute all operations every twenty-four hours at midnight UTC. When that happens... the world resets. That way tomorrow can never happen. The day starts over, all things are reset. Even memories."

Remy tapped at the band on his wrist. "This keeps me and the other devs out of the loop."

Oliver's expression reflected his confusion.

"At first," Remy continued. "I thought your proximity to me might have had an effect. But when so many people began to share their memories, it became... a problem. We call those, rollover minutes."

"Rollover?" was all Oliver could say as he felt a headache coming on.

"The period between the exact rotation of the planet and actual midnight is only a few minutes. Twenty-three hours, fifty-six minutes and four seconds and some change is a messy number. Cazzo doesn't like messy numbers and made the call for midnight UTC."

Oliver's headache was quickly in full force. "This is all a software bug?"

Remy shrugged.

"What would happen if I died?" Oliver said as his mind whirled. "Would I remember that? Does Leon even know?"

Remy shook his head. "No. He's in the loop, just like you. I have to stay outside and keep the satellites running."

"How long have we been in this?"

"Three months." Remy motioned to his laptop. "I've written a patch to correct the timings. Once it's uploaded, no more rollover minutes."

Remy watched silently as Oliver stood up and walked into the kitchen, soon returning with painkillers in hand. Neither of them spoke a word as Oliver downed some pills with his coffee, then stepped behind the counter, pulled cash out from the safe, and started counting the bills.

Oliver was the first to say anything. "How many times have we had this conversation?"

"You're upset, I get it."

"We must have talked a lot," Oliver said sadly. "It makes sense. The way you look at me, how you talk to me. I've just met you. At least that's what I think. But you've spent all this time with me. Remembering each one." He opened the cash drawer, put the bills inside, then closed it, before looking up at Remy, "What's the fucking point of this? Why do I bother even being at work? Everything resets anyway. I should just get blackout drunk and stay that way."

"I'm sorry," Remy said as he returned his laptop to his mag and put it over his shoulder. "I should go."

"Do we even age?" Oliver asked.

Remy shook his head. "You don't. But I do and the other devs do. Everyone else... stays the same."

"And how many people are gonna die today?"

"I, uh, don't know."

"Old age, disease, violence, wars, every day they die. Do they come back at the reset and die again?"

"Yeah," Remy slowly nodded.

"And how many people are born? They'll never grow. They'll never experience life, because your boss tricked the world so he can fuck off on a yacht for eternity."

"I didn't make this choice," Remy said. "It's just my job,"

Oliver let out a laugh. "Why do I care? I'm sure tomorrow, the next day, I'll be fine again. I won't remember any of this. Just in time for you to convince me to take the day off for a date at the park. But I guess I won't remember that either. Until I get flashes and get all confused, thinking I'm going mad."

"What would you have me do? If I do nothing, if this patch doesn't go through, the rollover minutes will get worse. People are losing their minds as is, can you imagine how it *could* get? I *have* to fix this."

"This isn't living, Remy," Oliver almost shouted. "Trapping people to an endless existence on repeat, well, I think that's a worse end of the world than it just stopping."

"I'm sorry." Remy adjusted his coat and made for the door.

* * *

A bundle of Chronicle newspapers slumped against the glass panel doors.

CAZZO DIED IN PLANE CRASH

A large photo filled most of the page below the headline, of somewhere in Arizona; the site where the plane went down. The bold paragraph read; *Leon Cazzo's private jet suffered a mechanical error while en route to California to see to the satellite outage.*

A smaller story at the bottom of the page read *"WAS THE SKY REALLY FALLING? DoJ opens a probe into the Nikola quantum prediction model and the global crisis that never occurred.*

It was Tuesday.

Oliver's phone buzzed with a message

> 350k babies were born yesterday.

> It's Remy BTW.

Of course, the man had Oliver's number.

What did you do? Did you do the patch?

Yes

...

Oliver waited a while for the next message to arrive.

Tiny bug was added. Sats are in a loop. Jobs never ran, memory leak, just space debris now. I might be in trouble lmao.

Oliver didn't understand much of what he read, so just typed a brave reply that he no longer felt any nerves about.

Why don't you tell me about it over a coffee?

Oliver the put the phone in his pocket, grabbed the newspaper bundle by the string, unlocked the door, then went inside to start the new day.

Chris Williams is a horror thriller author. His works include Antibody and Gold Rush.

He lives in Texas with his husband and their pack of rescue dogs.

chriswilliamsbooks.com

SOULS ADRIFT AT THE WORLD'S END

BY M.K. DOCKERY

A creeping numbness gripped his knees causing them to ache. They had been robbed of sensation by endless hours of stillness.

In this place, silence had long held dominion. Now, it had become a desolate void.

The four pillars encircling him, architectural, and strategically positioned, had once been the symbolic bedrock of ancient churches. They now stood as a symbol and a somber reminder of humanities audacious quest to touch the divine.

Through most his life he held unwavering faith in the attainability of such ideals that the church espoused. Now, in such days, it was all too easy to have long unshakable foundations crumble and wander like a lost soul.

Clad in black, his collar askew, he gazed up at the flickering flame, a symbol of God's presence within the lofty tabernacle alcove. His purpose for remaining was unclear, yet, his head remained reverently upturned with hope or bent with prayer.

Though the presence of that holy flame, which burned as resolutely as the expanding sun, almost mocking now as it hung over him, still he remained at his post. This was his appointed station and covenant in life.

He couldn't help but be struck by the hollow absence of sound that surrounded the space he occupied. In this church, silence reigned, yet this void was unlike any before. The peace was a gentle hum, while this was oppressively absent even that. The sacred walls felt bereft of their usual warmth and regular rustling. There was always solace to be found, a moment of comfort amidst the liturgy and Eucharist's rhythmic rituals. But after the announcement of the coming event that would end all god's creatures and creations the faithful attendance dwindled, and now... there was no one but the priest.

Midday cast a relentless glare upon the desolation, and the notion of surrender flickered in his weary mind. Hunger and thirst were nothing but earthly discomforts, ones that would soon be over. Even his regular devotions and attempts at penance couldn't alter the relentless orange hue of the burning sun seeping through the stained glass.

Then, in the midst of his stagnant vigil, a faint sound reached the weary priest's ears. It was the soft creak of the vestibule door. He spun around with effort, his back cracked audibly in protest from the hours of rigid stillness.

A man emerged from the shadows, his gaze silently locking onto his. The man was unfamiliar, a stranger to this parish, and yet he moved with the quiet determination of someone who knew his way around. He approached the water font, dipping his three fingers into its still depths before making the sign of the cross, a gesture familiar to the Orthodox, executing the movement from right to left.

The way the man rubbed his wet fingers together set the priest on edge, an unsettling feeling he couldn't quite put into words if he were to feel the need to speak.

As the newcomer completed his genuflection, the stranger found his place halfway down the aisle, his head bowed as if deep in prayer.

The priest wasn't immune to humanities desire for simple human connection, even he longed for basic companionship.

The priest had questions which he resisted the urge to ask, choosing instead to redirect his focus to the warm embrace of the sanctuary lamp, seeking in its flickering flame the same comfort that the mysterious soul behind him must also yearn for. With a heavy sigh, he offered thanks to the almighty for the presence of someone with him at the very end. Of that he could give thanks for.

He found that even with the stranger's quiet company, the unsettling silence only intensified, growing more uncomfortable with each passing minute. The skyline's glow deepened to a furious red that cast eerie shadows within the church. Though he was no longer alone, the past isolation was still haunting him.

The vestibule door swung open once again, this time it was with a resounding crash. As the priest turned again, his eyes met a striking sight—a woman clad in a short, iridescent silver slip of a thing. The tight fabric shimmered with its neon hues; her entrance and attire was anything but muted.

"Oops, my bad," she slurred, her platform heels echoed clumsily as she stumbled around the water font, entirely disregarding the tradition of dipping her fingers in to make the sign of the cross. "It's my first time," she admitted, her voice quivered with a hint of nervous laughter. Her eyes, however, told a different story, their puffiness betrayed recent tears she had shed, the make-up was smeared unevenly across her face.

In response to this most recent newcomer's presence, the priest attempts to stand proved difficult, as his legs had gone entirely numb all the way up to his hips. They barely registered the neurological commands; the blood having ceased its flow to those extremities hours before. His gaze darted toward the earlier visitor who so far hadn't acknowledged the woman's presence. The man remained with his head down, engrossed in his own world, unfazed by the new stranger in their midst.

"I expected this place to be packed," she slurred, her steps were unsteady. The priest noticed a bottle of whiskey was clutched in her hand and was likely the cause of her wobbly gait. "I thought there would at least be music. I was looking for music. The radios and power have all gone out."

The priest struggled to find words, but eventually managed to find a few. "There hasn't been a choir here in days."

The woman shrugged her thin shoulders, her neck rolling as she scanned the almost entirely empty church. "Lame," she drunkenly replied, before bringing the bottle to her lips and took a sip. Then she noticed the other stranger. The presence of the silent man seemed to pique her curiosity. "It's a little less creepy with company, I guess. No offense, father," she scoffed, her words ran together. "Or is it Reverend? Pastor?"

The priest raised his hand in a placating gesture. "I am Father Timons," he introduced himself, but the silence was like shadows, and they threatened to creep forward once again.

A slight misstep, a trip on her heel became almost symbolic as it triggered her to bend down and discard them. The weighty sigh she exhaled as she stepped over the cast offs was a clear farewell to a persona that no longer served her. "Mine is Celest," she stated flatly.

"How may I assist you?" Father Timons inquired as his brought his attention back to her and away from her strappy heels.

"Assist me?" She leaned on the edge of one of the pews, her eyes looked around. "Can you give me hope? I'm going to wake up from this, and be late for work, right?"

Father Timons opened his mouth to reply when Celeste continued, her voice echoing through the stone and stained glass. "I've probably mixed some meds and am lost in this crazy dream where it's the end of the world, and it just can't be. That's got to be it, right?"

Her deranged laughter sent shivers down the priest's

spine, more unsettling than the eerie silence that had pervaded the place moments before.

She shifted her focus to the man who had entered ahead of her. "Hey, big boy, what are you here for?" Her question hung in the air, and Father Timons noticed the man's contemplative gaze lift. The priest could sense the internal struggle within the man and wondered whether the stranger would choose to ignore her question or respond.

The priest could not deny that he was eager to learn more about these newcomers, but before that could happen the door swung open once more. This time a youth entered, appearing to be scarcely older than a teenager. Father Timons couldn't help but wonder where the young man's family was. No one of this youths age should face these dire circumstances alone.

"What can I do for you, young man?" Father Timons inquired. His gaze briefly fixated on the blood that spattered and marred the boy's shirt.

"What should I do?" The boy's trembling hand hovered above the water font, stained red with what appeared to be fresh blood. Father Timons noticed out of the periphery that the first man who entered flared his nostrils, and his expression took on a look as if he something pained him.

"The water?" Father Timons replied, demonstrating the process by dipping his own fingers and then gesturing to make the sign of the cross. Unspoken, blasphemous thoughts swirled within his mind as to the source of the blood on the boy's hands, but he tried to focus on helping him through the ritual.

The youth's hand trembled as it hovered in mid-air above the font. It shook, and at the last second he pulled his hand back and anxiously dragged it across the fabric of his once-white shirt, leaving a smear of faded red that spoke of horrors untold. His movements were clumsy, as if he desired to be clean before he dipped his fingers into the blessed waters.

Eventually he brought his hesitant hand to the bowl and dipped his fingers in and swirled them around a little before bringing them to his head, heart, then across his body in the motion shown to him.

"That right?" His voice was a sad whisper in the quiet sanctum, a faint inquiry of hope amid the overwhelming gloom.

Father Timons drew a deep breath as he grappled with the weight of his own doubts and fears. In this moment, as the world teetered on the brink of oblivion, his own thoughts clouded his reply. Did the sanctity of these rituals hold any power besides what they symbolized? To him, they seemed useless now, but to these lost souls who had found their refuge with him they must still be seen as tangible tools and so he didn't have the heart to leave behind the pretense.

Unable to reply, he simply gestured for the young man to come forward. Observing the sheen of perspiration on the youth's forehead, he offered him a seat. "Come, you look tired, sit," he suggested. "My benches are not particularly comfortable, but you can rest your legs."

The woman, her steps still uncertain followed suit. She collapsed onto the unforgiving wood with a heavy sigh. When she spoke again it was with a message soaked with drunken cynicism. "So, what's there to do now, besides wait for it to all burn up?"

Father Timons cast a weary glance around his church. "Before any of you arrived, I was at prayer," he confessed. The words tasted hollow in his mouth.

"Praying?" Celeste scoffed, disbelief coloring her tone as she tapped her foot against the cold stone. "On this stone? Bet that hurt." Her judgmental statement echoed off the walls. "I have spent a good amount of time on my knees, and I can tell you this, I am not about to be found on them right now," she declared. With a rebellious tilt of her head, she took a deep pull from her bottle, as if to drown the bitter taste of her words. "Not a chance," she muttered.

Between her flippant ramblings and the suggestive clothing she wore, Father Timons found himself inadvertently piecing together her story paired with the fragments she offered from her base innuendo. A crawling sense of guilt shadowed his thoughts as he realized he was teetering on the brink of judgment. She had come to his church for sanctuary, seeking solace or perhaps redemption. And who was he to judge her? He was only a mere custodian of faith in a world crumbling and struggling under the weight of personal despair.

The youth positioned himself just behind her. The woman extended the bottle towards him—like a makeshift olive branch. Father Timons initially felt an impulse to interject, to uphold the vestiges of decorum and rules that had governed their world. Yet, he restrained himself, understanding that in the twilight of humanity, the rigid frameworks that once defined sin and sanctity had blurred beyond recognition now that they were nearly upon the final moment. What did any rules matter at this point?

Celeste's next question was direct and unfiltered. "Why are you all bloody?"

The youth's eyes dropped to the crimson stains marring his shirt and legs of his pants. His gaze seemed strangely dazed. "Oh, I didn't think to change. I just left the house," he murmured, his voice was a whisper that held little emotion.

Father Timons felt an awkward sense of silence return and didn't know what to say. He almost went to turn back to his prayers, yet Celeste's voice tethered him to the moment.

"So what you do, fight some rough people off?" she probed, curious as to the young man's state.

His response came as a quiet confession. "We were all going out together. All of us were supposed to be gone now, but I couldn't." The air around them seemed to thicken with the meaning behind his words. Many were ending this day by their own hand.

Father Timons couldn't harbor judgment against those who choose their own terms of departure. It was for their own conscience to act in this world that was cascading towards oblivion. He knew that families would forge their own paths from his place of sermons. It had been with sadness that he noted the hopeless eyes and swelling bellies in his congregation, that babies would cry their first in the bright orange glow of the apocalypse, underscoring the futility of resistance against the unstoppable end that was to come. In that dire thought, he recognized the tragedy of existence, the persistent spirit of life, birthing amidst anarchy, entirely oblivious to the cataclysm that raced towards them. It was a strange conjunction of creation and destruction, a sad clash of beginnings and endings. Seeing the youth before him now reminded him of that bleak thought once again.

Celeste reclaimed the whiskey, her face contorting in a grimace. "Heavy. Now you are alone?" Her question, a mirror that reflected the isolation of each of their circumstances.

The young man's nod was barely perceptible, but they all noted the drop in his shoulders.

Father Timons refused to abandon his vocation entirely and allow the shadows of despair to envelop his last and final flock. "We are not alone now. We are here, together, in "his house" on the day of judgment." His voice carried a conviction that he was uncertain of, a mere flicker of faith amid the encroaching doom.

Celeste offered a snort, the armor of the cynical against the vulnerability of hope. Yet, she offered no counterargument. Instead, their attention collectively shifted to the silent figure among them, a presence who had yet to lend their voice to their shared ordeal. The man's demeanor was a mystery, his posture remained stiff, betraying neither interest in the others conversation nor concern for their collective eyes upon him. His head was trained forward, unnaturally steady.

"So, what's your story?" Celeste probed in her direct manner. Still, the man appeared impervious to her inquiry.

Before the tension could escalate, the unmistakable roar of jake breaks from a semi-truck, followed by the sound of compressed air from newly stationary heavy machinery shattered the strange silence. All heads, save for the man they had been questioning, snapped in the direction of the vestibule doors, anticipation and apprehension mingled in the air.

Moments later, both sanctuary door's swung open to reveal a new arrival. Wearing a plaid shirt and suspenders, his bulk filled the doorway, startling to those who looked.

"Guess I made it?" he declared. His voice cut through the uncertainty. "Highway was all choked up. Had to make my own way here, off road part the way."

Caught off guard by the newcomer's statement, Father Timons instinctively spread his hands in a gesture of welcome. "Yes, I suppose you did make it. We were just getting to know one another," he said, nodding towards the others seated on either side of the aisle.

The truck driver maneuvered his bulk across the threshold, sidestepping the baptismal font as if it were an obstacle rather than a usual stop in the procession of the faithful. "I came for confession, father," he stated simply.

The priest looked him over and observed him for a moment, the weight of the man's request settling between them. "And when was your last confession?" he finally inquired, adhering to the ritual despite the unconventional nature of their assembly.

The truck driver's response was a mixture of humility and stark honesty. "Never been to confession. Hardly been in a church since I was a kid." His admission was almost impatient.

Father Timons went against habit and gently dismissed the formalities of the sacrament. "Come, sit with us. I am not taking formal confession anymore, but I am pleased to welcome you into our Father's house," he offered in favor of human connection rather than the expected ritual used in the vain attempt to attain redemption. He felt less than qualified now to assist anyone towards god's grace.

Celeste turned with an inviting smile. "You can come sit by me, honey." With a playful flourish, she waved her bottle to the newcomer in an act of hospitality, highlighted by the glare of the relentlessly burning light that streamed in through the windows. "I have party favors."

The truck driver's response was a bitter confession, lowly muttered in the face of temptation. "Perfect, two of my weaknesses, under one roof," he whispered, a hint of rueful amusement in his voice. He wiped his mouth, his gaze holding a wild, untamed glint.

The truck driver found a seat directly in front of Celeste in the pew. His smile, unsettling in its intensity as he accepted the bottle with a nod. With a sigh, he quipped, "So much for AA." The liquid burned down his throat. "So what is this? Group therapy at world's end?" His words, filled with dark humor, echoed the collective resignation to their fate, a motley crew seeking solace not in salvation while the shadows shortened around them as the sun's rays burned brighter.

Father Timons was initially at a loss for words. The truck driver's sarcastic question had cut through their tense solemn gathering, yet in the silence that had followed, he could recognize the reality within the joke. This impromptu congregation, gathered not by faith but fate, could offer little beyond the comfort found in their shared humanity. In the absence of divine intervention, their collective resilience and companionship could become their sanctuary, a makeshift therapy for souls adrift at the world's end. Perhaps, he mused, in the face of ultimate doom, this was the most sacred offering they could extend to one another—a moment of connection amidst the chaos.

"My parents wanted me to go to therapy," the youth murmured, his voice was tinted with the bitter residue of a life interrupted, "That was before."

Celeste's response was immediate as she reclaimed the bottle from the driver, whose thirst had seemingly deepened their communal well of despair. "What? Was that before they realized we were all fucked?" Her tone wasn't padded with compassion but instead was filled with bitter humor as she leaned over the back of the pew, diminishing the physical distance. "Bet they were worried about themselves and forgot all about you." She reached over and handed him the whiskey again. "That what happened?"

He accepted the bottle. His reach was filled with reluctant resignation. "Yeah," he conceded.

Feeling a latent pull towards pastoral care, Father Timons stepped forward with intention softened by compassion. "What's your name, son?" he asked.

The young man flinched slightly at the question, as if sharing his name made the situation all the more real. With the bottle pressed to his lips, he offered his identity before he took a swig, "Taz. My name is Taz."

Reclaiming the bottle with a chuckle that seemed incompatible with the grim atmosphere, "Taz... That a nickname? Like Tasmanian Devil?" Celeste's laughter rang though the space, now a strangely rare sound since the beginning of the end.

Taz's gaze remained fixed on the ground, lost in either memories or thoughts. His silence stretched out leaving a gap.

Feeling uncomfortable, Celeste shifted the conversation. "So, what are we gonna do for the time we got left?" Her question cut through the heavy moment that had settled over them. "Play truth or dare?"

The trucker snatched the bottle from her grasp. Raising it, he declared, "I came for confession, so truth is fine with me. Dare is all I have done my whole life. I rather forgo that part if you don't mind."

Taz extended his hand this time, reaching out his wrist rested on the pew as if to anchor himself. "If I drink enough of that I won't care that this is all happening, right?" His words were almost a plea as they blurted from his mouth.

Before Father Timons could offer any words of either caution or comfort, the woman seized the bottle once more from the trucker. Celeste was about to take a deliberate swig herself while Taz's hand remained outstretched for the drink but answered first. "That's my goal," she stated, her reply was laced with defiant acceptance.

Flashing her drunken gaze towards Father Timons, she posed her question with a provocative edge, quirking her brow in challenge. "Alright, truth... priest," she said. With deliberate movement, she let her shoulder strap slip, an insinuation silently communicated wordlessly. "How do you wish to spend your last hour?" She leaned forward. "Do you have anything you want to do?" The implication could not be misunderstood. A daring temptation into the realms of sin long suppressed within the vocation of a man of the cloth.

Father Timons turned his head, his gaze once again fell on the sanctuary lamp and the symbol it had long represented. It flickered gently within the alcove above them, a silent witness to the end of all things they knew. Strangely bolstered he found his voice. "I have no use for earthly needs any longer," his voice was filled with calm strength. "I had debated the need for food or drink, but all I took was water. I will fast up until my last breath from food or any other pleasures."

Snorting with disbelief, Celeste pressed Father Timons for a truth unshackled by the constraints of his vows. "Yeah, but what do you want to do?" she asked, probing deeper as if she believed he was lying. "Tell me what you want if you were not afraid of hell."

Her question was a dare for him to strip away the layers of his faith and confront the primal desires and forget years of devotion and discipline, yet it held no temptation for him.

His response was heavy. "I no longer hold faith that there is a hell when this is how the world will end," he replied, his words echoed the profound shift that had evolved within him. The admission felt naked and unvarnished, but it was honest. It was what she wished from him.

Father Timons sought to change the focus. "And you? What about you...?"

The trucker exhaled deeply. His unease was apparent as the focus of the group noticeably shifted on him. His eyes darted around the room, as if he sought refuge in any corner that might offer escape from the sudden spotlight. "I guess I did come for confession."

Celeste, her interest piqued, leaned forward with anticipation gleaming in her eyes. "Ooh, I bet this is going to be good," her tone was laced with an edge of morbid excitement.

With another sigh, he scratched the back of his head. "You like true crime?" he asked, his query directed at the small audience before him. His gaze was reluctant, yet he sought some measure of understanding.

The atmosphere grew dense in light of the trucker's opening. Celeste found her casual curiosity begin to morph into apprehension. "Yeah, sure. I enjoy a good crime story," she replied.

With a heavy sigh, the trucker began the confession of his truth, "Well, I am one of the bad guys who was never found." The simplicity of his admission hung in the air.

What the trucker said was unanticipated and had managed to pierce even the apathy of the man who had thus far seemed disinterested in the eclectic assembly. His reaction was subtle, almost imperceptible. A mere turn of the head, a silent acknowledgment of the trucker's ominous words.

No one replied as fear of the trucker filled their hearts. Breaking the suffocating silence that had enveloped the room, the man who sat across the aisle finally lent his voice to the conversation, his Eastern European accent adding an unexpected depth. "I am intrigued," he declared. "You have already distracted me from my prayers, so, do go on. But first, who are you?"

The trucker was faced with the task of elaborating. Closing his eyes as if to shield himself from the weight of his own words, he began, "Nat. The name is Nat Bordaux. I am a long-haul trucker. I have committed terrible crimes all across America. Left bodies from Jacksonville all the way to the Puget Sound."

The man across the aisle offered only a wry smile. "To get away with such crimes, you must be rather good at it," he observed, his voice tinged with a macabre fascination that contrasted with the others who listened.

The trucker's response was a heavy sigh and Celeste behind him now retreated, her playful demeanor evaporated into the cold air of reality. "Why?" she whispered.

His answer was chilling in its simplicity. "Why does anyone do anything bad? Because we want to, because we can." It was a statement that laid bare the darkest aspects of himself and of human nature, an admission of guilt without remorse.

The man across the aisle, shook his head, offering a different perspective, a nuance in the wide spectrum of morality. "Certain men, but others do evil deeds because we must," he countered. "Because we have been forced to."

The addition of the silent man's voice combined with his words left the small gathering speechless. No one spoke for a moment, but eventually the trucker felt compelled to speak. "I am not one of those certain men I am afraid. I did not need to do the things I have done. I just did it."

Father Timons could only stand by as a silent witness to the exchange, speechless in the midst of the confession and ensuing discussion.

The man from across the aisle persisted with his questions. "Then why have you come for salvation when you did evil for nothing and deserve no grace?" The question cut to the core of the trucker's confession, challenging the very notion of forgiveness and redemption in the face of gratuitous evil.

The trucker's response was a desperate search for understanding, his voice low. "I don't know. I had a fucked-up life, I thought perhaps that might have some weight in the whole of it. But maybe I am just messed up." His admission, raw and devoid of self-pity revealed a man grappling with the enormity of his sins and the elusive possibility of redemption. But there was still a lack of regret.

Reaching for the whiskey bottle, and a fleeting attempt to drown the taste and weight of his confession, he caught the wide-eyed gaze of Celeste, her playful demeanor was now a thing of the past, entirely replaced with shock.

Her voice, heavy with a newfound perspective on her own life's choices shook when she spoke. "Who are you people?" she asked, her words reflected a sudden reevaluation of her circumstances. "I am just a stripper. I thought I was going to have a lot of explaining to do if there is something after this, but compared to you, I might be alright."

The quiet man's words were simple. "We all live surrounded and soaked in sin. Some more than others." His voice hinted at the inescapable nature of their flawed human existence.

Prompted by this comment, Taz turned, the bench beneath him protesting with a creak. His youthful curiosity, undimmed by the events that he had faced, now directed himself towards the mysterious man. "What about you? What is your story?"

The man's eyes narrowed into a smile, a flash of amusement—or perhaps challenge—crossing his features. His smile revealed pointed canines, sharp and distinct. "What do you think my story is?" he asked almost playfully.

Celeste reacted with a mix of fascination and alarm. "Woah, you got those tooth implants, huh?" Her voice carried a note of incredulous wonder, seeking a rational explanation for the unnerving display.

His hand reached up and pricked his finger until it bled. "These are natural." His assertion was delivered with an unsettling calm, transforming the atmosphere from one of mere survival to a chilling hint of otherworldly mysteries they might not have had time to hear.

Taz, with a fearless curiosity of youth, broke the tension with a question that would have been ludicrous in any other context. "Wait, so vampires actually exist?" His laughter, however, was short-lived as the man confirmed with a simple, "We do."

Celeste's retreat spoke volumes of her unease, yet it was Taz's forward lean that brought them all into a collective, breathless pause. "How old are you?" he asked, his interest ignited a spark of curiosity among the others.

The man's response, couched in a smile that revealed nothing and everything, "Does my age matter at a time like this?"

Nat cleared his throat and looked around him before he spoke. "Considering our lives are about to be cut short, you had a long one I suspect, we are naturally curious."

He shifted his eyes back up to the altar and shook his head, "I have walked the lands for over six hundred years."

Father Timons could only respond with disbelief. "Such a length is beyond the will of God." Yet, the vampire's retort, cold and measured, challenged the priest's conviction. "How would you know, Father? Through my long life I have learned to understand the limited understanding the mouthpieces of the church hold when it comes to the will of God."

Father Timons hand gripping the rosary at his side like a lifeline, dared to voice the question that hovered on everyone's lips. "What is your purpose here?" The tension in his voice betrayed a fear of the unknown, a fear of the very real darkness that sat before him in human guise.

The man's response was laced with amusement, a chilling smile played on his lips as he countered, "Are you afraid that I have come to consume you, Father?" The mockery in his tone added an edge to the already fraught atmosphere.

Taz leaned in, a spark of interest in his eyes. "Wait, the sun is out..." His gaze shifted towards the sunlight that bathed the church in its angry orange hue, growing brighter as the moments passed.

The vampire's laughter filled the space. "Vampires do not turn to dust by the light of day," he corrected the youth, a hint of bemusement in his voice. "But perhaps this day we will."

Standing, the vampire crossed himself, an action so incongruously human for a creature of nightmares, and he moved to the aisle. "I can tell by the looks on your faces that you think that I have come here looking for a last supper as our lord and savior had before his unfortunate end," he mused, a chuckle softening his words. "If it makes you feel better to know, I am a man of faith even if you have lost yours, father," he continued, placing a hand over his heart, "It is Lent, and I do not partake during that holy time, though it makes me weak."

Father Timons exchanged a glance with Celeste, before he looked at Nat the trucker and the youth Taz, their shared uncertainty mirroring the collective tension. Taz, ever the bold spirit, broke the silence. "Well, is anyone going to ask him?"

The vampire's gaze settled on Taz; curiosity piqued. "Ask me what?" he inquired, tilting his head in a gesture that belied his ancient nature.

Taz looked to be filled with a mix of both hope and fear. "Perhaps if we are turned, then we might survive?" The suggestion, borne of desperation, sought an escape in any form, from their impending doom.

The vampire's smile held an element of both sadness and knowledge. "And what would you eat after I turn you?

Nothing else will be alive. When there is nothing to live upon, there is no reason to live." His words highlighted the grim reality of their situation. "I hope my end comes with yours, for there is no point without the hunter and its prey to chase."

The trucker's reaction was serious as he silently reached out for the whiskey, and Celeste didn't flinch as her expression remained as still as a statue.

The brief encounter with the stripper seeking hope, the youth who clung to life, the serial killer trucker who desired absolution, and the ageless vampire who sought peace within the parish of the faithful Father Timons had lost faith, irrevocably shifted their perspectives on life, death, and the nature of humanity. The silence that once owned the sanctuary before their arrival settled once again, enveloping their senses as their hearts beat wildly in their chest.

Father Timons wondered about what would come next but concern over it or those who surrounded him dissipated as the ground underneath him began to rumble. With a weary sigh he turned around and looked up. His eyes again fixated on the hanging flame. "No matter what comes, it will be his will that is done... I heartily thank you for sitting vigil with me at the very end. I have been made all the braver for it."

M. K. Dockery, a wordsmith by night and mother of three by day; transformed her late-blooming passion for reading into a haven from life's challenges. Overcoming early struggles in literacy, she cultivated a deep love for history and an unquenchable thirst for knowledge. Her resilience against childhood bullying fueled her creativity, leading her to craft intricate worlds in her writing. These realms are not only reflections of reality but also emotional journeys that promise to either touch hearts or elevate spirits. Dockery's works are more than stories; they're portals to experiences resonating with the depths of the human condition.

beacons.ai/mkdockery

amazon.com/stores/M.-K.-Dockery/author/B0BK6BDD4P

EPILOGUE

As the light faded,
and as darkness set in,
Death closed its eyes.
It remembered all it had witnessed throughout its existence,
and a smile crept over its face.
The infinite memories: those it had ended, those it had
rebirthed, those it cradled, and those it had eviscerated. Every
instance, now a clear spark of recollection in the deathly
heralds consciousness.
As the sun paid its last respects, as the balance of dark and
light finally ended, what came next was something no being
could foresee... Not even Death.

TO BE CONTINUED...

Printed in Great Britain
by Amazon

56113971R00238